THE
UNKNOWN
BELOVED

ALSO BY AMY HARMON

Young Adult and Paranormal Romance

Slow Dance in Purgatory
Prom Night in Purgatory

Inspirational Romance

A Different Blue
Running Barefoot
Making Faces
Infinity + One
The Law of Moses
The Song of David
The Smallest Part

Historical Fiction

From Sand and Ash
What the Wind Knows
Where the Lost Wander
The Songbook of Benny Lament

Romantic Fantasy

The Bird and the Sword
The Queen and the Cure
The First Girl Child
The Second Blind Son

THE
UNKNOWN
BELOVED

a novel

AMY HARMON

Published by Lake Union Publishing, Seattle

www.apub.com

Amazon, the Amazon logo, and Lake Union Publishing are trademarks of Amazon.com, Inc., or its affiliates.

ISBN-13: 9781542033831
ISBN-10: 1542033837

Cover design by Laywan Kwan

Printed in the United States of America

To the real Michael Malone,
and all the names no one ever knows

Unable are the loved to die,
for love is immortality.

—Emily Dickinson

Prologue

January 1923

Her mother was sleeping now. A soft snore bubbled from her lips, and Dani patted her cheek. Mother and Daddy had fought all night. That's why Mother was tired. They'd fought, and then they'd hugged and kissed and slapped at each other, and then they fought some more. Daddy had been gone too long the last time, and Mother worried and paced and chewed on the sides of her fingers until they bled, though she never chewed her nails. They were pretty and painted for Daddy. Just like Mother's lips. Mother liked Daddy. Daddy liked Mother. They liked each other too much, Aunt Zuzana said. Aunt Zuzana didn't like Daddy. "He's a fool," she said.

None of Mother's aunts liked him. Aunt Lenka said he was too handsome, and Aunt Vera said he was too much trouble. "You should bring Daniela and come back to Cleveland, Aneta," they told Dani's mother. Mother had been raised by them so she was used to their opinions. But Mother just shook her head when the aunts said things like that.

"I chose George Flanagan, *Tety*. He's what I want. And I won't have you talk badly of him. I am George's wife. Daniela is George's daughter." Mother never called her Daniela except when she was talking to the aunts.

The aunts said she should be named after her great-grandfather, Daniel, the first Kos in Cleveland, and for some reason Mother and Daddy had agreed to it.

"Daniela Flanagan is a perfect name," Daddy always said.

"I'm not perfect," Daniela had informed him.

"Of course you are. Just like your mother. She has the perfect name too."

"Aneta means merciful," Dani had parroted, knowingly. The aunts had made sure she knew such things.

"It does. Such a smart girl you are. Your mother took mercy on me . . . and married me."

"Even though the aunts don't like you?"

"Yes. Even though the aunts don't like me."

"I like you, Daddy."

"I like you too, Dani Flanagan."

She liked the way the house rocked a little when Daddy was home. His heavy boots on the floor, his laugh, his smell, his inability to be quiet. Daddy was never quiet. He was yelling or laughing or stomping or snoring.

Mother snored now, but she snored softly. Mother was tired.

Dani slipped from her arms and gathered the books they'd purchased at O'Brien's. Mother had tried to stay busy all day even though she'd been weary. They'd gone to Holy Name Cathedral and lit a candle for Daddy. Then they'd visited Schofield's Flower Shop across the street just to smell the roses, bought a hot dog from a vendor, and finished their outing at O'Brien's Books, their favorite. Mother liked books, but she liked most when Dani told her what the books were about without even opening the covers.

The big blue book with the frayed cloth edges had once belonged to a boy with long, slim hands and a sickly cough. The story wasn't about him. But he had loved it . . . once. He had muttered to himself as he read, and his voice sounded like Mr. O'Brien's. Mother said Mr. O'Brien was from Ireland like Daddy . . . so maybe the boy who'd owned the book was from Ireland too. Maybe Mr. O'Brien had brought it across the sea, all the way to Chicago to sell in his bookstore.

The other books Mother bought hadn't been read by anyone else in so long. One brought a pair of squirming buttocks to mind—Dani giggled at that. She guessed that the book had been used to boost a small body at the dinner table. The last book, a new one, filled Dani's mind with gray. Nothing there. The book had not been opened or loved or even hated or held. At least not long enough for someone's story to sink into the threads or the paper.

Dani always told Mother what she saw, and Mother said she was good at telling stories. But Dani wasn't good at stories. She couldn't think of any stories by herself. She couldn't even think of anything to draw most of the time. But she'd drawn a picture of the kitten she wanted. *Charlie.* Mr. O'Brien had a box of kittens behind his store that were ready for homes. Dani wanted one. She wanted one badly. She'd drawn a dozen pictures of Charlie, and she'd put them all over the house.

Mother didn't really want her to have one. But Daddy said he would talk to Mother about the kittens. He said Dani would just have to wait until he got home again, and they would go get Charlie together.

Maybe she could go visit Charlie while Mother was napping. She wouldn't know.

Dani carried her shoes and her coat from the room. Mother would hear her rustling if she put them on beside the bed. Mother had good ears. But she didn't even stir when Dani eased the door closed. She was sound asleep.

Dani shoved her feet into her boots. They were getting too small. Daddy said she grew every time he was gone. Mother told him he better stop leaving then. Dani's coat fit fine, though. Her hat too, and she pulled the edges down over her ears so she wouldn't get cold on her walk. It was growing dark already. She would have to hurry so she could get a good look. Then she would come right back.

But Charlie was so sweet. And Dani stayed too long.

The clanging of police bells greeted her when she rounded the corner for her street. She began to run, certain that Mother would be awake. She would be angry and scared. Maybe the police were looking for Dani.

Two police cars were in front of her house, parked in haphazard fashion, their lights on and their doors open. As she watched, another car pulled up and three more officers tumbled out to join the two already standing in the yard. Daddy's car was there too.

The front door of Dani's house was open. Mrs. Thurston from next door was talking to the officers, hunched against the cold but gesticulating wildly.

"Oh no," Dani cried. They *were* looking for her. Mother would never let her have a kitty now.

Nobody had seen her. Not yet. Dani raced across the neighbor's yard and slipped quietly through the back door of her own house, the one that led into the kitchen, hoping she could find Mother first. Then mother could tell them all to leave because Dani had returned.

But the police were already inside. One man stood in the door between the kitchen and the sitting room. He wore a jaunty cap on his big head, and his long overcoat hung open, revealing two rows of brass buttons that marched down his big belly. A gold star peeked out from behind the lapel.

Someone had turned on the lamps in the house. *All* the lamps. The house blazed with light. Mother wouldn't like all the lights on and the doors open. The heat from the stove would be whisked out into the January evening.

The policeman was looking down at the floor, and his cap shielded the upper part of his face. He didn't look up when she entered the kitchen. The clanging from the front yard was enough to deafen the entire neighborhood.

Where was Mother?

Dani took another step and craned her neck, trying to see beyond the table between her and the policeman, to the sitting room and the front door.

Then she saw them.

Mother wasn't in her bed anymore, but she was still asleep. She and Daddy both were—lying in a tangle of limbs on the kitchen floor.

Mother would be so glad Daddy was home. She'd said he wouldn't be back for days.

Mother wasn't wearing any shoes, and Daddy still wore his overcoat and his hat, like he'd run in from outside and picked Mother up and spun her around, kissing her and swinging her until they both fell down. Maybe Daddy had left the front door open.

He was lying across Mother, and Dani couldn't see his face. She couldn't see Mother's face. Only her pretty, bare feet and the hem of her red dress. Mother's dress had ballooned around her, around her and Daddy both, framing them in a big, red heart.

The policeman lifted his head.

"Ah hell. I found the kid!" he shouted. "Malone, get in here."

Another officer in a matching uniform, this one younger and darker, appeared behind the first and strode through the kitchen, avoiding the crimson heart and the sleeping couple. He reached out a hand and set it on Dani's shoulder, urging her to turn away from the confusing display on the kitchen floor.

"Keep her outside until we can sort this out," the big-bellied policeman said, pointing toward the back door. "And see what she knows!"

Several more police officers entered the house through the front door. She heard their steps and felt their presence behind the first officer.

"Come with me now, lass," the young policeman said, and though his voice was low and kind, his big hand on her shoulder was insistent.

Sometimes Daddy called her *lass* like that. The policeman named Malone didn't have a voice like Daddy's, though. His voice was softer. Rumbly. Like he didn't use it very much. Like he didn't sing at the top of his lungs and shout whenever he spoke. He was much younger than Daddy too, though he seemed older somehow. He had a serious mouth and dark, drooping eyes that made him look a little like Mrs. Thurston's hound dog, Reggie.

"I need to tell my mother," Dani said. Her voice echoed oddly, like she was shouting in the church. "I already left once without telling her where I was going."

Malone crouched down so she wasn't looking up at him anymore, though he still blocked her view of everything else. She saw his momentary surprise and knew he'd noticed her eyes. The reaction was always the same.

"What's your name, kiddo?" he asked softly.

"Dani Flanagan." Again, the echo, and now she couldn't feel her toes. Her feet were cold and her chest was hot.

"I'm Officer Malone, Dani. We won't go far. Just out the back door. So we aren't underfoot."

"Will you tell her I'm here?" she said and clapped her hands over her ears. Something was wrong with her. Something was wrong with Mother and Daddy. The heat in her chest was rising to her eyes, and the ache in her toes was climbing up her legs. She didn't know if she could walk.

"Jaysus, Malone. Get her out of here," the first policeman yelled, and Officer Malone's mouth tightened. She didn't think he liked the big policeman.

"Come with me now, Dani," Malone urged.

She tried to move her feet, but she couldn't.

"Malone!"

Without another word, Malone scooped her up and stomped out into the cold night. When he reached the backyard, he stopped and looked around for some place to set her down.

"Here you go, Dani Flanagan," he said, and placed her on the bench where Daddy smoked.

She was stiff and cold on the outside, but inside she was on fire, and the fire was crackling and hissing like the logs in the stove. She began to shake, and Malone sat down beside her and shrugged out of his overcoat and wrapped it around her. He didn't tell her she was okay. He didn't pat her back or stroke the curls on her head the way Daddy did when she was upset. But his coat was warm and big, and it distracted her from the darkness in and all around her.

"Where were you?" he asked. "Before you came home. Where were you?"

"I w-walked down to O'Brien's. B-but I didn't go in. There are some k-k-kitties in a b-box in the alley behind the store. They're so cute. I was just going to visit them for a minute, but I stayed too long. Mother must be wondering w-where I am. She must b-be scared. She's been scared a lot lately."

"When you left . . . where was your mother?"

"She was asleep."

"And your pop? Where was your dad?"

"He wasn't home. He just left this morning with Uncle Darby and wasn't supposed to be back for a few days. He was going to miss my birthday, but he told me I could have one of the kittens when he got home. He said he'd talk to Mother."

"When's your birthday?"

"Tomorrow. I'm going to be ten."

She thought he swore, but the word was soft, and she wasn't sure.

"Have you picked one out? Do you know which one you want?"

"Yes. It's a little boy cat. Daddy said no girl cats allowed because we only need one. The boy cat can't have babies. But he was my favorite anyway. His eyes are like mine. One is brown. One is blue. It's very rare, Daddy says. Very rare and very special."

"What are you going to name him?"

"Charlie."

"That's a good name."

"They're dead, aren't they?" she asked. She didn't want to talk about Charlie. She wanted her mother. She wanted Daddy to come out and tell Malone and all the other policemen to go home.

Malone swore again, and this time she heard it. He crossed himself and looked down at her, and his eyes were shiny, and his lips wobbled.

"Yes, Dani. They are. I'm so sorry."

~

People died. Their hearts stopped. The breath rattled from their lips, and the light went out. It wasn't like a car stalling or a bulb flickering, though it was, in a way. Movement, motion, presence . . . and then nothing. A soiled glove in the road, the blown-off boot of a legless soldier. Michael Malone had seen more than his share of limbless men. Death was so unforgiving. So unforgiving. He had yet to see someone come back from it.

The soul was quick to flee. If there was a soul—whatever that strange phenomenon called consciousness was—it didn't linger with the body. It raced away. And death, gray-faced and foul-smelling, immediately claimed the flesh. He'd seen it a thousand times.

When he was young, he'd imagined he could see souls. He'd even told his mother about the colors that hovered like watercolor paints around some people's heads and shoulders. Pink and lavender, white and yellow, he saw them quite clearly, and he saw the light that shadowed him when he caught his reflection from the corner of his eye.

His mother had believed him, and said it was a gift. His light had been warm once, but it'd been years since he'd seen it. His mother's light was warm too, and he'd watched it fade. Maybe his mother took his gift when she went away.

He wasn't sure what happened to a soul when a person died in stages. His mother had died in stages. He supposed a soul was like a great fire, raging, roaring until nothing but embers remained, and embers weren't enough to subsist on. It was better for a man—or a woman—to go completely, for the soul to not sit with the body, but to leap out and let go.

He had worried that his mother's slow death had killed her spirit. He still worried about that. Was she free? He hoped she was. He wasn't. But he hoped she was. And he hoped little Mary was. And Baby James too. Maybe his mother and his children were together. That thought had brought him comfort when nothing else could.

But he didn't know how to comfort Dani Flanagan.

"They're dead, aren't they?" Dani asked. And he told her the truth. Yes. George and Aneta Flanagan were dead.

He thought how strange the girl was, asking something so unbearable with a soft and knowing voice. It made the hair rise on his neck, that calm composure, that emotionless statement. But then her eyes began to fill, and tears coursed silently down her cheeks. Shamed, he fished Bunny out of his pocket and handed it to her. He didn't even think. Afterward, he would curse himself for giving up the precious possession, but he'd wanted to give the girl *something*. It was the day before her birthday. Ten years old, and she was even more alone than he.

So he gave her Mary's pink rabbit.

It wasn't very big. It fit in his pocket. He'd carried it for the last six months. Dani accepted the toy and gripped it tightly, almost desperately, in both hands.

She looked up at him, eyes still streaming, and twisted the cloth rabbit nervously between swipes at her seeping eyes.

Then she looked away, still clutching his offering, but a vacant look stole across her face. Shock. Poor kid was going into shock.

"Bunny," she murmured.

"Yeah. It's a bunny. A lucky rabbit. You hold on to that for a minute, until we figure out what's going on, okay?"

"But this was Mary's," she said softly.

"What . . . what did you say?" he whispered.

She didn't answer.

Of course, he'd misunderstood her. It was his own madness. His own grief. His own guilt. She looked up at him again, her gaze still blank. Her eyes had shaken him in the kitchen. The left one was a clear, pale blue, and the right one as brown as his own. Here, in the meager light, he couldn't see the colors, but they glimmered, one much darker than the other.

"Do you have a d-daughter?" she asked.

His heart stilled in his chest. It happened every time. The same sensation. The same sinking in his belly and tightening in his throat.

"No," he whispered. "No. Not anymore."

"He's a sweet bunny," she said, stroking the nubby cloth. She brought the rabbit to her chest, like it comforted her, and pressed both hands over it, closing her eyes.

"The neighbor said she would take her, Malone. Family's being contacted," Murphy bellowed out the back door. He and Dani Flanagan both jerked at the sudden interruption. She opened her eyes again, and they locked on his.

"I want to see my mother and daddy, Mr. Malone. Please."

"No, kid. I'm sorry. But no."

"Please."

He needed to get a few more answers and didn't know how hard to press.

"Did you see what happened, Dani?"

"No. But you're here. And they're inside. And they would be calling for me if they could. They would be looking for me if they could. But they're just lying there. Aren't they?"

They wouldn't be lying there much longer. Murphy had declared it a murder/suicide the moment he'd walked through the door, and the neighbor, a Mrs. Jana Thurston, had confirmed there was trouble between the Flanagans.

George Flanagan was violent. He runs with the lads of Kilgubbin. The North Side Gang, I think they call them. Vicious lot. There was always yelling and fighting coming from that house. Aneta came to me in tears more than once. I heard shots. He's killed her, hasn't he?

"I'll take you next door to Mrs. Thurston," he offered. He was the low man on the ladder. He always got the shit assignments. This was, by far, the worst he'd ever had.

"I don't want to go to Mrs. Thurston," Dani said. "She doesn't like me or Mother."

He frowned. "Why not?" Mrs. Thurston had made it sound like she and Aneta Flanagan were close friends. She'd had plenty to say about all of it, but none of what Malone had seen in that kitchen had made much sense to him.

"She was jealous of Mother," the girl whispered. "She said mean things and tried to kiss Daddy one time. Don't believe the things she says. She's not a nice lady."

Well, damn. Malone had kind of thought as much as soon as Mrs. Thurston had opened her painted mouth.

"Do you have family you can go to?" he asked Dani. He hoped she did. God, he hoped she did.

"I have Uncle Darby and my *tety*," she said softly. "And my grand-father, though he's odd."

"Tety? Who's Tety?" He was good with languages, but he didn't know that word.

"Mother's aunts. Tetka Zuzana, Tetka Vera, and Tetka Lenka."

Her mother's family. The names sounded eastern European.

"Do your aunts love you?" he blurted. His question embarrassed him, but he needed to know.

"Yes. They love me." Her assurance eased the nerves in his belly. He didn't want the kid to be stuck with the likes of Darby O'Shea, if he was the Uncle Darby she was referring to.

"Then you will not have to be with Mrs. Thurston for too long," he said. "We'll call your aunts."

He'd taken the girl around to the front yard and stood beside her as her parents were carried out on stretchers, shrouded from view. The coroner was preparing to take them away, and though Malone had seen death up close in the Somme, he'd never witnessed a moment more tragic.

The little girl ran, breaking away from him, and begged the ambulance workers for a chance to say goodbye. The attendants, preparing to lift the stretchers into the back of the waiting truck, paused in discomfort.

"What the hell, Malone?" Murphy yelled, but Malone ignored him. He'd been twelve when his mother died, not much older than Dani. And he'd been allowed to say goodbye.

Malone followed the girl, and with great care and a quick crossing of his heart, folded the cloth down from George Flanagan's face first, and then did the same to his wife.

Dani Flanagan, still wearing his overcoat, pressed a kiss to their cheeks, her tears streaming but her sobs restrained. And then she stepped back, clutching Bunny in her hands, and watched as they were taken away.

1

January 1938

Michael Malone hadn't been back to Chicago since he'd helped bring down Al Capone in '31. Poor Big Al. He was currently sitting in a cell on Alcatraz. Malone thought even Alcatraz would be better than standing in a cemetery in Chicago on New Year's Day.

Malone had been in the Bahamas working a case involving offshore accounts and money laundering for most of the year, which meant that at the moment he was nut-brown and colder than he'd ever been in his whole life. He'd had no time to acclimate to Chicago, though he was well-adjusted to the fact that Irene was gone. She'd been gone for a long time.

His sister, Molly, had gotten a message to him two days after Christmas.

Irene is dead. What should I do?

He'd gone home to the house on the south side of Chicago, the house where he'd been raised, though it didn't feel like home anymore.

Molly was glad to see him. Her children had grown, and both she and her husband, Sean, were grayer and thinner.

"You've hardly aged at all, little brother," Molly had said, kissing his cheeks and holding him close. But they both knew he was a much different man.

Now he watched as the coffin he'd purchased, a white one with pink roses painted on the corners, was lowered into the ground beside Mary's little stone and the marker for James. Molly cried, though Michael suspected a little relief in her tears. Molly had always had too many people to look after, and Irene had been a burden. He'd always made sure there was a roof over Irene's head and money in her account, but Molly had cared about her. And caring was its own millstone.

No one but Father Kerrigan, Sean, and Molly came to the graveside service. There *was* no one else. And Michael just felt cold.

He would need to leave again. Soon. The old neighborhood wasn't safe for him anymore, though the Chicago Outfit was under new leadership and the Prohibition wars of the '20s were over. But he didn't like sleeping under Molly's roof. His presence, no matter how long it had been or how insulated he'd become, made her less safe. Not more.

Word got around, but it still surprised him to see Eliot Ness standing on the doorstep two days later, bags beneath his blue eyes and a file box under one arm.

"I heard about Irene, Mike. I'm sorry." He took off his hat when he said the words, paying his respects. He still parted his hair straight down the middle, and at thirty-four he still retained the boyishness that had caused so many to either underestimate or adore him.

Malone nodded, acknowledging the sentiment, and invited Eliot in by simply stepping aside. Molly rushed out from the kitchen and greeted the famed Prohibition agent, asking about his wife, Edna, who had grown up down the street, and giving her condolences for his mother, Emma, who had apparently passed away the month before. But Molly didn't linger. She left them alone with a couple of glasses and a bottle of malt whiskey, closing the sitting room door behind her. She knew the business they were both in. Or *had* been in. Ness had moved on from the Treasury Department.

"I heard you're in Cleveland now," Malone said, pouring as he talked.

"Yeah. I moved there in August of '34 when I was still working for the bureau. Got offered the job as safety director about a year after that," Eliot answered, taking the glass Malone handed him; he sipped it appreciatively. He never used to drink. He'd never wanted to be a hypocrite. But Prohibition was over.

"What the hell is a safety director, Ness?" Malone asked. He stared down into the amber liquid in his own glass. He didn't really want to drink right now. Once he started, he might not stop.

"I'm in charge of the police and the fire department. Basically . . . the public safety guy."

"You're the chief of chiefs?"

"Something like that." Eliot spoke in the same slow manner Malone remembered. It made him seem older than his years and forced patience and attention on the listener, and Malone had always found it endearing.

"Last I heard, you were hunting moonshiners in Kentucky," Malone pressed.

"Yeah. And I'm never going back." Ness set his empty glass on the table.

Malone added another finger. "That bad?" he asked.

"I'd take Al Capone and his boys any day."

"You got mob troubles in Cleveland?"

"Yeah. They're everywhere. But I have a whole new set of problems. You know what's going on in my city?"

Malone's brows shot up. "Your city? Cleveland is your city now? I thought Chicago was your city."

"I'm responsible to the people in Cleveland now. And Cleveland has a madman roaming the streets, cutting people's heads off."

"I've been a long ways from Cleveland," Malone said. "Are you talking about the murders? I know a little. But you're going to have to fill me in."

"They're calling him the Torso Killer. The Mad Butcher of Kingsbury Run. I've never seen the like. Not here. Not in Kentucky. Not ever." Ness sighed. "The thing is . . . I understood Capone. His crimes made sense. It was business. Money. Power. Control. I don't understand this guy. Chopping people up. Dumping their naked corpses in plain sight. Men. Women. Doesn't seem to matter."

Ness took another swallow like he needed the reinforcement. "Some of the bodies have been found by kids. Scarred for life now, those kids. You decide to skip school and go fishing and end up finding a human head, rolled up in a pair of trousers, sitting beneath a tree? How does a kid recover from that? Some other boys were playing ball near the Run, on a slope they call Jackass Hill. Their ball rolled down the hill; they chased it and found two dead men without heads or genitals, one of 'em still wearing his socks."

Malone winced.

"Oh, it gets worse," Eliot said. "The third victim, a woman named Flo Polillo, was chopped up and divided between two produce baskets. The woman who found the baskets thought the woman's torso was a couple of hams." He grimaced. "People are hungry right now, Malone. Luckily, the woman was not as desperate as some, and she went and told the butcher across the way that she thought he'd been robbed. Imagine her shock when she discovered the hams were human flanks. That's the garbage going on in Cleveland. Not raids on distilleries. Not disruption of supply lines. Not good old cops and robbers or gangsters and agents. I can handle all that."

"I can see why you miss Capone," Malone murmured.

"I do. Damn it. I do," Ness said. "Like most everywhere else, the food lines in Cleveland are long and jobs are few, and the misery is everywhere you look. And . . . all of that misery makes sense. I don't like it, but it makes sense."

For a moment both men were quiet, thoughtful.

"What doesn't make sense is a guy who chops people up for seemingly no rhyme or reason," Ness said, adding, "I don't even know where to *begin* with that."

"It doesn't make sense to you. But that doesn't mean it doesn't make sense," Malone offered. A wise little girl had said that to him once. He'd never forgotten it.

"Yeah?" Ness scoffed. "Well . . . so far it doesn't make sense to my guys either. We're all scratching our heads. All the old rules don't seem to apply with these murders."

"Like what?"

"The victims don't have any connection to each other, beyond the fact that they lived in or around Kingsbury Run. The papers have said all the victims were indigent, but that's not true, not exactly. They were poor, but not so much poorer than anyone else. They frequented establishments that aren't highbrow, but that's just the few we were able to identify. The rest could be saints and angels for all we really know."

"Do you think the Butcher knows them?" Malone pressed.

"You understand how these things usually work. Murders are almost never committed by strangers."

"But you don't think that's what's going on here?"

"No. None of the people who knew the first victim, Edward Andrassy, are even people of interest at this point. Andrassy wasn't an especially swell fella, but his family loved him. His parents grieved him. It's been hell on them, the endless interviews trying to turn something up, anything that would give us a clue as to who killed him so we can connect the dots to the others."

"How many now?"

"Ten. There was one in September of '34 that hasn't been included in the tally. A woman's torso was found on the shores of Lake Erie. She's never been identified, and they weren't even sure she was murdered. They thought it may have been someone who fell overboard, drowned, and her body was possibly torn up by a propeller."

"The Lady of the Lake." Malone remembered now. That scenario had never seemed likely to him. A woman falls out of a boat and drowns on Erie, and nobody comes forward?

"That's what the papers called her. Pretty name for something damn ugly. The man who found her torso was looking for driftwood and found a different kind of trunk."

"So you think that was the Butcher's first victim?"

"We didn't. Not for a long time. But now . . . with all the others since, yeah. I think she was his first."

Again silence settled around them. Malone rose and stoked the fire and Ness waited for him to return to his chair.

"Maybe he's showing off," Malone mused, sitting again.

"Who?" Ness frowned.

"Your Butcher."

"*My* Butcher?" Eliot grunted.

Malone shrugged and pushed the bottle toward his friend. "Your city. Your Butcher."

"Showing off for who?" Eliot said. He picked up the bottle but didn't take off the cap.

"You."

"Me?"

"Yeah. Didn't the bodies start turning up right around the time you got into town?"

Eliot frowned at him, his gaze sharp. He set the bottle down with a thump. "What?"

"The bodies started turning up right around the time you got into town, yeah? You said you moved to Cleveland in August of '34. Lady of the Lake turned up in September of '34."

"Ah hell, Malone." Ness rubbed at his eyes. "This has nothing to do with me. I didn't even take the job until December of '35." But he sounded tired, like he suddenly wasn't certain.

"The papers love you, Eliot. Young, good-looking, straight as an arrow. Took down Al Capone. Maybe this guy just wants to give you another challenge. I've seen plenty of gang hits where the heads are lopped off. What makes you think this isn't just more of the same stuff we faced here in Chicago?"

"I wish it were. But . . . it isn't. I've stayed out of it and let the dicks handle it. But the mayor, Harold Burton, told me I need to take a more active role."

"A more visible role?"

"Yeah. He says the whole reason I got the job was because the people believed I could clean things up. I didn't know I'd be cleaning up severed limbs and dead ends." He was so morose that Malone handed him his own glass. He wasn't going to drink it.

Eliot raised his blue eyes to Malone's almost like he was waiting for Malone to catch up. Malone glowered back.

"What's this all about, Eliot? I thought you came by because of Irene."

"I did. But her death . . . gave me an opening. I knew I had to move fast, or you'd be gone again."

"No," Malone said. He suddenly knew what Eliot was going to say, and he wasn't interested. Not at all.

"You've always been a details man. You know your onions, and I need some fresh eyes. Do you realize that you are the first person to connect me to the case? I can't say I like the idea, but it's a lead. Nobody else put that together. That's what I'm talking about."

"You've got good cops in Cleveland, don't you?"

Ness hesitated and Malone groaned. So that was it. That was *always* it. Corruption. Ness didn't trust the team that was in place.

"There are always good men. Always good cops," Eliot amended, judicious.

"So? Let them do their jobs."

"It's been more than two years, and we're no closer to solving this thing than we were the first day. The whole thing is rotten."

"It always is. The bad guy is never who the politicians need him to be. And the good guys are always a little dirty."

"And that's why I need you. A group of businessmen have put a fund together to hire some independent investigators to solve this thing. Separate from police. Just like we did when we took down Capone."

"I just put Irene in the ground."

Ness was silent, eyes clinging to Malone's face.

"You're free now, Mike."

"I won't ever be free, Ness. My job has made sure of that." He changed the subject. "What does Edna think of Cleveland?"

Ness hesitated again, and Malone had his answer. So the trouble persisted in the Ness marriage.

"So far she likes it better than Kentucky," Eliot said. "But she's lonely. We don't have any children. She doesn't like my work."

"Ah. Well. Can't argue with her there."

"No," Eliot sighed. "She's at her mother's. She sends her condolences."

"So you came all the way to Chicago when you heard about Irene?"

"No. We came for Christmas. We're heading back to Cleveland tomorrow. I need you, Malone."

"I already have a job, Ness."

"I talked to Elmer Irey before I came here."

"You talked to my boss?"

"He says you're between assignments. He can spare you for a bit. He said he could even make it official. There's no Treasury angle, at least not that we know of, but the big brass in Washington wants this thing put to bed. It's an embarrassment. The German papers are using it for propaganda. Savage Americans. Brutal Americans. 'The Americans can't stop one man; how do they think they can stop a single German tank?'"

Malone sighed. So much for going back to the Bahamas.

"Irey said you just wrapped up a case," Eliot added. "I heard you were on the Lindbergh kidnapping too. Terrible, that."

Malone said nothing. It *was* terrible. A toddler taken from his crib for ransom and killed. Left by the side of the road. But they'd caught the bastard. It had taken them two mind-numbing years, but they'd caught him. Malone had dreamed about Mary every night for those two years.

"Irey thinks the rest will do you good," Ness continued.

"Rest? In Cleveland? I don't think rest is what you have in mind."

"There won't be any pressure. It's all off the record. And like you said, you can't stay here. You know that. You're a wanted man in Chicago. Somebody recognizes you . . . you're dead. Capone might be at Alcatraz, but he still has reach, Malone."

"Why me, Ness?"

"You're perfect for the job."

Malone snorted in disbelief. "How do you figure?"

"You're not afraid of anything. You're patient. You know police work. You've got powerful resources. And at the moment, you've got nothing else to do."

"You mean if something goes wrong, and the Butcher decides to take me out, no real loss. No crying widow or fatherless children on your doorstep."

Ness shrugged. "It's how we decided on the Untouchables, you know that. You were there. If they'd ever have caught on to you, Malone, you'da been dead."

"That's the thing, Ness. I've been dead for a while. That's why I'm so good at my job. I don't give a damn."

"Cut the bull, Mike. If you didn't give a damn, you wouldn't be here. You took care of a woman you haven't lived with for fifteen years."

Malone picked up the glass he'd offered Ness and gulped the contents down. It burned, and he almost coughed, embarrassing himself. He didn't drink when he was working, and some cases lasted for years. He had some catching up to do.

"How old are you, Mike?" Eliot asked softly.

"I'm almost forty years old." He felt twenty-five. And ninety-two.

"Forty years old. Still got a full head of hair and a flat stomach. Still got that sour attitude that women inexplicably clamor to, and a face no one can place. You're free now, Mike. Come to Cleveland and help me catch a bad guy."

"There's not a single reason why I'd go to Cleveland, Eliot. Leave those files here. That's what's in the box, isn't it? I'll look them over. Give you my impressions."

"Nah. I'll leave the files. But you aren't going to solve this looking at files. That's not how it works, and you know it. Detective Merylo, a guy assigned to this case, seems to think the Butcher rides the train cars with the transients and bums, and that's how he finds his victims. Nobody is better at blending in than you are. And nobody will recognize you and blow your cover. We've had a few of our local guys try it only to be made pretty quickly."

"How much does it pay?" It was his first concession, and Ness was ready with the details.

"I'll take care of your room and board—already got a place picked out for you—and give you twenty a week until you, or someone else, gives me a suspect, wrapped up nice and tight. Or until Irey assigns you somewhere else."

"Who's going to talk to me? Nobody knows me in Cleveland."

"And you'll be able to get information others can't. The police chief, Matowitz, put two of his best men on this case, full time. And the next day it was announced in the papers. Big spread." Ness sighed.

"So everybody sees them coming a mile away and reporters dog their every step," Malone summarized.

"Yep. The papers have their purpose. Nobody knows that better than I do. But I need someone who isn't in their sights. Someone I trust. Someone who isn't connected to anyone in Cleveland. I was brought in by a Republican mayor. For some people, that means I'm the enemy, and they're always looking to bury me just to get at him."

"I hate politics. And politicians."

"You won't have to answer to any of them. Nobody will even know you're there. Or at least the reason you're there. Just me and maybe David Cowles. You remember David? He works for the Scientific Investigation Bureau, and he's been helping us out. But you won't have any of that old baggage."

"I've got plenty of baggage." But suddenly, it felt as though he didn't. He felt a spark, a glimmer of something he hadn't felt for a while. *Interest.* He was intrigued.

And Ness saw the moment he had him. His countenance lightened.

"I'm not working with anyone else, Ness," Malone warned, shaking his finger at him. "I'm not bunking with a ragtag bunch of trigger men."

"Calm down. This isn't the Untouchables . . . exactly. One of the backers suggested we call you the Unknowns. Unknown to the community, unknown to each other. You report to me—anything you find. That's it. And maybe to Irey, if he sees fit."

"The Unknowns. Oh, that's swell." Leave it up to a bunch of bored rich guys to come up with a name like that for their pet project. *The Unknowns.* And Ness said it wasn't the Untouchables.

"There's a room for rent in a house south of Kingsbury Run. Right across from St. Alexis Hospital in the Czech district. Big, swanky houses along there. Grand at one time. Now they've mostly been converted into businesses with living quarters above. But the street is well maintained, and the room will be decent." Ness shrugged. "Single rooms go fast because so many can't afford more, but no one wants to live near the Run. That will keep the price reasonable. I've put down a deposit to hold it."

"You were that sure of me?"

"No. I was pretty sure you'd refuse. But the room was too good a location to pass up. If not for you, for someone else."

"I can't promise you anything. I'll call Irey. Then I'll decide."

Ness nodded, but they both knew Malone was in.

"You've got until January tenth to get to Cleveland. They're holding the room. You call me when you're settled." Ness tapped the paper he'd clipped to the topmost file in the box. "I've written the number there, below the address." He cocked his head. "You still going by Malone? Or do you have a new name?"

"I'm between names."

"Well . . . use whatever name you want. I had a girl from the office take care of it so I'm not connected. The deposit is in her name. A reference from city hall should clear the way, even if it doesn't come directly from me."

"January in Cleveland," Malone muttered.

"It'll be fun, Malone."

"No it won't," Malone shot back, and Ness chuckled, satisfied.

"Nah. It probably won't. But it needs doing. That's what men like you and me are best at. Doing what needs doing." He shoved his hat back on his head and buttoned his overcoat. His cheeks were flushed and his eyes were bright from the booze. "Don't think too hard. You'll scare yourself. Isn't that what you used to tell me?"

"Yeah."

"It's good advice."

2

"I know it feels soon. But we've got to take on a boarder," Daniela Kos said, forcing a conversation she knew her two aging aunts did not want to have.

"We can't have a stranger in the house right now, Daniela. Not when we're all still grieving," Zuzana said.

"But, *Tetka*, Auntie, we will always grieve," Daniela replied gently. She was the youngest of the three women by more than fifty years, but even she knew that. Grief did not leave. It just became part of the patina.

Lenka's chin wobbled, and she pursed her wrinkled lips. She withdrew three of the straight pins from the waistband of the dress she was constructing and stuck them between her teeth to cover her distress.

For a moment, the three women were all quiet, letting their work distract them. Many days they had no work—no dresses to sew or alterations to make—and they were grateful for the holiday uptick in business. Once upon a time, when the Koses had made beautiful gowns and expensive suits, when there was more work than they could keep up with, they had turned commissions away. Now they took all comers.

Now they haggled over prices and settled for rates Zuzana said they hadn't seen since Daniel Kos had opened his shop in the old neighborhood on Croton Street. And now, Daniel, Eliska, Pavel, Aneta, and Vera Kos were gone.

The rows of mansions on Euclid Avenue were gone too, the ballrooms demolished. The wealthy people who once danced in them danced no more. Mark Twain had once called it one of the finest streets in America. But Millionaires' Row was now like the rest of downtown Cleveland. Penniless and abandoned by those who had built her.

The Koses had never lived on Euclid Avenue, though they had profited from her patrons. Instead, they'd saved and toiled and built a grand house on Broadway Street, not far from East Fifty-Fifth and Our Lady of Lourdes Church, and just across the street from St. Alexis Hospital. It was the community where the wealthiest Czech immigrants banked and lived and worshipped and became Americans. It was the home where they now sat, Daniel's great-granddaughter and his two remaining children, carrying on a legacy that would most likely die with them.

"It's a nice, big room . . . We can get a good price for it," Daniela attempted again. "A higher price will attract a certain sort, maybe a doctor. Dr. Peterka's never had any trouble renting out the rooms above his clinic. We're so close to the hospital. We'll rent it out in no time," Daniela explained. She omitted the fact that it was already done. She had until January 10 to get her aunts used to the idea.

"We'll be butchered in our sleep," Zuzana warned, not even looking up from the seam she was carefully unpicking.

Lenka moaned, the sound rising and falling like a yowling cat. She still had pins sticking out of her mouth and couldn't do much more than that.

"*Teta*," Daniela pled. "Please don't say things like that."

"We live right next door to a funeral home. If the Butcher lived here, he could throw his victims on the Rauses' front steps. Save everyone the trouble," Zuzana mumbled.

Daniela had known that convincing her two aging aunts would be difficult.

"No. I take that back. He would most likely only leave an arm or two," Zuzana muttered. "Or maybe a head, wrapped in the victim's trousers or chopped in half and put in a basket like poor Flo Polillo."

"You say her name like you knew her." Daniela sighed.

"I know she was a human being who didn't like having her head lopped off," Zuzana sniffed.

"They never found her head," Lenka said, tsking. "I wonder what in the world he did with it?"

"We need the money, *Tety*," Daniela said.

"We need our peace of mind more," Zuzana retorted.

"The papers say he's powerfully built—tall and strong. He would have to be to lug the bodies to the base of Jackass Hill. Maybe we should just rent the room to someone weak . . . and small," Lenka suggested, hopeful.

"I still think he rolled those men down the hill and then walked down to arrange his bit of theater," Zuzana inserted.

"The papers said there was no indication of that. No drag marks or broken underbrush. No sign on the bodies at all that they'd been dragged or tossed," Lenka argued. The two of them had speculated about this same thing a thousand times over the last two years, as had all the papers.

"I would feel so much better if he only killed men," Lenka confessed, and Daniela felt her lips twitch. Her aunts were delightfully undiplomatic.

"Well, so far, he doesn't seem to kill *old* ladies," Daniela said. "So I think you are safe."

"But you're not old, Daniela," Lenka argued. "It is you I am most afraid for."

"No. But I'm also not his type. And you know it."

"You're not a hobo," Lenka said.

"No. I am not."

"And you don't live in Kingsbury Run," Lenka said.

"Though we live mighty close to it," Zuzana interjected.

"And you don't frequent houses of ill-repute." Lenka kept her tally going.

"Not often." Daniela nodded.

Her aunts gaped at her, their stitches forgotten, momentarily stunned. Daniela grinned and their shoulders wilted.

"Though if we do not rent our empty room, I might have to consider it," Daniela warned.

Zuzana slapped her leg in censure. "Stop that. Now it's final. You are young and beautiful, and we can't have a boarder in this house while you are living here."

"I will always live here, *Tetka*."

"Oh, Daniela, my dear. Don't say that. Don't say that," Lenka chided. "There is a man out there for you. He is coming. I know it."

"Then he will have to move in with us," Daniela said. "Because I live here."

"A man in the house . . . imagine it," Lenka whispered. And they were right back where they started from.

~

Irene had a black 1935 Lincoln Model K town car parked in her garage that Malone could drive to Cleveland. He wanted something new. Something clean and shiny that hadn't been hers. But he settled for hardly used.

"You bought it, Michael. You might as well use it," Molly told him.

He thought about taking the train and then decided he'd want—and possibly need—his own wheels. He wouldn't be playing a specific part, and he had no identity to adopt. He would just be poking around to start. Elmer Irey, his boss with the agency, said he would expect updates and regular reports, though Malone's presence in Cleveland would not be official. *Officially*, he was on paid leave.

Molly had kept a few of his things from the years with Capone. Two silk suits, a white fedora, and a pair of glossy white-and-black spectators that he'd loved but that were too flashy for a man who constantly needed to blend in. He'd lived out of a suitcase for so long, buying what he needed when he arrived, and a year in the Bahamas had left him lacking for cold weather wear. He decided he would figure it out when he got to Cleveland. If he was going to be mingling with the shantytown crowd, he wouldn't want new. He packed the suits and the assorted items anyway. He might need them. A good silk suit opened certain doors, and he had no idea which doors he would be knocking on.

He thought he might enjoy the drive from Chicago to Cleveland. He liked to drive, but he hit snow and holed up for a long night in a roadside inn on Highway 20 that might as well have been Timbuktu for all the warmth and comfort it offered. He was so cold, he slept in the ill-fitting wool suit and the overcoat he'd bought for the funeral, wrapped in a ratty bedspread. He left as soon as the roads were clear, but not soon enough.

When he finally arrived in Cleveland, a day later than he'd intended, he was exhausted, angry, and in no mood for nightfall, which was rapidly approaching, though it was barely four o'clock. Euclid Avenue was still lit up for the holidays, but the city seemed tired, and the few folks he saw out and about moved quickly, faces down, hands shoved in their pockets.

Everything was dreary.

He turned south onto East Fifty-Fifth, following the map to the address he'd plotted out when he'd last stopped. It wasn't the most direct route, but it gave him a feel for the area, and looking around, he didn't feel so good. Broadway crossed East Fifty-Fifth on an angle, and he turned right again, studying the neighborhood, making a mental note. Bank, theater, library. He went a few blocks. The address should be on the south side of the street. He passed it once and flipped around at the intersection so he could approach on the right side.

The houses were handsome, as Eliot had promised, but the street-car line trundled past directly in front of them, ruining the effect and making the three-story Victorian ladies look more like funhouses at a carnival instead of the grand residences they once were.

St. Alexis Hospital, topped with crosses and sectioned with three identical Dutch gables, took up the entire block on the opposite side of the street, and a small café butted up into the first residence, furthering the impression that the neighborhood was crowding the old girls out and leaving them behind, though each seemed open for business.

Of the three on the block, one was a medical office, one was a funeral home, and one simply said *Kos*. The driveway on that one was large and empty, but he didn't pull in. He stayed on the street, his car idling in front of the house, and frowned at the sign. Where had he heard that name before?

He checked his map and Eliot's notes again.

This was it: 5054 Broadway. A tailor, Eliot had claimed. The name sounded more like a law firm. Wills and probate made more sense next to the funeral home.

He straightened his tie and checked his reflection, noting that the shadows below his eyes had become gullies, and his fresh shave was not nearly so fresh. He caught movement out the passenger-side window and watched as a woman made her way up the walk to the front porch. She moved quickly, which made him think she was young, though it was hard to tell the shape of her beneath the too-large overcoat that was rolled at the cuffs, a bulky brown scarf, and a crocheted cloche hat that hugged her cheeks and gave him only a glimpse of light brown curls beneath the flattened brim.

The bells on St. Alexis began to toll, and she looked back, pausing as though she appreciated the sound, showing him a slice of cheek and the red tip of her small nose. Then she turned back toward the house and entered the front door, which jangled merrily, suggesting the entrance was indeed open to the public.

He considered waiting for the woman to leave again. He didn't want to inquire about the room with people nosing about the shop. But perhaps she lived there. Or worked there. He grabbed the sheet of paper with the details about the deposit, stuffed it in his breast pocket, and strode up the walk, leaving his things in the car.

Inside, it smelled of leather and starch, and dress forms, mirrors, and racks of clothes were neatly arranged to give the impression of space and abundance, when in actuality there was little of either. Rows of hats, both men's and women's, ran along one side, and glass cabinets of buttons, spools of ribbon, and bolts of fabric occupied the other. A privacy screen and a tailor's stool were not in use, but he could hear rustling from behind a display case that also served as a counter. The bell had rung when he entered, and the woman he'd seen go into the shop before him bobbed up as if she'd been stowing her things, though she still wore her layers.

"Excuse me, sir, I'll be right with you," she said, placing a pair of round, yellow-lensed glasses on her nose. They only accentuated his impression of a small feathered owl, hunched against the cold. She ducked down again, and he thought he heard her tug a boot from her foot.

"I'm here about the room," he said, removing his overcoat and throwing it over his arm. He took the hat from his head as well. It felt ill-mannered to leave it on inside the shop, though the woman's next words made him think he'd been too hasty.

"Oh. Oh, I see. I'm so sorry, sir, but I've already rented it out."

"Daniela?" An old woman walked from the back of the shop, a cane clutched in her hand. Her dress looked like something from the previous century, and her hair was knotted at the back of her head, as if she was attempting to lift her papery skin back into place. But her eyes were bright, her cheekbones high, and her back straight.

"I'm right here, *Teta*," the younger woman called, bounding up again, still bundled, but he guessed she'd changed her shoes. The old woman gaped.

"You should not leave the shop looking like that, Daniela. We make clothes. *You* make clothes! People will not trust your judgment."

"It's cold outside." The girl named Daniela lifted her chin to free her mouth from the folds of her scarf and began to unwind it. It was a very pretty mouth, and Malone was instantly, and surprisingly, distracted. To be sidetracked by a pretty mouth was a pleasure he didn't often indulge in.

The buttons of her coat came next, and as she shrugged it off, she tossed her hat aside as well. Her chin-length hair was the color of shiny pennies, but the static from her hat made the copper coils writhe about her face.

The old woman glowered in disapproval, but the young woman smiled indulgently, ran her hands over her hair, and pushed her spectacles up on her nose. She was quite lovely now that Malone could see her. Her deep blue dress accentuated fine skin, full breasts, and a lithe figure, and he cleared his throat, drawing her attention back to him.

"Pardon me," he said. "I hope I'm in the right place."

The young woman stilled as if she'd forgotten he was there, and the old woman's frown became even more pronounced.

"How can we help you, sir?" the old woman asked.

"I'm here about the room," he repeated.

The young woman gasped. "I know you."

"You do?" the old woman asked.

"I most certainly do," Daniela whispered.

"I doubt that very much," he protested. It was a strange thing to say upon a first meeting, but she seemed too stunned to be embarrassed by her frankness.

The old woman peered at him, lifting a monocle she wore around her neck so she could study him more closely. "Well, I've never seen him before, Daniela," she protested. "And he needs a better suit. Perhaps you are also here for a suit, sir?"

He looked down at the fit of his off-the-rack suit and decided he probably did need a better one. Everyone needed new clothes these days, but he suspected few were buying them. He wondered how the poor women were making ends meet in such a business.

"You have good shoulders and a lean frame. At the very least, we can make that one fit better," the old woman mumbled.

"Yes, I'm sure . . . but I'm here about the room," he insisted.

The old woman frowned. "What room?"

"It's b-been rented, sir," the young woman stammered, still gaping at him. He wished she would take off her glasses. The yellow lenses hid her eyes. If he could see them, he might know her too, come to think of it. He pulled the paper out of his breast pocket and checked the name.

"A month's deposit was put down by a woman named Inez Staley. Could that be the mix-up?" he asked.

The young woman didn't answer. She simply continued to stare at him like she wasn't hearing him at all.

"Well, you are not Inez," the old woman said. She had a hint of an eastern European accent and an entirely American attitude.

"I am not Inez. No. But the deposit was made for me. On my behalf. I was told it would be ready today. Actually, yesterday." He was getting irritated.

"Malone?" the young woman said, her voice so faint he wasn't sure he heard her right.

"My name is Michael Malone. Yes." He'd been under the impression Ness's secretary had withheld his name, but maybe it was better that she hadn't.

The young woman sat abruptly as if she'd grown faint. He could barely see her head above the counter. There must have been a stool back there.

"Daniela Kos, what in the world has gotten into you?" the old woman snapped. "Are you ill?"

The woman named Daniela stood again, slowly, and her face was ashen.

"I'm fine, Zuzana. And yes. Inez Staley. Yes. That was the name." She walked out from behind the counter.

"I will show you the room, Mr. . . . Mr. . . . ." She let her voice run off like she wanted him to supply his name, even though she'd just said it.

"Malone."

"Yes. Malone. Michael Malone," she repeated, almost marveling. What a peculiar young woman.

"Daniela! What have you done? We must discuss this!" the old woman snapped.

"Is there a problem?" he asked. He kept his voice level, but he was seconds from exiting the premises.

"No. There's no problem," Daniela said, shaking her head emphatically. "I expected you yesterday. And I did not know . . . I did not know . . . it would be *you*." She closed the distance between them and took his coat and hat. He surrendered them hesitantly, but she gave him no choice.

"You didn't know it would be *who*? Who, Daniela? Who is this man?"

"Zuzana, Mr. Malone is our new boarder. He will be staying in the room downstairs. Just as we discussed. The deposit has been paid. Rent too. For the next six months. We're being very . . . rude."

The old woman looked at Daniela as if she'd sprouted two heads. He could hardly blame her. The whole thing was quite strange.

"Please follow me, Mr. Malone," Daniela instructed, still clutching his hat and coat.

The old woman—Zuzana—let Daniela pass, but she halted Malone with her cane.

"We need a reference, sir," she said imperiously. "Who are you, and what is it that you do?"

"My name is Michael Malone, like I said. I am a . . . consultant."

"And who is it you consult with, Mr. Malone?"

He hesitated. He did not know what had already been communicated and he did not want to contradict it.

"He is in policing," Daniela said softly. "Isn't that right, Mr. Malone?"

"Yes," he agreed. "In a manner of speaking." Inez Staley must have given her a backstory of some sort.

"You're cheating, Daniela," Zuzana snapped. "I would like to hear it from Mr. Malone, not from his garments."

Cheating? Malone looked at the women, dumbfounded.

"And you are unmarried?" Zuzana continued her grilling.

"I am a . . . recent . . . widower."

That seemed to mollify the old woman. Widowers were better than bachelors, apparently. Especially bachelors his age.

"Oh dear. That's terrible. I'm so sorry about Irene," Daniela blurted.

"Daniela," Zuzana chided. "Don't be so familiar."

Daniela looked at the floor, a deep blush staining her cheeks. Apparently, his backstory had also included his deceased wife's name, which was completely unacceptable. At the moment, he was very unhappy with Eliot Ness. Unhappy with the whole situation.

"I'm tired, ladies," he said to the women, voice sharp. "I've driven a long way, and I want the room. If I have to leave now, I won't be coming back. And I will expect to leave with the deposit in my hand."

"The name Malone is Irish. You don't look Irish," Zuzana said, undeterred by his threat. But she withdrew her cane, a signal that he could pass. "You look like a Gypsy. However, I prefer Gypsies to Irishmen."

Good God.

"Mr. Malone, please. Come this way," Daniela urged, tugging on his arm. "I'll show you the room." She still carried his coat and hat, clinging to them as if she were afraid he would leave. He desperately wanted to. But he followed her through the shop and down a long corridor, leaving the old woman to stare after them.

"The room is here on the main floor," Daniela called over her shoulder. "It's the only bedroom that is, and it's on the back of the house, giving you some privacy from the shop as well as proximity to the back door, just there, straight ahead, at the base of the stairs. The toilet is here." She pointed to a door on the right side of the hallway, directly across from a room that was crowded with sewing machines, dress forms, and a table stacked with bolts of cloth.

The door to the bathroom was open, and as they paused in the doorway, he noted the massive claw-footed tub, the pedestal sink, and their combined reflection in the mirror above it, a bright bluebird next to a careworn crow.

She was staring at him again.

"Miss Kos?" he said, urging her on.

"Um . . . yes. The laundry is there"—she pointed at the final door on the right—"and we will be glad to do your wash as part of your board. I noticed you have a car as well. You can pull that into the old stable around back if you like. On the covered end. There's room. You may also leave it in the drive or on the street if you are worried about customers boxing you in. Whatever you prefer." She spoke quickly, nervously, as she ushered him through the last door on the left side of the hall.

The room was large, with two big windows that faced west, giving him a view of the side of the funeral home when he parted the heavy drapes. A long drive wrapped around it and curved into what looked like a ramp to the funeral home's basement. It made sense. One did not bring the dead through the front door.

He let the curtains fall and appreciated the lack of dust on their thick folds. The room was clean. A fireplace and a desk ran along the south wall, across from an ornate wardrobe and a large bed made with a spread that matched the drapes. The floors were wood, the moldings thick, the rugs plush. Everything had aged, but it had aged well.

"My aunts—Zuzana and Lenka—and I are upstairs. You saw the stairs just beyond the door?"

He nodded.

"The kitchen and sitting room are upstairs as well, which you are welcome to use. You are also welcome to eat your meals with us—at least breakfast and supper. Or we will see that you have a tray brought down. We don't all stop at the same time for lunch, so you will be on your own. We also have some help—Margaret—who does much of the cleaning and the cooking. If you put your laundry in the hamper just inside the door, she will do that too."

"I don't know how long I'll need the room," he warned.

"We won't rent by the week." Her voice got defensive, and she was still clutching his hat and his coat. "Only by the month. And we need at least a month's notice if you want to leave. We'll keep the deposit too. For cleaning and . . . and . . ." Her voice faded off.

She was new to this, he could tell. He stepped forward and took his things from her arms.

"That's fine, miss. The six months is yours to keep, even if I leave next week. And I'll give notice when I go."

"That's very kind of you," she said on an exhale. "But . . . I hope you won't leave so soon." Her cheeks pinked again, and she took off her spectacles and tucked them into the pocket of her dress.

"It's a nice room," she continued, her eyes averted. "The biggest in the house. We typically use the bathroom down here during the day when we are in the shop or the sewing room, but now that you are here, we will go upstairs. It will be for your use alone."

"Won't that be difficult for the woman with the cane?" he asked, tossing his coat and hat across the bed so he could fiddle with the radiator in the corner. It hissed and clanked but seemed to be in working order.

He was freezing. There was a small stack of wood in the fireplace, and the tinderbox beside it looked full as well. He would need it.

"Zuzana is very able," Daniela answered belatedly, and he had to remind himself what they were talking about.

"Feel free to continue using the bathroom downstairs. I hardly need a private bath during the day."

"That is very gracious of you. But in the evenings, we will stay upstairs."

"All right."

"Will the room do, Mr. Malone?" she asked.

He nodded, his eyes taking another quick run around the space. "Yes. It'll do nicely." The proprietors themselves might take some getting used to, but he liked the room very much, and he could avoid them.

"I will get my belongings from my car. If I need something, I will ask. But I'm guessing you will hardly know I'm here."

Daniela nodded and folded her hands, but she made no motion to depart. He took a few steps toward the door, hoping she would get the hint that he was through with her.

She was studying him intently, her hands clasped in front of her, her jaw tight. It was as if she was waiting for something.

Her eyes were different colors. The left one was blue. The right one was brown.

She kept her gaze steady, allowing him to stare, and stare he did. He'd only seen such a thing once before . . . but he was being rude. He looked away, embarrassed, and grabbed his coat and hat from the bed.

"I'll just get my things from my car and pull it off the street. If you'll excuse me, Miss Kos."

"It's Flanagan, Mr. Malone," she said. "Not Kos. My name is Dani Flanagan. My aunts are named Kos. My mother was a Kos. But I am a Flanagan."

"Flanagan," he murmured. He looked at her again, and realization finally dawned, lighting his weary brain. All the little pieces became a picture.

"Dani Flanagan," he gasped.

"You remember me, then?" Her mouth bore a hint of a smile, but her brow was furrowed.

"Yes. I do."

"It's been fifteen years. It would be quite understandable if you didn't."

"Fifteen years," he repeated.

"Yes . . . to the day, actually. I met you fifteen years ago . . . today." She swallowed, and a shadow passed over her face. "Now you might not think me so strange. You gave me a bit of a shock out there."

To the day? Good grief. What were the odds of that?

"You look exactly the same," she said.

"Well, you don't!"

She laughed. "I hope not. I was ten years old. I'll be twenty-five—"

"Tomorrow," he finished for her. "You'll be twenty-five tomorrow."

"Yes." The shadow was back. Her birthday marked a terrible loss. He couldn't believe it. "Little Dani Flanagan," he breathed.

"Yes. And Officer Malone."

"Nobody calls me that anymore. I haven't been a patrolman for a very long time."

"Well, that's how I always think of you."

He cocked his head in question.

"I've thought of you often since then, and with great fondness."

"I can't imagine why. I would think you'd try not to think of me at all."

"You were kind. It doesn't take much to make a child love."

"You were a brave girl." Brave . . . and extraordinary. She'd said the strangest things. And she'd had the most *uncanny* ability. It was his turn to feel weak-kneed, and he sank to the bed.

"I'm tired, Miss Flanagan. Forgive me." He ran a hand over his face.

"Yes . . . I can see that you are." She searched his eyes and looked away at last. "I hope . . . I haven't upset you. Maybe we can talk more in the days to come. I would like that."

"Of course." He couldn't imagine what they would say, but he nodded agreeably.

"We will eat at seven. Please join us. It would be good if we all got to know each other a little. I'm afraid my aunts are very old fashioned, and the circumstances in Cleveland right now have made everyone a bit skittish. You have heard that we seem to have a . . . mad butcher . . . on the loose?"

He nodded, and with that she slipped out, closing the door behind her.

3

Malone didn't want to join the women for dinner, but he was famished, and the thought of going out into the wintry darkness to forage in unfamiliar surroundings was even more unappealing than a dinner with strangers. Better to break the ice anyway. If he was going to live in this house, even briefly, he'd best get past any awkwardness as soon as possible.

It took him two trips to empty out the trunk and park the car behind the house under the cover of the stable-like structure. The funeral home next door had removed whatever outbuildings had once existed on its property in favor of the wrap-around drive and the unloading ramp. The house beyond that, the one used as a medical practice, had a stable much like the Koses, though a wall between the two yards made it hard to see anything other than the roofline. The three houses were probably all built around the same time, so similar were their exteriors and style.

As he opened the back door on his last trip, the box of files in his arms, an orange cat shot past him and ran into the house. It startled him, and he danced sideways to avoid it, stepping on its tail. The cat shrieked in pain and raced into Malone's new quarters, disappearing under the bed to lick his wounds.

"Is that you, Charlie?" Malone asked, putting the files on the desk. He crouched down beside the bed and lifted up the spread to peer underneath it. A rumbling death rattle sounded from the feline form. Oh yeah. It was Charlie.

"You don't remember me, but I remember you," Malone muttered. "If it weren't for me, you'd still be living in Chicago and not hiding under this nice bed."

The cat hissed, staring back at Malone with odd-eyed outrage, and the memory of their first encounter surfaced like it was yesterday and not fifteen years ago.

The day after the Flanagan murders and two hours before his shift started, Malone went to O'Brien's Books, a mere block from the Flanagan residence and right next door to Schofield's Flower Shop. He and everyone else knew the flower shop was owned by the notorious Dean O'Banion, leader of the Irish gang that ran the whole area. But Malone didn't go to ask questions or pursue leads. He went to fetch the kitten Dani had talked about.

Connor O'Brien, the owner of the bookstore, had heard about the Flanagans, and when Malone told him who the cat was for, the man gave him an old birdcage Dani could transport him in.

"It'll do to get her wherever she's going," O'Brien said when the cat was settled. "I hear Aneta has family who will take the girl."

The little orange cat with his furry face and mismatched gaze would not fit in the birdcage for long, and he stared through the thin bars, unamused.

"George didn't kill her, did he?" O'Brien asked Malone as he turned to go. "They're saying he did. But I don't believe it. George Flanagan was a rascal, but he wasn't a killer. He worshipped the ground Aneta walked on. And right he should. She was too good for him by half. I just don't believe it."

Malone only nodded and thanked the man again. He didn't know George Flanagan, but he didn't need to. The whole thing was a rotting, stinking shame.

O'Brien clamped his lips shut like he'd said too much, but he had one more question. "What will happen to little Dani?"

"I don't know," Malone said, but it was her birthday, and he was going to make sure she had her cat.

He brought it to Mrs. Thurston's house and knocked on the door, dreading a slew of questions from the woman, but it was Dani who answered, almost like she'd seen him coming. She didn't look like she'd slept, poor thing. Her eyes were ringed with purple and the shocked glaze had not abated. When the glaze left, the grief would set in.

Her hair had not been tended to, and it was a riotous mass of reddish-gold curls that bounced around her shoulders. He hadn't noticed her hair the night before. She'd worn a stocking cap pulled low on her head, the curls barely peeping out here and there to frame her face.

"Your hair is almost the same color as Charlie's fur," he said by way of greeting. She'd taken one look at the cage and the little cat inside, and her face crumpled. He'd almost cried too.

"Is he mine now?" she asked, trying to control her tears.

"Yes. He's yours."

The cat, now ten pounds heavier and fifteen years older, spat at Malone again, bringing him back to present day.

"Don't give me your attitude, Charles. We have history. And yes, I will call you Charles. You've outgrown Charlie."

The cat didn't budge, and Malone left it alone while he went into the bathroom to wash and shave, hoping it would leave while the coast was clear.

He dealt with his two suitcases, one that held his clothing and another filled with the odds and ends of disguise. He didn't know yet what he would need, but he always traveled with some basics. When he opened the wardrobe, the scent of roses wafted around him, and he hung his suits and dress shirts on the rack and put his undershorts and pajamas in the fragrant drawers. He wondered who had inhabited the room before him. Clearly not a man. He tried to remember the details of young Dani's family situation and could not. He would find out soon enough.

He exchanged one white shirt for another. He doubted dinner would require it, but he wore a tie with his suspenders just to be safe, though he left his suitcoat in his room. As he climbed the stairs, Charlie swished by him, tail high, as if he hadn't just sulked beneath the bed for the last hour.

Malone followed the cat as well as the sound and smells of food and found three women—Dani, Zuzana, and one he'd not yet met—already seated in the small dining room off the kitchen. A place had been set for him at the end of the table, but Charlie beat him to it, hopping up onto the chair and eyeing Malone with disdain. Dani rose and scooped the indignant creature off the chair and took him into the kitchen where he heard her scolding him like a mother.

"Be nice, Charlie. You are not the guest."

Zuzana introduced her sister, Lenka, a shorter, plumper version of herself, but where Zuzana was prickly and dour, Lenka was all smiles and soft glances. They were both a million years old, with bright blue eyes and thick white hair, and they both stared at him throughout the entire meal, which was hot and filling but not worth enduring their attention or his own aggravation.

The resemblance between the three women was unmistakable. Zuzana and Lenka had the same pearly skin as Dani, though theirs had pooled beneath their eyes and around their mouths with age. They were wrinkled and bent, but their skin was still unspotted. He suspected that once they had both been quite beautiful. Maybe as beautiful as Dani.

He sneaked a quick look at her across the table, and her different-colored eyes met his before dancing back to her plate. Her skin was as buttery and poreless as whipped cream. He thought briefly that it might simply be her youth, and then had to remind himself that she was the same age he'd been when they met. When they'd met, he'd already been to war and back again. He'd already outlived his children and left his wife.

Dani had been a child when they met. She was not a child now.

What a strange vortex the years suddenly seemed. The jump from ten to twenty-five was a lifetime. The leap from twenty-five to forty was but a long weekend. It was like being trapped in a Jules Verne novel.

He caught his reflection in the big mirror that sat over the long sideboard, the same way he'd seen himself in the washroom mirror when Dani was showing him to his room. He made himself look harder, simply to ease his disorientation.

He didn't have a boyish face or a youthful glow, but he'd looked old when he was young, so aging wasn't as marked in him as it was in some. He had deep-set, downturned eyes that were always shadowed, and skin like leather. He was currently the color of a brown paper bag, but even without the tempering of a year in the sun, he never burned.

We thought you were a changeling, with your dark eyes and all that dark hair. But then you smiled, and Dad saw himself. Thank goodness for that. They might have left you for the faeries or given you to Father McDonough to raise.

Molly had always said this with great affection, but young Michael had worried about it. What if he was a changeling? His pop's skin was always pink, and his eyes were a vivid blue. How could Michael be the son of Martin and Kathleen Malone and look the way he did?

Have you ever seen a litter of pups where one is spotted and one is not? Where one is brown and one is gray? It's no different than that.

Molly always had an answer for everything. But Michael had taken his looks as something of a sign. He was the outsider. The black sheep.

"You must tell us about yourself, Mr. Malone," Lenka insisted, drawing his attention back to the dinner table and his present company. "Where are you from? And what brings you to Cleveland?"

He was ready for the questions now, though he would have to stay much closer to the truth of his life than he'd intended. Knowing Dani demanded it.

He gave a glancing biography: Raised in Chicago. Served in the Great War. No children. Wife deceased. Former policeman. Currently worked for the Department of the Treasury.

"And what is it you do for the Treasury Department?" Lenka asked.

"I'm essentially a tax man. I consult with local governments on receiving and meeting the requirements of federal assistance," he said, then droned on about budgets and public welfare just long enough and drearily enough that they wouldn't want to inquire again.

"How fascinating," Lenka said, though she didn't ask a follow-up question. None of the women did.

Daniela said little, Zuzana even less, though she reiterated that she did not like Irishmen and reacted in horror when he addressed Dani as Miss Flanagan. He didn't even know *what* to call her, and calling her Miss Kos felt ridiculous. They had too much history to address each other as strangers. It was like saying *Pardon me* in a foxhole.

He ate as quickly as was politely possible and excused himself as soon as he was finished. Then he bid the women good night and descended the stairs, knowing he would be the topic of discussion as soon as he shut his door.

~

"He has said we can keep the rent, all six months, even if he leaves before then," Dani told her aunts. "He will be a good boarder."

"Nobody has money like that these days. Not honest men," Zuzana said, tossing her napkin onto her plate.

"He works for the government," Lenka protested.

Zuzana scoffed. "So? Never trust the government."

"He's quite handsome," Lenka whispered, though her whisper was louder than her regular speaking voice. "I like a man with a good head of hair."

"He's handsome, is he?" Zuzana huffed. "What does he look like then, Lenka. Hmm? You can't see the buttons on your own frocks without your spectacles. He could look like the dog that hangs around the sandwich shop, and you wouldn't know the difference."

"But he doesn't look like the dog, does he? Not at all. He's handsome. And well put together. And he smells nice." Lenka drew in a deep, cleansing breath. "I can smell him all the way up the stairs. He must have just washed."

"Lenka. Good heavens," Zuzana snapped.

"It is good to have a man in the house again," Lenka said, defensive.

The last man in the house had been their brother, Pavel, Daniela's grandfather, almost fifteen years ago. The youngest, by far, of the four siblings, he'd been the only one to marry and have a family, though neither the marriage nor the family had lasted long. His wife died when his daughter, Aneta, Dani's mother, was three years old, and she had been raised, primarily, by his three older sisters who had never had families of their own.

"It most certainly is *not* good to have a man in the house," Zuzana said. "You'll not be so glad when he's chopping you up and throwing you in the Cuyahoga."

"Daniela says the plates on his car say Chicago," Lenka answered. "The Butcher's been carving people up for three years. I doubt Mr. Malone from Chicago is the Torso Killer of Kingsbury Run. And so far, the Butcher doesn't kill old ladies. You said so yourself, sister."

"No . . . I suppose not," Zuzana sulked, as if she enjoyed fearing for her life.

"He's awfully young to be a widower," Lenka said.

"I thought the same thing!" Zuzana said, wagging a finger. "He probably killed her too."

"Zuzana!" Dani gasped.

"I don't care what he says. He's shifty. He's probably running from the law."

"You heard him. He *is* the law. So you should be comforted by his presence. We are safer with him here."

That stumped Zuzana for a moment, but not for long. "You were acting so oddly when he came into the shop. I thought you were having a fit. The next thing I know, you're escorting him through the house and inviting him to dine with us."

"I admit . . . I was surprised," Dani confessed.

"By what?" Lenka asked.

"By him." Dani lifted her empty glass and set it down again. She might as well air it all out right now. Her aunts did not like talking about Chicago. Or her parents. But she should tell them about Michael Malone, if only to set their minds at ease.

"I met him a long time ago," Dani explained. "He was the policeman who escorted me here from Chicago after . . . after Mother died. He was very kind to me. He was the one who gave me Charlie, and he took very good care of me on the train. And so it was a surprise to see him today. A strange coincidence. But a welcome one too."

Zuzana and Lenka stared at her, their mouths gaping. Zuzana shut hers with a snap.

"Goodness gracious," Lenka breathed. "What a shock that must have been."

"Does he know who you are?" Zuzana asked.

"Yes. I told him when I showed him the room. He remembered me immediately. Of course, he knew me as Dani Flanagan, so you must forgive him when he calls me by that name. But . . . I think he was as stunned as I."

"Unbelievable," Lenka marveled, and Zuzana sniffed.

"That doesn't mean you know him. You were a child. We know nothing about him now," Zuzana argued, determined as always to be the voice of dissent.

"No, *Tetka*. You're wrong. I know a great deal about him. And he . . . knows . . . about me."

~

Malone took off his clothes and hung them in the wardrobe, noting the rosy fragrance once more. At least it didn't smell like cat. He had a feeling Charlie thought the room was his. That would change. The cat gave him the creeps. Or maybe it was the house. Or the women. Maybe it was just Dani, and the little girl she'd been.

"Poor Dani Flanagan. Strange little Dani Flanagan," he said aloud, and felt ashamed of himself for saying it. To call her strange was true. But it wasn't the whole truth. Words like "strange" reduced men and women to their oddities. To flat, unfeeling objects to be studied and dismissed. People deserved more than that. Dani Flanagan deserved more than that.

He crawled into bed and turned off the lamp, not caring that it was barely 8:00 p.m. He was bone-tired, and he did not want to think anymore. He wanted darkness and oblivion. But there, in the quiet of his new surroundings, his mind flew back to the long train ride to Cleveland, little Dani Flanagan beside him.

She was being sent to family, and he'd been given the assignment to accompany her.

She knows you now, Murphy had said. *It makes sense for you to go. Her family will have someone there to meet her at the station. You just have to see that she gets there.*

Dani held the birdcage on her lap, and the kitten inside seemed happy enough in his makeshift home. She got smiles from other passengers and a few comments at the incongruous occupant of the cage, but she was shy about making eye contact and replied mostly with a smile and a yes or no if she had to speak at all. Maybe it was weariness. She started nodding off right after the trip began. The whirring and clacking of the wheels chased thought away.

He made a pillow from his overcoat and set it on the top of the cage, and she leaned against it and slept for two hours, only rousing when the cat started to cry. She lifted her bleary eyes to his, as if she'd forgotten where she was, and he was struck again by their color, so distinct, one from the other.

He saw the moment she remembered. It would be like that for a while, that awful shock and pain each time she awakened. But eventually, even in sleep, she would know they were gone. Malone didn't know which was worse—to escape and return or to constantly remember.

"Do you think I could take Charlie out of the cage for a while?" she asked.

"No, Dani. If he gets loose, it won't be good."

"He's thirsty."

"I'm more worried about you. Are you hungry?"

She nodded. He brought out the sandwiches he'd purchased at the station and gave her one, along with a bottle of lemonade. He had water in his flask for the kitten.

"Cup your hand, like so." He showed Dani how to make a little well in the palm of her hand and then opened the door of the cage just far enough for her to ease her hand through. Charlie lapped up the water with his tiny tongue, and Dani laughed, delighted.

A woman joined them in their car soon after. Her eyes were hollow and her mouth pinched, and she stared at Dani as if she didn't like the look of her. Or maybe it was just the cat. She sneezed several times and asked the attendant if she could be seated somewhere else. When she rose to leave, her shawl fell from her shoulders and Dani shifted to pick it up.

"Ma'am?" Malone said, calling the woman's attention to her wrap.

The woman turned back around and yanked it from Dani's out-stretched hand.

"I'm sorry about your Jimmy," Dani said, her voice ringing with sweet sincerity. The woman blanched and her knees buckled. Malone reached for her arm, fearing she would fall, but she straightened almost immediately.

"What did you say, girl?" the woman cried.

"I'm sorry for your loss," Dani said, amending her words slightly.

"She's got the devil in her," the woman hissed at Malone, like he was to blame, but tears were streaming down her cheeks. She couldn't get away fast enough.

He looked down at the girl, incredulous. "Why did you say that, Dani? Who's Jimmy? Do you know that woman?"

"No. I don't know her." Dani wouldn't look at him.

He waited for her to expound, but she pulled out the last bite of her sandwich and pinched a piece off for Charlie, offering it to him through the bars.

"Dani, who's Jimmy?" he pressed.

She sighed heavily. "I don't know. Someone she lost. Someone she loved. He died. She's angry. And sad."

"I see. But how do you know that?"

"Her shawl told me."

"Her . . . shawl . . . told you," he repeated, his voice flat.

"Yes," she said.

He sat in stunned silence.

"I'm sorry, Mr. Malone. Mother said it's better if I don't tell my stories. But that lady was so sad . . . and the words just came out."

"Your stories." He felt like a babbling idiot, repeating everything she said, but he couldn't catch up. "They're just stories?"

"I suppose. But they're true stories, I think."

"Tell me another one."

"I can't think of them by myself."

"How do you think of them?"

"I have to touch something."

"Like what?"

"Cloth. Sometimes other things. But usually cloth. Cloth talks to me because I'm a Kos." She pronounced the word "Kosh" and said it like it was a grand thing to be.

"A Kos?" There he went again.

"My great-great-grandfather Kos made garments for the emperor."

"The emperor of where?"

"I don't know. A place not in America."

"Huh." He thought about that for a moment but circled back around to Dani. "So the woman's shawl told you that she lost someone named Jimmy."

"It's kind of hard to explain." She looked at him, eyes pleading. "I didn't mean to say anything. I know better. My brain is tired. Sometimes when my brain is tired, my words come loose."

"And you say things you don't mean?" he asked, hopeful.

"No. Not things I don't mean. Things I shouldn't say."

"Why shouldn't you say them?"

"Because people don't understand. And they are afraid of me."

"When I gave you Bunny—the little cloth rabbit—you said it was Mary's," he prodded softly. It had haunted him.

She nodded. "That's why I gave it back to you when you left."

He reached into his pocket and pulled it out. Then he held it out to her. She seemed hesitant to take it.

"Go on," he urged, and she obeyed, closing her hands around the little toy.

"Are you mad at me, Malone?" she asked.

"No. Why would I be mad?"

"Mother said people sometimes get mad when they're scared."

"I'm not mad. And I'm not scared."

She looked at him doubtfully and chewed on her lip, considering, as if she knew full well that he was scared.

"*Mary was my little girl,*" *he whispered.* "*You were right. That was her bunny.*"

"*She got sick,*" *Dani said. It wasn't a question, and he wondered how many stories the rabbit had to tell.*

"*Yeah. She did. And she died. About six months ago.*"

"*I'm sorry,*" *Dani said. And he could see that she was.*

"*Me too.*"

"*You sang her to sleep. But I only hear one song,*" *she murmured, still squeezing the little rabbit.*

"*I only ever sang one song.*"

She began to hum his lullaby. "*I've never heard it before.*"

Jesus, Mary, and Joseph. He'd lied. He was scared. Ice skittered down his back and heat pooled in his belly. He took the rabbit from Dani's hand, but he replaced it with the hanky from his pocket. It was the one Irene had given him before he went to France. Her initials were neatly intertwined with his.

"*Tell me another story,*" *he insisted.*

Dani took it and spread it out over her skinny knees. She stroked it a few times and traced the letters.

"*Is Irene your wife?*" *she asked.*

"*Irene who?*" *he asked, his voice soft and without inflection.*

"*Irene . . . the pretty lady who made these stitches,*" *she said, touching the initials.*

He wanted to jerk the handkerchief from Dani's lap and be done with the whole bizarre conversation. But damn if he didn't believe her. And damn if he wasn't fascinated.

"*Tell me more.*"

She wrinkled up her nose and tipped her head.

"*You were going to be away from her, and she was scared you wouldn't come back.*" *She drew the handkerchief to her nose and breathed deeply.* "*She put perfume on it so you would think of her. But I can't smell it. It must have been a long time ago.*"

"It was." It felt like a lifetime ago. And he'd never used the hanky. He hadn't wanted to soil it. He'd found it a few days ago at the bottom of a box of his things Molly had kept for him during the war. He'd been trying to get his affairs in order. He'd shoved it in his pocket with Mary's rabbit, caught in a fit of sentimentality.

"How could you possibly know any of that?" he mused aloud, but Dani thought it was a question for her.

"I just do."

"It doesn't make sense."

"Just because it doesn't make sense to you, doesn't mean it doesn't make sense," she whispered, and he couldn't argue with that.

"What else? What else do you see?" he asked.

She folded the handkerchief into a smaller square and held it a minute longer. "I don't see anything else. I just feel you." She shrugged. "That's probably because it's been in your pocket. But that's all."

"You feel me? What do you mean?"

She shrugged again. "Just . . . you. Kinda like I can feel you next to me without looking at you. You're warm and you're big and you smell clean."

"Huh," he grunted. He thought of the colors from his childhood, the hues that surrounded different people, and trying to describe it to his mother.

"Do you believe me, Malone?" she asked.

"Yeah, Dani," he whispered. "I guess I do."

She sighed like he'd given her a slice of pie with ice cream on top and closed her eyes. "Mother and Daddy said I shouldn't tell anyone my stories. So I don't. But I still know things. I can't help it."

"You ever told anyone else?"

"Not really. Mother tried to send me to school, but the nuns got mad at me. Mother said I could wear mittens, so I wouldn't touch something that would get me in trouble, but the nuns didn't like that either, and it made it hard to do my work. And sometimes the stories just popped right out of my mouth. The nuns told Mother I had an evil spirit. So Mother took me out of school."

He had let the conversation trail after that, but Dani had extracted a promise from him before they parted.

"Will you find the man who killed them?" she asked. He thought about evading her query with a pat on the head and a denial of the facts.

"I don't know, Dani. My captain thinks it was your pop who killed your mother. And then he killed himself." It was a brutal assessment, but Dani was not a child that could be easily lied to.

"But you don't think that. I wore your coat."

Malone stared at her, dumbfounded.

"You put your coat around me," she pressed.

"So?"

She sighed as if she knew he wasn't going to like what she said next.

"A man who wants to kill himself doesn't shoot himself in the chest. He shoots himself in the head. That's what you thought when you saw them . . . when you saw Daddy. Isn't it?"

"Good God, kid."

"Daddy didn't do it. Someone else did. You need to find him. If you don't do it, who will?"

4

Malone didn't join them for breakfast, so Dani made up a tray and knocked on his bedroom door. She knew he was up. She'd heard him moving around, and he'd been in and out of the bathroom. The smell of spice and soap wafted in the hall between his closed door and the sink.

Dani knocked again, balancing the tray against her chest. "Mr. Malone?"

He didn't answer.

"Mr. Malone? I brought you some breakfast. I can leave it here by the door. I just wanted you to know it's here."

The door swung open, and Malone stood on the other side, his jaw clean-shaven and his dark hair slicked straight back from his square forehead. The shadows beneath his hound dog eyes were considerably lighter, and he greeted her pleasantly, though he didn't smile. Dani would like to see him smile. She had a suspicion it might transform him. Maybe that's why he didn't do it. Transformation could be frightening.

Like last night, he was dressed in a white shirt and gray trousers with a pair of black suspenders that matched his shoes. He wasn't wearing a coat or tie. Not yet, though it looked as though he was pre-paring to go out.

"You didn't have to do that," he said, looking at the tray, but he rushed to clear off a stack of folders from the desk so she could set it down. "I would have come up . . . but I slept a little later than I planned."

"You look rested," she said. Rested . . . yet still uncomfortable in her presence.

She wondered if he remembered everything. She thought he might. He'd looked at her with a good amount of trepidation at supper. She'd seen the look before. Many times. It was the look that said he found her peculiar.

She'd kept her stories to herself as much as possible when she'd moved to Cleveland. But eventually the truth leaked out. Vera had believed her first. Then Lenka. And finally Zuzana. It was a family trait, Lenka said. But Mr. Malone did not have their history to reassure him.

She wondered if she could call him Michael. She didn't like calling him Mr. Malone. It put her back in the skin of her ten-year-old self, clutching the little rabbit, and looking up at him as he confirmed what she knew. *They're dead, aren't they?*

She cleared her throat and smoothed her skirt. "I have something that's yours, Mr. Malone." Better to get this out of the way. She reached into her pocket and pulled out his handkerchief and set it beside the breakfast tray. It was folded neatly, initials up, and he froze.

"I didn't mean to take it," she explained. "It was in my coat when I got off the train that day."

For a moment he didn't speak. He simply stared at the small white square, his hands in his pockets.

"You kept it all this time?" he asked, finally lifting his gaze to hers.

She shrugged. "I couldn't very well throw it away. It was yours."

"Huh."

"I'm very sorry. You must have wanted it back."

"No." He shook his head. "I didn't. It was an unhappy reminder."

She didn't know what to say. Should she take it back? The past was swirling around them. Questions and doubts. Disbelief and denial. She turned to go, unable to bear the awkward tension.

"When I called you Miss Flanagan last night, your aunt corrected me," he said, delaying her exit. "So now I don't know what to call you."

"My aunts think my father was a no-good bum who murdered my mother. They won't even say his name," she explained softly.

"I thought maybe that was it. I guess you can't blame them. They believe what they were told."

"Yes. I suppose. I go by Kos because they asked me to when I came to live with them. And it made me feel like I belonged to them, which I needed. But it bothers me still. I think of myself as Dani Flanagan. That is who I am in here." She patted her chest. "I tell myself it doesn't matter. Daddy and Mother would understand. But sometimes it still feels like a betrayal."

"What would you like me to call you?"

"You can call me Daniela . . . or Dani. I'd like to call you Michael . . . or at least Malone. It will feel less strange, I think."

"I can't imagine many things stranger than this," he said. But his mouth had softened. "Have you been all right, Dani? I have worried about you. Wondered about you."

"I've wondered about you as well. You believed me. I never forgot that." She didn't explain herself. She didn't think she had to.

He was quiet for a moment, and she thought he might pretend not to understand. He didn't.

"You were very convincing, kid. And you had no reason to lie."

"No. None at all. I still don't. At least, not with you."

"Why? Why not with me?"

"Because you . . . already know." She smiled, sheepish, but his hangdog expression didn't change.

"For what it's worth, Dani . . . I never thought your father killed your mother. I never believed it. I was just a beat cop. Young. Fairly new on the force. And I was told to shut my mouth. The case was closed, my captain said. But I knew. The whole damn precinct knew."

She reached for the wall to brace herself. He was almost as odd as she, saying such things. They were strangers having an intensely intimate conversation. No small talk. No niceties. Just murder and conspiracy, right out of the gates. She felt almost dizzy and suspected it was relief. *How good it felt to speak of it!*

"My aunts said my father was a rumrunner," she said. "Involved with the Irish gang. That's what the authorities told them. I think that might have been true. It makes sense. He was gone a lot and didn't work regular hours. Mother was nervous. That's why they fought, I think. But he would not have killed my mother. Himself? Maybe. But never her. He would not have done that to her. And he would not have done that to me."

He didn't argue.

"I was a child. I didn't know anything . . . except, they were crazy about each other. I saw that. I remember that. It comforts me now, thinking about how they were. Most people don't get that in a lifetime. Many of us get love. But not like that." She swallowed, trying to rein in her words. She sounded impassioned and . . . silly. But Malone nodded slowly.

"Mr. O'Brien said much the same thing when I went to get Charlie."

"Mr. O'Brien did?" Dani whispered. Bless him for that. "The police told my aunts that my father pulled up to the house in a hurry. They said he walked inside—ran inside—shouting her name. Angry. A few minutes later, gunshots. Is any of that true?"

"I think someone was already in the house when your father got there. Your father *was* a rumrunner, and he stepped on some toes. Tried to sway suppliers and buyers to give him their business. Maybe he crossed some of the big guys, the gangsters. Or maybe he thought he could be in business on his own, and they didn't like the competition. I don't know, honestly. But that was a hit. It wasn't even a very clean hit. But everyone fell into line. Neighbors. Cops. Newspapers. They told the story they were supposed to tell. And nobody else got hurt."

"Nobody else?"

"Nobody but you," he said gently. "I left Chicago not long after you did. But when I got the chance, I tried to make it right. In a roundabout way, George Flanagan got his justice."

"What do you mean?"

He sighed like the story was too big to tell. Then he shook his head, refusing to answer.

For a moment there was silence between them, but Dani's head was spinning.

"I haven't ever been back," she said. "I've never seen where they're buried. Never visited their graves."

"They share a stone. They're buried not far from my—" Malone hesitated, like he'd said something he didn't want to finish. But she knew. And she was too discombobulated not to follow where he'd led.

"From Irene?" she asked. She'd mentioned Irene yesterday in the shop. Maybe he hadn't understood then. But he did now, and his face went blank.

"I held y-your overcoat," she stammered. "You must have worn it to her service. It was her service . . . wasn't it?"

"Yes." He jerked his head once in assent. "It was Irene's service. I buried her on New Year's Day. But you might already know that." His answer was clipped and cold, and Dani flinched.

Too much, Dani. Too much truth. You're scaring him.

"No. I didn't know that. I don't see everything . . . and rarely do I understand the context of what I see. I also don't usually make those kinds of mistakes."

"What mistakes are those, Dani?"

"I shouldn't have blurted it out. I always keep what I see to myself. But your sudden appearance yesterday after all these years was . . . unnerving. I didn't handle it very well. I'm not handling it well now. Forgive me."

He nodded once, but the bubble of candor and intimacy between them had burst. They were strangers again. His eyes were wary, her arms were folded, and they'd both had enough. She hurried to the door.

"Dani?"

"Yes?"

"Happy birthday," he said softly.

She nodded, much the way he had done, and left him to his discomfort and his cold breakfast.

~

He had thought about denying it. It angered him that Dani would invade his privacy that way, and that she would *admit* it to him. The very least she could do was *pretend*. But he didn't want to lie about Irene. She was gone, and Dani clearly knew it. Dani knew a lot of things.

She hadn't outgrown her "stories."

He felt exposed, like he'd suddenly found himself in a shoot-out without his gun or in a room full of strangers without an exit door. His instincts were shrieking at him to get out, but he'd learned long ago that running drew attention and suspicion. Holding his ground when he'd wanted to bolt had saved his life a dozen times. But he was dazed and disoriented, and for the first time in fifteen years, he thought maybe he was out of his depth. He would have to tell Eliot he needed a different place to stay, or simply tell him he wasn't up to the job.

He waited until he heard their voices in the shop—Lenka and Zuzana were arguing and Dani was quiet, but he heard her quick, light tread come down the stairs and move hastily past his door. Another voice, this one singing in a language he didn't speak, came through the back door and remained in the laundry room long enough for him to deduce this was the help.

With all the women accounted for, he went into the sewing room to use the telephone Dani had pointed out the day before. He rang Eliot Ness's office and was put through immediately.

"Malone. Are you settled?"

"Yeah, though I'm wondering how you came across this rental."

"Why? What's the problem? No good?"

"No, the room's fine. I just . . . know the landlady."

"You know her?" Eliot's voice echoed his surprise.

"Yeah. And she knows me. From way back. Beat cop days."

Ness was silent, but Malone could hear him thinking.

"And you think that's a problem?" Eliot asked. "I can't think why it would be."

Malone didn't think he could explain. He kept it simple. "I'm just curious as to how it came about. I don't like surprises. And I don't trust coincidences."

"When I heard you might be available, I had my girl look for a place. She saw an ad in the *Plain Dealer* and jumped on it."

"Because it's close to the Run," Malone supplied.

"Yeah. And right across from St. Alexis Hospital."

"What does that have to do with anything?"

"I'll fill you in." Eliot didn't want to tell him over the phone. Malone could hear it in his tone. "I have some time Friday. Tell you what. I'll come by and grab you, say one o'clock. Watch for me, will ya? I don't want to knock on any doors."

"Why not?"

He sighed. "Because people recognize me. It's a damn pain, but if we want to be quiet about this, we're going to have to talk in the car, or you could come to my place after hours."

"All right. I'll see you then."

Malone walked out of the sewing room, preoccupied, and almost ran into a woman with cheeks as red as her hair and a frame that was round from every angle.

She screeched when she saw him but immediately stuck out her chubby arm to shake his hand.

"I'm Margaret," she said, all smiles, her accent thicker than Lenka's and Zuzana's combined. "You must be Mr. Malone. I'll take care of you, don't worry. Good food. Clean clothes, clean room. Anything you need, you ask Margaret." She nodded like it was agreed and bustled on without any comment from him, but he caught her peeking back at him when he slipped into his room. There would be no privacy in this house.

It was only ten o'clock, but he was antsy and troubled, and he didn't want to sit in his room, though the files he'd brought with him hadn't been thoroughly scoured. He would do that after Ness filled him in with whatever couldn't be said on the phone.

He decided he would walk for a bit, but not before locking the files in his car. The last thing he needed was for Margaret to see the photos of severed limbs and run to the Kos women. He would have to set some boundaries on her help; he didn't want her with unlimited access to his room. But he didn't want to deal with it now. He needed air, and he needed activity.

At the sandwich shop that butted up against the doctor's office on the corner of Broadway and Pershing, he ordered enough sandwiches to feed a small army. He didn't know what the women liked but figured it wouldn't matter all that much. If they were like the rest of the city—the rest of the whole country—what they didn't eat for lunch they'd save for tomorrow. Dani had delivered his breakfast, so he felt compelled to deliver her lunch. He always kept the scales balanced. It was something he was religious about.

He left the sandwiches on the counter in the shop and managed to get back out the front door without being subjected to conversation. Dani darted from a back room as he ducked out the jangling front door, and he just waved and called, "I brought lunch for later," before striding down the walk and continuing on his way.

Turning south, he walked along Broadway toward East Fifty-Fifth, where he could buy a few things and acclimate himself to the area. The two main thoroughfares came together on a well-dressed intersection. A theater, a grocery, a bank, and a library, all brick and edged in arches and quoins, anchored the corners with no setback from the streets. Just behind the theater on Fifty-Fifth was the Fifth Precinct—good to know—but he wandered south a block and found Our Lady of Lourdes Church and slipped in the back ahead of midday Mass.

He wasn't especially religious, though he supposed he might seem so on the surface, but he clung to the order of his faith, to the anchor it gave his feet upon a path. He needed it. He needed the rules and the rituals. He needed the quiet in his head and the unburdening in the confessional.

He always felt better when he walked out than when he went in. Not because the church had all the answers, but because it had better answers than he did. It kept him from blowing his head off. He'd come close a time or two. The day he met Dani Flanagan, fifteen years ago, he'd even had a plan.

He'd cleaned his weapon before his shift. It usually calmed him, taking his gun apart and putting it back together. But that day it didn't. That day it called to him instead. It would be so easy, and he wasn't afraid. He wouldn't feel anything, he knew that, and not feeling a damn thing sounded peaceful. It sounded right. Pull the trigger, and he'd be gone.

The thought had filled him with euphoria.

His affairs were in order. Irene would get his army stipend and a small payout from the police union. And she still lived with her parents. She was an only child and they doted on her. They'd doted on Mary too. When he'd come back from France, they'd even doted on him. He'd wanted their own place—a little home for his tiny family—but it had never happened. Life had gotten in the way, and Irene's parents had insisted there was plenty of room and plenty of time.

It turned out there wasn't nearly enough of either.

Still, when they were gone, Irene would get their house, three houses down from Molly and Sean, where he'd been living for the last two months. Irene would be looked after. His presence was not required.

So he went to work knowing it was his last time. Reveling in it. He'd ignored Murphy all shift, letting his partner's attitude roll off his back. Murphy wouldn't matter in mere hours. He would never have to look the other way or listen to Murphy's fat mouth again. Malone managed to be cheerful right up until they got the assignment at the end of their shift. A domestic situation on Dearborn; nearest intersection, Chicago Avenue.

They'd arrived after it was all over. Murphy wasn't even surprised. He'd known it was going down. He'd driven right to the home, pulled up, and went straight to the neighbor next door before going inside and seeing if there was anyone hurt or in need of assistance. The neighbor gave Murphy exactly what he wanted. An eyewitness account and plenty of bad blood to make it clean.

Malone had just wanted to go home. He'd just wanted to be done. He didn't want to care. But then Murphy had put him in charge of the kid. That poor little girl. And he'd cared. He'd cared enough that he'd changed his plan.

He postponed it. Just until he picked up a kitten named Charlie. Then he postponed it again. Just until he got back from taking a train, a kid, and a cat to Ohio.

But Dani Flanagan had looked into his eyes and said, "If you don't do it, who will?" And his plan had dissolved for good, leaving an odd, new purpose in its wake. Dani Flanagan didn't know it, but she'd saved his life.

5

Malone was waiting at the end of the driveway for Ness at exactly one o'clock on Friday. Eliot was punctual. Malone had always liked that about him. When he pulled up in front of the house in a nondescript black car, Malone climbed in and slammed the door, and Ness pulled away again, veering back into the traffic along Broadway without a hitch.

Malone pointed at the dashboard and the radio setup mounted like spaceship controls to the right of the wheel. "We goin' to another galaxy?"

"It's a two-way radio," Ness said proudly. "I've been working on getting them in all the cars. Future of policing right there." He shook his finger at it. "No more call boxes or blinking lights on street corners. Expensive as hell—this setup cost more than the car itself. But we've got at least one in every precinct." He turned the dials and flipped switches, demonstrating, and then turned them off after a few minutes of meaningless chatter.

They drove for an hour, winding in and out of the streets, across the bridges and over tracks, Ness pointing out places of interest and pockets of trouble. They drove past a line of men, most in caps and overalls, that extended half a block.

"Is that a soup line?" Malone asked.

"Nah. That's where they pick up their relief checks. Things are getting better, I think. I hope. But half the city is still unemployed, and the jobs they're getting don't pay enough to cover the rent. That's why the Run is full of shantytowns. A lot of folks who live there work; they just can't afford to live anywhere else."

"I plan to go down there and start picking around. Hop a train or two. Talk to the hobos. But I need to get some different clothes. And I admit, I'm not too eager to ride a train right now. I've gotten soft in the last year. I don't much like being cold or dirty, and I'm going to have to be both."

"I know a place where we can get a look of the whole Run without getting out of the car. It'll give you a bird's-eye view of what's down there."

Ness drove several blocks and turned off a paved road onto a dirt path. Had the ground not been frozen, it surely would have been inaccessible, but Ness seemed to know where he was going. Sure enough, when he stopped, the crater that was the Run—a dry riverbed crisscrossed with train tracks and cluttered with mountains of junk—stretched out below them.

"They tell me it used to be an oasis down there," Ness said. "Women would walk with their parasols on tree-lined paths. Families would push their babies in strollers, and couples would stroll along like it was Central Park."

"Huh. Hard to believe."

"Now we got railroad tracks, tin sheds, and pup tents. And that's just in the nicer sections." Ness's laugh didn't contain much mirth. "The rows of crates and cardboard boxes are a city of their own. I've thought more than once that I should go and just burn it all down.

People shouldn't live that way. I don't know how compassionate it is to just look the other way."

"Before you start burning things, you better have somewhere for them to go," Malone said.

"And that's why it's all still there." Eliot sighed. "Plenty of good people down there. Plenty of bad. Plenty of characters too."

"Characters?"

"The truly bizarre, Mike. There are all types, everywhere, but down there, it's not as easy to hide your proclivities. I got reports of a man beneath the Lorain Bridge that has a collection of shoes. Hundreds and hundreds of shoes. He doesn't sell them. He just sets them up, like they're being worn by his invisible friends. And he talks to them. We've tried a couple times to question him, just because he's so damn odd. But he's always cleared out when we go."

"It's not a crime to like shoes. I know a few women—and even more than a few gangsters—who would be guilty if it were."

"Yeah. Well . . . we were wondering if some of the shoes belonged to a few of our victims."

"How would you ever know? You don't know who most of your victims are. How in the world you gonna be able to identify their shoes?" Malone shot back.

"I just want to find the killer, Mike. That's all I want to do."

"You got any ideas? Any at all?"

"About eighteen months ago, we had what we called a Torso Clinic. Psychologists, coroners, scientists from the bureau, criminologists, pathologists, and of course the detectives on the case all attended. We even had some reporters from the different papers come. With everyone's help, we put together a profile of the Butcher."

"You've got a description?"

"Not eyewitness accounts, but yeah. An educated set of parameters telling us what kind of character is doing this."

"I'm guessing it's not one of your characters living down there." Malone pointed at the Run.

"It'd be easier if it were. But no. I don't think it is. We figure the man is either a butcher—an actual butcher—a doctor, or someone who has had experience that would provide him with the knowledge that the Butcher exhibits. He knows what he's doing when he starts dismembering. Where the joints are, how to cut around them. That kind of stuff."

"Is this why you didn't want to go into detail over the phone? You think your Butcher might be someone with some prestige?"

"That's one of the reasons. Mostly, there's people listening in. I don't say anything on the telephone I don't want to read in the papers. Learned my lesson with Capone always tapping my wires."

"What else did you come up with in your clinic?"

"He's smart. He's strong. Most definitely male. Everybody agreed on that aspect, though the emasculations of some of the victims made some folks wonder."

"It made me wonder."

Ness grimaced. "The medical practice next to Raus Funeral Home has five doctors on staff. And actually, a mortician is up there on the list of probable professions. So you're sitting right in the thick of it in that room we're renting on Broadway, not to mention you're right across from St. Alexis. We have a file on all of them." He jerked his thumb toward the back seat and the box on the floor.

Malone's eyebrows shot up. "I'm guessing that's for me."

"At this point, there isn't a doctor, butcher, orderly, or undertaker in town that we don't have some information on." Ness made a circle in the air with his pointer finger. "This is where he hunts, and this is where he dumps. Which makes me think this is also where he lives. Not in the Run, necessarily, but in the neighborhoods on the rim. He's comfortable here. He knows the hidey-holes and the shortcuts. He knows the routines and the businesses. He knows the people who won't be missed or searched for. He might not be a nobody . . . but he needs nobodies."

"So you want me snooping around the hospital, looking at who is on staff and trying to establish patterns, see if any alarm bells go off."

"Yeah. You'll want to do that. And you'll also want to go down there." Ness nodded toward the shantytowns below them. "You'll want to look into it all, I'm guessing. In your files is a whole list of leads the detectives on this case have run down in the last two years."

"I saw that. Haven't spent any time on it yet, though. I didn't want to put ideas in my head until I had my own impressions."

"Well, you're in for a treat. Just to give you an idea, we've looked into reports of a voodoo temple, an abortion clinic, a secret cult, and a self-confessed soul eater. We questioned a hunchback that eats his supper with a medieval sword and a hatchet, depending on the day of the week. A woman on Carnegie, not too far from where Victim Number Three lived, was reported for her collection of headless dolls. A couple detectives went by and questioned her. The dolls came in several variations. Some were simply missing their heads, but others were cut up in pieces and put in tiny burlap bags. Lots of amazing details," Ness said, the sarcasm dripping from his voice. "She sells them on Euclid Beach as souvenirs. Calls them Torso Dolls. People buy them. So she keeps making them."

"Hey . . . times are hard," Malone said, monotone. "A girl's gotta eat."

"We thought we had a lead when one of our complaints involved a man—a Negro named One-Armed Willie—who knew both Flo Polillo and Rose Wallace, Victim Number Three and Victim Number Eight. He has a sheet a mile long, and the brass got excited. But he has one goddamn arm. He gets by pretty well, considering, but there is no way in hell he's the Mad Butcher of Kingsbury Run. He isn't physically capable of it."

"Yeah. And the problem with scapegoats is the murders don't stop when you lock 'em up."

"Yeah. Inconvenient." Eliot smiled ruefully, but he was suddenly weary. He removed his hat and ran his fingers through his haystack hair.

"You okay, Ness?"

"I'm okay, Malone. Just haven't been sleeping a whole lot. And when I do, it's usually on the couch in my office."

"Edna kick you out?" Malone only asked because he knew Ness was going to tell him.

"No. She left. And I don't see the point in going home most nights."

"She left for good?"

"Yeah. She stayed at her mother's house after Christmas. I came back alone. She doesn't want to be here anymore."

"She doesn't want to be here? Why not?" Malone swept his hand toward the rows of shanties lining the base of the cliff below them. If he squinted, the clusters and outcroppings looked like a filthy, tattered quilt. A tattered quilt in a junkyard.

Ness was silent.

"I'm sorry, Ness," Malone grunted. He wasn't very good at sympathy.

Eliot sighed, wrapping his arms around the big wheel and staring down into the ramshackle jungle. "Yeah. Me too. But I'm also . . . relieved."

"I understand that." He did. When Irene had asked him to go, he'd been relieved too. It was exhausting being responsible for someone else's happiness.

"She said she would come back for some of the public functions I'll need her for. Keep the papers quiet. Not for me. I don't really care. But Congressman Sweeney keeps hammering Mayor Burton over this Butcher business. Democrats and Republicans, you know how it is. Everybody's always looking for an angle to bury each other. But I don't want to be a political liability."

"Gotta keep up appearances," Malone said, tone dry. Eliot knew all about appearances, and he juggled that part of the spotlight well, even though he'd never been very political himself. Politics and public service, even in the bureau, was all about appearance. Malone had learned that the images most people presented to the world didn't reflect reality. Which, for some reason, had his thoughts bouncing back to Dani Flanagan. She had her own methods of getting at the truth.

"Do you think there's such a thing as a . . . sixth sense?" he asked Eliot abruptly.

Eliot frowned at him, distracted from his marital woes. "Like prescience?"

"Nah. Not foreknowledge. Not that. More like . . . an ability to see things other people can't. Or maybe *see* isn't the right way to describe it either. It's more like a heightened sense of touch. You hold something and you know . . . where it's been." He didn't know if that was what Dani did, exactly, but he needed to keep it simple.

"I've never heard of anything like that before. Although, come to think of it, my mother seemed to always know where I'd been."

Malone sighed.

"Now what's this about?"

Malone waved his hand. "Nothing."

"You seeing things, Mike?" Ness felt his head like he was checking for fever. Malone swatted his hand away, but Eliot was smiling again.

"Not me. No. Though I used to see colors around people when I was younger. Some murky. Some bright. I always thought I was seeing the color of people's souls."

"Oh yeah? What color do you think my soul would be?"

"Green. Pea green, with a shot of shit brown," Malone said without hesitation or inflection.

"Ha!" Ness spat, laughing again.

It was actually the same blue as his eyes. He'd seen it a few times, hovering around Eliot like a shadow. Over the years, he'd glimpsed a few colored halos clinging to various people, but he always looked away.

He looked away again, staring at the window, but he couldn't let the subject rest. "I guess I'm just trying to decide what I believe and what I don't, Ness."

For a moment both men were silent, lost in the conundrum of personal faith.

"Capone had a guy—a numbers guy—who could do sums in his head," Malone continued, pensive. "Didn't matter what it was, he could spit it out. He was great at cards too. It wasn't magic. Wasn't voodoo. It was just . . . something he could do that the rest of us couldn't."

"They called him Count, didn't they?" Ness asked. "I think I remember him now. But I wouldn't rule out voodoo. That guy was a bad fella. He mighta made a deal with the devil. I think he's in the slammer now. I hope so."

"A deal with the devil, huh? You believe in the devil, Ness?"

"You can't be in our business and not believe in evil."

Malone nodded. "I believe in evil."

"Well, if you believe in evil, you gotta believe in good. Can't have one without the other."

"No. I guess not," Malone said.

Daniela Kos—Dani Flanagan—was not evil. He knew that. So whatever else she was, whatever confusion he was feeling about her abilities, it wasn't that. The tightness he'd carried in his chest since Dani had fled his room the other day eased with an almost audible *pop*.

"I gotta get back, Malone," Ness said, starting the car again. He eased away from the overhang, his eyes on his rearview mirror. "But let's do this again next week. Same time. Until we figure this thing out."

∼

Dani was fixing the display in the front window when a black Ford sedan pulled up in front of the house and Malone stepped out. He shut the door without a backward glance, and the car pulled away again without giving her any indication of who was driving it, beyond a felt hat and a male profile. It was the same car Malone had driven away in the week before, and the week before that. Always the same day and roughly the same time. He had kept to himself beyond mealtime, and even then, he hardly said a word. He'd asked that Margaret not tidy his room. He said he'd see to it himself. He left his laundry in a hamper in the hall, and when Margaret was finished with it, she slid a note beneath his door, and he retrieved his things from the laundry room.

Dani didn't blame him; Margaret was a gem, but she was also a snoop. Dani was certain Malone thought *she* was a snoop as well. And Dani was. But it was not intentional. She hadn't yet given in to the temptation to touch his things. At least . . . not much.

He'd left a pair of boots on the back stoop. They'd been covered with mud—from who knows where—and he'd cleaned them off at the outdoor pump and left them beside the door to dry.

Dani had not been able to help herself. She'd brought the boots inside, telling herself they would never dry outside in the cold damp of February. But when she'd slipped her hands in the openings and pressed her palms flat to the soles, she felt nothing but his frustration with the cold, his longing for sunshine, and his curiosity over the string of murders that had happened in the area. He could hardly help but think about murder. The entire city was caught in its grip.

And then there were the silk suits in his wardrobe. She hadn't meant to look at those either, but Charlie had gotten himself locked in Malone's room. It wasn't his fault, the poor baby. She'd switched rooms on him. He liked to take long naps beneath the bed and had managed to get himself locked in when Malone left one afternoon.

It was fortunate she had a key. She'd heard Charlie's pitiful yowling and let him out. She checked the room to make sure the cat hadn't left a mess behind—who knew how long he'd been trapped inside—and saw a few files open on the desk, a large map of Cleveland tacked to the wall above it. A few of the files were scattered on the floor. She wasn't sure if that was Charlie's doing or Malone's. From the tidiness of the rest of the room, she thought it was likely Charlie. She hurried forward and retrieved them, shoving the pages inside and stacking them with the others. She hesitated when she caught a glimpse of a house and a familiar face in her mind's eye.

Eliot Ness.

Michael Malone knew Eliot Ness. He was a popular figure in Cleveland. The papers covered his every move and clamored for his statements. She set the files down and stepped away. It wasn't so hard to believe. Malone said he worked with local governments.

She'd made a quick turn about the room, ignoring the lure of his private papers, but when she'd paused to close his wardrobe—which was slightly ajar—she'd seen the beautiful silk of the suits, one in a snappy chalk print, one in a navy so deep it looked like a jewel. She'd touched them, admiring the cut and the fabric. Suits like that cost more than most people made in a year.

But those had been the only times she'd slipped.

She'd tried to afford him the privacy he deserved, really she had, and she'd made a point to warn him to check for Charlie under the bed before leaving for the day.

Now Malone stood on the front walk, slightly hunched, with his hands on his hat. He still wore the same dark wool suit he'd worn the day he arrived. The pose made his overcoat pull at the seams, but she wasn't sure if it was the cold wind that bent him over or the weight he carried on his shoulders. He looked as though he wasn't sure whether to come inside or go for a walk, which was something else he did often. He walked for hours. Sometimes he took his car and went to places unknown, but more often he left on foot. He claimed he was a tax man, consulting with local agencies, but he kept odd hours. She knew he hadn't told the whole truth when the aunts had questioned him about his work—his silk suits told a different story—but that was a typical trait. No one gave detailed explanations about their lives or their pasts when asked. Especially not to strangers.

His overcoat swung around his legs as he sidestepped a puddle with the agility of a young man, though he no longer was, not like he'd been. Not like she remembered. He wasn't yet gray and his hair was still thick, but the lines were deeper around his eyes, the half-moons beneath them darker, like he didn't rest well. Or maybe that too was just the world. The times they were living in were not happy ones, or maybe such days had never existed. Not collectively. She knew there were pockets of peace and calm, of laughter and ease, but no one she knew lived in those alcoves. She had . . . once. Then Michael Malone had looked down into her eyes and told her the truth that had changed her life.

She hadn't blamed him, even then. In fact, before they'd parted, she had honestly loved him. It was a childish devotion, true, but deeply felt. Seeing him now, with adult eyes, she recognized that he was a rather sinister-looking character and not a hero type at all.

He was lean in the way a cat was lean, broad-shouldered and narrow-hipped, with a back that was longer than his legs and light feet that always seemed to know where to step.

He was also somber to the point of gloom. He was grim. She could think of no word that described him better. Oh, not in the way death was grim. She knew that darkness. Malone's darkness reminded her of deep waters and long nights. She suspected his darkness was loneliness, and it echoed in her own breast.

When she was a child, he had seemed almost towering. Solid and safe. Now he was merely a man, a shade too thin and a bit too old, at least . . . for her.

He loped for the rear of the house, his decision clearly influenced by the sudden crack of thunder and the rain that followed. With just a few steps, he was completely out of view. She listened for him and moments later heard the back door open and close—just a snick and a whine—and the faint tread of wet shoes on wood floors.

She would be wise to steer clear of him as much as possible, the voice that sounded like Zuzana said from her head.

But she feared she would not.

She feared she *could* not.

She already knew him too well.

6

They ate dinner in awkward silence, just as they'd done every night for the last month. Malone hardly raised his eyes from his plate. Dani suspected that was her fault, though maybe not. Her two aunts had lost the art of subtlety in their old age. They watched Malone with worried gazes and pinned him in baleful stares. She wouldn't blame him if he demanded a tray in his room, but he didn't. He joined them each night and ate with polite gusto, and he spoke only when he was questioned directly.

He always helped them clear the dishes away, despite their insistence that he go. He said he was used to cleaning up after himself and didn't like being waited on.

"Your wife didn't fuss over you, Mr. Malone?" Lenka asked.

"No. She didn't."

"And what about your mother? Surely she doted on you."

"My mother died when I was twelve, and I haven't had a woman fuss over me since."

It was the most personal information he'd offered yet, and Lenka looked at him sadly and clucked her tongue. "Poor tyke."

"I am forty years old, Miss Kos. I have not been a tyke for some time."

"We listen to *Dick Tracy* most nights if you'd like to join us around the radio," Dani invited. "Or perhaps you have your own favorite programs. You're welcome to listen to them here."

He hesitated, like he was considering it, but then shook his head. Lenka's shoulders sagged in disappointment, but Zuzana seemed relieved.

"I have work to do. So I'll say good night," he said, characteristically polite, characteristically guarded. But Malone had barely made it to the bottom of the stairs when the lights began to flicker. Lenka mumbled and crossed herself. Dani was tempted to do the same but instead rushed to gather the lanterns in case they lost power. Zuzana griped, trying to tune into her program, determined not to miss it, storm or no storm, and was met with static and nothing more.

"The radio towers are getting battered just like we are," Lenka explained, as if Zuzana wasn't well aware of the reason the radio wasn't working. Then the lights flickered and didn't come back on, and Lenka's moans and Zuzana's grumbling rose in volume. Dani heard Malone climbing back up the stairs.

He set about making a fire in the sitting room and even remained with them, keeping it stoked and hot, listening to them chatter over hems and darts and seams. Maybe the cold darkness of his room was the reason he stayed, but his presence was a welcome addition.

Lenka needed more light than the lanterns provided. She struggled in full light and glasses, so her ability to work in the current circumstances was limited. Zuzana wasn't nearly as visually impaired as Lenka and sat adjusting a pattern for their spring line.

Dani had a stack of piecework she needed to get through, mending mostly. Buttons and tears and holes to be patched. They didn't turn work away, even though it paid little and took precious time. Eventually, Dani would be doing it all alone. Her aunts would not live forever. When that day came, she would have to decide where to put her time and attention, and maybe then she wouldn't take on the patching and stitching of clothes that were hardly worth saving.

Malone sat near the fire, occasionally poking at the logs. He seemed content enough to listen to them chat as they worked, but Dani guessed he was simply reluctant to make another fire—or be cold—in his room.

"Stop slouching, Daniela," Zuzana said. "You have a spectacular figure, but no one would know, the way you hunch over."

Dani straightened her back and rolled her shoulders but didn't raise her eyes from her task. Zuzana said the same thing about once a day.

"Not one bit of you is not perfectly lovely. You look so much like Aneta. And Vera too when she was young," Lenka interjected, trying to soften Zuzana's criticism.

Dani darted a glance at Zuzana. Her blue eyes had begun to water, and she lifted a shaking hand, dabbing at them with the handkerchief she kept tucked in her blouse.

Daniela didn't argue with the claims of her loveliness or take offense at the nagging. It would only upset her aunt. Zuzana had not recovered from Vera's death. Daniela feared she never would. She would simply miss her terribly until they were reunited again.

"Tell us one of your stories, Daniela," Lenka said, yawning like she needed the story to stay upright. She was slouching too.

"Not tonight, Lenka," Dani said.

"I thought you said Mr. Malone knew all about you, Daniela," Zuzana commented dryly.

"All about Daniela?" he asked.

"Yes. That she has a feel for the cloth. It speaks to her. She said you know all about it," Zuzana replied.

Dani winced but didn't raise her eyes from her work. She wouldn't give Zuzana the satisfaction. The old woman was a bit of a troublemaker. She forgot nothing, she forgave nothing, and she missed nothing.

"Our father, Daniel Kos, had the same sense," Lenka said, shooting a warning look at Zuzana. "But Papa wasn't as good at the stories as Daniela. And our sister, Vera, knew what the cloth could be, how to use it to its full potential. A suit or a sail, she had an eye."

"You must demonstrate for our boarder, Daniela," Zuzana said. "He'll think we're telling tales."

"I cannot demonstrate the intangible," Dani mumbled. "And often it isn't remotely interesting."

In the flickering light, the shadows beneath Malone's eyes and the hollows of his cheeks were even more pronounced, and he regarded Dani in silence, his shoulder propped against the mantel, the poker gripped in his right hand.

"There are no stories in me tonight," she said. It was a lie. The skirt she was holding was ripe with a tantalizing tale. It belonged to a woman who was pregnant, and she wasn't sure the child was her husband's.

Zuzana harrumphed, not buying Daniela's protestations. Unless the fabric was new—and often not even then—there was something hiding in the weave. Family drama, secrets, guilt, love, and loss. There was always something, and though Dani was careful with confidences, she was liberal with her storytelling. Not tonight. Zuzana could sulk all she liked; Dani would not be the carnival barker with Malone watching.

"Tell me about your family," Malone said softly, making the request to no one in particular. "What is your story? The story of the Kos family? That I would like to hear."

Lenka, with no work in her lap and none of Dani's reticence or Zuzana's mistrust, responded eagerly to Malone's request. She regaled him with the exodus of the Kos family from Bohemia—Daniel, Eliska, and his three daughters. Pavel was born in America, and she glossed over his story, as was often the case with poor Pavel.

"Our grandfather, Daniel's father, was a clothier too. His name was Kristof Kos. He made clothes for Franz Joseph the First."

"Ahh. Yes. The emperor. I remember that part," Malone said.

Dani raised startled eyes from the hole she was mending. Malone regarded her with a small smile.

"He was the emperor of Austria and the king of Bohemia, Hungary, and Croatia," Zuzana retorted. "We have always moved among royalty. And what of your family, Mr. Malone?"

"They were farmers. No emperors in Ireland. Just Catholics and Protestants and the occasional English lord, though there are far fewer of those now, I'm guessing."

"And which are you? Catholic or Protestant?" Lenka asked.

"I was raised Catholic," Malone said.

"And do you still practice?" Lenka pressed.

"I suppose I do."

"Thank goodness for small mercies," Zuzana sniffed.

"We are—or were—a house divided between the Catholics and the freethinkers," Dani interjected, trying to move them from the sensitive subject.

"I can't be both?" Malone asked.

"No." Zuzana snorted. "You cannot. You clearly do not know Bohemian politics."

"No. But my parents were Irish. I understand familial divides well enough."

"Tell us more about your parents," Dani pleaded, dancing away from the topic before Zuzana gave Malone a very hostile primer.

"My father was from Belfast. My mother from Dublin. They came to America on the same ship when they were still in their teens. My father's accent was so thick you could hardly understand him. It never faded either."

"And your mother?" Dani asked. "Did she have an accent too?"

"The accents in Ireland vary, depending on where you're at. Dublin and Belfast aren't even one hundred miles apart, but the accents are distinct. Belfast sounds like Scotland. Dublin, more like England."

"I don't know about that. All Irishmen sound the same to me," Zuzana said.

Malone repeated what she'd said, his impersonation of her accent exact, his look sardonic. He even spoke with the same expressionless face, the barely moving mouth, and the sound at the back of his throat.

Zuzana gaped at him, her pale jowls quivering with outrage. "Do you think you are comical, Mr. Malone?"

"No, ma'am. I was just demonstrating my skill," he responded, dropping the eastern European accent, though he kept his gaze lifted to hers. "Accents are a hobby of mine." Dani guessed he'd grown weary of her gibes.

"He sounded just like you, Zuzana," Lenka snickered, waving her handkerchief in the air like she was surrendering. "Do it again, Mr. Malone."

"I'm going to bed," Zuzana said, pushing herself to her feet. She reached for her cane, her chin high and her nostrils flared.

"Good night, *Tetka*," Dani said.

"Good night, Miss Kos," Malone echoed.

"Good night, Zuzana dear," Lenka said cheerfully, but as soon as Zuzana had exited the room, she rose and made to depart as well. As she walked past Dani, she laid a hand on her bowed head.

"I'm going too, Daniela. Don't wear out your eyes, now. The work will keep until tomorrow." Lenka looked over at Malone and winked, as if the two of them had a secret. "Good night, Mr. Malone," she simpered.

"Good night, Miss Kos."

"Oh, please call me Lenka," she said, conspiratorial. "I am not a girl anymore."

"Good night, Lenka," he said dutifully.

He shifted, as if he too should leave, but he remained in front of the fire, his hands in his pockets, his expression thoughtful. Dani laid her mending aside and exhaled. It came out with more feeling than she'd planned, and Malone raised his eyes to hers.

"They are quite the pair," he said.

"Yes, they are. I love them dearly, but they wear me thin sometimes. Vera—the middle sister—balanced them out a little. She was the bridge between them. That role has now fallen to me, and I can't say I like being tread upon."

"None of you have talked about her. Not in detail."

"No . . . I guess we haven't. It is painful for us, I guess. It hasn't been very long. She died in October."

"So it is her room I am occupying." It was not a question but a statement.

"No. It is mine. I moved upstairs to Vera's room after she died. I wanted to be closer to my aunts. They are growing increasingly . . . frail. More obnoxious and more frail." She smiled to show she spoke in jest. "And it made more sense to rent out the room downstairs."

"I took your room?" he gasped.

"I have hardly been inconvenienced, Mr. Malone. I have a perfectly lovely room just down the hall," she soothed, but he did not seem reassured. He rubbed at his jaw, ill at ease.

"But surely . . . it is hard . . . to stay in her—your aunt's—room."

"No. Not really. I switched out the linens and the drapes—those are in your room—so I wouldn't be bombarded with her memories." She waved her hand in the air like it was just a small detail.

"Would you be? Bombarded, I mean."

"Yes. I would. And some distance, even from those you love, is good. You know the story of King Midas?"

"He turned everything to gold?"

"Yes. That is what my *sense*"—she emphasized the word—"feels like most of the time. As lovely as gold is . . . as lovely as memories are . . . both become much less so without moderation."

He folded his arms like he was trying to take that in. He didn't ask her to expound, though she sensed he wanted her to.

"Lenka said it was a family trait . . . the thing with the cloth."

"That's what I've been told, though my mother didn't have it. She was a capable seamstress and could mend and make alterations. She made *our* clothes, but she had no wish to dress the rich and famous. She had no wish to move among royalty." She could do a decent imitation of Zuzana too.

"And the rest of the family?"

"My grandfather and my great-grandfather both claimed to have a sense for the cloth, though they described it differently. Vera too. She always said the fabric told her what she should make. The style and the size. She said, 'The fabric knows what he wants to be. The fabric chooses.'"

"But she didn't sense things . . . about people."

"No. My great-grandfather, Daniel Kos, was a little more like me. Vera said he knew where the cloth had been—saw it—and liked working with bolts that were as new and pristine as possible."

"Why did she die? Vera?" he asked. The irony was not lost on her. Death was a more comfortable subject for him than her abilities. Maybe it was more comfortable for her too, and she answered his question.

"Her heart just stopped beating. She sat down in this chair, a dress in her lap, and she drifted off. It was easy. Quiet. It was a good death. Hard for us. But not for her."

"I hope it is not a burden to have me here," he said. "I would not want that."

"No. It is a relief. We need the money," she confessed. "Nobody is buying expensive clothes right now. My grandfather used to dress the Rockefellers, and we still benefit from his reputation. We have a few wealthy clients; it is the reason we have a roof over our heads and food in our bellies. But even the wealthy make do with less, and the Rockefellers hardly come back to Cleveland anymore. Most of the houses on Millionaires' Row are empty or gone. All those beautiful houses, all those beautiful clothes . . . gone."

He didn't seem to know what to say to that, and she hadn't meant to say so much. It was a bit of a soapbox topic for her, when someone would listen, and he seemed intent on listening. It was intoxicating, his attention. She wasn't used to it, and before she knew it, she was talking again.

"Cleveland is well-known for its garment districts. The factories have rows of sewing machines and giant presses, and they spit out hundreds of cheap suits every day. We can't really compete with that. The aunts have always worked hard, but they aren't particularly good at rustling up business. That was never their responsibility, and they are proud. I am not."

"No?"

"No. I think they'd rather die than do some of the things I've done." She laughed softly. She wasn't ashamed. Not at all. And she didn't think she was even especially defensive, but her words hung in the air, and Malone studied her, his eyes solemn. She expected him to leave, to retreat, but he stayed put.

"Tell me some of the things you've done," he insisted.

"I've gone to every business in this town, every business where uniforms are worn, and I've made them deals they can afford. I've sewn shirts with logos and badges and buttons. I've made aprons and caps and hairnets. It's boring, but it isn't hard, and I don't mind making the uniforms. No one's ever worn them before. It makes it a bit easier on me."

"No stories?" he asked quietly.

"No stories," she repeated. His understanding made her throat tighten, and she returned her gaze to her lap, composing herself. And still, he didn't bid her good night.

"There are also locals who bring me their mending," she added. "The church has sent me business as well."

"And your aunts are not too proud to help you with the work once you've acquired it?"

Dani picked up her mending again. She didn't know what to do with her hands. "There is one contract that my aunts refuse to help with. They are horrified by it. But sadly . . . it's steady work."

He raised his eyebrows, waiting. She bit her lip, wondering how she'd backed herself into this corner. She'd had no intention of telling him every detail of her dreary life. It was as if he'd turned a spigot inside her.

"There's a funeral home next door. Did you notice?" she hedged.

"Of course. And a doctor's office on the other side."

"Terribly crass, isn't it?" she asked.

"Pragmatic. If the doctors can't help you, do they just send you next door? Toss you over the fence?" His tone was dry, and she laughed.

"You sound like Zuzana."

"Oh no," he grunted, and that made her chuckle again.

"But only those that can afford the funeral home go to the funeral home," she explained. "This city has a great number of dead that are indigent. Often they are never identified. Some are, but there isn't any money for burial expenses, so even if they are known, the families do not claim them to avoid getting saddled with the cost. It is very sad."

His brow had furrowed while she talked, and she began to talk faster, fearing she was boring him to tears.

"The city has a small fund for the indigent dead. Mr. Raus, the owner of the mortuary, has a building over on Mead Avenue where those dead are brought. I clean them up, tidy their clothes, and keep a record before they are buried in a potter's field or donated to the Western Reserve University for medical study."

Malone's mouth dropped open. "You look after the dead?" he gasped.

"I don't look *after* them. No. I just keep records and . . . dress them . . . for burial."

"Good God, Dani."

It was her turn to gape. His response surprised her. "It's honest w-work," she stammered. "And I am a seamstress. Clothes are my business. Even the dead need clothes."

"Yes . . . but . . ." He seemed dumbfounded. "Is that where the stack of battered clothing comes from? The endless piles that poor Margaret is constantly laundering?"

Dani blinked at him. "Poor Margaret is grateful to have the work too. If it weren't for that stipend, we wouldn't be able to keep her on."

"Well. That's . . . good . . . then, I suppose." He seemed at a loss for words, and Dani reached for her button box, wishing she'd had the sense to just stay quiet. Every time they had the opportunity to visit, she stepped on a land mine and blew herself up.

Malone stoked the fire one last time and hung the poker from its hook. He seemed eager to go now.

"Good night, Dani," Malone said, taking the lantern she'd set aside for him.

"Good night . . . Michael," she responded, forcing herself to say his name, though it felt ridiculous on her tongue. She desperately wanted for them to be friends, and friends called each other by their names. But for all her bravery, she couldn't look at him as he left.

7

The storm howled and hovered all night, making the panes in Malone's room shake like someone stood outside with his hands pressed to the glass, trying to get in.

The house was so cold when he arose he could see his breath in the air. He pulled on two pairs of socks and as many layers as he could manage and shoved his feet into boots, his hands into gloves, and made a fire in his room before he lost his will to live. He then hurried up the stairs and stoked a new blaze in the fireplace they'd sat around the night before.

Dani hurried out of her room, her curls tousled, wearing as many layers as he, and thanked him effusively.

"There's more wood in the stable. I lock it in the back room, partly to keep it dry, partly to prevent it being stolen. Goodness, what a storm! Still no power. The pipes haven't frozen, but there's not a drop of hot water in the boiler."

He found two snow shovels along with the wood: driftwood and an assortment of sticks and logs and shipping crates that someone—Dani most likely—had carefully hoarded. It was a good thing. He wondered if her aunts knew how fortunate they were to have her.

He brought in an armful and then began clearing the drive, section by section, piling the snow along the edges.

Dani called him in for lunch, but he didn't want to have to come back to it. It was hard work, but the movement kept him from getting too cold.

When Dani joined him twenty minutes later, dragging another shovel behind her, he told her to go right back where she'd come from.

"I can do this," he said.

"And I can help," she said, cheerful. She began, moving in the opposite direction so they were clearing from the center to the sides. She knew what she was doing.

"Do you usually clear the snow by yourself?" he asked.

"No. I usually pay Harry Raus to do it for me. But he's off to college now. I haven't found a replacement shoveler."

Malone extended his hand like they were just meeting for the first time, but she was too far away to take it. "Michael Malone, replacement shoveler, at your service."

"You're never going to get warm at this rate," she said apologetically after several minutes. Her breath puffed out around her head, underscoring just how cold it was.

"No. I'm not. But the faster I shovel, the warmer I stay."

"It must be hard to adjust to Cleveland. Are the Bahamas beautiful? I've only seen pictures, and not many of those. I can't imagine. I've never seen the ocean. Or palm trees. Or pink sand. Do the Bahamas have pink sand?" She sounded wistful, but he'd ceased shoveling.

"How did you know I was in the Bahamas?" Nobody knew that. His boss, Elmer Irey, knew. Molly, probably, though they'd never discussed it. But nobody else.

"You must have mentioned it," Dani said, her eyes on her shoveling.

He hadn't. There was no way he'd said anything of the sort.

"My coat told you that too?" he asked, flabbergasted.

She wiped at her nose, still avoiding his gaze. "Perhaps."

"Perhaps," he whispered. He resumed shoveling, suddenly too stunned to be cold.

"What does a Treasury agent do in the Bahamas?" she asked after they'd cleared another few feet. "That's a long way from Washington."

"Vacation," he grunted.

"Oh."

He wondered if she knew he was lying. She didn't say anything more, and the camaraderie between them was gone. A few moments later, she stopped, her cheeks flushed with exertion, and asked him if he could finish up on his own.

"I did not ask for your assistance, Miss Flanagan," he said, sounding like a schoolteacher. What an ass. But she had discombobulated him. Again.

"No. That's true. But thank you." She went inside the house but came back moments later shouldering an enormous canvas laundry bag. She walked past him without pausing and turned west when she reached the street.

"Where are you going?" he called after her.

"It is not your concern, Mr. Malone." Her voice was as frosty as his had been.

He set his shovel against the side of the house and trotted to catch up with her.

"Let me carry that," he insisted, feeling like an apology was in order.

"No . . . thank you. I can manage," she huffed.

He took it from her arms with an impatient yank and settled it on his own shoulder, wondering in amazement how she'd managed it. It wasn't light.

"What is this?"

"Clothing. A lot of clothing. I never know what I will need."

"I see." He didn't, but that didn't matter. He could help. "Lead on," he directed. She didn't move.

"I usually pull a wagon," she said. "But with the snow, it would only get stuck, and I don't have too far to go. Just up two blocks and over another."

"Let's go then." He began walking in the direction she'd been headed. It was her turn to trot after him, but she seemed slightly panicked.

"Really, sir. I can manage," she said, hurrying alongside him, kicking up snow with every step. God, what a miserable place. And had she just called him "sir"?

"I thought you were going to try to call me Michael," he said.

"I was. But . . . it doesn't roll off my tongue."

"No. It doesn't roll off anyone's tongue." No one but Molly called him Michael.

"Perhaps that's because you've had so many names?"

"Good God, woman. How do you know these things?" he snapped, coming to a halt. The bag wobbled with his abrupt stop, and he almost dropped it.

Dani didn't answer for a moment, her eyes on her feet. She dusted off the snow that was clinging to her skirt. Then she looked up at him in apology, and she told him.

"Your hat. You must have thought about what name you would use when you walked into the shop that first day. When I took your things, all the names were there, clinging to the brim like little plastic monkeys."

Little plastic monkeys. He could picture them, the little monkeys, wearing his aliases.

"Like what? What names?" he asked, refusing to believe.

"Are you testing me?"

"Yes."

"Well, let me see if I can remember. Patrick O'Rourke. Mike Lepito. Mikey . . . or was it Micky? Micky Monahan? Michael Malone was the biggest monkey."

He would have laughed at that had he not been so flabbergasted.

"I mean the biggest name," she amended in a rush. "Most likely . . . you had spent a lot of time in that hat . . . thinking about who you are," she explained.

He trudged along beside her, hardly knowing where he stepped, feeling a bit like a plastic monkey himself.

"Where are we going?" he asked five minutes later as she slowed in front of a nondescript building. He followed her to the rear, stepping in the tracks she made in the unblemished snow.

"I told you last night . . . I ready the indigent dead for burial."

"Here?" he gasped, dropping the laundry bag with a grunt.

"Yes. Here." She began unlocking the door next to a single loading dock. From the outside, it appeared to be just another storage facility. It was unmarked, unassuming, and as dreary as every other structure on the short street.

He followed her inside but hovered at the door, brushing the snow from the bundle of clothes.

The light inside the warehouse was poor, and of course, the electricity was down. Dani was prepared, though, and lit the wicks on two lanterns that sat on a worktable just right of the entrance.

Two embalming tables, complete with gutters and drains, took up an area to the right. Thank God they were empty.

Along the left wall, metal tables, a dozen of them, were arranged. Only two of them were empty. Ten bodies were laid out on the others.

Surgeon's gowns hung from hooks, and Dani pulled one over her clothes, tying it at her waist and neck.

"Just set the clothes there." She pointed to a table to the left of the door. It was already stacked with neatly folded items that appeared to be organized by size and gender. He did as he was instructed but went no farther into the drafty space.

"If you're going to stay, Michael, you should change too. I don't do anything terribly messy . . . but they are *dead*. The rubber gloves are there too." She'd traded her stocking cap for a white scarf that she tied over her hair, giving her the look of a nun doing rounds at St. Alexis.

He walked to the hooks where the gowns were hung. He must have looked as hesitant as he felt, for she reassured him gently. "Everything is boiled and bleached after each session. Don't worry."

"Maybe I'll wait outside," he said. He wasn't squeamish. He couldn't afford to be in his line of work, but there was something intensely private and sad about preparing a body for burial, and he really didn't want to watch.

"It's freezing out there."

"It's freezing in here too. And there aren't any dead bodies out there."

"I don't know about that. This is Kingsbury Run, after all." Her voice was quiet.

He grunted, noncommittal. He wondered again what she knew and considered telling her about every single thing in his head just so he wasn't plagued by that question. Did she know why he was in Cleveland? Did she know how he spent his time? Did she know that he'd been casing the bars, learning the streets, and watching the people? Did she know he'd pored over Eliot's files for weeks and gotten nowhere? He could ask her. But he didn't. He turned back to the door. He should go.

"Will you have anything to carry back?" he asked.

"Yes. I will take the soiled things home to wash. But I can leave them here for the time being. At least until I can return with my wagon."

He hesitated again. He didn't feel right about leaving her.

"You can go, Michael. Really. I don't expect you to help me with this. It's not pleasant work. Though it's a lot better during the winter than the summer."

"You'll still have death all over you."

"I scrub down when I'm finished, and my clothes are covered. You don't have to help me. I've been doing it for years."

"Years?"

"Years."

He flinched. Dead bodies decomposed quickly in the heat. The cold was indeed good for something. He didn't know if this place would be tolerable in July. He stamped his feet to warm them, but he didn't leave.

Dani shrugged at his hesitance and filled up a wash bucket at the sink. She carried it to the tables holding the dead and came back for a clipboard, a ledger, and one of the lanterns, and began her work. She moved between the tables laden with the dead, taking quick assessment of what she needed, talking to herself and maybe to him, though he wasn't sure.

"New shirt and trousers. And he has no boots." She wrote it down and sighed like that was a problem, but moved on, calling out what articles of clothing each body needed or whether she could make do with what they already wore. When she pulled off her gloves and began peeling off a dead man's coat, Malone barked at her.

"Good God, Dani. Put your gloves back on."

"I did not ask you to come, Mr. Malone," she said quietly, and rolled the corpse onto its side, freeing the garment. She had clearly done it all before, but her work would be a good deal easier if he helped instead of watching.

He removed his coat, yanked a gown from the hook, tied it around himself with impatient hands, and then exchanged his mittens for a pair of the coldest rubber gloves he'd ever had the misfortune to don.

"So I'm Mr. Malone again?" he muttered as he moved to her side.

"I find it hard to be casual in these circumstances," she said, but her voice sounded odd. When he cocked his head to see her face, he saw that her cheeks were wet with tears. *Had he done that?*

"You should wear your gloves," he said, his tone apologetic.

"I do wear my gloves, but they're awkward, and they slow me down. And I can't hear their stories with my gloves on."

"Why do you want to?" he asked.

"Because . . . because no one else ever will."

"Do you always cry?"

"No. I do not," she sniffed. He dug a handkerchief from his pocket—a task not easily done with the layers he was wearing—and blotted at her cheeks like a nurse assisting a surgeon. He didn't want her wiping death all over her face.

"So why are you crying now?" he asked.

"Because this poor man . . . Ivan. His name was Ivan. He was in love. She died a while ago, and he . . . he was glad to go. He wanted to die. But his love for her is here."

"Here?"

"Here in the cloth."

"Oh." The man's coat—if it could even be called a coat—was so black with soot it could have been the color of apples and no one would know it. Malone stuffed his handkerchief back in his pocket and hoped he wouldn't need it again.

"The woman he loved was Johanna," Dani said, her voice rising like she needed to convince him. "She . . . had a lovely smile and she wore a flower in her hat. A poppy. One of those paper ones that you can buy on street corners. He gave it to her. And every time it wore out, he'd buy her another."

"All right," he said, guarded, and she sighed. She turned to her clipboard and made some notes, her handwriting graceful and neat, gliding across the page like she was writing invitations to a party instead of descriptions of the dead. Then she set the clipboard aside and added another set of notes to what appeared to be an official record.

He didn't ask about the particulars; he didn't find he cared all that much, but when they finished removing the outer layers of "Ivan's" attire and dressed him in a clean shirt and trousers, Dani removed a paper from her clipboard and tucked it in his breast pocket.

"What's that for?" Malone frowned.

"I write their stories—in a few words—and put them in their pockets."

"Why?"

"Nobody's going to say words at their unmarked graves. These are their eulogies."

"Is that part of the job?"

"No. And Mr. Raus—and the men who come to retrieve them for burial—probably think I'm mad. I don't know if they toss the papers I tuck inside their clothes. But it makes me feel better. I keep good records so that someday . . . if someone comes looking, they can be found."

"Good God, Dani."

"You say that a lot, Michael."

"Yeah. Well. I don't know what else to say."

"He'll have to wear those old boots. That is one thing I can't spare. Look at his poor toes," she mourned.

He had no wish to look at the man's toes protruding from the ends of the boots, but he obeyed and immediately wished he hadn't.

"Move along, Dani," he demanded, and she did.

She mended a button here and there, washed the grime from frozen faces, and tidied tangled hair. They rolled another man to his side, as filthy as the first, and removed his layers, one by one, and eased him into a new shirt, buttoning it to the top and tucking the tails into a clean pair of trousers.

"I think his name was Wally. I don't know if it was his first or last. He liked ragtime music and whistled wherever he went. Whistling Wally." She wrote his description in her book, tucked his eulogy in the man's pocket, and moved on to the next body.

Poor Wally, unlike Ivan, didn't even have a bad pair of boots, and Malone did his best not to look at his bare feet.

A woman with scraggly gray hair and no teeth was next. She wore so many layers, it took Dani and Malone both to strip her down to the blue dress with faded lilies that she wore next to her skin.

"We'll leave her in this. It's the nicest thing she had. That's why she put it on the bottom. It kept it from getting soiled or too worn. She liked it. It made her feel like a girl again." Dani said all this slowly, almost like she was repeating something that was whispered in her ear.

"What will you do with the rest of her clothes? With the rest of all their clothes?"

"She doesn't need those now. None of them do. Check her pockets for possessions. If it's something small, a picture or a trinket, I like to leave it with them for burial."

He did as he was instructed, trying not to breathe. It afforded him a bit of separation. He found nothing in the pockets but a butt of a stogie the woman was probably saving for a special occasion. He showed it to Dani. She took it and tucked it into the pocket of the dead woman's blue dress.

He didn't know what it was about that gesture, the returning of something saved and something valued, but emotion rose in his throat, sudden and sharp, and he gathered up the filthy pile of clothes and turned away, wondering if he would need his damn handkerchief again after all.

"You can put the soiled items in a pile by the clothing table," Dani said. "What is salvageable, I'll reuse. Some folks come in here in rags. I don't want them buried in rags."

"And what do you do with the stuff you can't salvage?" He needed to keep talking. It helped him avoid thinking too much. What could Dani do with the Butcher's victims? The thought made him pause . . . and shudder.

"There's a rag and paper company on Scovill," Dani replied. "The owner will pay a few pennies per pound. It adds up."

He walked to the pile, shook out the clothes, and folded them neatly, buying himself a little time to find his balance. When he walked back to Dani, she had washed the woman's face and hands and tidied her hair. Then she straightened the woman's clothes and folded her arms across her chest.

"What's her name?" he asked.

She didn't respond for a moment but pulled out her paper and pencil and prepared to write. She hesitated, though, her pencil poised.

"I don't know what her name was. I can't tell. Her light was . . . dim. She was sick and tired. I'm not sure what to write."

"Just write that she loved a good cigar and lilies, and her favorite color was blue," he said, gathering the details like he always did, from the things he observed.

"You're good at this." She smiled at him.

He cleared his throat again, embarrassed, but handed her a pair of socks for Wally.

"Where did you find those socks?"

"They were in the bottom of the bag," he said, not missing a beat.

"No, they weren't."

"Yes, they were."

"I packed that bag myself. There were no socks. I'd run out. I'm not terribly fond of darning socks or knitting new ones. It takes more time than I have." She stared at the socks, frowning, and then peered up at him, suspicious.

"Michael, did you give Wally your socks?"

"Of course not."

She bent over and yanked up his pant leg, checking to see.

"Good God, Dani," he snapped, embarrassed, and jerked away from her. "I put on two pair this morning."

She gazed up at him, her eyes wide and her mouth agape. "You have a good heart, Michael Malone. That much has not changed."

By the time they were finished, the pile of soiled clothing was high and the daylight was gone. They both scrubbed at their hands and forearms in the small sink, took off the surgeons' gowns, and tossed them on the pile for washing as well. Dani insisted they would wait to bring them home in the wagon. Then they donned their coats and hats and scarves and made their way out of the nondescript morgue.

"They'll come and get them in the morning," Dani said, referring to the dead. "And within a few days, there will be more for me to see to."

"Next time, I'll bring you in my car." He was already regretting the loss of his second pair of socks.

"I don't need a ride. I have my wagon. And you don't want to transport that clothing in your car. But thank you very much."

Their footsteps crunched on the ice-sharpened snow, warning the street that they were coming, and he rolled his shoulders, grateful for the gun tucked beneath his left arm. He wouldn't use it—he wouldn't be able to see who or what approached—but he was glad he had it all the same. Chicago was every bit as cold and windy as Cleveland. But it had never felt as dark.

"You shouldn't walk alone like this at night, even for a few blocks," he told Dani. She probably shouldn't walk alone, period. Especially not near the Run.

"I can't always finish before sundown, not this time of year. Someone has to do it. If not me, who?"

If you don't do it, who will?

"Nobody cares about those people . . . or their stories," she added.

"Yeah. Well . . . they all have their heads. That's the only story the papers care about right now. My question is, Why do *you* care so much about them?"

"I don't know. Maybe . . . because I *can*. It's hard to care if you don't know someone."

"And you know them?"

"I know them as well as they will ever be known." She shrugged.

That silenced him. In fact, it almost stopped him in his tracks. How very sad that was, to be unknown.

"I will come with you when I can," he offered, surprising himself. Surprising her.

"You will?" she gasped. "Why? Today you already volunteered to be my new shoveler. Now you're going to do dead duty with me?"

"Dead duty. It's got a ring to it."

She shook her head, incredulous. For once the tables were turned.

"So your aunts know where you go with your wagon and your bags of clothes?" he confirmed, changing the subject.

"Of course, though they've never set foot in the place."

"And they say nothing?"

"Oh, they say plenty."

He almost chuckled at that. He just bet they did. "That was the strangest experience I've ever had, and I used to know Al Capone," he said.

"You will have to tell me all about that," she said, but he wondered again how much she knew. He found that did not bother him like it should.

Something had shifted in him. He'd given dignity to those who had nothing. He'd hated every minute of it, but he'd liked it too. He liked the way he'd felt watching Dani attend to those who had, most likely, rarely been cared for. Those who could never thank her for the service rendered. He had liked helping her. And he had liked being with her.

He liked *her*.

8

Two weeks after the storm, Malone walked through the neighborhood near Sweeney, just off of East Fifty-Fifth where Jackass Hill sloped down into Kingsbury Run. He didn't talk to anyone or duck into the bars as he'd been doing since he'd arrived in January.

He'd been to all the haunts and hangouts of the rougher crowd and the working-class toughs, starting with every joint in the vicinity of the Run and in the neighborhoods known as the Flats. There were a bunch of them. And he'd been making lists.

Most nights he sat alone nursing a beer while he kept his ears and eyes open. He'd heard a few mentions of the Butcher, a few theories, but without a recent murder, folks weren't talking about it as much as they might have. He'd been propositioned a few times, threatened a few more, but so far he'd managed to make it back home every time without a tail or a tumble.

He was starting to know downtown Cleveland far better than he'd ever wanted to, yet he hadn't managed to make much progress. Everything he did felt redundant, like waiting for a mouse to scurry across the floor when thousands lived in the walls. Then again . . . he was only hunting one mouse, and it was often the smallest crumbs that lured them out.

He needed a closer look at where the first two victims were found. He had the pictures and the reports and a description of the location, but without going there himself, he had nothing but secondhand impressions and, in many cases, third-rate accounts.

It wasn't a nice neighborhood. Dogs and cats and children ran loose. He didn't want to think about the rats. He was reluctant to judge, but first impressions were that everyone was hanging on by their fingernails. No one made eye contact, but he could feel their gazes skitter off his back and down to his shoes. Shoes said a lot about a man. Did he work? Did he walk? Did he take the time to shine them up? And if he did, he didn't belong in the Run. He was wearing his spectators, the white-and-black paneled shoes that dressed up a suit and drew the eyes away from a man's face. Malone liked that and utilized clothes like a costume director. Wear the right clothes, and you could go anywhere, no questions.

He wasn't wearing the right clothes today. He'd been expecting to meet Ness and remain in the car. But Eliot hadn't shown—something must have come up—and Malone had set out on foot as he tended to do. The way he was dressed now, folks might remember him, or worse, corner him in an alley and shake him down.

He went back the way he'd come and turned north on Fifty-Fifth and went another block to Praha and turned west again until he reached Forty-Ninth. If memory served, it was the base of Forty-Ninth, near the Shaker Heights tracks, where Edward Andrassy and the second victim, still only known as Victim #2, were discovered by boys chasing after their ball. The ground was frozen, but again, he wasn't dressed right for a scavenge, and he surveyed the rather steep slope. There were no shadows. The day was too grim and shadows required sunlight. The reports and the newspapers had all marveled at the brazen act of the killer, "arranging his kills for all to see," but it was a fairly desolate patch bordered by a few homes, with tracks and trees spread across it. At night, the killer would stand little risk of being seen.

"Hey, mister!" someone yelled. "I'll show you around for a dime or two."

He turned and saw a kid—fourteen or fifteen—in a checkered cap and coveralls, his coat too thin and his face too grimy for a boy who should still be in school. The kid approached him cautiously and stopped when he was about ten feet away.

"You're kinda late, aren't you, mister? There's nothing left to see down there that hasn't already been seen," the kid said. "But I'm happy to tell you what I know. I'll even give you a discount. A nickel just for talking."

"Oh yeah? Who are you?" Malone asked.

"Steve Jeziorski." The kid said his name hopefully, like he thought Malone might recognize it. When Malone didn't, he sighed.

"My name was in some of the dailies a couple years back. You probably missed it. Wagner and Kostura got all the attention."

"Why were you in the papers?"

"I saw one of the dead guys—the second victim—from the top of the hill. We didn't go down. James and Pete took off that way." He pointed. "We hightailed it home. Leonard wouldn't let me go down."

"Leonard?"

"My brother. He's older. Thinks he's the boss of me."

"And Wagner and Kostura? Who are they?" Malone knew who they were. He recognized those names, but he played dumb.

"They're the kids who saw the first body. James Wagner and Peter Kostura. They got the police down here."

"I think I heard something about that."

The kid scoffed. "Of course you did. Why else would you be here?"

Malone took a dime from his pocket and tossed it to Steve.

"Why don't you tell me everything you saw."

The dime disappeared into Steve Jeziorski's pocket, and he smiled like he held a winning hand.

"For a while we had all kinds of folks wanting to solve the mystery. I charge everyone I talk to . . . but I always tell the truth."

Malone didn't react to that.

The kid had a canned presentation all ready, pointing out the spots in the bushes and brambles where the first two victims of the Mad Butcher of Kingsbury Run had been found, describing what he and Leonard had seen before they dashed off to tell their mother. Nothing in the kid's account challenged anything Malone had read in the police reports. But the kid didn't tell him anything new either.

"Whoever done it wasn't trying to hide those bodies. They weren't too hard to spot. The Butcher wanted people to see, I'm guessing," Steve finished off, nodding like he hadn't heard the exact assessment a thousand times.

"Hmm" was all Malone offered.

"He was proud of his work."

"All right. Well, thank you for your time, Steve Jeziorski," Malone said, turning away from the path that led down into the Run.

"You don't look like a reporter . . . or a detective," Steve said, following him.

"No?"

"Nah."

"What if I was the Butcher? Come back to the scene of the crime?"

"Nah. You ain't the Butcher either. I've thought about it. The Butcher . . . he thinks he's a real funny guy. He thinks he's smart too, but mostly he thinks he's funny. You don't seem like the kind of guy who laughs all that much. You could probably kill a fella. But you wouldn't enjoy it."

"That's an interesting take. And you're right. I wouldn't enjoy it."

"You look like a gangster."

"Yeah? What gave me away?"

"Your face. Everyone around here is Polish or Hungarian or Czech. You're slick. Your shoes . . . and your hat. You could be a banker, but nah. You look like a gangster."

"Noted. You want to trade me hats?"

The boy hesitated. That surprised Malone. Steve's hat was a checkered cap that had seen much better days. Malone's hat was a black felt with a matching ribbon, and it was brand new.

"Yeah. Okay. I'll trade," Steve said.

Malone tucked a card with his number in the ribbon of the hat and handed it to the boy.

"You keep an eye out, Steve. You're a smart kid. You think of something else, or you see someone prowling around here that doesn't belong, you call and ask for Mike. At 5054 Broadway."

"You'll pay?"

"I'll pay."

The kid handed him the checkered cap, and Malone pulled it on.

"Much better." Steve grinned. "Now you look like one of us."

"Ha," Malone grunted. "Give me your coat."

The kid frowned.

Malone shrugged off his overcoat and extended it to the gaping boy.

"Are you serious?" Steve gasped.

"I can't have folks thinking I'm a gangster."

Steve checked his coat pockets and shoved a few coins and a book of matches into his overalls and handed his tattered jacket to Malone. His eyes were wide, and his hands shook as he buttoned the overcoat. "It's too big, but I'll grow into it. Leonard and my dad are both big."

"What size are your feet?" Malone asked. He might as well go all the way.

Steve laughed, incredulous, but he shook his head. "I don't know . . . but I need my boots. I can't wear those to work." He pointed at the spectators Malone wore on his feet.

"Where do you work?"

"Hart Manufacturing, near Twentieth and Central. My dad and Leonard work there too. I'm learning to be a toolmaker. It's a good job. I'm lucky to have it."

But Malone was only half listening. *Hart Manufacturing.* Where had he heard that before?

"You know what, kid? Your coat isn't going to fit me. You keep it. You keep both of them. I'll take the hat. It might save me from getting jumped." He tossed the coat to Jeziorski, who caught it with the same ease with which he'd swiped the dime from the air.

"Ma's gonna think I lifted these," Steve Jeziorski said, his smile fading.

"Nah. You always tell the truth, remember? Tell her you helped a curious tourist."

"A tourist? In Cleveland?"

"Ya got me there, kid," Malone shot back, but he began to walk. Briskly. He didn't have a coat anymore, and he'd just remembered where he'd heard of Hart Manufacturing.

~

Malone came in the front door of the shop at a quarter of four, shivering from the cold and wearing a cap that made him look like a delivery boy. Dani was changing the display and poked her head out from behind a dress form to greet him.

"I need an overcoat. And a new hat," he said, clamping his hands beneath his armpits.

"Yes. I can see that you do. What happened to the ones you had?"

"I made a trade."

"Willingly?" Dani teased, and he gave her a glimmer of a smile. One of these days he would grin at her.

"Yeah. Well. The kid needed them more than I did."

He didn't explain who "the kid" was, or why he was now in possession of a checkered cap, but she walked to a display and tugged down a lined and fur-collared overcoat and a matching fedora.

"This one will keep you warm, and it will look good with that hat," she said, holding them out to him. He shook his head.

"Too flashy. I want to be warm and . . . nondescript."

She hung them back up. "All right. I think we have a dark gray one in the back. It goes with everything. It's a good neutral. It picks up the warmth when you're wearing brown and doesn't look too yellow when

you go with the cooler tones. And this hat is a good shape for your face."
She plucked a charcoal-gray felt hat from a peg.

"Oh yeah? What shape is that?"

"Angular. The homburg is a nice compromise between the fedora and the bowler."

"You sound like you've done this before."

"Yes. Well . . . clothes are my thing."

He handed Dani the checkered cap he wore and set the new one on his head.

It looked good on him, just as she'd thought it would, but she was immediately distracted by the dirty cap in her hands.

"I'll take it," Malone said. "And the coat in the back, if you say it'll work. I also might want to dig through your pile of castoffs from the morgue. I'll compensate you. I need some clothes I can work in . . . ones that I won't have to worry about ruining."

She heard him, and she nodded, but she wasn't listening. The cap in her hands was too loud. She rubbed her fingertips against the inside band, the place where the brim joined the crown, the spot that absorbed both perspiration and contemplation.

"Dani?"

"This cap isn't his," she murmured.

"Whose?"

"The boy. He found it the day the bodies were found, but higher up on the hill. He hasn't told anyone. Not even Leonard. He doesn't know why. When he wears it . . . it's like he has a secret. But it's too late to tell anyone now."

She dropped the hat like it was hot and pushed her glasses up with the back of her hand. For some reason, she felt soiled, and she wanted to wash.

Malone stooped to pick it up.

"I'll go get that coat," she said.

"Who, Dani? Who are you talking about?" He kept his face blank, but she thought he knew. She thought he knew a lot more than she did.

"I don't know. He didn't think about his name when he was wearing it. He thought about . . . the man who it might belong to. Where did you get that hat?" she asked, striving for the same placid tone he was so adept at.

"I got that hat from a boy named Steve. He mentioned a brother. Leonard."

She nodded slowly.

"But you said it didn't belong to Steve. Who does it belong to?" Malone handed her the hat once more, and she accepted it with all the enthusiasm of a child receiving a ruler across her palms. But Malone had asked her, and she was pleased by that, even if she didn't like the way the hat *felt*.

She breathed out and listened again. "His scent is faded."

"His scent?" Malone asked.

"The man who owned it before the boy."

Malone waited as she dug deeper.

"He drove a car. Not his own. He was a driver."

"A chauffeur?"

"Yes."

"He probably wore this hat hundreds of times. Maybe more. And his presence"—she was always frustrated by the words she had to use to describe it—"is layered beneath the boy."

"Steve?"

"Yes. That feels right. Steve." Steve was anxious about the hat, and she would rather not keep sniffing at it. The scent did not appeal. But Malone wanted to hear more. She could see it in his stillness and the tilt of his head.

"Who was he? The driver, I mean. Do you have a name?" he asked.

"He thought of himself as Eddie." The scent became a muddy mix of motor oil and dust, onions and life. She might see something else if she tried again later.

"That's all," she said.

She handed Malone the hat. He studied it with a frown and then raised his eyes to hers once more.

"'He *thought* of himself as Eddie.' What does that mean?"

She shrugged, trying to think of the right words. "What do you call yourself?" she asked him. "When you talk to yourself, who are you?"

It was his turn to shrug. "I don't know. I guess I call myself Malone when I call myself anything at all. Sometimes Michael Francis, in my mother's voice, when I've made a mess of things."

That made her smile. "And I call myself Dani. Daniela when I am cross with myself. And sometimes I am Kos . . . or Flanagan, with my father's lilt. It depends. Some people think of themselves as 'mother.' Or 'father.' Or 'darling' or 'dear.' I think it depends on the voice they hear in their head, just like you said."

"So you can't always get a name from the fabric." Malone said everything as if he was clarifying, not questioning.

"No. I can't. Not a proper name. The apron of a woman who is simply referred to as 'mother' all day, who doesn't interact much outside of her family, might be harder for me to name—I may only hear 'mother'—whereas a gentleman who works in a bank might own a tie that literally vibrates with 'sir.'"

"That makes sense." He sounded surprised.

"I don't think what I can do is so different from what anyone else does. Don't thoughts and memories and connections flash through our minds all day long, every day? It's called thinking. We observe and catalog and quantify and organize all day long, every day, and we hardly realize we are doing it. I just seem to have a keener sense when it comes to . . ." She truly wished she had a word for what she did. "See," "sense," and "smell" just weren't quite right.

"When it comes to clothes," he finished for her.

"Yes, well. Most of the time, it is quite . . . useless. Just a glimpse of faded moments. Like eavesdropping . . . only I don't know who or what I'm listening to. Who or what I'm looking at." She shrugged. "It might be the most useless talent known to man."

He grunted at that, not committing himself to an opinion on the matter, and she let it drop, grateful not to continue.

He followed her through the shop to the stockroom behind the counter, where she unearthed the gray overcoat from the racks that lined the walls. He pulled it on, shot his sleeves to test the fit, and nodded. "That'll do."

He peeled the cost of the hat and coat from a money clip in his breast pocket and handed it to her as they stepped back into the shop.

"If you are inclined to give clothes away, or you need something for yourself, please feel free to take from the items we . . . collect." "Collect" was an imprecise word for what she did, but Malone had helped her twice since the storm, and he had earned whatever she could offer him.

"I might do that. Thank you."

"I will go again tomorrow, first thing after breakfast if you are . . . free." She almost laughed at that. What a pathetic outing. "And please don't feel obligated. I am only telling you because you insisted I do."

He nodded. "I can do that."

He tipped his new hat, thanked her for the assistance with his clothes, and disappeared down the hallway toward his room, the dirty checkered hat still clasped in his hand.

~

At dinner, Malone was back to staring morosely at his plate, hardly commenting, barely listening. He was preoccupied, and Dani thought it might have something to do with that checkered cap.

"We listen to the Cleveland Orchestra from Severance Hall every Thursday evening. You must join us, Mr. Malone," Lenka insisted, pulling him from his introspection.

"Maybe Mr. Malone does not care for the symphony, Lenka," Zuzana said. "Many don't. It is a refined taste. The Irish tend to like bagpipes."

"Nonsense. Who is your favorite composer, Mr. Malone?"

Malone was silent for a moment, and Dani thought for sure he would excuse himself.

"I heard Sergei Rachmaninoff at the Lyric Opera House in Baltimore a few years ago," he said quietly. "It was wonderful."

Lenka crowed and clapped her hands like a child, and Dani found herself beaming.

"He is Dani's favorite," Lenka exclaimed. "She says his music makes her feel crazed."

"His *Rhapsody on a Theme of Paganini* is the most beautiful music I have ever heard," Dani said, trying not to gush. "Except perhaps his Adagio sostenuto."

"He premiered his *Rhapsody* that evening. I might have to agree with you," Malone said, and Dani could not contain herself.

"I heard him first on the Victrola when I was a girl," she breathed, remembering. "It must not have been long before . . . before I came here. It was a new recording. Mother played it for us. Daddy was there too. The music was so wonderful, that when it was done we all clapped, and Daddy lifted Mother up, right off the bench, and kissed her."

Malone was watching her, his droopy eyes kind.

"You know how I feel about that man being mentioned in this house," Zuzana said, popping the happy memory like a pin to a balloon, and Dani was instantly bereft, the joyful spot of color destroyed.

Malone put down his fork, his gaze narrowing on Zuzana.

"George Flanagan did not kill himself or his wife. I am certain of that," Malone said evenly. "Whatever else he was, whatever else he did, he did not do that."

"This is a private, family concern, Mr. Malone. Please do not interfere," Zuzana clipped.

"Mr. Malone worked on the case, and he thinks it was a mob hit," Dani said, doing her best to keep her voice even.

"That is not what we were told," Zuzana said, her jowls quivering.

Malone held Zuzana's gaze with calm candor. "I know."

"They *were* madly in love," Lenka said, caving first. If Vera had been present, she would have been as outraged as Zuzana. Vera had sworn never to let George Flanagan's name cross her lips.

"I don't believe it," Zuzana snapped.

"Your belief is not required for something to be true," Malone said. His eyes returned to his plate, and he resumed eating.

"I am weary of your company. So I'll bid you all good night." Zuzana stood from the table and stomped out, her cane rapping the wood floor much harder than necessary.

"I suppose we'll be doing the dishes without Madame Zuzana this evening." Lenka smiled, unconcerned. "Tell us more, Mr. Malone. Surely you have many things you enjoy. Things that make you feel crazed. Blissful."

Malone looked at Lenka like he had inadvertently walked into the ladies' powder room.

"I felt blissful today," Dani said, compelled to rescue him from Lenka.

"You must tell us," Lenka insisted.

"I ate a perfect apple," Dani said. "It wasn't too hard and it wasn't too soft. It had a lovely crunch and the juice was both sweet and tart."

"And you felt bliss?" Malone interjected, his tone wry.

"Yes. Especially on the first bite."

"An apple a day keeps the doctor away," Lenka said. "What else makes you happy, dear?"

"Socks," Dani said.

"Socks?" Malone repeated.

"Warm socks on needy feet."

"Socks make you feel crazed?" Malone asked, droll.

She laughed. Surely he knew which socks in particular had made her happy.

"Can you imagine life without socks?" she challenged.

He picked up his napkin and wiped his mouth. "No."

"Your turn, Mr. Malone." Lenka was not going to give up, and Malone sat back in his chair.

"I like a good cigar," he said slowly. "The first drag. The way it smells, the way it feels in my mouth. If I smoke too often, I don't appreciate it as much. So I savor them and only indulge once in a while."

Lenka was beaming at him like he was a prized pupil. "Go on," she urged. He thought for a few seconds, and his list got much longer.

"I hate being cold, but I like sunshine in January. When it's so frigid it bites, yet the sun shines off the snow and warms the top of your hat and the tip of your nose.

"I like the smell of the sea on my sheets and bacon on the stove. I like a close shave and a hot towel around my face. A good pair of socks"—he glanced at Dani—"and peppermint drops. I have a sweet tooth. I don't think about food all that much. I'm not picky. But if you buy me a bag of candy, I'll eat it all."

"Noted," Lenka said.

"I don't care for John Philip Sousa or marching bands, but I get excited when I hear a storm. God's cymbals, my father used to say," Malone added.

"Excellent!" Lenka clapped. "Anything else?"

"I like an empty church and big dogs. I don't like small ones. They look too much like rats, and I don't like rats. And I prefer brown eyes to blue, though if you can have one of each, that's even better."

"Oh my," Lenka said, and Dani felt the heat rise in her cheeks. He was just being kind, but his face was completely serious. He didn't wink at her or even smile, but stood, signaling he was finished, and began clearing his dishes.

"Oh my," Lenka said again. "That was wonderful." But her gaze had grown speculative.

9

Malone spent the morning at the morgue with Dani, who had five bodies to tidy, dress, and write eulogies for. It took them three hours from the moment they left the house, pulling the wagon, until they were back again, mission accomplished. He bathed because it all made his skin crawl, and then spent the rest of the day poring over the files behind his locked door.

Between his long walks and his late nights, he'd begun to chip away at the list of "suspicious professions" in the surrounding areas. There were hundreds of them. He started at St. Alexis Hospital, just because it was nearby, and began putting faces to names and personalities to people. He sat in waiting rooms and roamed corridors and ate in the dining hall, listening to gossip and gathering data.

But today he went back to the files, searching for crumbs and taking notes.

He read and reread, setting the files aside and writing pages of ideas before reading again. Writing wasn't something he was particularly skilled at, not in the literary sense. He would never be a Shakespeare or a Dickens. But he found that the process of writing down what he thought he knew—facts, impressions, even the order of events—revealed what he didn't know and guided his steps.

When he was finished writing, he checked himself, going back into the files to see if what he'd written was there, in the pages, or if it was something he'd misunderstood or misremembered. What you thought you knew could lead you down paths that led to nowhere fast or, worse, to somewhere you never should have gone.

He was good at making lists. Even the kind that Lenka seemed to appreciate.

When he began feeling lost in the details, he backed up and started again, paring his lists to the bare bones. He took out a fresh pad of paper and limited himself to one-dimensional descriptions, no speculation allowed. He wrote only what was known and documented, and he did his best to keep it brief.

He started with Victim #1, Edward Andrassy, the man detectives kept circling back around to. Andrassy was a good-looking twenty-nine-year-old with a tall, lean build, brown hair, and blue eyes. He was the son of working-class Hungarian immigrants, and was well-known in the Roaring Third, a rough stretch of bars and tenements sandwiched between the Run and East Fifty-Fifth that extended up to Prospect Avenue. No one went to the Third if they wanted to stay out of trouble.

Andrassy hadn't stayed out of trouble. He had a criminal record, a reputation with the local cops, and a spotty employment history.

He'd been emasculated and beheaded, but not at the foot of Jackass Hill, where his remains were found. His body had been left—posed even—on his side, naked but for his black socks. His head was buried so his hair sprouted above the ground, and his genitals were found nearby. Both he and Victim #2 were discovered on September 23, 1935. He'd been dead between two or three days when he was found. Last seen getting into a long black car on September 19 near his parents' home on Fulton Road.

Malone ripped off the page and set it aside and started a new list for the second victim.

Victim #2: Short, stocky, age thirty-five to forty, emasculated. Headless. Both his buried head and his unburied genitals—found in a pile with Andrassy's—had been recovered in the area. His left testicle was missing.

Victim #2 had died at least a week (reports set the range to as many as thirty days) before Andrassy but was found approximately thirty feet from him. He, like Andrassy, had been killed somewhere else, but unlike Andrassy, his skin had been treated with something, giving it the appearance of red leather. A later report found that the second corpse had been braised, most likely with the railroad torch and the oil found in a two-gallon bucket at the scene. A pair of white trousers and a white shirt thought to be the second victim's had also been recovered in the vicinity. His identity was still unknown.

Malone set the second list aside and started another.

Flo Polillo, identified by the fingerprints on her severed right hand, was labeled Victim #3. She was in her early forties and roughly 160 pounds. She'd been arrested a few times for selling booze from her residence and selling herself in both Cleveland and Washington, DC.

A mugshot was included with her file. She looked tired but smiled slightly, incongruously, which made the picture seem more an awkward portrait than a mugshot. She did not look as if the arrest upset her at all; in his own experience there were two types of criminals: those who enjoyed it, and those who felt they had no other choice. Flo Polillo seemed the latter, but Malone didn't write that down on his current list. Instead, he added the produce baskets that held some of her dismembered pieces, and where and when she was found, which was behind Hart Manufacturing on January 26, 1936. Hart Manufacturing, the place where the kid Steve Jeziorski worked along with his father and his brother.

It was an interesting connection, but likely coincidental. The remarkable thing was that the kid had been wearing "Eddie's" cap. Malone could almost guarantee that Eddie was Edward Andrassy, Victim #1. Malone hadn't decided what to make of that, but if Dani's impressions were correct, the kid hadn't done anything criminal. He'd just failed to speak up and turn over the cap when he should have. Still, Malone would be swinging back to the neighborhood and having another conversation with Steve Jeziorski.

Half of Flo Polillo's headless torso, along with legs and her left arm, had been dumped at a different location, behind an empty house on Orange Avenue, and discovered on February 7, 1936. Her head had not yet been found.

That made it all the more interesting that *only* the head of Victim #4 was discovered on June 5, 1936, by two young boys. It'd been wrapped in a pair of trousers, and when they'd checked the pockets for change, it had rolled out. The rest of the man had been found, fully intact, genitals and all, the following day just east of the Fifty-Fifth Street bridge. The blood at the scene indicated he lay where he'd died. Why the killer had carried his head—and clothing—to a different location was anybody's guess.

Victim #4 was known only as the tattooed man. He was handsome, and that was saying something, considering the only pictures they had of him were of his severed head. Eyelashes like a child's, strong face, even features, and thick ruddy-brown hair. The coroner had made a diagram of the man's six tattoos, and the papers had distributed it widely. But still . . . nobody had come forward to claim him.

He kills nobodies.

Malone's lists tended to get longer and longer with every victim, his need to include the smallest details derailing him. He resisted the urge to describe the tattoos for his current list and wrote down the man's age, height, and weight—between twenty and twenty-five, five eleven, 165 pounds—and moved on to Victim #5.

Victim #5, yet another male with longish brown hair—this one estimated to be about forty years old, five foot five inches tall, and 145 pounds—was found about six weeks after the tattooed man. On July 22, 1936, the body was discovered in a wooded area by a seventeen-year-old girl out for a walk. Time of death put the deaths of Victim #4 and Victim #5 right around the same time. Had they died together and their remains been separated? From the file, it seemed the authorities—both police and coroners—were becoming numb to it all.

There was nothing on #5 to identify him. Fingerprints were impossible because the body was badly decomposed, except for the man's back, legs, and buttocks, which looked like seared hot dogs in the crime scene photo. He lay on his chest, though not facedown because his head had been removed. A detective found it about twenty feet away sitting merrily on top of what appeared to be a pile of the man's clothing, which included a double-breasted gray suit. His shirt and socks had matched; both were pale blue.

A man who matched his shirt and his socks cared about more than daily survival. Victim #5 was no Flo Polillo trying to get through each day in a beat-down, alcoholic fog. Malone had already noted that observation on a different list.

The police determined the man had died at the scene, just like Victim #4, and he too was in possession of all his limbs and his genitals. He was also the only victim found on the West Side, outside Cleveland city proper. Malone found that fascinating. The westsiders were a little "higher class," though the naked body had been found among the remains of hobo campfires. Still, it was like the Butcher was leaving folks where he thought they belonged, and some victims had been treated with more savagery than the others. Victims #4 and #5 were decapitated, which was hardly humane, but they hadn't been hacked up or emasculated, and that was new. Malone put that in his pile of unsubstantiated opinions and stood from his desk, in need of a break.

He checked the clock on his wall. Dinner was at seven and it was a quarter till. Close enough. He washed, then climbed the stairs, but Lenka was the only one seated at the dining room table.

"Sit down, Mr. Malone. Daniela had a late fitting. Zuzana is in a snit. So it is just you and me for supper." He groaned inwardly. He would have stayed in his room had he known. He liked Lenka well enough, better than Zuzana, though he preferred Zuzana's disdain to Lenka's keen interest.

Margaret was a welcome third, though she simply bustled about them and retreated to the kitchen when the food was on the table.

"I'll be going home now, Miss Lenka," she said, reappearing a moment later. "I'll see you tomorrow."

"Good night, dear."

"I didn't put a note beneath your door, Mr. Malone. But your laundry is done and hanging in the washroom."

"Thank you, Margaret," he said, and Lenka shooed her away.

"We are a little too casual around here, aren't we?" Lenka sipped at her soup, her pinky finger lifted as though she drank tea with the queen. He cleared his throat.

"We talk about laundry at the dinner table." She sighed. "When I was a young woman, dinner was a formal event. My mother would have dismissed Margaret on the spot for what she just did. But I prefer straight talk. Don't you, Mr. Malone?"

He really didn't. Not with nosy old women who had obvious agendas.

"Hmm," he replied, and continued spooning up his own soup.

"You should not doubt her, Mr. Malone."

"Hmm?" he said.

"Daniela. You should not doubt her."

He nodded and stuffed a hunk of bread in his mouth, hoping Lenka Kos would leave him alone.

"She is quite beautiful, isn't she?"

The bite caught in his throat, and he reached for his coffee, frantic, sloshing it over the edge and onto his hand. It burned and he swore, and Lenka let him recover.

He apologized for the curse when he'd taken a sufficient, crumb-free breath.

"She hasn't had many suitors. Men are fools. And opportunities are limited."

"I see," he said. He didn't. Not really. He didn't want to talk about Dani's suitors. He ate faster.

"My husband was three decades older than me," Lenka said.

He choked again. That comment seemed very pointed.

"For goodness' sake, Mr. Malone," she chided. "Slow down. Enjoy your meal."

"I was not aware you had ever married," he said.

Her lips quirked. "He did die rather early in the relationship. It was never even consummated. I never forgave him for that."

Good Lord. "A reason, perhaps, that young girls should not marry old men," he said.

"Hmm," she murmured, foiled, and she was mercifully silent for several minutes.

"Do you want children, Mr. Malone?" she asked, circling again.

He sighed and finished his mouthful. She waited, her fork in the air, her eyes trained on his face.

"I did. Once."

"But not anymore?"

"I had two children. Both are dead. My wife is dead too. And I have no wish to replace her." Better that he make that clear, as long as they were being bold.

"My dear, poor man." She sighed again. "Yet you like Daniela, don't you? You think she is beautiful. I saw it in your face the very first day."

Had she? How humiliating if so. He prided himself on being a bit harder to read.

"I am here to do a job, Miss Kos," he said, throwing his napkin down and pushing back his chair. "That is all."

"And what job is that, Mr. Malone? I have not been able to puzzle that out. I'm guessing Daniela knows. She's a terrible snoop, though it's not her fault."

"It seems to be a family trait," he said, his voice perfectly mild.

Lenka blinked at him, stunned, and then she snickered.

"I like you, Mr. Malone," she said. "I like you very much. I think you are exactly what the doctor ordered."

"Yes. Well. If you'll excuse me," he said. "I have work to do, hours of tedious work, and I'd very much like to finish. The sooner the better."

"Of course, darling," Lenka said, all sweetness and light. "But don't be in too big a hurry. And don't dismiss Daniela. You might miss something important."

Dani was coming up the stairs when he was going down. She greeted him sedately. He greeted her in the same manner. And they both continued on their way.

~

The first evidence that there was a Victim #6 had come when pieces of a man's pale white torso bobbed up in the waters of a stagnant pool vagrants called "the creek" in Kingsbury Run. A vagrant named Jerry Harris, waiting on the banks to hitch a ride on the train, was the lucky witness. That was September 10, 1936.

For a month, authorities dragged the filthy pool with hooks looking for the rest. They found the thighs, the right one and then the left, but never found the man's arms or his head.

They even sent down a marine diver.

Malone had marveled at that, especially when he read a quote by the man hired to do the job. It was an article published with a picture of onlookers lining the banks of the pond.

"We can't see anything," the diver reportedly said. "We're used to that, having worked in the Cuyahoga River. We operate by sense of touch."

Reading the article again made Malone think of Dani. What would she have been able to determine if she'd held the clothes the detectives had found in the weeds near the pool?

His heart started to pound at the thought. It wasn't the first time he'd considered it. Dani would be able to tell him things he couldn't possibly uncover any way else, just like she'd done with the kid's cap. He would just have to get his hands on the evidence. Ness could help with that. Maybe sneak them into the evidence locker for an hour or two.

Malone rescanned the list of clothing found with Victim #6, his excitement building. Some items were wrapped in newspaper as if they were gifts for the police. A felt hat, a patched-up work shirt, and a partial pair of underwear with a laundry mark of "JW." There was blood on the shirt, slash marks too, and blood on the underwear. Like Andrassy and Victim #2, Victim #6 had been emasculated. The coroner's report claimed that the thin, five ten, twenty-five to thirty-year-old man had been alive when the dismemberment started.

Malone's excitement crashed like it had been doused in ice water.

No, he wouldn't want Dani touching the clothes. He didn't want her anywhere near this case. She'd cried because a dead vagrant had worn his lost love on his dirty sleeve. He did not want her seeing—or feeling—anything to do with the Butcher or the Butcher's dead.

He sighed, sickened, and tore off the page to start a new one.

On February 23, 1937, the lower half of a woman's torso washed up on the beach at the foot of East 156th Street. The county pathologist guessed that the woman had been between twenty-five to thirty years old with light brown hair. She'd weighed about 120 pounds and was between five foot five and five foot eight inches tall, which were estimates and extrapolations, and not on actual measurements, as they had only half a torso, and no arms, legs, or head.

On May 5, 1937, almost three months later, the upper half of a torso rolled up on the beach and bottomed out a few feet from the shore. Cold Lake Erie had kept the flesh preserved, and when it was taken to the city morgue, it was a perfect match with the bottom half. The woman was never identified, and no one came forward to claim her. This time there wasn't even the victim's clothing from which to draw clues. Dani would be as blind as the rest of them.

But the coroner was reluctant to add the woman to the Butcher's tally, arguing she hadn't been found in the Run and that she'd already been dead when she was decapitated. The cuts were less controlled and precise, making the findings easy to waffle over.

The truth they didn't want to acknowledge was that the first Lady of the Lake had washed up in the exact same place, in roughly the same condition, her torso cut in half. Police didn't just have a seventh victim, they had an eighth; all indications were that the first Lady of the Lake in '34 had been the Butcher's work too.

The papers had begun to refer to the Lady of the Lake in some accounts as Victim Zero so as to not change the original numbering of the dead. Since numbers were all they had, in most cases, to keep their victims straight, Malone could understand why.

The remains of the official Victim #8—tentively identified as Rose Wallace—were found by another kid. Kids meandered. Kids explored. Kids played where adults rushed. Her torso, not much more than a skeleton, was found in a partially buried burlap bag under the Lorain-Carnegie Bridge. Her skull had been set atop it. It was her three gold teeth, winking in the late-day sun, that caught the eye of the boy traipsing across the trash-littered field beneath the bridge.

The coroner estimated time of death to be about a year earlier, though Rose Wallace had only been missing ten months, according to those who had last seen her. But the height, weight, age, and ethnicity of the remains all matched up to missing Rose Wallace. Forty-year-old Rose was a tiny Negro lady, barely five feet tall and a hundred pounds, and according to her dental records, she had three gold crowns. In the reports the police used words like "allegedly Rose Wallace," but it was her. The coroner had just gotten the death estimate wrong. Maybe it was the advanced decomposition of the skeleton; lime was found in the bag, which aided the breakdown of the body.

Rose Wallace had purportedly been doing her laundry at home when a friend dropped in and told her someone was asking for her at a nearby bar. Wallace left her laundry and went straight away. Various sightings of Rose with different men were made that night, but no one seemed to know any of them by name, and no one saw Rose again.

That was August of 1936. She was discovered June 6, 1937, but authorities didn't believe she'd died in the trash-strewn field, and they didn't know when her remains had been placed there.

Exactly one month later, on July 6, 1937, another body turned up, floating in the Cuyahoga, taking the attention from Rose Wallace, and shining it on a man still known only as Victim #9.

Like Victim #6, who was found in the pond, Victim #9 was discovered bit by bit. A burlap bag was spotted and fished out of the water first. The bag, which had once held chicken feed, now contained a woman's silk stocking and the top half of a man's torso wrapped in newspapers dated three weeks earlier. The bottom half of the torso was dragged out a few hours later after multiple sightings. One man saw it while watching a tugboat pass beneath the West Third Street Bridge.

A day later, the forearms with their hands still attached were found. A few days after that, the upper part of the right arm, and on July 14, the lower part of the right leg was recovered. And that was all. No head. No clothes. No other identifying items. The fingerprints they were able to get from the hands didn't match any records.

From the pieces they discovered, a general description was formed: white man, about forty years old, approximately five foot eight or nine with a good build, genitals intact. The coroner's report claimed that this victim had been "hacked up" in new ways, however. His heart had been removed. Lower organs too. And not neatly. The pathologist used the word "wrenched." The cut marks at the neck and joints were not nearly as precise or deliberate either. Ness had speculated that the Butcher was losing control.

Maybe so. But it was now March of 1938, and no bodies had been discovered in the last eight months. The Mad Butcher of Kingsbury Run hadn't completely gone mad. Not mad enough to make a blunder that would reveal him.

Malone arranged his bare descriptions in a row of ten pages across his bedroom floor and stood over them, his hands in his pockets, his eyes jumping from sheet to sheet.

One of the difficulties with having so many unidentified victims was that police couldn't retrace their steps. When something was lost, thinking back to where you had it last was usually the most effective strategy for finding it. But nobody knew where the majority of the victims had been.

Rose Wallace was believed to have been at a bar on Scovill and East Nineteenth, not far from where she lived the last time she was seen. Flo Polillo had left the rooming house where she lived on Carnegie at about eight thirty in the morning the day before her remains were found, according to her landlady. Both women had lived very similar existences. Lots of alcohol, lots of addresses, lots of unsavory men. One-Armed Willie, the suspect Ness had mentioned, had been involved with both women, but a dirtbag didn't a murderer make.

Unfortunately, the connections between the two women hadn't turned up another viable suspect, not one with the characteristics to implicate him in the murder of all the others as well.

The benefit—Malone used the word loosely—of having ten murders was that patterns emerged. The most glaring consistency was that all the victims had been found headless. The men weren't all emasculated, and they weren't all dismembered. The women were, though, every one of them. But they were *all* decapitated.

Malone added another thing to his list of consistencies. They had all been found naked, though Edward Andrassy had still been wearing his socks.

They weren't all the same age, sex, or race. Rose Wallace had been the outlier on race. But none of them were old and none of them were children. Between twenty and forty seemed to be the general age range. That was a pattern, though a minor one.

Most had been found in and around the Run, but not all.

The only other thing that remained consistent across the ten dead was that all of them appeared to be alone in the world. It might be argued that Andrassy was the exception, with a family who loved and mourned him, but he too was alone, if only due to his habits and his choices.

More than anything else, and it was something Malone kept circling around, the murders didn't feel *personal*. Vicious, yes. Horrific, absolutely. But he didn't think the murders were about the slain themselves. They were nobodies. To the killer, they were nobodies, chosen specifically for that one detail.

The Butcher killed the people he killed because he could. Because no one would really care if they were gone. And after Andrassy, he'd never made the same mistake again; he'd never killed anyone with a family who might come looking for them, raise a fuss, or even know they were missing.

No, the murders weren't about the victims. Malone was convinced the murders were about the killer himself.

10

Malone put the lists away, needing space and perspective, but he didn't want to sleep. Instead, he took out his gun and the rifle he'd brought back from France. It'd been at Molly's with his suits, and he'd brought it along for the hell of it. He hung his white dress shirt to keep it from getting stained and sat in his trousers and his undershirt, taking his weapons apart before he cleaned and reassembled them. He put his revolver away but took his rifle apart and reassembled it once more, this time faster. It was something they'd done in the army. It narrowed his focus and emptied his head, allowing him to stew without thinking and relax without drinking. He hadn't held the rifle in years, and he enjoyed getting reacquainted.

Snap, click, click, snap. Crack, snap, bang, smack. He repeated the process over and over again until a tapping at his door pulled him out of his rhythm. He put down the rifle and checked his timepiece with a frown.

It was midnight.

The tapping came again. He rose, walked to the door, and opened it reluctantly. His suspenders were still keeping his pants up, but his undershirt was a little informal for company.

Dani stood on the other side, covered from neck to toe in a pale blue dressing gown, even more informal than he was. Charlie the cat was in her arms, a witch and her familiar with matching gazes.

"Do you think you might be done soon?" she asked hesitantly. Her hair was a tangle of coppery curls, and he was reminded of the girl who'd greeted him the morning after her parents died. Her multicolored eyes had been just as heavy then, and he felt instant remorse. Her room was above his, and he hadn't tried to be quiet.

"I've kept you awake, haven't I?" he asked. "I didn't think. I'm sorry. It won't happen again."

She nodded, acknowledging his apology, and turned to go back up the stairs. The cat had other ideas. He bounded from her arms, shot through the open door, and disappeared under Malone's bed.

"Charlie," Dani groaned, her arms falling to her sides.

"I'll get him," Malone said, but when he kneeled down and peered beneath the bed, he couldn't make out a thing, and the cat didn't budge. When Dani knelt beside him and tried to coax the stubborn beast to come, cooing into the darkness, Charlie ignored her too.

"He goes wherever he pleases. I'm sorry." Dani sighed. "If I don't get him now, he'll yowl at your door in a few hours, demanding to be let out."

That sounded unpleasant. Malone wouldn't sleep a wink if the cat was in his room. The cat reminded him a little of Zuzana.

"You could sleep with your door open," Dani suggested. "Then he could just let himself out."

No. He couldn't. He pictured Margaret arriving in the morning and watching him sleep, that is if he was able to sleep at all. He did not go to bed with his door open. Ever. He tried fishing the cat out once more. When he was unsuccessful, he got his rifle and used it to extend his reach. He got nothing for his trouble but a stiff neck and squeals of protest from Dani.

"I'm not going to shoot him, Dani. I just want him to get out of my room."

Dani left and came back later with a bowl filled with cream. She set it down on the floor and tapped a spoon against the side, trying to lure the cat with food, but the cat ignored her kindness and Malone's threats and stayed put.

"I'm sorry," she said again. "This is new for all of us. He's been spoiled all of his life and had full run of the house."

He stood and put his rifle away, tidying his space and retreating to the bathroom to ready himself for bed. When he returned, washed, with a fresh undershirt beneath his suspenders, Dani was still sitting by his bed, her legs folded beneath her, her head against the side. She looked tumbled and tired and a little too young, in her dressing gown and bare feet, for his comfort.

He turned the chair at his desk toward her and sat down, his elbows to his knees, his hands clasped.

"Go," he said. "I'll let him out when he decides to show himself."

She'd seen his hesitation before and could not be convinced that he was sincere.

"Do you have work to do?" she asked. "I'll just sit here quietly while you do it. Or . . . if you're tired, I'll come back in an hour or so and check on him. I'll just open the door a little, and if he doesn't come, I'll try again an hour after that."

"You know this is ridiculous, right?"

"I really am sorry," she said, but she didn't go, and for a moment silence fell between them.

"Why are you still here, Dani?" he asked softly.

She frowned at him, not understanding, and he clarified his meaning.

"Why do you live with your aunts? Don't you want a home of your own? You're a beautiful woman. Charlie can't be the only man in your life. Surely you've had a string of young men lined up for your attention."

"No."

"No, you haven't, or no, you don't want a home of your own?"

"No, I haven't. And this is my home."

"You don't have anyone?" he pressed. He couldn't believe that.

"I'm odd . . . and I'm usually uninterested. That combination seems to be hard on men."

He laughed, surprised. She was right. How intuitive of her. Men needed a great deal of encouragement, and an average woman was difficult enough. Add *odd* onto *beautiful*, and most men would steer clear. Partly out of respect. Partly out of self-preservation. He laughed again, her honesty and perception delightful to him.

Dani was gaping at him, and his smile faded. "What?" he asked.

"I thought that might happen."

"What?"

"When you smile, your whole face changes. It's like the sun breaking through the clouds or . . . or a log catching flame. Whoosh." She emphasized the word with her hands, making a starburst motion. "Please do it again."

"I can't just smile on demand."

"Of course you can. You must have smiled on demand a million times."

"When?"

"It's just like playing a role . . . and you have played so many. Michael Lepito must have smiled at Al Capone. A smile is a language all its own."

He frowned at her.

"You told me you once worked for Al Capone," she said.

"Yeah. But I don't recall telling you about Michael Lepito, though he was one of the plastic monkeys, if I remember."

"I touched your suit. Your . . . suits. They are beautiful. My grandfather used to make silk suits for John Rockefeller, but those . . . those are lovely."

He looked at his wardrobe. He'd left it open when he'd prepared for bed.

He sat back in the wooden chair and rubbed his eyes.

"I was not trying to pry . . . I promise."

Had it been anyone else, looking at the quality of a fine suit, it wouldn't have been a big deal. But it was Dani, and it felt a little like he'd caught her reading his journal, and he didn't keep one on purpose.

"What did you see?" he asked. "And you better tell me all of it."

"May I please look at them again?"

He shot his hand toward the suits. "By all means."

She rose, invigorated, and threw the door of the wardrobe wide. Taking a suitcoat from its hanger, she slipped her hands into the sleeves so it was hanging from her forearms.

"The stitching is perfect, and the color is sublime," she marveled. "Nothing feels like silk. Nothing in the world."

"Dani." He didn't want to hear the tailor's opinion. He wanted to hear the soothsayer so he could assess the damage. He rose and stood in front of her. "Tell me."

She was quiet for several seconds, gazing up at him but not really seeing him at all. Her pupils grew so large the iris of her blue eye was reduced to a narrow ring. The brown eye just got darker. It was the first time he'd looked directly into her face, close-up, while she'd done her thing. The hairs rose on his arms.

"You make yourself be still and read the paper. But you aren't reading, you're watching. You tell yourself to turn the page. You know better than to use the paper as a prop. They're watching you too. You have to be natural. And patient. You are so patient." She paused and he swallowed.

"You like the suit. It makes you feel safe. Good clothes do that. Make us feel safe. Seen, but unseen. It's magic, really." Her voice was dreamy, like she was interpreting a painting on a gallery wall.

"I can smell newsprint." She inhaled deeply. "And cigars. You *do* love them. The best part of the job, you think."

"You can smell a memory?" he gasped, unable to help himself.

"That's what makes it so clear. And it is *. . . so . . .* clear. You must have sat in this suit, in that hotel, reading the paper and smoking many times."

"That suit and a few others. What hotel?"

She blinked several times, thinking, and then handed him the suitcoat.

"That's all I see . . . for now."

"What do you mean?"

"I can only see in pieces. Or parts. One layer at a time. And I grow desensitized to the fabric the longer I hold it. The way you notice a smell when you first walk in the room but don't notice it the longer you're there."

He glowered at her. He hated it when she made perfect sense with such nonsensical things. He hung the silk suitcoat back in his closet.

"It's not there in the suit, but I think I know where you were. It was in all the papers. Al Capone lived at the Lexington Hotel," she said.

"Yes, he did."

"Will you please tell me about it?" She sounded like a kid begging for a bedtime story.

"Oh, what the hell," he relented on a gusty exhale.

She turned and scampered to his bed and sat down, folding her hands in her lap and crossing her bare feet. He supposed that meant he got the desk chair. He sat back down, but he didn't really know where to start. He admitted as much.

"I'm not as good at . . . stories . . . as you are."

"How did you come to work for Al Capone?" she asked, coaching him along.

"I guess it's because I look like this." He waved a hand over his face.

"You don't have Irish eyes."

"Nope."

"Or Irish skin."

"No. I'm brown. My dad turned pink in the sun, and his hair was full-on white by the time he was forty. That's what I am now." He shook his head with the realization. "If I didn't have my dad's nose and his stubborn chin, I mighta been thrown out sooner than I was."

"You were thrown out?"

"No. That was just something my sister, Molly, always said. I went willingly. Joined the army when I was eighteen. My mother died when I was twelve. My father kind of lost interest in life after that. Molly was older, and she always tried to look out for me, but she was just a kid herself. The army made sense for me."

"Where is Molly now?"

"My clothes haven't told you about Molly?" he asked.

"No, Michael," she said, enduring his sarcasm with her usual aplomb. "They haven't told me about Molly or your mother or your father or most of your life."

"She's an angel, Molly. And she's still in Chicago. And lucky for her, we look nothing alike."

"She looks Irish?"

"Yeah. All Irish."

"So Capone hired you because he thought you were Italian?"

"He didn't . . . hire me."

"Start at the beginning."

The beginning. He wasn't even sure where that was. "Capone thought I was Italian . . . but that's what I wanted him to think. That's what I made him think. And it took a long time to make him believe it."

"You were patient. I saw that in the silk."

"Yeah. Well." He cleared his throat. "I look like I could be from anywhere. Or nowhere. And I'm good with language too. In the army, I used to copy accents. Some guys tell jokes. Some guys can sing. Some guys have the gift of gab. They can talk their way out of anything. I couldn't do that." He shook his head. "I'm not a talker. I'm a listener. I've got a good set of ears. And I could mimic anyone."

"As you have demonstrated." She smiled, encouraging him.

"The guys loved it. They'd call out the accent, and I'd give it to them. Yiddish, Philly, the Bronx, Boston. The ones I didn't know, I learned. Soldiers were from everywhere. I'd get them talking, and I'd listen. My mother spoke Gaelic, so I had that in my arsenal when I needed it. I can pass as Greek too, so I learned Greek. I can speak Italian, Spanish, and Yiddish too."

"You learned all of that in the army?" she gasped.

"Nah. The languages came before . . . and after. It's part of my job." His affinity for language was what had gotten him in the door, he had no doubt.

"In Cleveland, you'll find Poles and Hungarians—more Hungarians than in any city except Budapest—and Czechs," Dani said. "You'll have to brush up on your eastern European languages."

"I probably won't be here that long," he said.

A shadow flickered across Dani's face, as if that bothered her. He liked that it did. And that bothered *him*.

"Do you really work for the Treasury Department?" she asked.

"Yes."

"Are you really a . . . tax man?"

"No. Not . . . really. But kind of."

"And you were a policeman."

He nodded. "I didn't mind military life. Didn't mind taking orders. Didn't mind fighting either, though I didn't love it like some of the guys. When I got home, police work just made sense. I was already married. Had a family to support."

"You must have been very young when you married."

"I married Irene six months after I joined the army. We were both eighteen. We grew up together. Lived on the same street. When I went to France, she stayed with her parents. When I came home . . . I moved in too." It felt odd to talk about it. In so many ways, he did not recognize the Michael Malone in his memories. It was as if he'd split in two or left himself behind in the old neighborhood, on the street where they'd lived. The street Irene had never left.

"We got married, and three days later I left for France for more than two years. When I got home in early 1919, Mary was almost eighteen months old," he said. It'd been surreal, meeting his child for the first time, and what a lovely little girl she'd been. She'd had Irene's blue eyes but none of her blondness. Mary was dark like him.

"It wasn't just Mary that you lost. There was another little stone at the cemetery when you were burying Irene," Dani said, almost apologetic, like she was confessing something she wished she didn't have to.

"This was not the story I wanted to tell," he murmured.

"I know."

He didn't want to tell it, but it was all connected. There would have been no Al Capone in his life without the army, without Irene and Mary and James, without . . . Dani. He supposed it was best to just lay it all out, which he did, quickly. Three deaths and the birth of the man he now was.

"Irene got pregnant again about a year after I came home from France. Everything was fine right up until the end. I don't know what went wrong. But the baby—a boy—was stillborn. Then Mary died of pneumonia about a year and a half after that. Irene kinda broke. She was always a little high strung, but she just crashed. And she really never recovered. I made it worse, she said. I made her anxious and upset. We didn't divorce . . . but we've lived apart for the last fifteen years." That was very good. Very matter-of-fact. Unemotional. He was proud of himself. He didn't even break eye contact with Dani. Of course, she had more questions.

"How did she die?"

"She liked the laudanum. It caught up with her, I guess. Or she mixed it with something. We don't know if she did it on purpose. She was in her bed. Molly said it looked like she just died in her sleep."

"I'm sorry."

"I didn't feel anything. I still don't." He shoved his hands into his pockets and met her gaze with resignation. He was not deserving of sympathy nor did he particularly need it.

"When a lake freezes over, it doesn't freeze all the way to the bottom," Dani said.

"What?"

"It just freezes on the surface. The ice can be really thick . . . but there's always water moving below it. You feel something. It's just below the ice," she said softly.

"Yeah. Well." He shrugged.

"How does all this lead to Al Capone?" she asked, allowing him to return to the original tale.

"This is where you come in."

"Me?" she gasped.

"You. And your father."

Her gaze was riveted to his face.

"Your father was running on routes that had already been claimed. It was early days yet, and everyone was trying to get their foot in the door. Claiming territory. Supply lines. Paying off cops and judges and funneling money to whoever they needed to look the other way.

"I don't know if your dad was with O'Banion's gang. With a name like Flanagan, probably. But Johnny Torrio—the boss before Capone—sent a message."

"My father was the message?"

"Yeah. And the cops heard it loud and clear. Murder, suicide, case closed. I saw it over and over again. And there you were, a little girl with mismatched eyes who needed justice. And I knew you weren't going to get it. Your mother wasn't going to get it. And your dad, for all his mistakes, wasn't going to get it either."

"What did you do?" she whispered.

"I'd heard about the work the Treasury boys were doing. T-men, they called them. I thought maybe it was something I could do. I didn't want to be one of the bad guys, and everywhere I looked there were bad guys, and nobody was stopping them. And I had nothing . . . better . . . to do."

"Because your family was gone," she summarized, her mouth sad.

He nodded, the movement terse. "Yeah. So I . . . signed up."

"That easy?"

"No." He laughed, though the action didn't curve his lips. "It wasn't easy. But I'm not going to break it all down for you either. Jump ahead to Capone in '29."

"All right."

"The department needed an inside man."

"One that looked like an Italian and had a gift for accents?"

"Yeah. They had a plan that I would slowly infiltrate Capone's inner circle. I pretended to be a mobster from Philly named Michael Lepito who was lying low at the Lexington Hotel in Chicago until my lawyers could work out a deal so I could go back home."

"Where did you get the suits?" she asked. Of course Dani would want to know that.

"They were provided to me. I had to look the part, and bosses don't wear cheap suits. Cops wear cheap suits. Capone had to be absolutely convinced."

"And was he?"

"I guess so. Though when he found out I wasn't a wop—that was his word, not mine—he couldn't believe it."

"He found out?"

"Not until it was too late. I was undercover for a year and a half. He found out about me at his trial. He saw me coming out of the elevator with the prosecutor." For eighteen months he'd kept his cover. He listened, he played his part, and he never broke. Then something as simple as a courthouse conversation had blown it.

"You must have been scared."

"I got out of town after that, yeah. But Capone's at Alcatraz now. His organization was rattled to its roots. And so far . . . nobody's caught up to Michael Lepito."

"Or Michael Malone?"

"Just you, Dani. Just you."

"That was a very good story," she said slowly, her attention trained beyond him, mulling it all over.

"A very *long* story." He glanced at the clock on the wall.

Dani lifted up the skirt of the bed and peered beneath it once more. Charlie strolled out like he'd been waiting for his cue. Then he sat, directly in the center of the floor, and began washing himself.

Dani swooped him up, triumphant, and Malone just shook his head.

"What a pain in the rump he is," he growled, rising.

"If he weren't, I wouldn't love him so much."

"I would like him a great deal more, however."

She snickered but kept a firm hold on Charlie as she left the room.

"Good night, Michael," she called.

He sighed, feeling like he'd just been subjected to a pat down and a cavity search.

"Good night, Dani."

11

By late March, the temperature had risen enough that when Dani and Malone walked to the morgue on a Thursday morning, Dani pulling the wagon behind her, there was a decided feeling of spring in the air.

Michael had remarked on it, tipping his face to the sky and unbuttoning his coat. They'd developed a rapport and a comfort level that she enjoyed. His humor was decidedly dry and his demeanor consistently guarded, but he was gentle and attentive too. Kind even, though she suspected he thought himself quite the villain.

He seemed very mindful of keeping his distance, never displaying any sort of physical affection or attraction, yet he seemed genuinely intrigued by her. She did her best to keep her hands to herself as well, her Midas touch in check, but she looked forward to the two mornings a week when she had him all to herself, even if she had to share him with the dead. And the dead provided plenty of distraction.

Their only "customer" that morning was a woman wrapped in a colorful patchwork quilt and nothing else. The tag on her toe told the address where she'd been discovered, and if her death had been ruled a homicide, she would not have been turned over to the indigent facility.

She was relatively young and slim, and her hair, though unkempt, was bobbed at her shoulders, indicative of some level of attention.

Dani found something for her to wear and ran a brush through the matted strands before they unwound the quilt from around her gray limbs.

"What happened to her?" he grunted. The woman had no clothes to provide clues, and no apparent injuries.

"I don't know, Michael. I am not a coroner," she reminded.

"What does the cloth say?" he asked, no hesitation. He'd become used to her ways.

The quilt was tattered but not dirty, and Dani clasped the folds, allowing her mind to empty and her eyes to see.

"If this is hers . . . her name is Nettie. And she's had this quilt since she was a girl." She was quiet, watching the flickering images. Tears, shouting, hiding, holding, loving. Distance. The woman had taken the quilt from one day, one decade, to the next, and before that, the squares had belonged to a hundred different stories carefully stitched together by a freckled hand.

"There is care in the stitching. It is well made." Dani's eyes told her that much. She didn't even need to touch the cloth. "When the world is dark, look at the colors, Nettie," she whispered, hearing the echo of the words pressed upon the girl.

Malone cleared his throat, and Dani let go of the blanket. She hoped whoever had made a quilt of many colors for Nettie had welcomed her home.

She took up her log and made careful notes, engulfed by the sadness that often accompanied such glimpses.

"She's naked. Is that what she did for a living?" Malone asked quietly.

"I think so. Yes." She swallowed back the emotion in her throat. If she had been alone, she might have shed a tear, but Michael had seen her cry over too many, and it distressed him, though he usually scolded her to cover his discomfort.

"Is that what killed her?" he asked, grim.

"I don't know. She didn't know."

"She didn't know she was dying?"

"It doesn't feel that way. No. She was . . . floating."

He sighed. "Well that's good."

"We will dress her, but let's fold the quilt and put it in her arms. She should have it."

They finished in silence, and Dani made her obituary, tucking it into the folds of the quilt Malone had placed on the woman's chest. It was not until they were walking back toward home that they spoke again.

"My father called my mother Nettie sometimes," Dani said.

"Aneta," Michael supplied. "Nettie makes sense."

"Yes. Aneta Kos Flanagan. Aneta and George. What a pair."

He said nothing, but he was listening, and she found herself falling into his attention. He always had the same effect on her.

"It didn't fit. Nettie didn't fit. She was too regal for it."

"Ah. You must get that from her," he said softly, and her heart warmed in her chest.

"Thank you. I don't think my aunts agree. I think they worry that I have too much of my father in me."

"How so?"

"He was wild. And strapping, I think, is the word one would use. He was loud. And jolly, and . . . passionate."

"Were his eyes like yours?"

"One of them," she shot back, not missing a beat. Her mouth quirked in a self-deprecating grin, and he laughed out loud, tossing his head back. The somber mood dissipated with the sound. She loved making him laugh.

"Ah, Dani. That was funny, lass. You got me. So which eye is your father's?"

"He had blue eyes. My mother brown, though her hair was blond. A beautiful combination, I think. I got one of each, I suppose."

"It's not as uncommon as one might think, your eyes," he said. "I've done a bit of reading on it."

"Oh yes? Have you ever seen it before?" she said, wry.

"No," he admitted. "Not like yours."

"Ireland is a land of faeries. Daddy said I had fae blood. Mother always said, no. I have Kos blood."

"You said he had an accent. When did he come to America?"

"He was born in Ireland and he came to the States when he was fourteen, though he lied and said he was eighteen. He talked about Cork. But not about his family. At least not to me. Mother and I were his family. I knew of no one else except Uncle Darby."

He raised his brows in question.

"Darby. Darby O'Shea. His mother was a Flanagan too, I think, but I don't know for sure. He was just Uncle Darby, though he wasn't really an uncle, but a cousin. He and Daddy came to America together. I remember that Mother didn't like him. She thought he was trouble. But Dad and Darby were close. He said he and Darby had always looked after each other, and they always would."

"Darby O'Shea," Malone mused. Something about the way he said it made her think he knew the name and had not been greatly impressed by the man, but she'd been fond of Darby.

"He showed up at the shop a few months after I moved to Cleveland. He brought me a St. Christopher medal and a picture of him and my father. The aunts wouldn't let him see me, though. They threatened to send for the police, and he left. I would have liked to visit with him. I think he loved my dad, so it was hard for me not to love him. He sends a postcard every now and again, so I know he's still out there."

"From Cork to Chicago at fourteen," Malone marveled, shifting the subject back to her father.

She nodded. "Dad and Darby lived in Kilgubbin. You know Kilgubbin?"

"I do indeed. They don't call it Little Hell for nothing. It's a pit."

"Beware the lads from Kilgubbin," Dani sang. "They'll take what isn't movin'. With a glint in their eyes and a glint of the knife, you can bet your life you'll be losin'."

"The lads of Kilgubbin were what the North Side Gang called themselves," Malone said. "I'm surprised you know the song."

"Daddy sang it all the time. He had a song for everything."

"So how did he meet your mother? An Irish boy from Kilgubbin in Chicago and a Czech girl from Cleveland? Doesn't seem like they would run into each other."

"He and Darby came into the shop to buy hats. She was working."

"That was all it took, eh?"

She peered up at him. The brim of his hat shadowed his face, but he had stopped.

"Apparently . . . yes. They went for a stroll, much to my aunts' dismay. And my dad came to see her every day for a week. Then he had to go back to Chicago. And my mother went with him . . . and never looked back."

∼

On Thursday night, they set Malone a place for dinner, just as they always did, but he never came home. Zuzana claimed good riddance, Lenka sulked, and Dani wondered. Charlie curled up on his chair and promptly fell asleep in a furry coil, happy to have his spot back.

He didn't eat with them Friday either. Not for breakfast or dinner.

"He doesn't always come to dinner, Lenka," Dani reassured her aunt, who worried that he would have to eat his dinner cold, and Margaret had prepared his favorite.

"But he isn't in his room . . . is he? He hasn't been here all day. I'm not sure he ever came home last night either," Lenka fretted.

He hadn't. Dani had checked his room first thing in the morning.

"He's a grown man," Zuzana said. "He doesn't need you fussing over him. One would think he is a member of the family."

He did not have to report to Dani, nor did he owe her an explanation. He'd said nothing about his plans for the day, but he never did, and she hadn't seen him leave. She must have been occupied elsewhere when he departed, but his car was still in the carriage house.

Sometimes he went out after dinner and came back with his clothes smelling like smoke and cheap booze. Margaret had remarked on it, but Dani had never once seen him drink or appear drunk. She was almost certain his late-night activities were more about work than recreation. And he had always come home. Not once since his arrival more than two months earlier had he failed to be there the next morning.

Maybe Eliot Ness had come to retrieve him. Friday was their usual meeting day. At least, she thought the man Malone regularly met with was Eliot Ness. She'd never actually seen him up close. He never got out of the car, and Michael had not once mentioned him. Not once. He did not talk about his current assignment at all, though she had a fairly good idea what he was doing.

She reassured herself that must be it, that he and the safety director had gone somewhere together. But when he didn't return Saturday, she grew frantic, fearing that he'd met with something nefarious. And she had no idea what to do.

Lenka thought they should contact the authorities. "There is a butcher cutting off the heads of handsome young men in this city, Dani," she cried.

"He isn't handsome and he isn't young," Zuzana snapped.

"I'm sure he's all right, Lenka," Dani soothed, tamping down her own fears to ease Lenka's agitation. But she wasn't sure of that at all.

She found the sheet of paper Inez Staley had filled out upon securing the room. The telephone number she'd left routed Dani to city hall, and surprisingly, the call was answered by Inez herself, who sounded efficient but impatient, but perhaps that was because she was fielding calls on a Saturday.

"Director Ness's office, this is Miss Staley. How may I help you?"

"Oh! Um. I would like to speak with Mr. Ness, please," Dani said, her mind racing. *Mr. Ness's office!*

"Mr. Ness is not available. May I ask who's speaking?"

"Uh, Mr. . . . Mr. Malone."

"Mr. Malone?" Inez Staley asked, exasperation creeping into her voice.

"Uh, Mr. Michael Malone would like to speak with Mr. Ness," she amended. "It is quite urgent."

"I'm sorry, but Mr. Ness is not here."

"Would you tell him Michael Malone would like to speak with him at his earliest convenience? I believe Mr. Ness has the number, but just in case . . ." Dani dictated the number slowly.

"I'll give him your message, miss. But I don't know when he'll be back."

Dani returned the handset back to the cradle and sat, staring at the telephone, willing it to ring. When it didn't, she reluctantly returned to the shop but was silent all day, straining to hear, shushing her aunts when they spoke and listening to customers with half an ear. They received five calls all day, and each time, Dani dashed to answer it, making Zuzana scold and Lenka gasp. None of the callers were Eliot Ness.

It wasn't until they sat down for supper Sunday afternoon that Dani heard the telephone pealing from the sewing room. She flew down the stairs, through the hall, and into the sewing room before it had completed its fourth chime.

"Kos Clothiers," she answered, her heart in her throat, the way it had been for days.

"This is Eliot Ness calling for Mr. Malone, please."

"Mr. Ness, my name is Daniela Kos. It was I who called you. Mr. Michael Malone is a boarder in my home."

"Is he all right?" Eliot Ness's voice was sharp.

Dani's heart sank. "I was hoping you could tell me, Mr. Ness. He left sometime on Thursday—I thought maybe you had come to fetch him on Friday—and he hasn't been seen since. He hasn't been home. He didn't take his car. I wanted to file a missing person's report but thought maybe I should talk to you first."

Silence shimmered through the line.

"Mr. Ness?"

"Malone is fine. I can promise you that."

"Then you know where he is?"

"No, ma'am. But I wouldn't be surprised if he just took the train back to Washington, DC, on business."

"But . . . are you sure? I'm concerned. If he is in trouble, he is very much alone."

"What did you say your name was?" Eliot Ness asked, his voice mild.

"I'm Daniela Kos, uh, Dani."

"Dani," he repeated. "And you're the . . . proprietor of the house?"

"Yes, sir. I suppose I am."

"I see. And Mr. Malone told you we were acquainted?"

Dani didn't want to lie to the man, but she also didn't quite know how to explain her knowledge. "That's right," she said. "He listed you as a reference."

"Huh." He left the word dangling like a hook in the water.

"We were very impressed, Mr. Ness. Very impressed b-by that," she stammered.

"We?"

"My aunts and I."

She could hear his questions pulsing through the line, but he hesitated as if he didn't know how to ask them.

"He mentioned that he knew you many years ago. Is that right, Miss Kos?" he asked, so polite, so pleasant, but Dani wasn't fooled. He was suspicious of her.

"Uh, yes, sir. That's true." She was surprised Malone had mentioned her.

"Quite the coincidence," he remarked.

"Yes, sir. It was."

"He was a patrolman then."

"Yes."

"Did you know him from his beat?"

"Not exactly. He was assigned to me . . . to my case . . . when my parents were murdered." That seemed safe enough to reveal.

"I'm so sorry. Odd. I lived in Chicago during that time. I don't remember a case with the name Kos."

"Kos was my mother's maiden name. My father was George Flanagan."

"Flanagan," he repeated slowly, like he was searching his memory. "I might remember something about that after all. You say Michael was assigned to the case?"

"Yes, sir."

"And you were just a child?"

"Yes. I was ten." She didn't see what that had to do with Malone's whereabouts and said as much.

"No, it doesn't. You're right. I was just curious. Such an odd coincidence."

"We thought it strange as well, as it was fifteen years to the day when we first met." She didn't know why she told him that. It was completely irrelevant, but he made her nervous with his slow speech and mild questions. She was spilling information like a sieve. She wondered if he had that effect on everyone. He was quite the interrogator.

"Huh," he murmured. And was silent for several seconds. "Well, don't worry too much. He's a very capable man," he concluded.

"Yes, sir. He certainly is."

"How well do you know Malone, Miss Kos?" he asked, keeping that conversational, I'm-only-asking-to-be-polite, tone.

She hesitated. She supposed she didn't know him very well at all. And yet, she suspected she knew him better than anyone did.

"W-well enough, sir," she babbled.

He waited for her to elaborate, but she bit her lip, screwed up her face, and kept the words from bubbling out. She already felt like a fool.

"Tell you what. I'll make some calls and see if I can locate him. And I'll tell him to ring and check in. Don't expect me to call back tonight unless I get lucky. Most likely it will be tomorrow morning, but I will try to call you back, even if I don't have any news. But don't worry. He's fine."

"I certainly hope so. Thank you, Mr. Ness."

She put the receiver back in its cradle and turned to find her aunts looking at her with matching befuddlement. They had entered the sewing room without her even being aware.

"Mr. Ness?" Lenka gasped.

"Why were you talking to Eliot Ness, Daniela?" Zuzana pressed.

"I thought he might know where Mr. Malone is."

"So you contacted the safety director?" Zuzana asked, dumbfounded.

"Yes. I did. And he was very nice. He says he is certain Mr. Malone is fine, but he will make some inquiries and ring me back tomorrow."

"Oh my," Lenka exclaimed. "How exciting."

"When he rings again, I want to talk to him," Zuzana insisted. "If he can locate one ugly boarder, he can certainly find the man who's chopping people up in my backyard."

"Don't say that, Zuzana," Lenka said, shuddering. "Can you imagine if we actually found a body in our yard?"

The old women tottered back down the hallway and climbed the stairs to their interrupted supper. Dani followed them, but she was too nervous to eat.

~

The next morning, she found herself hovering near the phone again, neglecting the shop, her errands, and the visit she needed to make to the morgue. But Mr. Ness did not call. She finally left Lenka stationed in the sewing room and set out for the medical office to return the Peterkas' mending.

Over the years, Dr. Peterka and his family had been by the shop dozens of times for fittings and alterations, but since moving to Shaker Heights and converting his house on Broadway into his medical practice, the visits were much less frequent. Dani was grateful Dr. Peterka continued his patronage at all. Margaret had even secured a small income washing the doctors' white coats, which she did along with all the other wash in the Kos laundry room.

Margaret picked up the wash from the practice on Fridays and dropped it off on Mondays, but because Dani had the mending to return to Libbie Peterka, she loaded the laundered white coats into her wagon and delivered them to save Margaret a trip.

Dr. Peterka's office manager was a woman named Sybil who never remembered Daniela's name, even though she'd been working at the medical practice, two houses down from the Koses, since it had opened in 1930.

"Will you take them around to the back, Donna?" Sybil said, waving a hand at her from behind the counter where she sat. Dani didn't correct her but exited the small waiting area; she pulled her wagon around to the back door and let herself into the lounge where the doctors donned their white coats, drank their coffee, and read the newspaper between patients.

She left the mending in the tote it'd been delivered in and trudged back toward her house, certain that Ness had called the moment she left. Her head was aching from loss of sleep, and the sun was bright in her face. She shielded her eyes with one hand as she pulled her wagon with the other and noticed a man—a boy on further study—had stopped in front of her house.

He had come from the opposite direction, his too big overcoat and black fedora making him look like a child in a school production.

He pulled a bit of paper from his pocket before studying the place once more. She didn't think he'd come to buy a Kos original.

"Can I help you?" she called, continuing toward him.

He glanced at her, uncomfortable, and tugged at the lapels of his coat, pulling it more firmly onto his narrow shoulders.

"I'm looking for Mike," he said cautiously, when she stopped beside him.

"Mike?"

"Yeah. Uh. Dark eyes. Kinda dark skin too, I guess. Looks tough but not mean."

"Are you Steve?" she asked. The hat gave him away. She suspected he would look far better in the checkered cap he'd traded Malone, though that hat wasn't his either.

"You know who I am?" he gasped.

"You're wearing . . . Mike's . . . hat. He mentioned you. He isn't here right now, but you've got the right place. Can I relay a message for you when he returns?" If he returned. Her stomach twisted with three-day-old worry.

"Are you his old lady?" Steve asked. She wasn't wearing her glasses, and he had noticed her eyes. He avoided her gaze as if he didn't trust himself not to stare.

"No. No. But I . . . I live here too."

"Will you give him a message for me?"

"Of course. Would you like to come inside, maybe write something down?"

"I'm not much of a writer," he said. "Maybe I could just tell you?"

"All right."

"Tell him . . . Steve Jeziorski came by, just like he said I should do. And tell him I have some information he might want. He told me he'd pay me for information."

She dug into her coat pocket and pulled out a dime. "I don't know what he pays, but this is all I've got. You'll have to wait and tell him yourself if it's not enough."

He chewed on his lip, taking her measure. Whatever his qualms were, he took the coin and began to talk.

"You hear about Pete Kostura?"

The name was familiar, but she shook her head. "I'm not sure who he is."

"He and James Wagner found that first victim by Jackass Hill."

Ah. That was it. The poor boys had been front page news for weeks. "I remember now."

"Well . . . Pete got killed."

"What?" she gasped.

"Yeah. Just a few months ago. December. A big black car hit him. Fancy, like the kind the mayor would be driven around in. Whoever it was hit him and just drove away. They brought Pete to St. Alexis, but he died."

"And no one knows who did it?" Dani asked, sickened.

"No. His sister saw the car, but not the driver. And the police haven't done much to find him that I can see."

"That's terrible."

"Pete didn't like to talk about finding those bodies. It scared him. And after the first couple of weeks, when the police had to ask him questions, he just stopped saying anything at all."

"I can imagine."

"Talking can get you killed."

"You said he was hit by a car," she said.

"Yeah . . . but I don't think it was an accident."

"Why?"

"Pete was talking about it again. He was talking to the safety director himself. Ness is working on reforming the boy gangs. Putting them on patrol, giving them incentives to stay out of trouble. That stuff."

"Eliot Ness?" Dani whispered.

"That's right."

"Is that what you want me to tell Mike?"

"Nah. I mean. Sure. But he needs to know what I'm risking giving him information."

"I don't have any more money to give you, Steve."

He stewed. "All right. I'll give you this one for free. But you tell Mike he owes me."

"I will."

"After I talked to him the other day, another guy showed up, right after, asking about him."

"About who?"

"About Mike," he said, scoffing like she was slow. "Fella asked if I knew who Mike was and what he wanted. See, Mike didn't blend in. An Italian guy in a Slav neighborhood, you know?"

"Yes. I know."

"The thing is . . . this other guy didn't really belong either. So he wasn't just somebody curious about a stranger poking around."

"What did he look like?" she asked.

"Trouble. He definitely wasn't a copper. But that's all the freebies I'm giving. Just tell Mike he has a tail. He can come talk to me if he wants me to find out more. He knows where to find me."

He turned away, yanking on his lapels so the top button didn't choke him. Michael's coat didn't fit. He tossed the dime she'd given him into the air and caught it again, repeating the action as he headed back in the direction he'd come, a boy playing a big man's game.

12

Malone was filthy. He walked through the back door and directly into the laundry room where he pulled off everything he'd been wearing for the last few days while sleeping on trains, squatting by hobo fires, and talking to whoever wanted to talk, which were many. He smelled like burning rubber; tires kept the fires hot but created a stench like no other. He also reeked of rodents and body odor and every other bad smell related to blending in and staying alive while hitching a ride on the trains with all the other down-and-outers.

With the weather improving, he had decided he couldn't postpone riding the trains any longer. A series of murders in a New Castle, Pennsylvania, swamp had people talking about the possibility of the Butcher having moved to new territory. He'd intended to start slow, just take one stretch east to Youngstown, find the hobo camps, and come back the following morning. But it hadn't worked out that way.

He'd caught a freight by running at full speed alongside it, grabbing the ladder on the side of a car, and swinging himself up. He'd spent two hours watching other men do the same on earlier trains, but it wasn't as easy as it looked. Nothing ever was. The action nearly pulled his arms from their sockets and dragged him under the wheels. Adrenaline and outrage were the only things that saved him, and he heaved himself up onto the tanker and inched his way along the top of the thundering train until he found an opening he could swing into. He swung a little too hard and landed in a heap at the back of the car. He'd wanted to kiss the floor and shout the Rosary, but the car he climbed into was occupied, and the three men inside weren't especially welcoming. He'd had to bribe them with cigarettes and polish his very big, very sharp knife to make them more accepting and considerate.

Two of the men had the swinging tones of Louisiana, peppered with Creole spice, and they'd huddled together in the farthest corner, accepting a cigarette but only talking to each other. The third man had a bit of "Missouruh" in his thank-you when he'd accepted a cigarette, and he'd taken the opposite corner from Malone when the Cajuns started fighting. When he jumped off the train just outside of Youngstown, he invited Malone to tag along.

"It's not the worst camp and not the best, but it's better than staying on the train," he said, "and the jump ain't bad if you hit it just right." Malone hadn't hit it just right or even mostly right, but he'd survived without major injury, and the Missourian—whose name was Sully—provided the opening he hadn't even dared hope for.

It turned out Sully wasn't a bad sort, though it took three cans of beans, all Malone's potatoes, and two days of sleeping with one eye open in a hobo jungle for Sully to ease up on his guard. He hadn't minded the whiskey Malone had added to his flask either.

On the second night, he and Sully shared a fire with a ragtag assortment of residents and travelers before they dispersed to their own primitive lodgings. Malone introduced himself as Micky from Chicago and let the vagrants think they were dealing with a low-level gangster looking for a hideout. But they didn't press, and he didn't oversell.

Malone was adept at judging bullshit and who was full of it. Some people talked because they were lonely and some because they were liars, but neither was a good source of information. He'd gotten some of both, sitting around the fire with Sully and his cohorts, but he'd also heard a story that had made the hair stand up on his arms.

"I knew a guy, used to ride the trains like us. He's doing okay now. Got a job in Chicago on the docks. Emil Fronek. You ever know him?" Sully's friend, Chester, asked him. Chester was the proud owner of the tin shed and the hole in the ground they sat beside. His Boston accent and scraggly red beard made him seem more like a lost sailor than a jungle dweller.

"Nah. Can't say I did," Malone said. "Chicago's a big town."

"Yeah. This was back in the fall of '34. Long time ago, now."

Malone feigned a yawn, though he was too uncomfortable for sleep.

"Emil jumped off in Cleveland. Had an old friend in one of the camps he thought might still be around. But he wasn't. And a nor'easter was blowing in too. Fronek hadn't eaten in days, and he needed a new pair of shoes."

Malone thought of the dead in Dani's morgue, their toes hanging out of their boots.

"He said he thought maybe he could go to St. Wenceslas church since he'd been there before. Big one on Broadway. You know it? I got a damn good bowl of soup there once. Big loaf of bread too, all to myself."

"Sure." Malone knew it. It was northwest of the Kos house in the direction of downtown, the first Catholic church to serve the Bohemian community in Cleveland, according to Zuzana. Our Lady of Lourdes on East Fifty-Fifth was closer, and Dani and her aunts attended Mass there, but he'd seen Wenceslas. It was a massive brick edifice with two belfries, one shorter than the other, like a crowned king and his queen separated by the pope in his pointed hat.

"Yeah . . . well, Wenceslas was all locked up. So Fronek kept going. Didn't know what else to do. Ended up in front of a café, but it was closed up too. He walked around back to see if there was something in the trash. He doesn't remember exactly what happened. He's foggy on some of the details. But he says he could smell food. Went up some stairs and through an open door and realized he'd walked right into someone's place.

"A man walks out of the kitchen and sees him. But he doesn't get mad or even scared that Fronek's in his house. Fella tells him to sit and he'll get him something to eat. Get him some shoes. So Fronek does. He's frozen and hungry. Fella brings him a glass of wine and a plate of food—good stuff, like he'd been making dinner and just gave Fronek his own plate. Tells him to eat up."

"Damn fool," Sully said, as if he'd heard the story already. He was shoveling Malone's beans into his mouth with two fingers, the irony lost on him.

"I don't know any man that's hungry woulda turned down food and shelter in the same situation," Chester said. "It doesn't make him a fool."

"So what happened?" Malone pressed.

"Fronek starts feeling kind of sick, light-headed. Maybe eating too fast. Maybe his stomach can't handle so much so quick when he hasn't eaten for so long. But despite what Sully here says, Fronek isn't a fool. He's pretty sure the man put something in the grub or the drink."

"Why would someone do that? Fronek didn't have anything to steal," Sully said, licking his fingers. Chester ignored him.

"Fronek bolts, runs down the stairs and back out onto the street, and he keeps going. Guy calls after him, but Fronek keeps going, somehow. He climbed into an old boxcar by some tracks and passed right out."

"I think he drank too much and dreamed it all." Sully burped and lay back, folding his arms over his chest.

"He slept for three days." Chester held up three dirty fingers in front of Malone's face. "Whatever was in the food or booze the guy gave him knocked him out cold. When he finally came to, he tried to retrace his steps. Fronek is tough. He wanted a piece of the guy. But he couldn't figure out where he'd been."

"He thinks that guy was the Butcher?" Malone asked.

"Yeah. That's exactly what he thinks."

"Did him a favor, if you wanna know the truth," Sully said, still listening though his eyes were now closed.

"How's that?" Chester scowled.

"Fronek stopped hitching the freights, didn't he?" Sully said.

"Emil Fronek, huh?" Malone asked, making a mental note. "Name does kinda sound familiar. Maybe I did meet him some time or another," Malone fibbed. "He should tell the police. I hear there's a reward. A big one."

"Ha! Nobody will believe him. I sure don't," Sully said.

"The details were foggy," Chester admitted. "Probably the drugs. All he remembered is Broadway and a café. Couldn't even describe what the guy looked like except he was ordinary. Maybe a little bigger than average. Brown hair. Glasses."

"All I know is the Butcher ain't one of us," Sully added.

"One of us?" Malone asked.

"A transient. A homeless guy. We don't have enough time to think about killing. Not like that. Not for sport. Not for pleasure." Sully scratched at his head and shook his hat, as if that would shake the itch loose, and shoved it back on his head.

"I'd have to agree with you there, Sully," Chester admitted. "Everyone talks about it, everyone has their opinions, and everybody points their fingers at each other. There've been police and patrols crawling all over the Run for three years now. It can't be that hard to find a mad butcher. They're just looking in the wrong place. I'd say they'll find someone to pin it on, but the problem with pinning it on someone is that the killing won't end. So they can't fudge it."

The sentiment was so close to what Malone and Ness had discussed that Malone could only nod in agreement.

"Still, someone like that wants to be caught," Sully said, inserting himself back into the conversation. "Else they wouldn't leave the parts scattered where people can find them."

"He throws them in the water," another man scoffed.

"Some of them. Yeah," Sully said. "Others he buries with their heads aboveground or wrapped in their clothing, like he's giving the world a gift. And do you notice how he chops up the ladies into smaller sections? He's not happy with the ladies." Sully hooted like he had his own history with women.

"It doesn't feel personal to me," Chester argued. "I think he just likes killing."

"Oh, it's personal," Sully said. "But it's definitely not specific."

"How does he lure them in?" Malone asked, fascinated by the exchange. He'd had many of the same impressions.

"He offers them what they want," Chester said, no hesitation. "What they need. A ride. A drink. Food. I'm guessing he's fed them all. That's all a body can think of when he's hungry. We eat fast and taste later. They fall asleep, and he cuts 'em up. That's how he almost got old Emil, isn't it? I bet that's how he's got 'em all."

The conversation had quieted after that, each man lost in his own thoughts on the matter, and Malone had closed his eyes and feigned sleep until morning came.

He'd hit pay dirt, he was sure of it. There was a sandwich shop on Broadway, right around the corner from the house, where the lights of St. Alexis were easy to see. The story gave Malone a jumpy feeling in his gut, the kind of feeling he didn't ignore.

He would tell Ness about Fronek. Maybe one of the detectives could hunt him down and get his story. Or maybe Malone would have to do it himself. He also wanted someone to track down Darby O'Shea, as long as they were sniffing in Chicago. It wouldn't hurt to find out what had happened to George Flanagan's cousin, for Dani's sake.

He hadn't let on when she'd mentioned him, but he'd known all about Darby O'Shea, even as a young patrolman. Dani's mother was right. O'Shea was trouble, not that it mattered now. He also had nine lives. He'd avoided the hit that had taken out George Flanagan, though they were partners. When Dean O'Banion, the leader of the North Side Gang, was taken out at the flower shop in '24, O'Shea had supposedly been on his way to meet him. O'Shea had even managed to avoid getting mowed down in the St. Valentine's Day Massacre in '29, though five of his known "associates" had not fared so well. Malone had been sent to infiltrate Capone's organization not long after the slaughter, and O'Shea's name had popped up time and time again in the investigation, though Malone had never run into him, as far as he knew.

But first, after four days without a shower and a shave, two of them spent just trying to get home, he needed to wash, and he needed to sleep.

It was late, the house was quiet and welcoming, and he was so relieved to be back he spent an hour in the bathroom scrubbing and shaving, in no hurry whatsoever. He padded to his room at 2:00 a.m., his soiled clothes wrapped in a towel so he didn't have to touch them, another towel wrapped around his waist. But he hesitated outside his door.

He'd left it locked, but it wasn't locked anymore. He eased the bundle of clothes to the floor, and pushed the door open slowly, one hand on his towel, one hand on the knob. The lamp beside his bed burned softly, and Dani was waiting.

Unlike him, she was fully dressed and curled on his bed, Charlie cocooned in the curve of her body. Both cat and woman were deeply asleep.

He hesitated, caught with his pants down, literally, and then moved with quiet tread to retrieve some clean clothes.

She'd been through his things.

His wardrobe was open, his suits pushed to the side as if she'd run her hands over them, searching for something. He'd put the files in the trunk of his car before he'd left, but his notepad with his lists, which he kept tucked into the narrow desk drawer, was now sitting atop it. He'd been careless to leave it behind, even in a drawer, even with a locked door. But he'd had some expectation of privacy, damn it.

She didn't wake as he yanked on his shorts and undershirt, along with a pair of trousers for modesty, and snapped his suspenders in place. She slept like poor, drugged Emil Fronek.

"Dani," he said. She didn't stir. He said her name again. "Dani." Nothing. He walked to the bed and shook her gently, jostling Charlie in the process. The cat lifted his head and regarded Malone in narrow-eyed disdain before setting his head back down.

"Dani," Malone said again, and she blinked, coming awake slowly. The mellow glow of the small lamp lit her hair like a halo around her face, and when she finally looked up at him, still half asleep, still hazy, he felt a pang of reluctant affection. God, she was pretty.

"Dani . . . why are you in my room?"

She frowned and blinked again, and then she sat up suddenly, spooking her cat. Charlie shot beneath the bed, but Dani ignored him.

She stood with a cry and threw her arms around Malone's waist.

"I will scold you later. Right now I'm too grateful you are all right to be angry," she moaned.

Her curls tickled his chin, and her words were muffled against his shirt. He froze, not certain what he should do with his arms. He laid his palms carefully against her narrow back, hoping she would release him before he grew too attached to her nearness.

"Where have you been?" she chided. "I called Eliot Ness and told him you were missing. I've been sick with worry. Sick. I thought something terrible had happened to you."

"You called Eliot Ness?" The anger that had abated in the face of her cherubic slumbering now returned. "And why in the world would you think that?"

She pulled back enough to stare up into his face. He could see himself mirrored in blue and brown. This close, her eyes were even more fascinating than before, but he was too irritated to enjoy them.

"Why? Because you're hunting the Mad Butcher of Kingsbury Run," she said, clearly flabbergasted by his very logical question. "You left your car. You didn't say a word to me about where you were going or how long you'd be gone. You've been gone for four days, Michael. Four days. Why in heaven's name didn't you say something?"

"Because it never occurred to me to do so." And how had she known to call *Eliot*?

She gasped, outraged, but did not step away from the loose circle of his arms. They were arguing within inches of each other, their voices pitched low.

"It never *occurred* to you?" she cried.

"No. I knew you wouldn't need me at the morgue. I suppose it would have been polite to tell Margaret I would not need dinner, but extras always get eaten, don't they? You were with a customer when I left. I let you do your job, and I went to do mine. That's all."

"That's all?" she repeated, her voice high and her eyes wide.

"Yes. And you called Eliot?" he repeated.

"He was nice. He made me feel much better . . . but even still, he didn't know where you were either. I got the feeling he had some ideas but wasn't willing to tell me. And he didn't call me back like he said he would. I was going to go to city hall tomorrow and demand an audience with him."

Malone shook his head, trying to decide which part of that he should respond to first. "How did you know I was working with Eliot Ness? I see you went through my things and searched my drawers, not to mention making yourself at home on my bed. Is that how you knew? And have I told you I'm not crazy about cat hair? Because I'm not."

"You're angry?" Dani asked, incredulous.

"Yes, I'm angry. I expected a certain amount of privacy when I rented this room."

"*You're* angry?" Dani repeated, louder. "I have been in agony for days. I've hardly slept. I sewed a sleeve closed yesterday and hemmed a pair of trousers for a boy with twelve-inch legs. Sadly, they are far too short for him because he doesn't *have* twelve-inch legs. I am angry with *you*, Michael Malone." Each word was punctuated.

"And I was angry first," she added, "so you are going to have to wait your turn, or even better, try some introspection and ask yourself why you have any cause to be angry at me for *caring* about you." Her mouth trembled, and she gripped his undershirt like she wanted to rip it in two.

"You've got my shirt in your hands," he snapped. "So where have I been? What have I been doing? Why do I need to tell you? You know everything already." He peeled her hands from his clothes, caught between his extreme annoyance and his terrifying adoration. It was an odd, prickling sensation, like walking barefoot on the sand. It had been there from the day he walked into the shop, and it grew worse by the second. His shirt freed from her grasp, he clutched her shoulders, intending to put some space between them.

"I don't know everything!" she cried. "It doesn't work that way. And right now . . . I only feel you." She crossed her hands over her heart like he had hurt her feelings, like she was trying not to touch him. But she held his gaze, defiant, and she was still too close.

He was weary, frustrated, and out of his depth. Instead of shaking her, he kissed her, his lips hard and his eyes open, trying to assert a dominance he didn't feel. Better to demonstrate the disappointment he would be to her—in every aspect—than to let her think they were friends.

But her lips weren't hard or angry or mean.

She was soft and warm. Real and eager.

He gasped, and her sweetness filled his lungs and flowered on his tongue. He closed his eyes and chased the flavor, wanting more of it, and his will dissolved in a hunger-induced fog.

Sweet Mary, Mother of God.

His hands slid from her shoulders to her back, pulling her up and into his body. He was a starving man given a loaf of bread and told to eat his fill.

He had not kissed a woman for so long. When had he last kissed Irene? Irene had not wanted passion, even before he left, and he had bridled his. Now he had no idea what to do with it.

He pulled back abruptly and let Dani go, embarrassed by his inability to act the part he'd been trying to play. Long ago, he'd learned to keep his cool in every circumstance. He'd gotten so good at it. But he was not cool now. He was sweating, and his heart was pounding. And he was still *famished*.

"Please leave, Dani," he begged, not really meaning it.

She hesitated, her shoulders wilting. Then she took a deep breath, straightened, and rose up on her toes, pressing her lips to his once more.

"What are you doing?" he moaned against her mouth. "I am not the man for you. I am not."

"I think you very well might be," she said, withdrawing a hairsbreadth, just enough to speak. Her voice was plaintive. "And I'm trying to decide whether you don't like me or if you just . . . don't trust me."

"I like you." And he did. He liked her very much. Oh God, he liked her very, very much. "And I don't trust anyone," he added. That part really wasn't personal.

She sighed, her breath tickling his lips, but she didn't move away and neither did he. "How typical," she whispered.

He pressed his forehead to hers, trying desperately to be strong, but his arms had crept back around her.

"If I were not . . . *me*, would you want me?" she said. Her hands had climbed to his face.

He wasn't sure what she meant. He was quite sure that he couldn't possibly want anyone more.

"There are some women you don't . . . you don't . . . dabble with," he said, talking more to himself than to her. They were speaking with their foreheads pressed together, her hands cradling his cheeks, his arms wrapped around her slim waist.

"The world would be so much better if we didn't *dabble* with anyone," she said.

"Yes. Exactly. It would be. So I won't be . . . dabbling . . . with you," he said, but his mouth had inched down to hers, sneaking a taste of her bottom lip. She moaned like he was feeding her grapes, and he spent the next minute gulping the wine of her mouth, sipping and suckling, pouring himself another and another.

It was Dani who finally broke away, panting and rosy-lipped.

It was a good thing she did because he was drunk already. Years without kisses had made him a terrible lightweight.

"You're probably right," she gasped, resting her brow against his chest, her hands sliding from his cheeks and back to her own heart.

"I am?" he whispered, trying not to slur his words.

"Yes. I don't think I will survive a dabbling."

"No?" Now *what* were they talking about? He couldn't think straight.

"No," she whispered. "Because I will fall in love with you."

The word *love* woke him up a bit, and he took a moment to order his thoughts. *No, no, no. This would not do at all.*

He released her decidedly and stepped back, ending the torture. "No, you won't, Dani. You'll just think you're in love with me because you have no one and nothing to compare it to."

She seemed to consider that, her eyes searching his, her lips parted, and he almost returned to them.

"Must we try everything to know something is wonderful?" she asked softly. "I don't think so."

She had him there. He took another step back from her and shoved his hands into his trouser pockets, determined not to think about how truly wonderful it had been.

"Do you think you might be afraid of falling in love with me too?" she asked, her voice trembling. Was it fear that he would say yes? Or fear he would say no?

"Oh, Dani," he said, feeling an ache in his chest that he couldn't readily identify. But again, he could not answer her question.

"Is it too soon?" she asked gently. "Irene has not been gone very long."

"Yes, it's too soon," he said. It would always be too soon. And it didn't really have anything to do with Irene. At least . . . not in the way Dani meant.

She nodded, accepting that in silence, and he stared past her face for several seconds, collecting himself. He needed her to go, but she remained where she was, hands clasped and her eyes on the floor.

"Steve came by when you were gone," she said in a rush.

"Steve?" He frowned, reeling at the change of subject. His legs were still trembling from that kiss.

"The boy who gave you the checkered cap? He was wearing your fedora and your overcoat. I found him standing in front of the house. He wanted to talk to *Mike*. I assumed that was you."

He waited.

"He said he would check back, but he had some information you might want to know. He also said you would pay him. So I gave him a dime, and he told me instead. I promised to pass along the information."

"W-what?" Malone sputtered.

"He seemed eager to tell someone."

"Dani!"

"Yes?" Her brow furrowed.

"This is not a game. You shouldn't have done that."

"Do you want to know what he said or not?" she snapped, throwing up her hands, revealing her own loss of equilibrium. "And you owe me a dime."

"Tell me," he ground out, clenching his teeth over a sudden urge to laugh, and she obeyed, parroting the conversation seemingly word for word—*he said, then I said*—like she was afraid of missing something.

"I don't think the boy—Steve—is really afraid he'll be run down like Pete Kostura," she finished, worrying her lower lip.

"No?"

"No. Otherwise he would have told you about Kostura's death when you first met. I think he wants to string you along, keep you coming back to him for information."

"Yeah, well that's the life of a snitch. He's figured it out early."

"But, Michael . . . when he said someone was asking questions about you, and you didn't come home . . . I was afraid."

He sighed, ashamed of himself. None of this was Dani's fault. Not really. But he needed her to keep her distance from him and from his work.

"I am sorry I frightened you. I will be more mindful in the future," he promised. He made himself meet her gaze, and the weakness in his limbs immediately returned. He sat down on his bed, suddenly too weary to stand. "We still have to talk about you . . . touching my things. But not now. Tomorrow."

She looked like she wanted to defend herself, to continue hashing it all out mere feet from each other, but she swallowed back whatever it was that bubbled in her throat and let it be.

"Good night then, Michael," she whispered.

"Good night, Dani."

She left the room with an averted gaze and clenched hands, and pulled the door closed behind her. But when he turned out the lamp and climbed into his bed, no longer tired and longing for things he thought he'd moved beyond, he remembered the cat beneath it.

"Damn it, Charlie," he sighed. But he rose once more and, padding to the door, left it ajar for the first time.

13

Malone came to breakfast the morning following his return, but he ignored Dani so thoroughly she wished he'd stayed away. Lenka beamed and Zuzana scowled, and Michael apologized to the women for any worry he'd caused. He included Dani in his comments, though he never looked directly at her.

"I confess I'm not accustomed to logging my whereabouts with anyone, but I should have mentioned that my work would lead to frequent and sometimes prolonged absences," he began.

"Surely your wife minded you flitting off for days without a word," Zuzana said, slathering butter on a bit of toast, her tone as crusty as the bread.

"My wife and I were estranged for many years. So no. She did not mind," Michael said, voice equally dry.

"I can't say I am surprised," Zuzana retorted, blotting at the crumbs on her lips. "You're a very difficult man to live with."

"*Tetka*," Dani cautioned. "He is not."

"I have never seen you fret the way you fretted," Zuzana argued. "It was very rude of Mr. Malone to gallivant off like that."

"I will try to be more courteous in the future," Michael said stiffly. He swallowed his orange juice in a single gulp, cleared his plate with the focus of a starving, harried man, and pushed back from the table.

"Daniela called Eliot Ness," Lenka chirped, not ready to let him go. "Did he find you?"

"No. He did not. I did not need to be found, as I'm sure he was aware. But I will call Mr. Ness right away and reassure him that I am quite all right. And I will be in and out all week, so don't expect me at meals."

"We will have Margaret leave something for you in the icebox," Lenka said cheerily, and smiled at him like she was thrilled to have him back. He strode from the room without a backward glance.

He'd told her it was too soon, and Dani had no choice but to believe him. But as the week passed and another began with Malone keeping his distance, she became more and more embarrassed. She liked him too much, and she was humiliated by her response to him and his avoidance of her. By the end of the next week, she'd worked herself into a lather over his dismissiveness, making her mission all the easier to perform.

The boots he'd worn to wherever he'd gone were sitting on the back porch, the thin soles and battered leather calling to her like sea sirens. If he was not going to talk to her like he'd promised, she was not going to respect his privacy.

She strode out onto the porch, shoved her hands into his boots, and banged them together to dislodge the dried mud from their treads. Then she sank down on the step, raised her chin to the cold spring sun, closed her eyes to the glare, and listened. She immediately heard the roar of a train, the clatter of wheels, and the burr of soft voices. Cigarettes. Sweat. A man named Chester who insisted "the Butcher isn't one of us," and Malone's musings about a hungry man named Emil Fronek.

"What are you doing to my boots?" Malone asked, his voice mild, but she jerked and yelped like he'd yelled in her ear. He'd returned without her hearing him and stood looking at her, his hands in his pockets, his eyes shaded by the brim of his hat. Spring was here. She should urge him to buy a straw one. The dark homburg was too warm for summer.

"I was c-cleaning them," she said. She banged them together once more, quite convincingly, she thought, and set them beside her on the step. "I thought they could use a shine as well."

"Part of the room and board?"

"I just noticed they were worn."

"Yes. They are. Very worn, which is why they don't need to be shined."

"Have you h-had these ones long?" she stammered. His voice was hard, and she wasn't wearing her glasses, so she pulled them from her pocket and sat them on her nose, needing protection from his disapproval.

"Years."

She scrambled to her feet, but not before scooping up his boots again. "I'll have them looking brand new . . . and I'll bring them back when I'm done."

"Leave them. They have a hole in the sole. Polish won't fix that. I wear them for dirty work. Nothing more."

She didn't want to put them down. There was more to see from the boots.

Malone strode forward and tugged them out of her insistent hands. "I can look after my own things. And I know what you're doing."

"What am I doing?"

"Snooping, Dani-style."

Her cheeks burned and tears threatened. Her reaction made her even angrier than his. "You said we would talk. We haven't. It's been more than a week. So I thought I would see for myself where you'd gone, so that next time you go, I'll know where you are." She swallowed the angry lump of emotion in her throat.

"I was riding the trains with the bums, all right? I couldn't call. And it will most likely happen again."

"Riding the rails and trying to find the Mad Butcher?" she challenged.

He glowered at her. "I have tried to keep my work confidential, but you don't seem to have any concept of that word."

"You've been avoiding me," she said. "You haven't come to dinner. Or breakfast. Or to the morgue, though I don't expect that." She bit her lip and added, "Lenka misses you."

And *she* missed him. Dreadfully.

"Yes, I've been avoiding you," he agreed. He tossed his boots aside and then sat down on the steps.

"Please sit, Dani."

She sat beside him, a couple of feet between them. He reached for her glasses, slipped them from her nose, and put them in her lap. She glanced at him, surprised, but he looked away, clasping his hands between his knees.

"I've been avoiding you because I'm embarrassed. And I'm confused. I don't do well with either emotion."

"Why are *you* embarrassed?" she asked. She was embarrassed, but she hadn't for a minute considered he was.

He rubbed at the grooves between his eyes. "Do you know that I have not kissed a woman in fifteen years?"

"No. I didn't know that." She was shocked. And thrilled.

"Really? You really didn't know?" He sounded doubtful. "I've started to think I am an open book with you."

"Yes, really. Do you assume I'm omniscient? I told you I don't know everything. I don't even know *most* things."

"But you know so much. And I am not accustomed to it. I don't . . . like it."

Her heart plummeted.

"I am not accustomed to anyone knowing me so well."

"Oh, Michael. Do you want to be like those poor unknowns at the morgue without a friend in the world?"

"I have friends," he protested. "Just not one who . . . who . . ." He let his words trail off. She knew what he meant. He didn't have friends like her.

"Is Eliot Ness your friend?" she asked.

"Yes," he confessed. "I know the safety director. Eliot Ness and I grew up in the same part of Chicago. I'm older, but our families were acquainted. And we knew each other later through our work."

"I thought so."

"You thought so?"

She flinched. He made her squirm like the nuns at her first school. It was the way he picked apart her words, repeating them back to her with an inflection that said, *Explain yourself.*

She rarely could. But unlike the nuns, Michael was not in a position of authority over her, and she didn't have to comply. She straightened her spine and glared at him.

"He's the one who picks you up every Friday. And I saw the place where you lived," she said.

"The place where I lived?"

"Oh, will you stop doing that!"

"Doing what?"

"Repeating everything I say."

"I'm trying to understand. You aren't surprised I know Eliot Ness because you 'saw the place where I lived'?" His brows were lowered so much it appeared his brown eyes wore Russian hats. The thought made her smile, just a bit.

"Are you teasing me?"

"No. I saw . . . er . . . the connection between you when I touched the files in your room not long after you arrived. Charlie had gotten locked in there one morning and was scratching and meowing at the door. I simply let him out and did a quick turn about the room to make sure he hadn't left anything . . . behind. I didn't know how long he'd been in there."

"Wasn't the door locked?"

"Yes. But I have a key."

"And you use it anytime you want?" he snapped.

She sighed. "You are a boarder in my house, Michael. I went into your room for a good reason. And the files were on the floor. I simply straightened them. Mr. Ness must have given them to you. Paper is not so different from cloth, you know." She waved her hand like it was obvious.

"No, I don't know." He sounded so irked.

"Paper is very absorbent. Mr. Ness must have looked through the files before he gave them to you. He must have held them and looked through them right before he brought them to you in Chicago. I also saw his wife . . . Edna. Are they having difficulties?"

He rubbed at his neck as if she'd given him cold chills.

"I've frightened you. I'm sorry." She put her glasses on again. "I don't need these," she babbled. "Not at all. I have excellent eyesight. But they hide my eyes a bit. I make people uncomfortable."

"Yes. You do."

She winced, and he swore.

"Sorry. I'm sorry, Dani. I *am* trying."

"Yes. I know you are. But I will make sure to wear my glasses around you if it makes you feel better."

"That's not what I meant. I'm not talking about the color of your eyes." He removed her glasses once more and glowered at her. "The problem is, there is no pretense between us."

"Isn't that a *good* thing?" she asked slowly.

"I don't like it."

"You want pretense?" she squeaked. It was the exact opposite of what she wanted.

"*Some* pretense, yes! I am completely exposed. It is like being in a dream where everyone else is clothed and I am standing naked, with nothing but my wits about me."

"At least you have your wits," she said, biting her lip against an urge to snicker. Malone did not look like he thought any of this was funny.

"What is that supposed to mean?" he asked.

"I do not have dreams where I am naked," she said, frank.

"No? I thought that was fairly common."

"No. In my nightmares, I'm surrounded by nothing but clothes. Mountains and mountains of clothes, all talking to me. No quiet. No peace. And no one who wants to listen when I speak."

He sighed, but there was no more exasperation in the sound, and she was encouraged to tell him another truth.

"But you do listen, Michael. You are a marvelous listener. It is my favorite thing about you. And even though it's hard for you, you believe me."

"Yeah, well. Belief is not my problem," he muttered.

She did not want to ask him what his problem was. She was afraid it would crush her.

For a moment they sat in silence, and she screwed up her courage for the next round. "I think I can help you. With your case."

He waited, his eyes on his feet as if he hadn't heard her at all.

"The thought must have occurred to you," she pressed.

"Why would it?"

"That is why you're here, in Cleveland, isn't it? You're trying to find the Butcher, and I have a certain set of skills. Surely you have considered asking for my help."

"I'm not going to talk about my work."

"But . . ."

"I don't need your help."

"You don't need it, or you don't want it?"

"I don't need it, and I don't want it," he shot back, irritable. "We're not talking about this."

Dani wanted to slap him. She was not going to be dismissed, and they were going to talk about this. Right. Now.

"I bother you," she said.

"Yeah. You do," he muttered, and she tried not to flinch. "You bother me a great deal."

"Is that why you don't want my help?"

He didn't answer but lowered his hands and regarded her with his hound dog eyes.

"I am odd," she said stiffly. "I know that. I make you uncomfortable. But . . . you are quite odd yourself."

"I am?" He sounded surprised. Then he laughed, making her legs turn to liquid and her heart bounce in her chest, but she didn't take it back.

"Yes. You are. You are extremely odd. And I don't hold it against you." Her chin shot up in defiance, and she folded her arms, expecting him to argue. He laughed again, soft lips curling over his straight white teeth. He stared down at her as if he expected her to explain, but she didn't. She just let the accusation hang between them. His smile faded but his eyes still danced, and his next words were gentle.

"You don't have time to help me. You have more on your shoulders than any woman should have to carry."

Her folded arms fell to her lap, and she forgave him instantly. She forgave him for his rejection and for his absence, and for not wanting her company the way she wanted his.

"It wouldn't take too much time. If you could get me some of the items you wrote in your notepad, things that were found at the scenes, maybe I could help you learn the victims' names."

"You looked at my lists." Voice flat.

"Yes."

"That was not an innocent transfer of information. That was not something you couldn't help."

"No. It wasn't. But you have to remember that I was afraid you were in trouble."

"And what would you have done if I was, huh?" He shook his head like she was hopeless.

"I would have come looking, can't you see that by now? I would have done my best for you."

He looked taken aback and his throat worked up and down as he stared at her. She felt like crying for the umpteenth time in the last week. She looked away and steadied herself, pulling her knees further into her chest and looping her arms around them. His legs were spread wide, his oxfords planted on the ground, his hands clasped between his knees, and they both fell into silence once more, and although neither of them moved closer, the air between them had warmed.

"The saddest part of it all," she whispered, returning the conversation to the victims, "the saddest part, even sadder than their deaths, is that no one knows who most of them were. You know I can help with that, Michael. Even if I can't help you find the Butcher, I can give his victims back their names. That is important. That is important . . . to me."

"I don't want you touched by any of it. This isn't writing love notes for the dead, Dani. You don't know what you're asking for. You might see things that haunt you for the rest of your life. That hurt you for the rest of your life. You want that?"

She looked at him then, tipping her head to the side to study his sober countenance. "It will hurt me more to know I could have done something, and I did nothing. You have given your whole life to your work. Surely you can understand me wanting to do this one, small thing."

"It is not a small thing," he mumbled, but she detected concession in his sigh. She jumped on it.

"I will try harder not to touch your things. I've actually *been* trying."

He scoffed, incredulous.

"I have! But . . . you are a fascinating man, Michael Malone. And, in my defense, I can't really help it."

"You can't stop yourself from shoving your hands in my old boots?"

She blushed. "Well, yes. I can. But sometimes . . . sometimes it's as simple as catching a whiff of something. You can't stop your nose from smelling. Can you? Or your ears from hearing or your eyes from seeing?"

"So you are a Peeping Tom—a Peeping Dani—of a different sort."

The blush intensified; she could feel it seeping down her throat and over her chest. She supposed that was as good a description as any, though she didn't care for it. "You help people. I just want to help people too. And who is . . . Emil Fronek?" She might as well get it all out in the open.

He gaped, and then closed his mouth and shook his head. He threw up his hands, relenting. "All right. I'll answer every last one of your questions. I'll tell you everything. All of it. At least that way I won't be driven crazy wondering what you already know." He shook his finger in her face, his eyes narrowed on hers. "And you will not tell anyone. Not those two old ladies upstairs or Margaret downstairs. Not even Charlie. What I say doesn't get repeated. Ever. And what I say goes. Do you understand? You go only as far as I say. And when I say don't touch? You. Don't. Touch."

"Okay," she whispered. She zipped her lips, showed him her palms and, folding her arms, tucked them under her armpits, signaling she was locked down tight.

"This is a mistake," he muttered, but a grin tugged at the corners of his mouth, and she wished he'd just let it go so she could bask in it. Malone's smile was something to behold.

He didn't let it go, though. He banked it like he always did and scowled at her. "This is a mistake," he repeated. "But I don't think I have much choice in the matter."

~

Malone didn't give Dani a rundown of the murders or the steps he'd taken since arriving in Cleveland. He figured she could ask what she wanted to know. Otherwise, he was just going to assume that she knew it all. But he did tell her the story about Emil Fronek.

He'd told Eliot about Steve Jeziorski's assertions. He'd also told him about Emil Fronek's odd encounter with what might prove to be the Butcher, and Eliot had promised to take the "tip" to the detectives assigned to the case. Locating a particular transient in Chicago wouldn't be easy, but they had a lot more resources and manpower than Malone did. And in Chicago it wasn't exactly safe for him to go snooping around, asking questions, drawing attention to himself. Especially in the shipyards. The mob had a major presence on the docks. Better to let the Cleveland police reach out to the Chicago police and see what they could find. As far as he knew, Fronek hadn't been located, but that fact didn't take away from the impact of the account.

Dani's eyes got big during the telling, but she held her questions until he relayed the whole thing.

"The sandwich shop butts right up next to Peterka's," she gasped. "And there are stairs that lead up to the second floor from outside. If it was dark and Mr. Fronek had walked around the south side of the café, he would run right into those stairs."

"Yeah. I know. I thought of that too. Tell me about Peterka."

"Dr. Edward Peterka. It's his home—he grew up in that house—and it's now his practice. He hasn't lived there for a long time. It's been years. Almost a decade, I would think."

"So who lives there now?"

"I don't think anyone does. But there have been quite a few renters, I believe. Mostly interns at St. Alexis. I could ask Dr. Peterka. He was the same age as my mother. They grew up together and were friends."

He's been good to my aunts and me, and I think he would tell me whatever we need to know."

"No. I don't want the doctor—any of the doctors—getting wind that you were asking questions."

Dani seemed shocked by that, and her brows rose. Good. She needed to be aware that killers lurked behind friendly faces and innocuous fronts.

"I could get you inside. Just to have a look around," she said. "There's an interior staircase too. It's laid out very similar to our home. They added the stairs and the upper outside entrance later, so someone renting the room wouldn't have to enter the business."

"I'll have a look around tonight. If it's empty, I won't have any trouble getting in and out."

"It will be locked."

"Yes. I'm sure it will be." He could pick a lock in about ten seconds with one hand, but he didn't tell Dani that. She looked at him, her eyes still wide, and he guessed he didn't have to spell it out. It didn't stop her stream of suggestions, however.

"What if we go to the office tomorrow and talk to Sybil?" she said. "I will introduce you, and we will tell her you are looking for a place to rent, some place with more space than what we have here. She won't be suspicious. She can't ever even remember my name."

He mulled that over. It couldn't hurt. Picking locks and snooping around wouldn't tell him who'd been in the space in 1934, but Sybil might. "All right. But it might have to wait until Monday. I have to meet Eliot tomorrow afternoon. But I can go with you in the morning to the morgue. You are going tomorrow?"

She nodded. "But you don't have to help me."

"You help me, I help you."

She smiled like it was Christmas Eve and she couldn't wait for the morning. His heart flipped and sank simultaneously. He wasn't going to be able to avoid Dani anymore. He didn't *want* to avoid Dani. But he should. He knew he should.

"And can I please come with you when you pick the lock?" she pled.

"No."

"Please, Michael?"

And that's all it took for him to capitulate. *Please, Michael.* Please, Michael, and a pair of pleading, mismatched eyes framed in thick lashes and winged red-gold brows.

"All right, Dani. All right."

14

He came to dinner that night and stayed to listen to the Cleveland Orchestra play Debussy, stretched out on the rug, feet crossed, his hands clasped behind his head, his eyes closed. He fell asleep that way and didn't awake, even when Zuzana flipped off the radio and Lenka sighed that it had been the best ever.

"He has made himself quite at home, hasn't he?" Zuzana muttered, scowling at him.

"Shh, Zuzana," Lenka hissed. "Let him be. I like looking at him."

"Good grief, Lenka. What a thing to say," Zuzana said, shaking her head.

"He has beautiful lips. Did you notice that, Daniela? And lovely teeth too when he decides to smile."

"God save me," Zuzana groaned.

"Well, it's true, Zuzana," Lenka argued. "And the truth is never unwelcome."

"The truth is *always* unwelcome." Zuzana snorted. "One would think you were born yesterday, sister. I'm going to bed. You two can gawk at the man, but I'd rather look at my eyelids."

"Good night, Zu," Lenka said, unbothered.

"Good night, *Tetka*," Daniela added.

Lenka sat for a minute more, her hands in her lap, her eyes on Malone, the same soft smile on her lips that she'd worn while listening to the orchestra. "He likes you, Daniela," she purred.

"Shh, Lenka. Shh," Dani whispered, embarrassed but pleased.

"Did I not tell you there was a man for you?" Lenka said, not altering her voice at all.

"Aunt. Stop."

"Do not be shy with him, darling. Sometimes we women must be very direct."

"Zuzana clearly does not think so."

"I know. Funny that. She is so direct in every other way. But Zu didn't speak up when she should have. Now she lives with that regret."

Dani knew this story, though she was not certain Lenka's version was the truth. Perception was everything. Zuzana had never expressed regret.

"She was in love once with a man named Viktor," Lenka continued. "A long time ago. I think Viktor loved her too. But she was coy. And cold. And he never knew how she felt." She was silent for a moment, studying the past like it hovered in the corner of the room.

"Mr. Malone does not know how you feel, Daniela," she warned.

"Yes he does," Dani muttered.

Lenka's brows rose and she blinked, surprised. "I doubt very much that's true. I wasn't certain, darling, and I know you very well. Sometimes you assume the world can see you as clearly as you see it. But you are a lovely mystery to most. Don't be mysterious with Mr. Malone." Lenka rose and stayed bent for a minute, letting her back catch up.

"Are you going to wake him?" she asked Dani.

"No. He will wake when he's ready. He can't be very comfortable there on the floor, so I doubt it will be long. Go on, now. I'll finish up here and get the lights when I'm through."

Lenka blew her a kiss from the ends of her fingertips and hobbled down the hallway to her room. Dani kept working, her eyes on the wide lace collar she was adding to the bodice of a client's dress. But she was listening to Malone's breaths.

Malone had been relaxed at dinner, more so than she'd ever seen him, as if he too had been burdened by the strain between them and felt the relief of reconciliation. But she was afraid if she went to bed, he would leave her behind and explore the apartment in Peterka's upstairs without her.

She finished the blouse and set it aside. He had not moved, not even to shift his hands from beneath his head. His arms were going to fall asleep, and the night was cold and the floor hard.

A soft snore escaped his lips, signaling he was well and truly out.

She turned off two of the lamps nearest her but left the light glowing on the side table. She took a throw pillow from the sofa and made sure there were no stray pins or needles jabbed into it, a hazard when three seamstresses lived together, and crouched beside him, trying to decide whether she could ease the cushion beneath his head. He would sleep much more comfortably if she did.

Lifting his head with her right hand, she shoved the cushion under his head with her left. His arms, now free, unfurled at his sides, and she thought for sure he would wake. But he didn't.

She went to her room and drew a blanket from the end of her bed and lay down beside him, not too close, but close enough that she could share the edge of her blanket with him. This way, if he woke up she would hear him, and he wouldn't go without her.

He rolled away from her, burrowing down in her blanket and gathering it around him. She moved a little closer, just to stay under the covers. He rolled again, this time toward her, and her half of the blanket became his too. His eyes were closed and his breathing slow and deep or she might have thought he was playing possum. She didn't think Malone capable of that kind of silliness.

She inched her pillow closer and tried to free enough of her blanket to just put it around her shoulders, but it brought her so close that she could count his eyelashes, and his exhalations tickled her lips. She lay beside him for several deep breaths, too out of her element to know what to do, or even if she was allowed to enjoy it.

She should just wake him up. She couldn't sleep on the floor, and he *shouldn't* sleep on the floor. She put her hand on his cheek, not wanting to startle him . . . and not really wanting to wake him either.

His skin was warmer than hers. Considerably warmer. Her skin was always cool. He kept his face and neck clean-shaven, but the sandpaper roughness of his skin tickled her palm and made her fingers long to explore. His ears were small and the lobes oddly silky compared to the sharp stubble of his squared-off sideburns and the shortly cropped hair at the base of his neck. Like most men, he wore the top longer, but slicked it back from his brow. A vein snaked from his hairline to the deep groove between his brows.

She traced the furrow, still prominent even in sleep, but didn't press her finger into the indentation or try to smooth it out. Surely that would wake him. His lashes were short and dark but as thick as the bristles on a shoeshine brush. She studied them but didn't touch.

She moved the tip of her finger to the bump on his nose. It was slight, just a wider ridge that preceded the slope of an otherwise unre-markable feature. His mouth was wide above a clefted chin, the furrow in his chin almost identical to the one between his brows and the crease in his lower lip, like God had drawn his finger down the center of his face, marking him.

His face was one of peaks and valleys, horizontal and vertical—the ridges of his cheeks and jaw and brow, the blade of his nose, the creases beside his unsmiling mouth. The lines would only deepen, but his skin was still taut over sturdy bones and tight sinews. It was far different from her own in color and texture, and far different from the paper-frail skin of her aunts.

She found him fascinating and longed to touch all his edges, jagged and smooth. Warm and weathered. She had spent very little time around men and had little to compare him to—Michael was right about that—but she'd also had very little desire to know a man before. She had much more experience with dead men than living ones. She grimaced at that. *What must Michael think of her?*

He had kissed her as though he liked her. He kissed her as though he liked her very much. But he'd told her it was too soon. She wasn't certain she believed him—he'd said he and Irene were estranged for fifteen years—but it was not her right to question it.

How many times had she repeated his words in her head in the last week? *It's too soon. It's too soon. It's too soon.* It definitely wasn't too soon for her. She had no doubt about the way she felt. None at all.

She desperately wanted to kiss him again. She was lying next to him, his lips mere inches away. And Lenka was right. He had beautiful lips. She inched closer, closer, closer, until her mouth was positioned a breath from his. He smelled like the licorice tea he was fond of. He'd sipped at a cup after dinner, listening to "Clair de lune" and eating one of Margaret's gingerbread cookies.

She brushed her lips against his, puckering gently, and then withdrew enough to see his eyes. They remained closed and he was still breathing regularly. No twitching. She leaned in again, determined this time to not be so frightened that she wouldn't enjoy it.

She moved her lips so they hugged the curve of his top lip ever so gently, and then slid down to savor the fuller swell of the bottom one. She stayed too long, savoring the sensation, but she didn't increase the pressure or even purse her lips. When she pulled away again, incredibly proud of herself and the enjoyment she'd taken, she was met with a pair of sleepy, brooding eyes and a confused scowl.

She didn't immediately start to babble or make excuses. What could she say? She'd kissed him while he was sleeping. She was quite certain that was wrong. She met his gaze instead, measuring his response. The room was shadowed, but not dark. And he was awake, but not alert.

His hand rose and cupped the back of her head. And he brought her mouth back to his.

She swallowed her surprise, and his hand tightened in her hair.

He was no longer the sleeping beauty of the fairy tale but an eager participant. He kissed her with almost dreamlike ferocity, the hand in her hair keeping her face where he liked it, her chin tipped up to him. For an endless moment, he nibbled and bit and suckled like he dreamed of tropical beaches and ripe fruit dripping over his fingers.

Her clothes grew too tight and her skin too sensitive, and she could not have lifted her eyelids or withdrawn her mouth from his had the room been on fire. She was not convinced it wasn't. The flames licked at the pit of her belly, tickled the arches of her feet, and curled her fingers into her palms.

It was late and the house was dark, and the darkness made each act easier to perform. They didn't say a word. They simply kissed, mouths moving and silent, until his hand shifted from her hair and began to mold her hips and trace the curve of her spine, his thumb stroking the underside of her breast. Dani began to tug at his clothes, wanting relief from the flames, and that's when Malone rolled away, sprang to his feet, and walked down the stairs without so much as a good night.

She lay in stunned silence, panting. She heard him below, the snick of the bathroom door, the sound of water in the pipes, the house shifting around him.

She waited until her heart settled and the flames cooled. If he was going to leave her behind, there was nothing she could do about it now.

She rose from the floor, began her own toilette, and crawled into her bed to the sound of Malone pacing below her. Charlie leapt up and settled himself on her feet, anchoring her to the present. She closed her eyes and willed herself to sleep.

~

She was sure he would avoid her again and fretted over her impulsive act for half the night. She wanted his kisses, but she wanted his company even more. If he made himself scarce again, she would not be able to endure it.

But he was ready to go to the morgue after breakfast, just as he'd said he would, and other than a reluctance to meet her gaze, he was his helpful, if grumpy, self.

"Remember the woman wrapped in the quilt her grandmother made?" she asked him as they walked, needing something to talk about that had nothing to do with stolen kisses or regret.

"Nettie?" he replied.

"Yes, Nettie." It pleased her that he would remember the woman's name.

"How could I forget?"

"Well . . . something strange happened."

He finally looked at her directly, intently, and heat suffused her cheeks from the welcome weight of his stare, but she made herself continue with her story.

"When the gravediggers came to retrieve her, she wasn't there."

He frowned, his eyes still holding hers. "Nettie . . . The woman who was wrapped in the quilt and nothing else . . . and dead from unknown causes?"

"Yes."

"That was two weeks ago."

"Yes. We prepared her Thursday morning. They came to retrieve her Saturday evening."

"And she wasn't there?" He had stopped walking.

"That's what I was told. They saw my record, and it matched their order, but the morgue was empty. They assumed it was a mistake, though Mr. Raus called me. I came down, and sure enough, Nettie was gone. Her quilt was gone too. If you had not been with me, I might have thought I was going mad."

"Maybe someone claimed her after all."

"How? When? I'm not exactly sure how it all works. That's never been my responsibility. But there's a process for identification, I'm sure, at the city morgue. We don't see the bodies at the indigent facility until that process is over."

"That *is* bizarre. I'm surprised you're just telling me about it now." There was a distinct note of censure in his tone. He began walking again. She hurried to catch up and stumbled, partly from affront, partly from haste. His hand shot out to steady her, wrapping around her arm. He immediately let go.

"You were not here, Michael. And when you returned . . . I was distracted." She tripped again when she thought about why she'd been so distracted, and he gripped her elbow.

"If you keep tripping, I'm going to insist on pulling you in the wagon."

"I can walk fine. You just keep . . . infuriating me."

"Yeah. Well," he muttered, shoving his hands into his pockets.

For a moment she stewed, and it wasn't until she was unlocking the door to the facility that she shared her other question, one that had persisted since the body had gone missing. She knew she might sound like a fool, but her naivete was becoming a common theme. She might as well ask.

"That's the first time something like that has happened here," she began, pushing into the dark warehouse. "A body disappearing, I mean.

It made me wonder. Is the Butcher killing people, or is he working his experiments on people who are already dead?"

"You think he might be chopping people up after they're already dead?" Michael asked, incredulous, following her inside.

She flipped on the lights and waited for her eyes to adjust. "Has that been ruled out?"

He nodded. "It's been ruled out. I wish that were the case, gruesome as it still is. But he's killing people."

"How do you know?" she challenged, curious.

"Because the victims of the Butcher are drained of blood."

She stared at him, not understanding.

"If they were already dead when he began hacking away, Dani, there would still be blood in their veins," he explained. "Blood that isn't circulating coagulates. The Butcher's victims die from decapitation while they are still alive, while their hearts are still beating. There is no blood left in the bodies he's discarded."

Dani felt a little faint and steadied herself internally. "But when a body is embalmed, it too is drained of blood," she persisted.

"And replaced with an embalming solution. It wouldn't take long for a coroner to note the difference between loss of blood from decapitation versus the absence of blood from embalming. Not to mention, there is blood evidence in many of the cases. There would be no blood evidence if the Butcher was simply chopping up the embalmed."

"And there would be reports of bodies disappearing from the labs and mortuaries too," she conceded. "That wouldn't go unnoticed." She picked up her clipboard and studied the orders that had been left. There were eight today. Eight unknowns to clean and clothe. Eight lives to remember.

Malone shrugged off his coat and his hat and rolled his sleeves before donning a covering. He allowed her to tie it closed in the back before doing the same for her.

"Why?" she whispered, her chin to her chest as he tied her strings. "Why does the Butcher do what he does?"

"Just because it doesn't make sense to you, doesn't mean it doesn't make sense," he retorted.

She tossed a narrow-eyed look over her shoulder and tucked her hair inside a scarf with practiced efficiency. "That is something my mother always said."

"Yeah. Something she taught you and something you told me when you were ten years old. I've never forgotten it."

"I told you that?"

"Yeah. You did."

"Smart little thing, wasn't I?" She grinned at him.

His mouth lifted slightly at the left corner, but that was all. "Yeah. You were a smart little thing. Still are. Too smart for the likes of me."

She felt the double meaning in his words but ignored it.

"Saying that something doesn't make sense is lazy talk," he continued. "It's the speech of the defeated. Too many cops do that. My job is to *find* the sense in it. To make sense of the incomprehensible."

She nodded, agreeing. It wasn't until they had made their way through half the dead that her thoughts returned to the Butcher.

"Have you made sense of him then, Michael?" she asked. He didn't seem to need clarification.

His dark eyes were morose when they touched hers. "No. But one thing I'm not doing is ruling anyone out."

"They call him a monster," she said.

"Yes."

"And a madman."

"Yeah. That's not all he is, though."

She waited for him to elaborate.

"They will never find him if they're looking for a monster. It's never that obvious."

When she was silent, he continued. "Have you ever looked at a painting that up close is just a blur of color and smudges? Thousands of strokes and dabs, paint layered on paint . . . and then you step back from it and discover that all those parts create an actual picture?"

"Yes."

"Well . . . that's kind of what I mean. And sometimes we look at the pieces with a picture already in mind. We think we know what we're looking for."

"Looking for a monster and missing the man?"

"Exactly."

"But . . . the problem now, according to the papers, is that there *are* no suspects. No one has any idea who is doing this."

"I'm not at all convinced anyone really wants to know," he muttered. "It's more exciting that way. The papers are full of assumptions. Assumptions are bad information. Bad information is worse than no information. Bad information makes you blind to the truth when it comes along."

"What about feelings. Are feelings bad information?" she asked.

"Sometimes feelings are the worst information. Because we are attached to them. If you're going to do this with me, Dani, you have to turn your feelings off."

"Is that what you do?" she asked.

"Yeah. That's what I do."

"How convenient," she murmured.

"I think so. It's kept me from getting killed more times than I can count. It's kept me alive. And I find that being alive is a great deal more convenient than being six feet under."

She loosened the ties from her covering and pulled the scarf from her hair, thinking about that statement. Malone removed his own covering and washed up beside her at the sink, as silent as she.

"You said turning off your feelings has kept you alive. I'm not sure that's true, Michael. Plus . . . a man without feelings might as well be dead," she said, locking the door behind them.

He sighed. "Your heart is too soft for this, Dani Flanagan."

"Hmm. Maybe so. But perhaps your heart is too hard." She smiled a little to take the sting out of her words. "The truth is, the harder we are, the easier we shatter. It takes some softness to absorb life's blows."

15

He had two hours between the time they finished at the morgue and his weekly meeting with Eliot. They'd missed the week before due to Eliot's schedule and had talked only briefly on the telephone the morning Malone had returned. Eliot had been curious about his train-hopping and also about a certain Miss Daniela Kos who had called him in great concern, but neither subject had been delved into. They'd kept it light and nonspecific, as they usually did, but there was much to discuss and Michael kept an eye on the time.

He accompanied Dani to the medical office to inquire about the apartment upstairs, just as she'd proposed. Their plan to poke around in the apartment the night before had been thwarted. But he wasn't going to think—or talk—about last night. Dani seemed eager to steer clear of it as well.

The woman at the counter was applying a coat of lipstick when they walked into the small waiting area. The place had the smell of bleach and cheap perfume. He guessed the cheap perfume came from the woman who didn't even bother to look up.

"Sign in, please," she droned.

"Hello, Sybil," Dani said, trying to maintain waiting room decorum, though no one was in the reception area but them. "This is Mr. Malone. He is our boarder. But he's looking for a place with a bit more space. I was wondering if the upstairs apartment was available."

The woman looked up from her compact, popping her lips to blot them. Her eyes bounced off Dani immediately and locked on him. He saw the moment she decided she was interested, because her back arched and her chest lifted. He could see her tongue probing her teeth for lipstick.

"I would think you would want to keep him, Della," she purred.

"Daniela," he corrected. "Her name is Daniela. And I have some questions I'm going to need you to answer."

She frowned and Dani stilled beside him. He was not acting according to plan. He flashed his credentials at the receptionist, not giving her time to study them.

"I work for the Bureau of Internal Revenue. Who owns this establishment?" he asked, firm.

She gaped.

"Uh . . . Dr. Peterka. He's not here right now, though. You should come back and talk to him."

"I'd rather talk to you. Who lives upstairs?"

"No one. Dr. Peterka is planning to convert it to more office space."

"He's never lived in this house then?" Dani had already given him the answer, but it was a convenient segue into who else had lived there.

"He grew up here. When his parents moved out, he stayed with his own family with the practice beneath. But he moved out years ago."

"How many years?" He asked his questions fast, wanting her to answer just as quickly. He was more likely to get honesty that way. Plus, it kept her off guard.

"I don't know. About the time I was hired. 1930 or so."

"So the upstairs has been empty ever since?"

"No. We usually have several interns renting the space."

"Interns?" Again, he knew the answer.

"At St. Alexis."

"How many interns?"

"There has to have been a dozen, at least, over the years."

"Do you think you could make me a list?"

"Perhaps. I hardly see why you're asking me these questions. Donna could have told you all of this. She's lived next door longer than I've worked here."

"Daniela," he corrected. "So how long has it been since it was occupied?"

"Six months."

"But no one now?" he pressed.

"No. It's got a kitchen and an indoor toilet. But Dr. Peterka says he wants to put private offices upstairs. He wants it for himself if you ask me. A bachelor pad." She gauged his response to her gossip.

"But Edward isn't a bachelor," Dani said, frowning. Her innocence had Sybil rolling her eyes.

She reminded him of Dani's old neighbor, Mrs. Thurston, full of suggestion and innuendo, trying to find an angle. He also didn't like that she couldn't remember Dani's name. People did that on purpose. You didn't consistently get someone's name wrong unless you were trying to insult them. The woman was probably jealous. Women were odd that way. Maybe it was instinctual, but it wasn't attractive.

"I want a list of who has stayed up there, Sable."

"Sybil. It's Sybil."

"That's right," he said, level-eyed.

"Dr. Peterka's brother-in-law lived there last."

"Good. And what was his name?"

"Bartunek. Jacob Bartunek."

"How long ago was that?"

"He . . . left . . . last summer." She wasn't telling him something.

"And how long did he live here?"

"It wasn't very long. Four or five months. Six at the most."

"I'd like to talk to him. Could you get me an address?"

"No." She frowned, but her eyes were lively with a secret she couldn't wait to tell.

"Why not?" he grunted. "He was related to Dr. Peterka. A brother-in-law, you said? Surely you can get me an address."

"The poor dear is dead. Suicide. Not here, thank goodness. Can you imagine finding the body? It was after he left. When he gave up his internship and went back home. Dr. Peterka was devastated."

"Oh no," Dani cried. "How terrible."

"It really was," Sybil said, shaking her head.

Malone studied the woman for a moment, not sure if he could believe anything that came out of her mouth. "That's a shame. Who lived there before Bartunek?"

"There have been a few every year." She shrugged. "Just like I told you."

"Anyone ever live up there all alone? I mean . . . before Bartunek. I'm thinking as far back as '34. Dr. Peterka didn't claim income on the space that year. If I can clear that up, it'll save him an audit."

He could almost hear her inward groan. Her pique at his questions became a grimace of dread. An audit would mean more work for her, no doubt.

She screwed up her red lips and tapped her chin.

"I can't say for sure. Dr. Peterka handles the renters. It's his house. Maybe that was when Dr. Frank was here."

"Dr. Frank?"

"He stayed there for a while when he and his wife split. He didn't stay long either. Maybe a year. It's hard to remember."

"Where is he now?"

"I wouldn't know," she pouted. He thought she probably did. He thought she probably made it her business to know every detail about the doctors in the practice.

"You wouldn't or you don't?" he pressed.

"I wouldn't and I don't." Her red lips were turned down and her chin was puckered with distaste. She'd decided she wasn't interested in him after all, or maybe she'd divined his complete disinterest in her.

"Why did he leave?" he asked, mild. Time to play on her vanity. "I'm guessing not much happens around here without your supervision."

Slight hesitation and a darting look at Dani. Dani shrugged, indicating she couldn't answer the question. The volume of Sybil's voice dropped. She enjoyed gossip. "He drank too much, I think. And he wrote some prescriptions for people who . . . didn't need what he was prescribing. Dr. Peterka felt bad that he had to force him out. They grew up together. Old friends, you know? Dr. Peterka told Dr. Frank he could come back when he dried out. I think it was probably the reason his marriage failed too, though he always seemed so sweet to me. And funny too. I liked him."

"But he hasn't? He hasn't come back?"

"No. I haven't seen him since." Sybil sighed, as if it were a terrible tragedy that she regretted relaying.

Malone thanked her and tucked his credentials back in his pocket, tipping his hat as he led Dani out of the establishment.

"I'll be back to talk to Dr. Peterka, Sable. But you've saved him a lot of trouble. I'll make sure to tell him how helpful you were." She frowned and he winked, pulling the door closed behind him.

"You didn't stick to the plan," Dani said, descending the front steps. He waited until they were beyond the front windows of the practice.

"No. That plan wasn't going to give me names and dates. And she made me angry."

"But . . . what if she tells Dr. Peterka that a tax man was here, asking questions?"

"Is Dr. Peterka the one chopping people up and throwing their bagged bodies into the Cuyahoga?" he asked her, tone dry.

Dani took the question literally. "No. I don't think he is."

"And what about the others on staff?"

"I've never felt anything suspicious on the coats."

"The coats?" His eyebrows shot up.

"Margaret launders the doctors' coats every week. I gather them sometimes, from the doctor's lounge. But only for the last two years. Before that, I think the partners must have brought their coats home to their wives."

He drew up short and stared down at her.

Then he took her by the hand and turned back toward the practice. "Show me."

Her hand felt right in his, and he didn't let it go, even when it was clear where she was leading. The back door of the establishment was unlocked, just like the front.

"The doctors all come and go this way," Dani said in explanation. She stuck her head inside to see if the coast was clear. Then she darted in to survey the contents of the bin.

It was Friday and the bin was full.

"We'll save Margaret a trip if we take them now, but I don't have my wagon or any laundry bags," she worried. "There are too many to carry, and they're soiled, though not terribly."

He strode in, picked up the bin, and walked back out again. It wasn't heavy, only awkward.

"That will work too," Dani said, hurrying after him.

"The coats are interchangeable, for the most part, and they're laundered every week," Dani explained when they were back at the house, the bin of white coats sitting beside the table Margaret used for folding. Margaret was presently upstairs in the kitchen, and he and Dani wasted no time with their search. Actually, Dani searched, and he watched her, his hands shoved in his trouser pockets, his gaze on her face. She never closed her eyes when she read the cloth, which always unnerved him. Instead her face went soft and her pupils expanded, crowding out the colors.

He imagined it was how she would look if he made love to her.

"What are you seeing?" His voice was harsh and impatient, and she flinched. He had embarrassed himself and taken it out on her. "Eliot will be here soon. I haven't got much time," he added, adjusting his tone.

She set one coat aside and picked up another. "Well . . . There are little things. Exasperation. Stomach discomfort. One of the doctors has heartburn. This one enjoyed a delicious ham sandwich for lunch yesterday."

"Oh yeah?"

"Yes. See how helpful my gift is?" She smiled, sheepish, and he snorted at her sweet self-deprecation. She surprised him sometimes. She surprised him often. Caught him off guard. Made him hope. Made him afraid. Made him foolish. Made him yearn.

"Keep going," he insisted, quelling his thoughts once again. She did as he asked, shaking out the white coats and shoving her hands into the sleeves to listen for whatever it was she heard.

A moment later she grimaced and withdrew her arms, hugging herself.

"What?"

"Dr. Peterka knows his patient has cancer. He is sending the man to St. Alexis for tests, but he knows." She sounded aggrieved, like the knowledge pained her.

"So Peterka wore that one?" he asked, taking it from her. He didn't like the sorrow that rippled over her features.

"Yes. That image is clear. It's a strong emotion, and fresh." She turned to wash her hands like the scent of sadness clung to them, but she returned to the pile.

She picked through every one of the coats, telling him what she felt and saw, but there was little of substance—nothing of substance—and he mentally moved the doctors at Peterka's practice onto his unlikely list. Ness had given him a list of medical professionals a mile long. It would take him ages to work his way through them.

"I'm not sure what I would feel . . . or see, Michael, even if one of these men *was* the Butcher. The cloth is not a mirror for men's souls or their lives. Unless someone was killed in one of these coats, I doubt I would see a thing."

He moved the doctors back into the "maybe" column and sighed.

"It would be much more effective . . . I would be much more effective . . . if you could get me items from the victims. At least I could give them names," she said.

Dani and her names. Dani and her dead. Her beloved unknowns. The idea made his stomach twist. "We'll see."

"And, Michael?"

"Yes?"

"Should you want to go exploring tonight . . . you will take me, won't you?"

"Yes, Dani. I'll take you. I said I would."

"Okay. Good." She smiled and set the coats back in the bin. "I'll tell Margaret these are here. And I'll see you later."

She went one way and he went the other, exiting into the tepid shine of midday to walk around the house to the street. Eliot was already waiting.

~

They had a lot of ground to cover, and Eliot was always short on time. He parked in an empty lot, turned off the engine, and rolled down the window before taking a lunch box from the back seat and offering Malone two of his sandwiches.

"I made them myself. Even the bread. My father would be proud. He always wanted me to go into the family business." He took a big bite and sighed. Eliot's parents had owned a bakery in Chicago, but the fact that Eliot had made the bread—and his sandwiches—told another story.

"Edna hasn't come back?" Malone asked.

"Nah. She's not coming back. It's over." Eliot's voice was resigned. "And I've got that damned gala at the end of the month. The press—and Congressman Sweeney—are going to have a field day when I show up in tails by myself."

"Better than showing up with another woman. And why does Congressman Sweeney care?"

"I told you. Politics. It's all about demonizing the other side. Pointing out the flaws of the opposite team to distract from your own. He hates Burton . . . so he hates me." He took a big bite of his sandwich and urged Malone to dig in.

"Go ahead. I made extra just for you," he said around his mouthful. "Peanut butter and honey. They taste like dessert."

Malone shrugged and accepted. Breakfast had been a long time ago, and he'd been too uptight to eat his fill. He'd been wracked with guilt about kissing Dani. Again.

Amid sticky bites, Malone outlined everything he'd learned in the last few weeks, focusing primarily on the story of Emil Fronek—who still hadn't been located, according to Eliot—in relation to the medical practice on the corner of Pershing and Broadway and the café butting right up to the stairs.

"It was in '34, but it seems to me that's when the Butcher got started. That apartment has seen a stream of characters with medical training. I'll just have to track them all down. It's empty now, but I can get in. Poke around. See what's there."

"If we can find Fronek and get him here, let him retrace his steps, and even get a description of the guy he thinks drugged him, that'd be something concrete," Ness said. "We could show him pictures. St. Alexis has photographs of all their staff on file. Even interns. We need to narrow the field. And we need evidence."

Malone nodded, chewing. Thinking.

"I checked into the kid's story," Ness said, moving on. "Pete Kostura *was* killed in a hit-and-run in December. Damn tragic. He was in one of the boy gangs I've been working with. I lit a fire under the detectives on his case. But I don't know how his death has anything to do with the Butcher."

"Why? 'Cause his head wasn't chopped off?"

"Yeah. Not the Butcher's style," Eliot said, his cheeks bulging.

"Well, someone ran that kid over. Someone who didn't live in that neighborhood. Someone with a big, fancy car, like the mayor drives," Malone said, quoting Dani, who'd been quoting Steve Jeziorski. "Maybe Kostura thought he could squeeze someone for money, the way Steve does. Maybe he threatened someone important with something he saw the day he found those bodies . . . or with something he learned since. And instead of paying up, they took him out."

Something flickered across Eliot's face, and he stopped chewing.

"What?" Malone pressed.

Ness busied himself with his thermos and shook his head like it was nothing.

"Eliot," Malone said, insistent. "What?"

"Nothing. Any luck finding your shadow?" Ness said, changing the subject.

"No. I talked to the kid—Steve Jeziorski—again. He works at the plant Flo Polillo's remains were found behind. How's that for a coincidence?" He sighed. "I'm not worried about it. Jeziorski could have been describing half the men in this city. He said he'd try to get the guy's name—if there really was a guy—for a price. I told him to forget about it. The kid's a bit of a con artist, but I don't want *him* getting run down too."

Eliot didn't rise to the bait but sloshed some lukewarm coffee into the cup from his thermos and offered it to Malone.

Malone drank it down in one gulp. Then he took out his hand-kerchief and wiped at his hands, removing the crumbs and the sticky residue, and swiped at his mouth. Eliot didn't want to tell him, fine. He had a bigger ask.

"I want to see the items that were found at the scenes. Can you get me into the evidence locker?"

"Yeah. But why?" Eliot asked, eyes narrowed, the big black car forgotten. "The descriptions are pretty complete. That stuff has been combed over."

Malone considered not answering, the way Eliot had just done. But he couldn't show up with Dani and not provide any explanation. Special precautions would need to be taken.

He chose his next words carefully. "I have my own expert. Someone I want to have a look at the clothing, in particular."

"Your own expert?" Ness said slowly.

"Yeah . . . you'll see. It will be better if you just trust me. You can watch."

"What's the expert going to do?"

"She's a tailor. I think she can tell us things that someone else might miss."

"She?" Eliot crowed.

"Yes. She."

"A tailor, you say?"

"A tailor. A seamstress. Whatever you want to call it."

"This seamstress . . . she wouldn't happen to be Daniela Kos, would she?" Eliot asked. The man was no dummy. Malone had to give him that. And he also shared his sandwiches.

"Yes. Daniela Kos," he said.

"Your concerned landlady?"

"Yes. The same. She's very . . . skilled. I think she can help."

"Well, I'll be," Eliot marveled. "You've got me curious. I'll talk to Cowles. We'll figure something out."

"Good. You do that," Malone said.

"She was very concerned about you, old boy." Ness winked at him. "I thought it was sweet."

"She's a very . . . nice . . . woman. I wish she hadn't called you, but . . ." He shrugged, staring out the window. It was too warm in the car.

"She knows you well then?"

"I told you she did," Malone said, guarded. "I told you about her on day one."

"Is she nice looking? She sounded nice looking." Eliot was grinning. Malone could hear it without even looking at him. But he was reluctant to answer. Yes, Dani was nice looking. Beautiful, in fact. Perfectly, imperfectly, beautiful. And he could not say so without making it seem too important. Or *all* important. And as much as he liked Eliot Ness, and as innocent a question as it was, Malone couldn't talk about the way Dani looked. He could not . . . reduce her . . . to that. He met Eliot's gaze.

"No. She isn't," Malone said, tone terse, though his voice rang with truth. The lie comforted him immediately, as if he'd defended her virtue, and Ness blushed. It was endearing, his boyish ability to still be shamed.

Ness's grin flipped even as his brows rose, tugging his face in opposite directions. "Well, then. I almost feel sorry for the old girl now. You sure don't mince words, Mike."

Malone grunted.

Eliot started the car, his lunch break over. The speaker mounted above the windshield crackled and hissed.

"Calling Director Ness," a male voice insisted, and Eliot reached for the handset with the curling cord and flipped a switch.

"This is Ness," he said, a trifle too loud, like he was excited to finally be using his new contraption.

"We just got a call from the bridge tender at the end of Superior Avenue in the Flats. A severed leg has reportedly been found on the bank of the river not far from the storm drain. Sergeant Hogan and Chief Matowitz have been advised. Search teams are en route. Scientific Bureau already on scene."

"Son of a gun," Malone cursed beneath his breath.

"I'm not far," Eliot barked into the mouthpiece. "Five minutes out."

He hung up the gadget, squealed out of the parking lot, and headed north, eyes grim, both hands on the wheel.

"Nine months. Nine months and nothing. I had hoped that he was through," Malone said.

"Yeah. Me too. But we found a bundle of clothes in January, right around the time you got into town. Women's clothing, all neatly packaged in newsprint . . . kinda like Flo Polillo in the produce baskets. No body parts, though. Just bloody clothing. We've been holding our breath. What do you want to bet the leg belongs to a woman?"

"What? When were you going to tell me about that?" Malone asked, incredulous. A bundle of clothing. His thoughts instantly went to Dani.

"I didn't purposely *not* tell you, Mike. There just wasn't much to go on. It got added to the long list of things we don't know."

"Let me out here," Malone demanded as they neared their destination. "I don't want people seeing me with you. And keep me in the goddamn loop," he snarled. "I want everything you know, the minute you know it."

Ness dropped him off about a block from the already gathering crowd and proceeded down the street without him.

16

By the time Malone worked his way into a position where he could see the water and the police presence, he'd heard several versions of what had happened and what had been discovered.

"It's a woman's calf. Severed below the knee and above the ankle. No foot," someone said. "Joe said Steve poked at it with a stick thinking it might be a fish."

The waterway where the leg had been spotted was not much more than a big ditch with steep embankments and a bad bridge. A storm drain fed into it, and men were already in waders trying to see if other "pieces" had been caught in the grate. No efforts were being made to keep the crowd back, and people swarmed the banks looking for the rest of the woman. It was no way to conduct a thorough—or clean—investigation.

"It might not even be the Butcher," someone said, hopeful.

"It's him all right. You just wait. They'll find more. They always do."

"How many is it now?" someone else wailed.

"Eleven, if you count the Lady of the Lake."

"I heard them say whoever it belongs to hasn't been dead for very long."

"Steve" turned out to be Steve Morosky, a railroad worker, who at about 2:00 p.m. had walked to the end of Superior Avenue to visit a friend who lived in a shanty nearby. He was surrounded by a crowd, telling his story with wide gestures. He'd probably had to tell it several times already and seemed to be enjoying the attention. Two detectives in matching white straw hats and baggy suits were plying him with questions.

"I saw a guy drop a burlap bag into the water about a month ago off the Jefferson Street Bridge. He was driving a Lincoln. Real suspicious," a man called out, and one of the detectives peeled away to get his statement.

Malone saw David Cowles of the Scientific Bureau leaving the scene and ran to catch up with him. He'd known David since their Capone days, and when he called out to him, David turned and greeted him in surprise. The man's face was wreathed in worry and strain, and his trousers were streaked with mud.

"Mike," he said. "Ness said you were in town. Bad business, this. Bad."

"What do you know, David?"

"Not much. I'm heading to the lab at the morgue right now. That'll tell us more. But unless we find the rest, we aren't going to ever know much."

"Can I ride along?" Malone asked. No one was paying attention to him or Cowles. Eliot was already being trailed by cameras and hounded by reporters with pencils and notepads, even though he hadn't been on the scene for more than fifteen minutes.

"Yeah. You can. Jump in."

They drove to the city morgue, Cowles talking all the way, Malone digesting his initial findings. David was as level-headed and unpretentious as they came, and he and Eliot Ness were tied at the hip. He knew all about the "Unknowns" and Malone's assignment.

"It's a woman. White. Young. Slim. Blond," David rattled off.

"Blond?" Malone said, surprised. "How did you get that from her calf?"

"I found some long blond hairs wrapped around it," he said, grim. "Leg hasn't been in the river that long. Woman dead at the most a week, I'd say. And no abrasions—besides the amputation marks—on the skin. I doubt the piece went through the storm grate."

Cowles didn't want to introduce him to the inner circle, and Malone didn't care to be noticed or made, so he hung back when they reached the city morgue, lurking across the street until, just like at the Superior Avenue site, a crowd began to form, awaiting word from the coroner. He watched Eliot arrive an hour later and swing into a parking spot near the entrance. He was accompanied by men Malone didn't know, and all walked swiftly into the building, ignoring the questions and the shouted pleas for information.

It wasn't until nearly eight o'clock that the newly elected Cuyahoga County coroner, Samuel Gerber, tall, prematurely gray, and distinguished in his red-ribboned straw hat, white shoes, and tan suit, addressed the gathering, standing in the glow of the entrance lights, his hands clasped behind his back, his countenance sober. He was only Malone's age, but his silver hair gave him an air of gravitas his years might not. Eliot said he'd only gained the position in November on the Democratic ticket, which would mean this was his first case as coroner in the string of killings.

"We're awaiting the results from additional tests and X-rays," Gerber began, projecting his voice. "But, having studied each of the previous murders, I do believe this is the work of the Butcher."

The crowd moaned in terror and delight. That would get printed on the front page of every newspaper in Cleveland and beyond. It reminded him of a radio serial. *"Tune in next time, folks, for the continuing adventures of . . . the Torso Killer!"*

The coroner continued after his weighty pause. "The specimen discovered on the banks of the Cuyahoga near Superior Avenue is the lower left leg, severed above the ankle and below the knee. Our preliminary findings are that the victim was female, between twenty-five and thirty, about five feet two inches tall, and approximately a hundred and twenty pounds. Knife marks on the bones are consistent with other victims, though it does appear that the slayer was more frenzied in this killing than in the past."

The press pool gasped, and their hands shot up, but the coroner raised one hand, halting questions. He'd given them some red meat, teased them, and now he was cutting them off.

"That is all I can tell you at this time," he added, firm. Malone guessed, based on the past victims, it might be all he would *ever* be able to tell them.

Malone waited for an hour more, listening to the talk and the speculation among those that lingered, hoping for another statement. Eliot exited the building again, this time with Cowles, and the two men parted ways at the door, each climbing into their respective cars without acknowledging the crowd. It was dark, and Malone was starving. Nothing more would be learned this night, and Dani would be wondering where he was.

He scowled, embarrassed at that thought. One would think he had a ring on his finger. But he headed home, catching a streetcar from Public Square to Broadway, standing among passengers who looked as weary and rumpled as he felt.

The house was dark and quiet when he let himself through the back door at ten o'clock. The women hadn't waited up. He felt a flash of disappointment and doused it with a bath and a shave before heading up the stairs to the kitchen, desperate for dinner.

He stuffed a hunk of cold turkey in his mouth and slapped together two pieces of bread slathered in peanut butter and honey—Eliot had definitely started something—before sitting down at the table with a glass of milk and his plate.

"We heard the Butcher has struck again," Dani said from the doorway, startling him.

She was dressed for bed, her long white nightgown covered with her blue dressing gown. The normally neat coils of her hair were rumpled like she'd been asleep and heard him poking about in the kitchen.

"Word travels fast," he muttered, taking a big bite out of his sandwich. Dani sat down across from him, her gaze expectant, her hands in her lap.

"Did I wake you?" he asked.

"Yes," she admitted, no pretense. Never any pretense. "But I'm glad."

He was glad too, damn it.

"Will you tell me what you know?" she entreated.

So he did. He told her every single thing he knew, down to the blond hairs and the color of Samuel Gerber's shoes.

"That's quite a lot of information from a bit of leg," she said when he was finished relating the coroner's findings.

"Well . . . they can't tell whether she had a ham sandwich for lunch, like someone else I know, but they can tell a lot by the length of the bone, the weight of the calf, and the age and composition of the skin."

His reference to the ham sandwich fell flat and his appetite fled. He pushed his plate away. For a moment, he and Dani sat quietly, each tangled in their own contemplation.

"Are you all right, Michael?" she asked gently.

He looked up, surprised as always by her perception. "I'm fine. I wasn't the one running the tests on a woman's hacked-off leg. But I'm running in circles like the rest of them. I don't get the impression anyone knows—or even wants to know—anything. It's a goddamn carnival. And I don't like carnivals." He ran a hand over his face and apologized for his language.

"Neither do I," she said. "The world is frightening enough without clowns and distorted mirrors."

"I asked Ness if I could see the other evidence, Dani. And I told him I would be bringing . . . my own expert. He agreed, though he's got his hands full at the moment. Who knows when he'll get back to me."

"Your own expert?" she repeated.

"You said you wanted to come."

"I did! I do." She nodded, emphatic, and her curls bounced in agreement. "Did you tell him what I . . . do?"

"Not exactly. He might have me committed when it's all said and done."

She looked stricken, and he was immediately remorseful.

"Don't worry, sweetheart," he muttered. "Ness is unconventional. He's always been unconventional. He'll get a kick out of you."

Her cheeks flooded, and his neck got hot. He hadn't meant to call her sweetheart.

She reached across the table and picked up his sandwich with both hands. Without asking, she took a big bite out of it and set it back down on his plate, her cheeks bulging.

He laughed. "Hungry?"

She nodded again, her hand in front of her mouth to hide her anxious chewing. She was too damn cute. He slid his plate to her. She took two more bites before he won—or lost—the argument he'd been having with himself since she'd appeared in the kitchen.

"You want to go exploring?" he asked softly. It was almost midnight, but he was antsy, and he didn't want to wait any longer to see what clues the apartment turned up.

Her mouth was still full, but she immediately stood.

He stood too, feeling suddenly cheerful. He told himself it was because he'd always enjoyed breaking and entering. It probably had more to do with spending another hour or two with Dani, but he didn't think about it too hard.

"I'll meet you downstairs in five. And wear something dark," he said.

~

Nothing remained in the space but a single wooden chair and a sofa with a torn cushion, frayed arms, and a missing leg. It had been propped on a medical book to keep it from listing to the side. Dark curtains hung at the window in the sitting area, but the bedrooms, two of them, held nothing but empty springs on bed frames and dust balls that scurried like spiders when Malone caught them in the beam of his light.

He'd had no trouble jimmying the lock, and they'd slipped into the apartment almost as quickly as if they'd had a key. But there wasn't much to see.

It smelled like sour socks and bacon grease, and the only light in the place was a bulb hanging on a long, stringy wire above the shallow basin in the bathroom. Malone pulled the little chain, giving them a bit of light to search by, but used his flashlight to study the other rooms.

"I don't suppose you could run your hands along the walls and tell us this was the lair of a killer at one point?" he asked, grim.

"No. Hard surfaces don't speak to me."

They walked back into the sitting room, his light pinging from corner to corner, and Dani walked to the old sofa. It was soiled and sad, but it was cloth.

"I might be able to get something from the curtains or even the couch. It's upholstered, and it's never been washed. That will make it easier . . . and harder, depending on use."

"Why harder?"

"Everyone who has lived here most likely sat here. It didn't belong to just one person, wasn't worn or held or touched by a single hand."

"Like fingerprints on a door handle."

"Yes. Exactly. Hard to tell the layers apart. The curtains have probably been washed, though not often. But the same problem exists. The couch would have absorbed more. No one wraps themselves in the curtains."

He shrugged and pointed his beam at the sofa. "Give it a try."

She started by running her hands in a grid-like pattern, up and down, up and down, working her way across the length of the old couch. Images flashed, but they were blurred and indecipherable. A watercolor painting smeared with grime. When she hissed and swayed, yanking her hands back, Malone took her arm, steadying her.

"What's wrong?" he asked.

"It's like being jostled by a crowd. Or spun in circles. It's making me dizzy," she said, sheepish, but she tried again, moving her hands more slowly, trying to make sense of the colors and shapes.

"Diagrams. Anatomy. Da Vinci's proportions of the human body," she reported, but the man in the circle spun away and a sobbing intern—Jacob?—took his place. Jacob didn't want to be a doctor. He dreamed of blood, dripping limbs, and pustules oozing with terms he—Jacob?—repeated in monotone, as though he studied for an exam.

"Jacob lived here last," she said. "Isn't that what Sybil said?"

"Yeah. Jacob Bartunek."

"He's . . . miserable." She slid her hands to the left, but there was nothing else to see but the muddied wash of too many memories. Her stomach lurched again, and she clutched at it.

"What do you see?" Malone asked.

"This isn't going to work, I'm afraid." She closed her eyes, trying to settle the spinning wheel in her head. "Will you let me hold on to you for a minute?"

"Hold on to me?"

"I need a clean slate," she whispered. "Let me hold your hands . . . just until my mind clears."

213

He shoved his flashlight in his trouser pocket and did as she asked, enveloping her palms in his. His hands were rough and raw-boned, his father's hands, he'd said. He'd seemed proud of that, maybe because he resembled his father in so few ways.

His hands anchored her instantly, and the murky miasma dissipated, as if he'd wiped it away. She'd never had someone to hold her hands after a bad spell before. She'd always had to recenter herself.

"Is that better?" he asked, as though he thought he might be doing it wrong.

"Yes. Much better," she whispered, but she tightened her fingers so he wouldn't let go. Just a minute more. "I know you think when I touch you, I'm divining all your secrets," she said.

"You are." His voice was mild, but she could feel the tension in his grip.

"I'm not. I don't read skin, and I don't hear your clothes when you're wearing them. I tried to explain when . . . when we argued." Better to say "argued" than "kissed." "You said I was touching your shirt, so I knew everything."

"And you don't?" he murmured.

"I can't hear the cloth against . . . living . . . flesh. It's like the warmth and heat of the real thing—of life—is too loud. It's rather nice, really." It made fittings a pleasure when every other aspect of her profession was fraught with snags and the pinpricks of private thoughts.

He cocked his head, turning toward the door, her hands still clutched between his. She'd expected a different reaction.

"Michael?"

He stepped forward suddenly and clapped his hand over her mouth, sliding his other arm around her waist as he did.

"Shh, Dani."

She jerked in affront, and then she heard it too. The groaning of the stairs beneath a heavy tread and the rattle of keys. Malone was suddenly moving, running, pulling her behind him down the hall. He yanked at the dangling chain hanging from the bulb in the bathroom and pushed her toward the first bedroom. He dove after her, shutting the door behind him as the front door screeched and swung open, indicating they had company.

Whoever it is has a key, she thought. *He belongs here. We are the trespassers.*

Malone was rigid against her, hardly breathing, his cheek against her hair. She heard the snick of Malone turning the lock on the door. She flinched, certain the stranger had heard it too.

Whoever had entered the apartment proceeded through the space without hesitation, the tread heavy and slow but the steps sure, as if the darkness were of no consequence and the visitor was at home.

The footsteps stopped on the other side of the door they stood behind. A hand slapped against it, as if the stranger was surprised to find it closed. The knob turned and held. The stranger grunted, confused. He rattled the knob, insistent, and Dani bit back a scream, burying her face in Malone's chest. His heart drummed and his arms tightened, but he didn't move.

The person on the other side of the door grumbled again, but he didn't tarry. Three footfalls and a tug later, the light from the bathroom seeped through the crack beneath the door and touched their feet. The slap of water hitting water came seconds later and continued for a solid minute. The stranger was making use of the facilities. The whoosh of the toilet and the footsteps retreating down the hallway were followed by a long groan and the scrape of clawed feet against wood floors.

He'd settled on the sofa.

Flatulence, belching, another scrape, and a series of squeaks as the couch protested the weight of its occupant. Then all grew quiet.

Malone spoke directly into her ear, his voice a rumble instead of a hiss. "He's drunk. We'll wait."

Wait till what? she wanted to ask, but she just nodded, and they stood straining to track the stranger's breaths, their arms around each other. Malone's pocket watch ticked away the seconds that turned into minutes, and still they waited, uncertain whether the man slept or simply sat as silently as they stood. Was he waiting for them? And why had he tried the locked bedroom door? There was nothing in the space but a bed frame. Did he know they were there? He had not moved cautiously or with obvious awareness, and he had urinated like he had a belly full of booze. But they had to get past him to leave.

Malone shifted her away from the door and turned the lock, one hand on the knob, one hand on the frame. Then he listened. He took her hand, swung the door wide with a swift, smooth movement so the hinges had no time to whine. He waited again, standing in the opening.

He touched her mouth with the pad of his thumb and leaned in until his lips touched her ear. "Stay behind me."

She nodded once, just a brisk jerk of her chin, and together they moved down the hall, the shifting floorboards tattling on them, but Malone didn't stop or even hesitate. He walked straight to the door, tucking her in front of him as he disengaged the lock.

The sofa moaned, and Dani darted a look at the shadowy figure sprawled across it. His face was turned into the back, his legs and arms tucked close. The couch was too small for him and his hind end jutted out over the edge, tempting gravity. Should he shift, he would find himself on his back on the floor. Nothing about him was familiar, but she hadn't made a regular study of the male backside. His face and his head were obscured. Even his hands and his shoes weren't visible, though he appeared to be wearing a dark suit and not the clothes of a laborer.

Then Malone was pushing her out onto the landing and pulling the door closed behind them. She flew down the stairs, Malone at her heels, and together they fled across the grass, out into the street, and back home, tumbling through the door like they were being chased by Satan himself.

17

"Any idea who that was?" Malone asked, pacing back and forth from his wardrobe to his desk. He'd not been afraid for himself. Had he been alone, he might have enjoyed the encounter. He'd been cornered and surrounded in worse situations than that, more times than he could count, but he'd never had a woman he cared about—anyone he cared about—caught with him.

Dani had collapsed onto his bed and was now laughing in relief. Her cheeks were flushed, and her eyes and curls gleamed, but Malone was not amused.

"Dani," he sighed. "It isn't funny."

"No. You're right. It definitely isn't funny." But she continued laughing away her nerves, and he waited, his hands on his hips, his narrowed eyes on the window, though he couldn't see anything but the Rauses' backyard.

"Who was he?" he asked.

"I don't know," she hiccuped. "But he didn't move like Edward Peterka. Dr. Peterka's slim and tall and light on his feet."

"Liquor can make every man sound like an elephant if he's had too much."

"He had a key," she said. "It was probably one of the doctors on staff."

"Any doctor drinking in this neighborhood and crashing in that apartment is hiding something."

"St. Alexis is right across the street. Where do those doctors drink?"

"Not in the bars around here. Not if they are doctors in good standing. I've been in all of them, and there is a distinct clientele."

"You say he's hiding something. Maybe he's simply hiding the fact that he drinks too much."

"From who?"

"His wife?"

"Would you rather your husband come home drunk or not come home?" he asked.

"I'd rather he come home drunk," she said, no hesitation.

"Yeah. I'm guessing that's the way most women feel. Better the devil you know than the one you don't. So I'm guessing it isn't a wife he's hiding from."

"Sybil said Dr. Frank drank too much. That he was fired, and his marriage failed because of it. Maybe that man was Dr. Frank."

"You don't think Peterka has changed the locks in all these years? Peterka fires him but lets him access the building to sleep off a drunk?"

She shrugged. "Dr. Peterka is a good man. He looks out for the people in this community. He's on the board at St. Alexis and is constantly raising money with the diocese for meals, medical care, and shelter for Cleveland's poor. It wouldn't surprise me if he went very easy on Dr. Frank."

"A regular St. Peter," Malone muttered. "But he's a very foolish man if he isn't running a tighter ship."

"People aren't dying in that apartment, Michael." She said it with such confidence that he stopped pacing and scowled at her, even though he agreed with her.

"No?" he pressed. "You get something from that couch you aren't telling me?"

"No." She shook her head. "It was just as I said. It was unpleasant. But I'm used to that. My ability is unpleasant . . . *often*. The brush of a memory, the brush of a moment, that's fine. But the layers of a life? It's like peeling an onion. And I'd rather not do it."

"You could have fooled me, kid," he snapped.

She was quiet for a moment, studying him.

"Are you angry with me, Michael?"

"I'm angry with myself."

"Because you let me come with you?"

"Yes! Because I let you come with me." He walked to his desk and took out the notepad with his lists. He turned a few pages and found the list he wanted and handed it to her.

"Read this. And tell me what the Butcher's victims all have in common."

She looked it over quietly.

"Dani? Read it."

"They all lost their heads."

"They didn't *lose* their heads." He tapped the sentence she'd restated.

"They all had their heads cut off," she amended.

"Yes. Correct. What else?"

"They were all relatively . . . unknown."

"Yeah. Unknown. Down-and-out. Nobodies."

"They are all people. Human beings. Please don't call them nobodies," she said.

"To him, that is what they are. Nobodies. No ties. No family. Nobody to miss them when they disappear. Many of them led miserable lives, filled with abuse and addiction, and they frequented unsavory places. He's doing them a favor, you see. He's giving them notoriety in death. He's making people care. He's making people notice what they often ignore."

"He's not making people care about the victims," Dani argued. "He wouldn't make them so hard to identify if he wanted people to care about them. He's making people care about *him*. He wants them to notice *him*."

He took the pad from her hands and threw it on the desk.

"Bottom line, you aren't the kind of woman the Butcher kills, Dani. I'd like to keep it that way. So I won't be bringing you to any unsavory places or putting you in danger again. I don't care how pretty you are when you beg." He was suddenly dying of thirst. He wrenched his tie from around his neck and tossed it toward the bed. It slid onto the floor and Dani retrieved it.

She rose silently and left the room. He could hear her splashing in the bathroom—most likely washing the sofa from her hands—but a moment later she returned smelling of his soap and carrying a glass of water that she insisted he drink.

"You didn't put me in any danger, Michael. That man was not there to harm us . . . and no one has been killed in that apartment. They might have been drugged there, like Emil Fronek. But not killed."

He gulped down the water like an obedient child, swiping at his mouth and glaring at her because she'd "read" his tie. "How could you possibly know that?"

"You said all the blood is drained out of the victims. Wouldn't that be very messy?" she said simply, sitting down on his bed once more.

"Yeah. It would be," he admitted, relieved that her answer was common sense and not voodoo.

"So where is the Butcher killing them?" she asked. "That might be easier to narrow down than who or why."

"One of the detectives on the case is convinced he's riding the trains and killing transients in boxcars."

"I don't imagine that Rose Wallace, Flo Polillo, or the other women were riding the rails," she said, doubtful, and he almost smiled at her agile mind. His Dani was nothing if not sensible. He grimaced instead, not liking the way he thought about her as *his*.

"I don't imagine that either," he said. "My guess is he's killing them where death is common, and the refuse of death easily disposed of. A morgue. A hospital. A mortuary. You live conveniently close to all three," Malone said. "Every single doctor at St. Alexis would have access—at least *some* access—to all three as well."

Dani flopped back against his pillows, her eyes troubled. Her hands were folded over her heart and her hair made a golden circle around her pale face, like one of the saints in the stained glass at Our Lady of Lourdes.

"If I admit that I'm scared, will you hold it against me?" she asked after a quiet moment.

"No," he said, sitting down beside her. She scooted over, making room for him, but he didn't lie down. He was scared too. The skittering beneath his skin had not ebbed. "I tried to warn you, Dani."

"I won't be scared when it's morning. But I don't want to be alone right now. And I don't want you going out again without me. That's what you're going to do, isn't it?"

That was exactly what he'd planned on doing.

"We will go back together," Dani pleaded. "Tomorrow night. And I will tell you who he is. His scent on the couch will be new, and I will be able to give you answers."

He hadn't even thought of that, and the idea made his pulse quicken. "We'll go back tomorrow," he agreed. "Besides, there isn't anywhere to wait unobtrusively with a clear view of the stairway."

She exhaled in relief and closed her eyes.

"But you should go back to your room," he added. "What if your aunts check your bed?"

Dani lifted her head and stared at him, her brow furrowed like he was being ridiculous. "You act as though I am a child who needs tucking in. I am twenty-five years old, Mr. Malone. The aunts don't check on me. I check on them."

"I am forty years old, Miss Flanagan," he reminded her, addressing her as she addressed him. "And Zuzana is a terrifying woman. Lenka too, but for different reasons."

"My aunts are old enough to be your grandmothers. And they are harmless."

"I disagree. And *you* are young enough to be my daughter."

"For goodness' sake, I am not. You can be so stuffy, Michael. We talk about death and murder and beheading, and we have just escaped a harrowing situation, yet you are too nervous to be near me."

"I'm not stuffy," he argued, sounding very stodgy indeed. He kicked off his shoes and lay down on the bed, arms folded over his chest, but he left the lamp burning.

"You don't have to worry. I will not throw myself at you again. I promise. I am embarrassed too, you know," she said, her voice small.

That surprised him.

"I kissed *you*," he grunted. "You didn't throw yourself at me."

"You kissed me because you were angry . . . and then because you were half asleep. I kissed you because I wanted to. Both times." She looked away as she confessed the last bit, thank God. He hadn't had time to school his expression. "But I won't kiss you again. I promise. We will just be . . . friends. We are friends, aren't we, Michael?"

He couldn't think of a single woman that he'd ever been friends with, beyond his sister, Molly. The way he felt about Dani was hardly sisterly . . . or even . . . friendly.

"Have you had many male friends?" he asked, stiff. "Suitors?"

"There have been a few," she replied.

"A few?"

"Karl Raus grew up next door. He pursued me for a while. We went to the local dances together, and we both liked the pictures. I don't know of anyone who doesn't, though."

She sounded weary, and he knew it wasn't any of his business. But he couldn't help himself from pressing. "You said there had been a few."

"There was another gentleman last year. He was a widower with a passel of children. I didn't mind the idea on its face. Having children from the get-go, I mean. But it was more a business arrangement for him. I think he found me pretty. But if it's just a transaction, I'm not interested in making it. I have my aunts. I have my home. I have my work."

"You have your dead."

"You aren't a man who says much."

"Not usually. No."

"Yet . . . you are very opinionated where I am concerned."

He was. He couldn't help himself, and he still wasn't ready to let the conversation rest. "How old was this . . . gentleman?"

"About your age. He was surprised when I turned him down. He told me I wouldn't get a better offer."

The thought made him instantly angry, and he fought the urge to get up from the bed and pace the room. "Shame on him," he growled.

"Why shame?" she gasped.

"Asking a beautiful girl to come take care of his children and warm his bed and then being angry when she declines? I ought to find him in a dark alley one of these nights and take him down a few pegs."

"I was flattered, and I told him so. Then I told him no, and that was that."

He scowled. "And the Raus kid? What did you tell him?"

"He's hardly a kid. He's a year older than I am. He never asked, but I would have refused him. He's married now with a child on the way."

"Why didn't you want him?"

"Because I felt nothing, absolutely nothing, when I was with him. When he kissed me, I might as well have been kissing the back of my hand. In fact, I enjoy kissing the back of my hand much more." She yawned widely.

Suddenly, he wanted to kiss her hand more than he'd wanted anything else in the whole world. He gritted his teeth and thought about dark alleys and bringing wisdom and justice to fools. He must have radiated tension because Dani resumed her pleading, not realizing he had absolutely no desire to oust her.

"Just let me stay until the sun comes up. Please, Michael?" she coaxed wearily. "I'll be gone when you wake."

He wondered if he would ever be able to tell her no again. "All right, Dani."

He sat up and turned out the lamp. Charlie bounded up and settled at his feet like it was a slumber party. Malone nudged him over with his foot just to remind the old boy whose bed he was in, but he didn't oust him.

"Michael?" Dani murmured as he stretched out beside her.

"Yes?"

"Will you hold my hand? I keep seeing poor Jacob Bartunek, crying over his medical books."

He huffed like it was a bother but reached out immediately, wrapping her slim fingers in his. "No snooping," he grumbled.

"I told you. It doesn't work that way, you silly old man." She curled toward him. "What do I have to do to convince you?"

He didn't answer. Her voice was already drowsy, and he didn't really need to be persuaded. He believed her completely; he just wasn't very good at admitting it. Like he'd said before, belief wasn't his problem.

Her fingers grew lax against his, and he lay quietly, comforted by her presence beside him, by the weight of her hand, and by the cadence of her breathing. When he was sure she was asleep, he brought their clasped hands to his mouth and placed a kiss above her knuckles.

"I see what you mean, Dani. It's lovely," he murmured, and kissed her hand again. In fact, he might be happy kissing the back of her hand for the rest of his life.

Charlie protested deep in his throat, his hackles rising as though Malone were about to take a bite from Dani's flesh.

"Be quiet, Charles," Malone said, but he settled her hand in the space between them on the bed and pulled the edge of the comforter around her. Then he slept, surprisingly content.

~

He'd fallen asleep on the edge of the bed, as far from her as he could get. One arm was slung across his eyes, one arm hung off the side. One of his stockinged feet was on the floor as if he needed to ground himself to the earth while he slept. She understood that. She often feared being lost to dreams.

She pulled on her shoes and listened for Margaret. She didn't want the woman to see her leaving Michael's room. When she heard no sounds of movement or mumbled singing, she tiptoed out. Charlie followed, having completed his duty as chaperone. She ducked into Malone's bathroom and tidied her curls with a wet comb and a touch of his pomade. She borrowed a bit of his tooth powder as well and scrubbed at her teeth with the end of her finger. It would do until she'd had her breakfast.

As soon as she reached the base of the stairs, she could hear her aunts and Margaret conversing above her and dishes clanking with the sounds of breakfast being prepared. Dani was still dressed in a deep blue dress, the "something dark" Michael had insisted she wear. It was a little too heavy for a Saturday spring morning, but her aunts wouldn't notice, nor would they assume anything by her presence downstairs. She often began her day in the sewing room, the first to rise and the last to retire.

The women had the papers spread over the kitchen table, and Margaret was reading aloud, her voice suitably horrified.

"All they found was half of her leg," she summarized. "Nothing else. They'll be combing the banks all week for more. Coroner Gerber says it's him again. It's the Butcher."

"Now the city will be in an uproar and Holy Week will be ruined," Zuzana complained. "He might have waited until after Easter."

"Good morning, *Tety*," Dani said, pulling out her chair. "Margaret."

"Good morning, Daniela," the women said in tandem, but none of them gave her more than a passing glance.

"Will Mr. Malone be joining us?" Margaret asked.

"I don't know. We will prepare him a tray if he doesn't," Dani answered.

Zuzana sneered. "There is little worse than a lazy man. Pavel, even when he was so ill he could hardly eat, did not make us serve him in bed."

"Nobody is serving him, *Tetka*," Dani said, wondering why Pavel was being brought into the conversation.

"I would be happy to serve him." Lenka smiled, cutting her poached egg into dainty pieces.

Margaret snickered, but Zuzana leveled her with a silencing frown.

"Poor Pavel," Margaret said, clearing her throat. "What a valiant man. It's a pity I never knew him. What was it that ailed him? I don't think you've ever said."

"The voices in his head," Zuzana said. "Poor dear. He died in agony."

Margaret gaped, wanting more information, but when Malone's tread was heard on the stairs, she rushed to the kitchen to fill his plate, forgetting all about poor Pavel.

Lenka preened and Dani's heart galloped in anticipation as Malone walked into the room, but she kept her greeting mild and her glance fleeting.

Unlike her, he had changed his clothes, and his hair was freshly slicked in dark waves, and his appearance drew more than a mere *Good morning* among the women. Margaret buzzed around him, and Lenka beamed at him with so much pleasure that Zuzana swatted at her with the newspaper. He accepted the brimming plate from Margaret with a soft thank-you. She blushed a cherry red, retied her apron, and bustled down the stairs humming Benny Goodman's latest.

"We missed you at supper last night, Mr. Malone," Lenka said as he took the seat next to Dani. "Daniela waited up for you for the longest time."

"Lenka," Dani reproached, shaking her head. "I did not."

Malone swallowed and shot a look at Dani. "Yes. Well. Duty called."

"We are a family in mourning today, Mr. Malone," Zuzana said. "I would ask that you be mindful of that."

"We are?" Dani asked, frowning.

"Yes. We are," Zuzana huffed. "You were late to breakfast as well, Daniela, and missed our brief memorial. Today marks fifteen years since Pavel passed away. April ninth is a very hard day for us."

Dani said nothing. She had known her grandfather very little. He'd passed away only months after her parents died, and her aunts had never made a fuss on the anniversary of his death before. She suspected it was simply an opportunity for her aunt to make Malone uncomfortable.

"Pavel?" Malone asked.

"Pavel Kos. My grandfather. Their younger brother," Dani provided.

"Ahh. I see." He inclined his head to the aunts. "My condolences to you all."

"He had the Kos curse, I fear. And did not tolerate it well," Zuzana said, frank. "It was a mercy that he was taken. But we still grieve him."

"Zuzana!" Lenka gasped.

Malone looked from one old woman to the next. "'The Kos curse'?"

"He had a feel for the cloth," Lenka rushed to explain. "He also had a stroke. I doubt the two were related."

"He was stark raving mad. And it does no good for any of us to pretend he wasn't," Zuzana said, face blank, but her eyes were bright with troublemaking.

Dani felt the color drain from her face and embarrassment bubble in her chest.

"Mr. Malone?" Margaret called up the stairs. "You are wanted on the telephone. Shall I take a message?"

Malone was no fool. He pushed back from the table, leaving his half-eaten breakfast, and excused himself with obvious relief and hurried down the stairs.

"I'll take it, Margaret. Thank you," he called.

"What are you up to, Zuzana?" Lenka hissed the moment Malone had descended the stairs.

"I don't know what you mean, sister," Zuzana retorted, blotting her lips with her napkin. But she didn't look at Dani.

"'The Kos curse'? Do you want Mr. Malone to be afraid of Daniela?" Lenka asked, flabbergasted.

"It is only . . . right . . . that he know what he is getting into. I have not said anything that is not true. Daniela is a Kos. She suffers from the same ailment as Pavel did. Mr. Malone should be aware."

"What do you mean, *Tetka*?" Dani whispered. She thought she might be sick.

"You know what I mean. Don't look at me like that," Zuzana snapped. "You are taken with Mr. Malone. You are besotted. It is plain to see. Just like your mother was taken with George Flanagan. She ran off. So might you. And Lenka, fool that she is, has been encouraging you. Don't think I don't know these things." She tapped her temple and lifted her chin, haughty. But her mouth trembled, giving her away.

"That was cruel, Zuzana," Lenka said, shaking her head. "You are many things. But I didn't think you were cruel."

Zuzana sniffed, dismissive, but she didn't deny it.

"So you mean to scare him away from me?" Dani asked quietly. "Make him think I am mad, so he doesn't want me? Is that it?"

"Yes. Better he go than we lose you." The trembling in Zuzana's lips spread to her chin.

"Oh, Zu," Lenka cried, reproachful.

"I know it is selfish. But it is how I feel," Zuzana confessed, finally meeting Dani's gaze. "I fear he will take you away, dear girl."

"I will not leave you, *Tetka*," Dani said, her compassion welling in spite of her pique. It wasn't like she didn't know. Since Vera died, Zuzana's fear and grief had begun to permeate her clothes and leave a trace on everything she touched.

Lenka tsked and threw up her hands. "Shame on you, Zuzana."

"You are afraid too, Lenka. You just aren't as forthright," Zuzana shot back. "We are old, and we are alone, and we need Daniela."

"Then you'd better put your mind to making Mr. Malone stay, you old fool. Daniela might forgive you if he leaves, but if you run him off, I never will."

~

The call was from his boss, Elmer Irey, the director of the Treasury's intelligence division. He wasn't happy.

"What the hell is going on there? The big guy himself is breathing down my neck on this."

Malone knew of only one "big guy" who could make Elmer Irey sweat.

Malone had been sending weekly updates since arriving in January. It was unlike any case he'd been on, mostly because the Treasury Department didn't have an angle, and he wasn't digging into financial records or getting cozy with suspects to gain insider information. His reports outlined what he was doing, what he'd learned, and frankly, why it mattered that he continue spending the intelligence division's resources—meaning Malone himself—investigating a series of murders in Cleveland. So far, he hadn't gotten any pushback from his boss or any real indication of interest. He'd figured the request for reports was just Elmer's desire to keep tabs on his agent. He'd also assumed he'd eventually be yanked and reassigned, but he had hoped for more time.

"I've only been here for three months, Boss. We were on the Lindy case for years. You know how this works."

"You hear the news out of Germany, Mike?" Elmer always called him Mike over the telephone. Mike was about as generic as it came.

"What news, specifically?" He was sure Irey would tell him.

"Elections are being held tomorrow. The big guy says the Nazi Party will win ninety-nine percent of the vote. That's the kind of confidence Hitler inspires. More people have died in Cleveland at the hands of this Butcher than died when tanks rolled into Austria last month. He was welcomed with parades."

"That's all bullshit, sir."

"No, it's perception, Mike. A worldwide perception that Germany is in control, and we aren't. We can't find our asses with two hands, and Hitler doesn't miss. And he's making sure everyone knows it. The Cleveland Butcher is headline news in Berlin. It's being used as anti-American propaganda."

"What do you want me to do, Boss?"

Irey was silent. They'd spoken in generalities, and Irey wouldn't spell anything out over the telephone, even though he spoke from the securest of lines.

"When you know something, I'd better know it within the hour. No more of these weekly reports. I'd like to avoid sending a team in if I can help it, but the way the big guy's talking, Ness is about to get fired, and the whole state of Ohio is being written out of the New Deal. Whatever you have to do to wrap it up, do it. And for God's sake, keep me posted."

18

Malone decided they didn't need to wait until dark to visit the apartment for the second time. The medical office was closed for the weekend, and Dani had a reason to be there, should someone see them or tell Dr. Peterka. Plus, looking the place over in the light would be helpful.

The shop was busy all morning with the Easter rush. They sold every hat in stock plus three off-the-rack suits with minor alterations, a dozen blouses, and four skirts in their new spring line. Still, Malone waited for her until she closed the shop at six, giving them an hour of late afternoon sunshine with which to explore.

He'd been on the telephone throughout the day, though with whom she wasn't certain. She thought he referred to his "boss" and a man named Cowles, as well as mentioning a few of the victims by their numbers. Three, seven, eight, and ten, specifically. If she remembered right, those victims were all women. It was most likely that he spoke with Eliot Ness, though she never heard Malone address him directly.

She didn't actively try to listen, but she couldn't very well help it if the telephone was in the sewing room and that she, Lenka, and Zuzana weren't on speaking terms at the moment, making them all more prone to listen than chatter between fittings and customers. But Malone's countenance was as dark as her mood when they left the shop together. She didn't know if it was his work or if it was her that made it so.

Dani knew the subject of Pavel would have to be broached with Malone, but she would do it in her own good time and deeply resented Zuzana's attempts at sabotage, understandable though they may be. She lied and told her aunts they were off to the morgue, and the two should eat supper without them. Zuzana pretended like she hadn't heard her, and Lenka replied that "in that case, I will be eating in my room." She hadn't forgiven Zuzana either.

Malone insisted they circle the premises, testing the entrance and exit doors and checking the street for cars. Then they approached the rear staircase the way Emil Fronek would have done, behind the empty café, and climbed the stairs like they had every right to be there. Malone knocked on the door, surprising Dani.

"Do you think he's still here?" Dani gasped.

"No," Malone said. "But if he is, and he's entitled to the space, he'll answer. If he's trespassing, he'll scramble. Either way, we'll know soon enough. But I doubt he's here. Stand behind me please, and hold on to the rail, just in case he comes barreling out. I don't want him knocking you down the stairs."

Malone rapped on the door again and called out, "Hello?" letting anyone who might still be inside know they were aware of him.

No one came to the door.

Malone slipped his tools from a slim pouch in his pocket, and mere seconds later, the lock released.

The smell hit them the moment the door swung inward.

They peered into the dark room, their hands over their noses and mouths.

"Someone was sick," Malone hissed through his teeth. "Someone was sick all over the couch. I'm guessing it was our drunk visitor."

"I'm not touching it," Dani moaned through her hands.

"Me neither." He pointed at the trail of water leading from the bathroom to the door. "But maybe he left some of his clothes behind."

Malone walked through the apartment, telling Dani to stay put, and she heard him yank the chain dangling from the bathroom light. No glow emanated from the space.

"It's burnt out. But there's nothing in here but more puke and bathwater," he called. "He must have cleaned up enough to leave."

She made her way to the couch, her nose tucked into her shoulder to relieve some of her discomfort. The end of the sofa, where his feet had been, was splattered with vomit too, all but the arm rest. She touched it tentatively, grimacing, trying to listen amid the rancid distraction. She felt nothing but sadness. Confusion. And layer upon layer of life, none of it specific. None of it helpful. She thought she heard Jacob again, chanting his terms in the same hopeless monotone.

"Nothing?" Malone asked.

She shook her head.

She stepped away and reached for the drapes. Malone moved beside her, his arm wrapped around his lower face so he could breathe into his elbow.

The curtains were dark and warm, absorbing the light from the window, and for a minute their warmth obscured what was beneath. Like clothing on a corpse.

Dani shuddered and let go. Her palms stung as though she'd fallen on frozen ground, and she rubbed them down her skirt. It was a sensation she was not accustomed to, that undercurrent of cold, and she didn't know what to make of it.

"Let's get out of here," Malone insisted. But she shook her head and reached for the panels once more, bracing herself like one would brace for the wind. The sun was too bright, and she grimaced against it, the rays turning the backs of her lids red. She buried her face in the dusty cloth, and the red became black. She coughed and the cold skittered over her cheeks and down her throat, burning her the way ice burned.

She just needed a name, and then she would let go.

"Jacob?" she murmured. "Is that you?"

He'd contemplated death here. Standing right here. His own. His father's. His mother's. So much death. And he did not fear it. He longed for it.

No. Not Jacob. This was not the hopelessness of a drained medical student teetering on the edge of severe depression.

This was different.

Someone else had stood, clinging to these drapes, waiting for the darkness to lift. Many times. Her fingers felt like claws, rigid and cold, but she climbed higher, finding her grip. Right there. He was taller than she, and his hands had twisted in the folds above her head. His hands . . . whose hands?

"Dani?" Malone's voice seemed far away, a voice in the mouth of a cave, but she moved deeper into the frigid darkness, the cold seeping into her limbs and slowing her heartbeat.

"He doesn't know who he is," she said, but her voice was small and hollow, the cavern growing bigger and bigger around her, and she wasn't sure Michael even heard her. She tried harder, pushing around her frozen tongue.

"He's many people."

"Who?" Malone's voice was as distorted and faint as her own, and she tried to answer, to tell him to wait. She tried to let go, but she couldn't feel the curtains anymore. She couldn't feel her *self*. She was just one of the many, hovering in the icy dark.

"Who are you?" she asked them. "What are your names?"

One whisper, then another, like a colony of bats dripping from the stony darkness above her head. But the murmurs told her nothing. She only knew she was not alone.

"I will help you find your names," she said, but the words were whisked away as soon as she formed them.

She needed to touch them. She could not help them if she could not touch them. But she had no hands. No eyes. No ears. No tongue. And no names.

~

Dani wouldn't let go of the drapes. Her hands were clamped around the folds and she clung, her eyes closed, her legs buckling, a golden-haloed witch tied to a whipping post, barely conscious. This did not resemble the dreamy Dani with her enlarged pupils and her searching touch. This was something else.

He swept her up in his arms and stepped away from the drapes, attempting to pull her hands free.

"Let go, Dani," he roared, but she didn't react. Her fingers were like icicles, sharp and frail, and he feared he would break them if he forced them free.

He sank down to his knees, bringing her with him, using her body weight to assist his efforts. She jerked, her arms fully extended, her grip unyielding, but the fabric was taut. He wrapped his fingers around her wrist and tugged at the cloth, freeing one hand and then the other before scooping her up again and staggering for the door, half convinced the curtains would twine around his legs and pull them both down into whatever pit he'd dragged her from.

He didn't close the door behind him, and he hardly remembered descending the stairs, Dani cold and motionless in his arms. Goddamn it, she was so cold. He had to get her warm. It was all he knew to do. Get her warm and wake her up.

He must have looked a sight, half running, his arms full of unconscious woman as he cut across the Rauses' lawn, which was wholly visible from the busy street. It was a wonder no one honked or stopped or contacted the authorities. But the sun was sinking, and the sky was a frothy pink, and maybe he simply looked like a man clinging to his love, and not a man running for his life, though later it would occur to him he was doing both.

He crashed through the laundry room door and barreled down the hall and into the bathroom, this time pausing long enough to secure the door and thank providence that Margaret would have gone home, and the aunts would most likely be upstairs.

He toed off his shoes and stepped into the wide tub and settled her between his legs, turning on the water as hot as he could bear it. Her head lolled against him and he tightened his arms, but breath fluttered between her lips, and when he pressed his fingers to the column of her throat, he could feel her heartbeat.

"Dani," he begged. "Dani, where are you?"

He made a quick inventory. Three of her nails on her left hand and all of the nails on her right were bleeding and they would be sore, but her fingers appeared unbroken. He pressed them to his lips, the way a parent does with a child, though he knew he was consoling himself. Was it just last night he'd kissed her hand? Good God, he'd aged ten years in mere hours.

"Dani?" he repeated, smoothing her hair back from her brow. The water was rising, steam billowed around them, and her skin was starting to pinken.

Then her eyes opened, and awareness descended. She blinked, blinked again, and then lifted her head slightly from the crook of his shoulder, her expression bemused. A damp tendril clung to her cheek and she swiped at it.

"I haven't missed my room . . . but I have missed this tub," she murmured.

He almost laughed in sheer relief. "Oh yeah?"

"Yes. It's delightfully large. As you can see. And very comfortable for a long soak."

"It is. I've enjoyed it very much."

"Hmm. Good. That's good. I'm glad," she said. "But why . . . why exactly . . . are we here?" she asked. "In our clothes?"

He wiped at the bead of sweat trickling down his nose and reached for the faucet, turning it off. Dani's dress tangled around his legs, and he'd lost two buttons on his shirt in the scuffle. It gaped, revealing his sodden undershirt beneath.

"What's the last thing you remember?" he asked.

She puzzled over that question and then laid her head down against him again.

"Zuzana is scared. That's why she said those things at breakfast. She's afraid I will leave her. Like my mother did."

"And that's the last thing you remember?" he asked, dumbfounded.

"No," she said. "But now . . . now you're going to think she's right."

Breakfast seemed like a lifetime ago, and it was hardly relevant to the current situation. "Right about what?"

"That's never happened to me before," she whispered, not answering him directly. "I promise I'm not crazy."

"What's never happened to you before?" he pushed.

"I've never fainted before." She stopped talking and burrowed down into him, the water sloshing over the side and hitting the floor with a wet slap.

"You're going to have to do better than that, sweetheart. You scared the hell out of me." His voice was sharp, but his hands were gentle as he lifted her off him, setting her back against the opposite side of the tub so he could assess her condition. So he could consider his own.

"I'm sorry, Michael," she said, but it wasn't an apology he was looking for. It was an explanation.

"You grabbed hold of those drapes . . . and something grabbed ahold of you."

"It wasn't like that. Not exactly." She began to shake again, and he turned the water on once more, pulling her beneath the spout so the hot water streamed down her back.

"Tell me what you saw," he insisted.

"I didn't *see* anything." She shook her head, but her denial was belied by the fear in her eyes. "It was dark. And cold. And there were no names. Or faces, or memories. There was no love or life."

"You said, 'He doesn't know who he is,'" he reminded her, keeping his voice hard. He wanted to comfort her. He wanted to draw her into his arms and stroke her back and kiss her brow. But that would solve nothing. He turned off the spigot again.

"There were no names," Dani said, shifting and sinking down so her shoulders were below the surface. She clung to the sides, her knees drawn up against her chest, and he stretched out his legs, bracketing her between them again.

"He is many people," Malone challenged softly. "You said that too."

"I think that is what he believes."

"What does that mean, Dani?" He was trying so hard to be patient, but he was lost.

"I don't know. Maybe he is like Pavel. Maybe he is like . . . me." She winced.

"Like you?" he repeated.

"Like a . . . Kos."

"How so?" He frowned.

"Pavel described his ability—or ailment—as hearing voices. Vera described it the same way, but the voice she heard was always the cloth itself, telling her what it wanted to be. Pavel said the cloth yammered at him and stole all his ideas. He had a stroke and died three months after I came to live here, but I think he was mad long before that. Maybe the Butcher hears voices too."

"Do you hear voices, Dani?" he asked. "Do you believe you are many people?"

"No. It isn't like that for me. It has *never* been like that for me." She was almost pleading with him.

"Well then. He's not like you, now is he?" he said simply.

"No," she sighed. "No. I don't think he is. But he is odd, Michael. He is very . . . odd." She sounded precariously close to tears, though her face did not crumple and her gaze did not waver.

Ah. He thought maybe he understood now. She wasn't upset by what she saw—or not entirely. She was afraid of what *he* was going to think of it all. *Good God.*

"When I was young . . . I could see things others couldn't," he said.

"Like what?"

"Colors, mostly. Auras. I thought everyone could see them . . . until my mother explained that I was special."

"Auras?"

"That was her word for it. I called them shadows, though they were colorful, and often not dark at all."

"What kind of colors?" she breathed.

"Every shade and hue. Even colors that don't have names. Everyone had their own. My mother's was grass green. My father's, a rusty red. Molly's was violet . . . like the sky right before sunrise. I couldn't see them all the time, but often enough that it was very normal for me. When my mother died, the colors went away. Or maybe I simply stopped acknowledging them."

"You don't see them anymore?"

"Sometimes I do. Yours is warm . . . amber . . . like sunlight on honey."

She stared at him, dumbfounded, but there was a flush to her cheeks and a softness in her gaze.

He cleared his throat. Enough of that. "You are not odd, Dani," he said. "Not in the way you mean. You always say that. But you are strong and good and wise. And you are kind. Those things are not odd. They are precious."

She smiled like he had set her free, her off-kilter eyes brimming as she beamed at him, and he stood abruptly, the water sluicing from his clothes. He unbuttoned his shirt and shrugged it off, wringing it out before tossing it into the sink. He started pulling off his undershirt and Dani's jaw dropped.

"Cover your eyes," he barked. She did so immediately, and he peeled off his undershirt and gave it the same treatment. His trousers and socks followed, but he left on his shorts, wringing them out by the fistfuls before he stepped out of the tub and pulled a towel from the cupboard across from the sink. He mopped at the floor so she would not slip when she alighted and wrapped another towel around his waist before setting one within her reach.

"I will go dress and then bring you my robe so you can get out of those clothes. Are you steady now?"

"Yes," she promised, still covering her eyes. Her nails were shredded, but she hadn't complained. The sight of her raw fingers made his stomach roil, and he turned toward the door, suddenly reeling once more. Maybe *he* wasn't steady. He stepped out into the hall, filling his lungs with cooler air, and pulled the door closed behind him. But he did not leave his post. Instead, he listened for Dani, fearful she would fall. The sounds of wringing and wiggling and the weight of wet clothes being discarded reassured him, and he left her to retrieve his robe as he had promised.

Lenka and Zuzana had retreated to their quiet corners when he climbed the stairs, but there was cold ham and potatoes in the icebox. He made two plates and poured two glasses of milk, and ate his while he waited for Dani, listening to her movements while he filled the hollows of his anxious belly.

She was clear-eyed and composed when she joined him at the kitchen table a half hour later, but she used her fingers gingerly and ate like she was forcing herself to do so. He waited on her, counting her bites and clearing the dishes when she was through. And when she excused herself with a wan smile, pleading for sleep, he trailed behind her like a hovering nursemaid.

"Michael. I am simply tired. That is all," she said.

"I know," he said, defensive, and he said good night, but he lingered outside her door and waited for her to put out her light. She didn't.

He knocked softly and, when she bid him come in, stuck his head around the frame.

"Can I just sit with you for a bit?" he asked, his chest hot and his palms wet. "I . . . I am unsettled, I suppose."

"All right," she said, folding her hands beneath her cheek. She yawned and closed her eyes, and he sat down on the chair by her door. The seat was upholstered with twining vines and little yellow flowers, and a fat spool of thread and a stack of doilies sat in a basket beside it. He'd seen Dani's fingers flying with needle and thread, creating her lace. Her hands were always busy, always working, and he wondered briefly if she enjoyed it or if she'd never had another choice.

He clasped his hands in his lap and rested his head against her wall beneath the picture of George Flanagan and Darby O'Shea wearing new suits and matching smirks. A St. Christopher medallion on a chain was looped around the corner of the frame. Dani's deference to her aunts had not extended to O'Shea's gifts, clearly.

It was a good picture. A hopeful one. And terribly sad. George Flanagan was gone, and neither of the men in the picture or the little medallion would protect her. He certainly hadn't. Every time he shut his eyes, he saw Dani, hanging limply with her hands tangled in the drapes.

"Michael?" She was watching him, her brow furrowed but her lips soft.

"Hmm?"

"Sometimes the dead, their humanity roars into me, like a stack of old papers catching fire. And other times . . . there is no glow at all. There are simply flickering images, flat and cold and impersonal. A candle in a far-off window, yet not even *that* hopeful. Not even that warm."

"It takes a lot of fuel to keep a fire burning. People are suffering."

"It is not suffering that stamps out the flame. It is hopelessness. When we stop believing . . . it seems like we slowly lose our humanity."

"Stop believing in what?"

"Love."

He sighed, a great whooshing of air, a gusty protest. "You lost me there."

"You think I'm a fool."

"No. Just . . . young."

"It was him. The Butcher. He lived in those rooms."

"You think what you felt—*who* you felt—was the Butcher?" he clarified.

"Yes. There is no light in him at all. I've never felt quite that level of dissonance . . . or disassociation, especially in the living. He is living, isn't he? What I felt did not feel human . . . though I'm sure it was. What do you call a human when they've rejected their humanity and everyone else's too?"

"A monster."

"Yes." She hesitated and then pushed herself up, like she needed to be upright for what came next. Her voice was apologetic. "And I was not prepared for a monster and didn't handle it well. I frightened you, and I'm sorry. But I *will* recognize him when I feel him again. And next time . . . I will know to let go immediately." She seemed sheepish, like she'd tripped or misjudged her own strength.

He groaned out loud and pressed his palms into his eyes. *Next time.* God forbid. He would not survive a next time.

"We're never going back into that apartment, Dani Flanagan."

"No, I didn't think we would. And I confess, I don't want to. But you *will* take me to see Mr. Ness? Won't you? You'll let me touch the victims' things? We're going to catch him, Michael. We've found him."

"But you did catch him!" he shot back, almost accusing. "You caught him. That's what you felt. You locked hands with pure evil, and it almost dragged you under."

"And you dragged me back," she said quietly, like he was the brave hero, and all was well. He rose, unable to sit with his disquiet and her beatific confidence. He paced, five steps one way, five steps the next, and Dani watched him, her eyes gentle. The gold from her hair seeped out around her, limning her, and he rubbed at his temples, though he knew it wouldn't help. Her light was impossible to ignore.

He was weary. She was weary. He should let her sleep.

Terror rose in his breast once more. He didn't want her to sleep. He didn't want her to be still and quiet.

"I have never been so afraid in my whole life," he ground out. "Not when I went to France, not when my wife told me to leave, not even when my Mary died. I was too naive to be afraid, and I expected all to be well. But she died, and I realized all is not well. All is *never* well. I've been a fatalist ever since. But tonight, I was afraid."

"Oh, my darling. Forgive me," she begged softly.

He gazed at her, dumbfounded. She'd called him "darling."

"I know it is hard to understand. What I see. And what I feel. It is even harder to explain," she said, rueful. "Tonight was a new experience for both of us. But I don't think I was in any real danger. Not from the Butcher. He was not there . . . not physically. I was just taken by surprise, sent into shock, I suppose, and I . . . fainted. It's embarrassing, really. I feel silly. I was quite the damsel in distress, wasn't I?"

"You scared me," he repeated.

"But you're not scared *of* me?" she clarified.

"No, Dani. I'm not scared *of* you." Not in the way she meant. The simplicity and frankness with which she described her abilities, and herself, was what had made him believe her on that train a decade and a half ago. It was what made him believe her now.

In many ways, she was the most remarkably untangled human being he'd ever encountered. Complex but not complicated. Deep but not dark. It was as if she stood with her arms wide open and said, *Here I am*, and the world nodded and said, *Yes, you are*, and gave her a wide berth, not out of fear, but out of reverence.

To not believe in her would be like not believing in the sun. The sun simply was—it shined, it set, it rose, it waned—and it had no need to please or persuade. That was Dani. And he suspected he was in love with her. So no, he was not afraid.

He was terrified.

"Will you let me hold on to you for a minute?" he asked, voice strained, echoing her request from the previous evening. "Just for a while. I'll be gone when you wake."

Her throat moved and then she nodded.

She rolled to the other side of the bed and he turned off the lamp, stretching out beside her. When he pulled her into his arms, her back to his chest, she came willingly, and sleep found them both.

19

Dani stayed in bed all Sunday. The last time she could remember doing such a thing was when she'd contracted the chicken pox at twelve and been covered with pink blisters. Different-colored eyes, orange hair, and spots were too much for the public, and she'd been relegated to her room, though she'd felt just fine, beyond the intolerable itch.

She didn't feel "just fine" today. She couldn't bear the thimble on her thumb or thread a needle with her sore fingers, but worse than that was the bone-deep weariness and the throbbing in her head. So she slept, and no one complained. Michael checked on her, the aunts too, but then the aunts went to Mass—it was Palm Sunday after all—and Michael went back to his old ways.

In the days that followed, he was watchful and grim and careful not to get too close. She'd seen something in his face when he'd asked to hold on to her, the way she'd asked to hold on to him. But the next morning the look was gone. Or shuttered. He was good at setting aside his feelings. He boxed them up tight and labeled them neatly, the way he made his lists and organized his details.

She'd tried to catch his scent on her sheets and see his thoughts by pressing her palm into the indentation of his head on her pillow, but the longing she felt was inseparable from her own.

The Easter rush continued at the shop, and Michael accompanied her to the morgue twice, but he was stiff and short on conversation, and when she pressed him again about seeing the evidence, he avoided setting a firm date.

"I have a few other ideas we will try first," he hedged. "I need Eliot's help to get into the evidence room at headquarters, and he's being hounded at the moment. I thought we might visit the rooms Flo Polillo and Rose Wallace rented and see if their landlords still have any of their things. Clothing and the like. You could go through that, see if you catch a hint of something. Though . . . you are forbidden from touching the drapes."

She'd smiled at his attempt to jest, but the quirk of his lips didn't reach his eyes.

"And maybe something more will be found of the woman—Victim Number Ten—and there will be something new for you to examine," he added. "Something that hasn't been combed over and handled and mislabeled. I don't have much confidence that you'll learn anything we can use from old evidence."

"Are you sure? Because I think that's exactly what you're afraid of," she broached gently. "I will be fine, Malone. You must believe me."

He'd simply grunted and turned back to his morning newspaper, and she let it go.

All week long, search parties dragged the river and walked the banks, their eyes on the ground, looking for bits of flesh the way the children scoured the grass in Euclid Beach Park for colored eggs. But Easter came and went without a single find. No flesh. No matching leg or severed feet. No head or bisected torso, and no clues about who was dead and who had done it.

Michael must have told Ness about Emil Fronek and the apartment above the clinic because detectives came and searched the premises, interviewing Dr. Peterka and the whole staff. Sybil had come to the shop in a huff looking for Malone and had left with a new hat and a pair of gloves, slightly mollified by her purchases and the chance to spill every morsel of gossip she'd collected. Dani had listened raptly to the office intrigue: the doctors were offended by the detectives' questions, Peterka had provided police with a list of renters for the last ten years, and they had to close the office for the rest of the week to deal with the upheaval.

The couch had been carried out, the drapes too, and workmen had come in to begin Dr. Peterka's remodel of the space and change the locks on the door. Malone had made good and sure she wouldn't be tangling with the curtains again or catching the scent of a killer.

~

Eliot didn't know anything more two weeks after the discovery of the woman's calf than Malone had learned from Coroner Gerber's press conference the night it was found. But the papers led with the story of the left leg and the latest "work of the Butcher" every single day, rehashing the previous cases, and castigating everyone from President Roosevelt to railroad security for turning their backs on "Cleveland's most vulnerable." Cleveland's *Plain Dealer* ran a sprawling front page letter to the editor penned by none other than Martin L. Sweeney, congressman of the Twentieth District. He claimed Eliot Ness was more interested in traffic control and courting the press than protecting Clevelanders from madmen.

"He's playing with his police radio, wasting taxpayer dollars, and organizing wayward boys while the people of this city cower in their homes, wondering who will be next. Cleveland deserves better," he wrote.

Cleveland did deserve better—nobody deserved what the Butcher did to them—but Malone knew people rarely got what they deserved, good or bad, and Eliot was neither Cleveland's problem nor Cleveland's solution, though he'd been hailed as one. Maybe that was the rub. Everyone wanted the man who took down Al Capone, and the Butcher was an entirely different beast. Capone had also been in the government's crosshairs. This time, there was no target. The Butcher was a phantom nobody wanted to name.

Malone and Ness had a sit-down with David Cowles on Friday, April 22, in Eliot's office at city hall. It wasn't the most private of locations, especially going in and out, but Eliot had picked up some persistent tagalongs in the last week and told Malone he better come to him until the storm passed. Malone hadn't yet told Ness about the "big guy's" interest or Irey's ultimatum. Ness didn't need the added pressure, but at the rate it was going, the storm wasn't going to pass without a major break.

Cowles was consulting with crime labs and criminologists all over the country, and he brought Malone up to speed on their mostly unhelpful assessments. Eliot listened to the conversation with bruised eyes and slumped shoulders but added little. There was simply no real news and no developments.

"Eliot says you have an expert," Cowles said to Malone, his gaze curious. Hopeful.

"Yeah. I do," Malone replied, glancing at Ness. He'd thought maybe Eliot had forgotten the conversation with all the chaos. He obviously hadn't. Dani hadn't forgotten either, and she was persistent, even eager, about getting her magic hands on the evidence. But with the new victim and no new information in the last two weeks, reporters were rabid, and Malone had become more and more opposed to the idea of bringing Dani into the investigation in any way.

"I don't want anyone getting curious about her. It wouldn't be good for Ness." It wouldn't be good for Dani either.

Cowles frowned and Eliot straightened in his chair. "How so?" Cowles asked.

"The papers are clamoring for information. They want stories. They get a whiff of her—if anyone gets a whiff of her—they'll put it in the papers. They've got nothing else to talk about," Malone said. "So we need to keep it quiet. And private."

"What kind of expert are we talking about?" Cowles pressed.

"She's an ugly seamstress," Eliot said, straight-faced but with a twinkle in his eye. It was the first sign of good humor Malone had seen in him since the leg had been discovered.

"Huh," Cowles grunted. "All right. Guess it can't hurt. We've traced the laundry marks, though, in the few items that have them. So far nothing's come of it."

"Say when, Mike," Ness said.

"Next Saturday night," Malone said. "You can get us into the evidence locker without anybody getting too nosy about what we're doing, right?"

"Next Saturday is the damn Spring Gala at St. Alexis." Eliot sighed. "Press. Politicos. Fundraising. The diocese and the nuns have turned it into an annual arm twisting, and nobody gets out of it without a public shaming or a huge check, but it keeps the hospital and Catholic charities going, and I have to make an appearance."

"Even better. It'll be a good distraction," Malone said. "We can do it after."

"You're right," Ness agreed. "Everyone will be there, occupied and accounted for. Staff will be light at headquarters, even lighter than usual on a Saturday night. And we won't have any reporters lurking with the gala in swing."

"Can you get me two tickets?" Malone asked, an idea surfacing.

Ness raised his brows, surprised. "You want to come to the gala?"

"It's at St. Alexis itself, the hospital?"

"Yeah. The dining hall doubles as a ballroom. It has a stage where the orchestra sits, and they clear the center of tables for dancing. People dress to the nines—full tails and evening gowns—and it's quite the event. It wouldn't be so bad if I had a wife."

Cowles shifted uncomfortably, and Ness blushed like he hadn't meant to say that last bit. He laughed at himself, sheepish. "On the bright side . . . maybe after the gala the papers will be talking about my love life and ignoring the fact that I can't seem to find the Mad Butcher of Kingsbury Run."

Cowles didn't look optimistic. "Can't we do it any sooner? Next Saturday is more than a week away. We need a direction, Malone. We've got nothing. If you think your expert can give us something new, I want to talk to her now. Tonight."

"You get a call from Irey, Cowles?" Malone asked. Ness's eyebrows shot up, and the bureau man's shoulders sank.

"Yeah. I did. Lotta talk about Germany winning the propaganda war and Cleveland getting their federal contracts pulled if this thing doesn't go away immediately."

"I got that call too," Malone said. "David's right, Ness. Sooner is better."

"Well, damn." Ness sighed, scrubbing at his face. "So that's how it is? I've been wondering when the brass was going to start throwing their weight around. How long do I have?"

"We need a break," Cowles said. "We need it now."

"Or what?" Ness pressed, grim.

"Or all your programs—work with the boy gangs, traffic safety, police reform—it won't mean a thing," David answered, frank. "Mayor Burton will let you take the fall just to make it look like somebody's doing something. I heard he's going to run for Senate next go-round, just to get out of Cleveland. But everyone's gunning for you, Ness."

Ness looked at Malone. Malone stared back. Ness didn't get petulant or accusatory. He just clasped his hands and crossed his legs. "Well . . .

then we better not wait. Can you get Miss Kos back here tonight, Mike? This place will be a ghost town by eight o'clock. Cowles can arrange for the evidence to be brought here. He'll vouch for chain of custody, and we'll keep it by the book. That way you don't have to deal with anyone but us and maybe a couple officers to escort the boxes back and forth, but they can be outside the room. That way no clerk working the evidence locker will know you and Miss Kos are involved, and we won't have any detectives dropping by and seeing us there."

Malone promised to have Dani at city hall at eight o'clock. He had no doubt she would be willing and eager. But he felt sick. He'd been dragging his feet, trying to get out of it, and now he was committed. The truth was, he wasn't sure he could endure another encounter with whatever had dropped Dani in a cold faint.

～

Dani told her aunts Malone was taking her to the picture show after dinner. Lenka looked so tickled and Zuzana so stricken that Malone almost confessed, not sure which reaction alarmed him most. But Dani couldn't very well tell them the truth, so they left the house at seven thirty, too early for the eight o'clock show at the Olympia, but it worked as an alibi.

"Don't wait up," Dani told them, and Malone studiously avoided looking directly at either aunt.

Dani was excited, her cheeks bright and her back so straight it didn't touch the seat. He did his best to give her an idea of what he thought she could expect, and when they pulled up in front of city hall, he didn't bring her in through the entrance but circled around the massive edifice to an unmarked side door, where Ness was waiting, having a smoke, just as they'd planned.

He didn't make introductions—that could happen inside—but Ness glanced at him as she stepped past, a darting look of bafflement, and Malone knew what he was thinking. Dani wasn't at all what Malone had led him to believe.

They were met by Cowles in a room filled with a long conference table stacked with boxes marked with case numbers, and Malone shrugged off his overcoat and took Dani's, tossing them over a chair.

"How do we want to do this, Miss Kos?" Ness asked. "The victims are numbered, and we don't have evidence—not clothing, at least—from all of them. Do you have a preference for the order or way in which we proceed, and do you mind if David and I take notes?"

"Uh, no. Of course not. I'm sure Michael will as well. He has a penchant for lists." She blushed as if she'd said too much. "But I would actually prefer . . . not to know which victim the item was found with. I don't want to know anything that might cause me to make . . . assumptions about what I'm seeing. I would really rather not know anything at all."

It was a good idea. Malone should have thought of it himself.

"The case numbers won't give that away," Cowles said. "And I haven't organized the evidence, as I wasn't certain about how we would proceed. It's all just . . . here." He indicated the boxes. "We'll be able to cross reference what the items are after you have a look, so that we know which victims we're dealing with."

"So . . . just garments?" Ness asked.

"Leather. Burlap. Cloth. Anything fabric," Malone instructed. "Just let her hold on to it for a minute and give us her impressions. I'll jot down what she says and put a description and a case number notation along with it. You and David can do the same if you like. But I'll be taking my notes with me, for my own reference."

"Let's proceed then," David said, the expression on his face an indicator that he didn't expect much. Malone's stomach twisted, but he took a seat and accepted the pad of paper and the pencil Eliot offered him. Dani remained standing beside him.

Her cap of red-gold hair, parted at the side and waving to her shoulders, was in deep contrast to the icy blue of her dress and the deep red of her lips. Her hands were clasped behind her back, drawing the eye to the shape of her bust and the pale length of her throat. She didn't stand that way for effect, he knew. It was her habit, a way to avoid touching what might distract her.

Eliot cleared his throat but took a seat at the head of the table, steering clear of the boxes. David Cowles remained standing as well, across from Dani, and pulled the first box toward him. He picked through it, pushed it aside, and moved on to the next. He placed a pair of plain white underpants on the table—Malone knew immediately which victim they'd been found with—and read the case number off, his voice ringing with discomfort.

~

Dani didn't want to embarrass Malone. She knew he'd put himself in a vulnerable position. The two men wouldn't believe her, and he would bear the brunt of that disbelief. She would simply go back home to her life and her work, but this *was* his life and work, and yet here he was, sitting beside her, waiting for her to do her voodoo, as he liked to call it.

She reached for the pair of panties, her face hot and her fingers cold. She pressed the fabric between her palms and, like a stone dropped in a pool, allowed her own thoughts to ripple away and the cloth in her hand to pull her under.

"She never wore these," she said at once.

"Who?" Ness asked.

She thought she knew; she'd read Michael's lists, though now she wished she hadn't, but she wasn't getting the name from the cloth. "I don't know," she said truthfully.

"They were found with Florence Polillo, Victim Number Three," Cowles told Ness.

"David," Malone grunted.

David looked baffled, and Dani continued, searching the fabric for something more. "She put them in her coat pocket when she left home. She thought she might need them. But they were . . . new. She never wore them."

"How do you know that?" Cowles interjected. "You aren't even looking at them."

"David, if you can't shut up, we're going to go. Okay?" Malone snapped.

His eyes widened. Michael hadn't clarified what she could do, obviously, and the tension in the room was already palpable.

"People—all people—have an essence." She attempted a brief explanation. "Like a . . . signature scent. The things they touch, especially for a long period of time, absorb that essence. You smoke in a room once . . . it fades. You smoke in a room every day? That scent never leaves."

"You can smell Florence Polillo?" Cowles asked.

Malone vibrated beside her, but she didn't think the man was being disrespectful. Not really. He'd just been caught unawares. Ness was observing silently, but his eyes, as blue and guileless as a child's, were wide.

"Sort of," she said. "It's a bit . . . hard to explain. But these are new. So there isn't much . . . there."

"Can we proceed?" Malone asked. "This will go much quicker if you don't interrupt. You'll start to understand. And keep in mind, she's helping us."

Dani set the item down. When Cowles reached for it, she entreated, "Don't put them back. Please. I'd like to come back to them, if I could."

He shrugged and went on to the next item from a different box and read the evidence number. He turned over a large envelope, and a pair of men's black socks slid out onto the table. Malone swore, and she sat down on the chair she'd pushed aside, a little weak in the knees.

Again, she knew too much. Edward Andrassy, the first victim, had been found wearing only his socks. She suspected these were his.

"Something else," Malone barked, but Dani reached forward and took them. Holding a sock in each hand, she braced herself for something similar to the cold she'd felt in the drapes. But the socks had not been handled or worn in a long time. She bore down and was met with a weary haze.

"He was drunk. Or . . . dizzy. And he was tired." She tried to look beneath the fog. "And his toes were cold. Dr. Frank put his socks back on when he begged."

Sadness welled, but it was her own.

"Dr. Frank?" Ness asked.

"Yes." She nodded. "That's what he thought. He was grateful." The impressions were brief, faint pinpricks in the night sky.

"What's his name, Dani?" Malone asked softly.

"Andrassy. He's proud of his name, but he's not proud of himself."

She felt a flash of fear, a tug on her wrists, and the smell of something sharp and chemical bit her nostrils before the ripples ceased. She cataloged each impression for the men. Eliot Ness was scribbling notes and David Cowles was frowning.

"You can *smell* it?" Cowles asked, still stuck on that word.

She looked at Malone, helpless, but then shrugged and nodded. It was too simplistic an explanation, but it worked.

"Scent fades. But imagine that you have gasoline on your hands when you touch someone's coat. That scent will stay for a long time. Some things are like gasoline. Fear is like gasoline."

She set the socks down.

"Hold my hands for a minute, Michael," she asked, and he obeyed, engulfing her hands in his.

"And why do you do that?" Ness asked, surprise in every word, but she didn't look at him.

"It . . . um . . . cleanses the palate," Malone said, gruff, and he didn't look at him either. The tips of his ears were a deep red, but he held her hands until she pulled away and moved on to the next items.

A small stack of clothing belonged to a man named Eddie. Eddie, who drove the ladies all over town. Victim #2, who'd never been named, whose checkered hat was found by Steve Jeziorski. She did her best to separate what she already knew from what the cloth told her and was confident in his name.

"The guy who wore those is Eddie too?" Malone clarified. "Not Andrassy?"

She picked up a bit of cloth she thought was a rag, and realized it was yet another pair of underpants, though just a piece.

"Ready Eddie," she said, listening. "That's how he thought of himself. The chauffeur. Steve Jeziorski gave you his cap." She felt herself blanch.

"What?" Malone asked.

"I saw his . . . um. His male part. He was quite proud of it."

The room was silent.

"Ready Eddie," she murmured. "He was always . . . ready."

"Wasn't he emasculated?" Cowles asked.

"He wasn't aware of that," she whispered. "I believe that happened . . . after." She dropped the piece of cloth.

"Next," Malone ground out. She thought he was going to march her out of the room after that, but he sat stoically, listening, holding her hands, and writing his notes as she continued.

For the most part, the images faded quickly, and nothing that remained was especially potent or powerful. Time had left its own layers on the cloth. But there was a whisper of cold she began to recognize, an icy fingerprint that glanced off her pulse.

Sometimes she felt nothing at all, and sometimes a snippet sprang to mind before it dissolved. She repeated each impression dutifully, resisting the need to sway or convince the two men who listened and doubted. She was not there for herself. She was not even there for Michael, though she cared far too much about what he thought. She was there for the nameless.

"He was good at cards," she said after a particularly fruitless stretch. "But not good enough. He lost more than he won. But at least they never hid their faces."

"Who?"

"The cards." She changed her grip, trying to chase the impression, but it was gone, snuffed out.

"Got a name?"

She ran her fingers lightly over the inside of the shirt collar, where it would rub against the back of the neck. It was a place that often yielded something.

"Robert Weitzel," she said, grasping the whisper that brought a draft, gossamer and glancing. Then both were gone.

"You sure?" Malone asked.

She tried to confirm it, then shook her head. "I heard it, but it was faint."

"Anything else?" he asked, but she shook her head again. "These things sat awhile in the sun and rain. Just like colors fade, so do memories."

There were some boxes that held several items—shoes, belt, trousers, shorts, suitcoats—but the impressions from each tended to be the same, though some were easier to read. A pair of russet-brown oxfords in one such box flooded her thoughts with a burst of color followed by a persistent pricking sensation. She dropped the shoes with a yelp and tried again, careful not to press her palms so firmly against the soles.

"He has no pictures of the things he loves. The people he loves. So he put them on his skin. It was the way he carried them with him."

"The tattooed man?" Ness asked.

"Yes." She nodded eagerly. "Tattoos. He has plans for more. Many more."

She searched through his other things, looking for clues that came in complete thoughts.

"He thought of himself as Chuck . . . and Grift. Sometimes Grift," she added.

"Any idea about the initials, WCG?" Malone asked.

She listened, but the impression stayed the same. "Chuck and Grift."

"The name William Charles Griffiths came up somewhere—a tip or a telegraph," Malone said. "Make a note for your detectives to revisit that tip."

Toward the end of the night, a grayish knit cap, tasseled and filthy, netted a name and a flash of insight that burned a little brighter and longer than the rest.

"She sang when she was alone. Hymns. She loves the hymns. She knew she shouldn't. Sinner that she was. Hymns were for the believers. Sometimes she sang the hymns when she was with a man. Sometimes the men laughed, like she was singing their praises. Most of the time they made her stop. Hymns strip us down. Naked men don't want their souls on display." She spoke quickly, almost babbling, but she was trying to keep up with the swell before it crashed and receded.

"She has a son who's all grown up, but she doesn't tell anyone. They'll think she's old, and she needs to stay young and pretty . . . like her name. Rose. Her name is Rose Wallace. She looks better than the white girls. Her skin is holding up. Her figure too. But she feels old inside."

The room was silent as she chased the current, but it was gone as quickly as it had come.

"Why do you get more with some things?" Eliot asked.

"She liked this hat. Wore it often, I suspect. And hats don't get laundered much . . . if at all."

"None of these things have been laundered," Cowles argued.

"No. But a hat isn't laundered hardly ever. Even a knit cap like this. Washing doesn't remove the ground-in memories, ones reinforced and layered over the years. But it can—and does—obscure details and specifics. If an item is freshly laundered, often I'm just left with a sense—not a specific scent—of the person who owned it."

"So some things . . . reveal more?"

"Yes. Shoes. Coats. A hat one wears every day. Hats sit on our heads too, where thought is centered. A pillow can be quite telling. A handkerchief that is carried in the same pocket, year after year." Malone shifted in his chair.

"And some fabrics reveal more. Cotton talks. It absorbs everything. Silk is a little more coy. It clings, but it's fragile too, and the weave is very tight. Very small. It doesn't absorb anything."

"And leather?" Ness asked, intrigued.

"Leather takes time. It's tougher. But I could probably get something from a belt someone's owned for a while. Or a holster."

"Even an empty one?" Cowles asked, his tone wry. "Eliot wears a holster but never carries a gun."

"Let her hold your holster, Eliot. Maybe she can explain that one to us," Malone said.

"I'm not letting her anywhere near me," Eliot said, a small smile playing around his lips. "That was impressive, Miss Kos."

"Thank you. Is there anything else?" She desperately hoped there was nothing else. Her head ached and her stomach was gnawing a hole in her back.

"Just one more. On January seventeenth, someone found some bloody women's clothing in an empty lot on East Sixty-Fifth, not too far from Jackass Hill. There's a coat among the items. People don't abandon their coats. They don't generally bleed on them either. We've been waiting for a body to turn up."

"A body did turn up," Cowles said. "Remember Victim Number Ten?"

"We don't know if they're even connected to the Butcher at all. But . . . maybe you can tell us something," Ness said.

"All right."

Cowles moved to the end of the table and took a black coat from a box. He set it in front of her and then added a black cloche hat beside it. Both were caked and stiff in areas, though with filth or blood, she didn't know. She closed her eyes, trying to ease the pounding for one last look.

"You don't have to do anything you don't want to do, Dani," Malone reminded her, his voice low. "And don't forget to let go."

She reached for the coat with timid hands. She immediately smelled coal and newsprint, sharp and black and tinged with . . . glee?

"He thinks he is very funny. He leaves these things for you, Mr. Ness. Along with lots of fun clues that mean nothing at all."

"Dani?" Malone warned.

"Who?" Ness asked.

"I'm not sure. It was just an impression of amusement and your name in the papers."

The ink and merriment were quickly drowned out by stronger currents.

"These belong to Flo Polillo," she said. She felt the woman's weariness and her thirst. But both were old. Older than years. She'd worn this coat through many disappointing, parched days. Dani made herself hold it until she was sure there was nothing else to see and picked up the hat.

"She hopes he'll be quick," she said. The weariness again. The thirst. "The last time Frank bought her a drink, he didn't make her earn it. She's surprised he's insisting tonight." She waited. Turned the hat in her hands. "She hopes the little girls will take good care of her dolls."

Silence.

"That's all," she said, and she heard the note of pleading in her voice.

Ness exhaled and Malone reached for her hand as Cowles placed the coat and hat back into the evidence box.

"Is there a place I can wash my hands please, Mr. Ness? A bathroom perhaps?"

"Just around the corner, Miss Kos. On your left. Take your time. I think that's enough for tonight, don't you?"

"Yes. Please. I mean, thank you." She rose, testing the strength in her legs, and all three men rose as well, the way good-mannered men do, and Malone pulled back her chair so she could step away from the table.

"I'll just be a few minutes," she said, and he nodded, his eyes searching her face. He looked as wrung out as she felt.

"You steady?" he asked softly.

"I'm steady."

20

"You're a damn liar, Malone," Ness said the moment Dani left the room.

"Yeah," Malone agreed. He was too tired to argue about the truth. He sank back into his chair. Eliot and David did the same.

"Did I miss something?" Cowles asked, looking from one man to the other.

"Does that woman look like an ugly seamstress to you?" Ness said.

"Her eyes are different colors," Cowles said. Malone considered punching him in the face. He wasn't too tired for that.

"Yeah. They are. You got a problem with that, David?" he asked.

"No. No problem. Just . . . haven't seen it before," Cowles muttered.

"That was something else," Ness said, throwing down the pencil he'd been using.

"Do you really believe her, Malone?" Cowles pressed.

"If I didn't believe her, I wouldn't have brought her here," Malone enunciated, wondering when David had become so obnoxious.

"None of this stuff is evidence we can use," Cowles said. "She can't testify for us. And we sure as hell can't tell anyone we entertained her."

"It's not about making a case, David," Ness said. "Not at this point. Right now, we need a direction, just like you said. We need to find this guy."

"Well . . . she didn't give us that," Cowles said, shrugging. "I admit, I'm intrigued. She made the hair stand up on my arms. But she really didn't tell us much."

Malone gaped. Then he started listing exactly what she *had* told them. "You now have names for several of the victims. Who is Robert Weitzel? You have confirmation on Rose Wallace. Maybe look into finding her son? You have professions, pastimes. The second victim was a chauffeur. You also have chloroform as a method for submission—that's what she was describing with Andrassy. Chloroform on a rag. And you have Dr. Frank."

Ness was studying him through steepled fingers. Cowles rose and started putting the rest of the evidence away.

"You got a list from Dr. Peterka," Malone added. "Previous renters. Is there a Dr. Frank on it? His secretary referred to a Dr. Frank when I talked to her. I've been asking for a copy of that list, Eliot. I want it."

Ness and Cowles exchanged a look.

"What?" Malone ground out, and Eliot lifted a reassuring palm.

"Nobody with the last name Frank. But Francis, yeah. We have a Francis. A couple of them, actually. We're tracking them down," Ness said.

"That reminds me . . . who is Steve . . ." Cowles consulted his own notes. "Steve Jeziorski?"

"He's a nosy kid," Malone said, not liking the way he'd been sidestepped, but Steve Jeziorski needed to be discussed too. "He lives around East Forty-Ninth, near the Run. Knew Peter Kostura, one of the kids who found the first two victims. Kostura was killed in a hit-and-run in December. I've been trying to check on Jeziorski for weeks, but I haven't been able to. I don't know if he's giving me the slip or if I'm just missing him. But he thinks Kostura was run down because he was talking to Ness. I feel responsible for him, I guess."

"Peter Kostura was in our program for the boy gangs," Ness told Cowles. "Along with a whole bunch of others. He was on a community patrol. Sad business, tragic, but I don't know how his death would be connected to all this . . . madness." He tossed his hand toward the boxes.

"The Butcher is playing with you, Ness. Just like I said he was, goddamn it," Malone muttered. "I would check to see if your name was mentioned in the newspaper articles and pages left with the victims."

"You really think this is about me, Mike?" Ness asked, baffled.

"Not entirely. But damn if this guy doesn't love that you're chasing your tail."

Dani returned to the room, her eyes cautious, her curls combed, and her lipstick fresh. Eliot rose, and Malone knew the conversation was over. He rose as well, and when Eliot offered to walk them out the same way they'd come in, he shook his head.

"Just keep me in the loop, Eliot." He shot a look toward Cowles, including him in the directive. He helped Dani with her coat and slipped his arms into his own before putting his hat on his head and reaching for the door.

"Ah. Wait. Here are those tickets you asked for," Eliot said, pulling two white strips from his inner breast pocket. "That is . . . if you still want them?"

Malone took them and shoved them into his own pocket, avoiding the blatant curiosity in Eliot's gaze.

"So I'll see you both there?" Ness asked.

"Yes," Malone grunted. Dani's brow furrowed.

Eliot gave him a ghost of a grin. "It was nice to meet you, Miss Kos."

"Please call me Dani. And likewise, Mr. Ness. Likewise." Malone put his hand against her back and steered her out.

"Goodbye, Mr. Cowles. It was lovely to meet you as well," Dani said, throwing a look around her shoulder. It hadn't been lovely at all, but David Cowles nodded and thanked her, and then they were free. Malone made use of the toilet and washed his hands and face with haste. He didn't want Eliot finding Dani alone in the hallway and engaging her in conversation. He was too skilled at gently wheedling information from the unsuspecting.

"Can we walk for a minute?" Dani asked as they exited the building. "I need to move for a bit. I'm feeling a little raw. And the night is nice."

"You *do* know that Cleveland is the most dangerous city in America," Malone said.

"Yes. And I also know *your* holster isn't empty."

He harrumphed, and she slid her hand into his. He stiffened, and she immediately released it. He grabbed her hand and wrapped it around his arm. He didn't try to explain himself. Even a welcome touch took some getting used to.

"All right. Let's walk. I could stand to clear my head too."

Willard Park was just east of city hall, but he didn't like parks at night. Too much draw for people who had nowhere else to go and way too much to drink. He steered Dani forward instead, staying where the streetlights lined the streets and the hotels jutted up around them.

"They were all so unhappy," she said quietly. "I didn't make an issue of it—it wasn't specific enough, but it struck me, all the same."

He didn't need to ask her who. He knew. The Butcher picked on the down-and-out.

"The world is an unhappy place, Dani."

"Yes. I know. But they were scared and tired and . . . dulled. And I don't mean scared of whoever killed them. I think they were just scared. Of life. Of all the tomorrows. Now they don't have any tomorrows."

"No," he agreed. "They don't." There wasn't much more to say, and for a moment they walked in silence, heading down East Sixth Street toward Euclid. He could feel her tension in the clutch of her hand and the rigidity of her spine. It would take her a while to come down, so he kept walking, letting her set their pace and the duration of their stroll.

"God, Cleveland is ugly," he sighed, wishing he could walk with her on a secluded beach somewhere and let her sink her toes in the sand.

"Cleveland isn't ugly," she said, like he'd insulted her child.

"No?"

"No. Cleveland is poor."

"Everyone is poor."

"Only the honest."

"You're starting to sound like me, sweetheart," he said, bumping her a little. She was morose. He could hardly blame her after what she'd seen. But he immediately took the opposite argument. It was just his way.

"Cleveland killed the golden goose," he said. "Governments are good at that. They thought they could squeeze the wealthy for more. They squeezed too hard, and the wealthy went elsewhere. There's always a balance. Maybe Cleveland will find it again, and coax them back."

They walked past a crumbling, columned edifice marked for demolition, one of the remaining mansions from the days of Millionaires' Row, and she sighed.

"In Europe there are buildings that are hundreds of years old. In Rome, one church is built on top of another. The whole city is layers upon layers of old and older. Here . . . we tear things down when we're through. We tear them down and clear them away, and what once was is no longer. I hate that."

"Why? Crumbling cities and outdated infrastructure isn't good for anybody."

"It makes me tired. Nothing lasts. Not clothes. Not people. Not buildings."

"You're too young to think like that," he said.

"The very best things are old," she said. "And we let nothing grow old here."

"Old things take extra care. Sometimes . . . it's better to start fresh."
She frowned up at him.

"What?" he said, smirking at her stormy expression.

"Of course things of value take extra care. That's what gives them their value . . . we *care* about them. Starting fresh sounds like an excuse to not care."

"Don't put words in my mouth, Dani Flanagan."

"Nobody cared about them."

"What are we talking about now?" he asked gently. "Are we back to square one? Unhappy people?"

"Yes," she whispered. "Unhappy people that nobody cares about."

"Nobody? You mean me? Or Eliot? Or just the whole rotten system called life?"

"The whole rotten system. How do you make people care?"

"You can't."

"Then how do we, at the very least, make things more equitable?" she said.

"Equity is impossible. There is inequity in all things."

"Why can't you just agree with me, Michael?" she asked, and he laughed.

"Because it's actually comforting when you think about it. Much more comforting than whining about fairness," he said.

"I'm not whining."

"Humans are complex creatures. We want to belong, but we can't stand to be the same. How in the world do you *force* equity on humankind, when we try at every turn to differentiate ourselves from each other? You can do things others cannot, Dani. Where is the equity in that?"

"Maybe the equity is that every gift has a price. I've certainly paid it."

"Ah. Now you're talking. Now you're on the trolley," he said, nodding. "Everything has a price."

They walked in companionable silence for another minute.

"Do you think we might get something to eat? I'm so hungry," she asked, her voice plaintive, and he was mortified that he hadn't thought to ask. The poor thing was running on empty, and he'd been mindlessly yapping.

"Yeah. Sure." He looked around at the dark facades and the shuttered businesses. "But where?"

"Short Vincent isn't far," she said, hopeful. "In fact, it's just ahead, isn't it?"

"You want me to take you to Short Vincent?" he scoffed. Short Vincent, the street between East Sixth and East Ninth, was a single city block where Clevelanders of influence but not innocence went to play. The stretch of bawdy businesses—burlesque shows, gambling halls, and beer joints—was infused with money from more respectable operations, giving the crass an uptown veneer. It catered to a certain kind of guy and doll, but sprinkled in with the gin joints and the dancing girls was good food and lots of it. At the Coney Island Café, you could eat fried eggs and jelly toast at any hour, and they would just keep bringing it. His stomach rumbled at the thought. Dani heard it.

"The Theatrical Grill opened last year with all kinds of big acts and real-life stars. Frank Sinatra himself sang there."

"It's a Friday night. We'll never get a seat at a joint like that," he said, shaking his head. "But I'll buy you a plate of eggs and a coffee at Coney Island."

He'd been right about the crowds. He picked up his pace, pulling Dani alongside him, and claimed a booth at Coney Island, right beside the Roxy Theater, seconds before the place was overrun.

"We'll have the house special," he said to the harried waitress, who nodded, not even bothering to write it down. It was the standard fare, and it was thirty-nine cents flat, no matter how many times you asked for more.

"Of course you will," the woman said. "Coming right up."

"You've been here before," Dani said, her eyes scanning the teeming café. Her back was straight—Zuzana would have approved—and she kept her hands in her lap. She stood out like a sore thumb, and he felt his first twinge of unease.

"Yeah. I've been here before." He'd downed three plates of eggs waiting for Maxie Diamond—a Cleveland gangster and racketeer Irey had been sniffing at—to come out of the Roxy. Malone had just finished up the Lindbergh case and was brought in last minute; Irey though he might need a "gangster" for the job. Two days later, the sting was dropped, and Irey sent him to the Bahamas. Malone hadn't complained, but the outgoing Ohio governor had commuted the sentence of one of Diamond's boys on his last day in office, and Malone had wondered if some kind of deal had been struck. It wouldn't surprise him. It was the kind of stuff he tried not to think about. If he thought too hard or looked too long, he wouldn't be able to do his job.

"I've never been here," Dani said. "Can you believe it?"

"Yeah. I can. It's not the kind of street where a good girl goes by herself."

The waitress placed two plates in front of them and filled two cups with coffee before dashing away. It didn't take long to get your food when you kept it simple. He buttered his bread between bites of fried egg and soaked up the yolk with his second piece.

"I thought you were hungry," he said, looking up from his shoveling to see that Dani hadn't touched her plate. She was too busy gawking. He signaled the waitress for another round.

"Dani. Sweetheart. I brought you here to eat. And I'm going to march you right outta here as soon as I'm done. It isn't a nice place, and these folks aren't nice people, if you know what I'm saying."

She took several bites to please him and chased a dollop of jelly that wouldn't stay on her knife. He took it from her, slathering her bread with quivering, purple sweetness, just to move her along.

"There," he said, handing it to her. "Try that."

"It's good," she said, licking her lips, and the bottom dropped out of his stomach. He didn't know where to look, and his own plate was empty. She took another happy bite.

"It's delicious, in fact."

"Yeah. It is. So get eating." He took a pull of his coffee, too much, too deep, and burned his mouth.

"Don't rush me, Michael. This is the most excitement I've had in ages. And I'm going to stuff myself. You'll have to go get the car and come and fetch me. I won't be able to move."

He stared at her balefully, and she winked at him.

"You're a funny bird, Dani Flanagan. You've just spent the evening combing over bloodstained clothing with none other than Eliot Ness, and Short Vincent ranks higher?"

"It's more fun. That's for sure. Do you see anyone famous?" she whispered after the waitress whisked their plates away and set new ones down, topping off their coffee.

"No," he said, though he hadn't been looking. He had a better view of the room than Dani did. It was a habit to put his back to the wall, and she kept craning her neck to check out the constant flow.

He cleared his second plate and dressed another piece of bread for Dani, though there was no way she was going to eat it at the rate she was going. Her brow was creased, a line of demarcation between blue and brown, and he tapped her plate with his sticky knife, bringing her attention back to her food.

"I thought I saw my uncle Darby," she said, her gaze swinging back to his. "Isn't that strange?"

With the ease of long practice, he tossed his napkin on the table and shifted in his seat like he was sitting back for a smoke. He scanned the room with disinterest, patting his pockets. Every table was full, and folks were standing outside the entrance, but nobody was looking at him or Dani, and nobody in the room resembled Darby O'Shea.

"No. Not here. Outside the window straight across from you, having a cigarette. He wore a cap like Darby always wore, pulled down low so I couldn't see his eyes, but he had the same snub nose, and the same dimple in his chin. Isn't that how life is? You don't think of someone for eons, and as soon as you do, you start seeing them in random faces."

"Was it him or not?" he pressed softly, searching the dark windows and the ruddy lights that reflected off the pavement. Shadows shifted and people passed, but he couldn't see the man she'd described. Still, he was a fool for coming to a place like this, full of the same type of goons and gangsters he'd been spying on for most of his career. Full of people like Darby O'Shea.

"I haven't seen him since I was ten years old, Michael. I'm not certain. And, if you haven't noticed . . . I'm prone to seeing things that aren't actually there."

"You hadn't seen me since you were ten years old either, and you knew me right away."

"Well, that's . . . true. But you were standing right in front of me with the same grumpy look on your face you're wearing now. I just caught a *glimpse* of him."

"Are you done?" he asked, rising. He put a dollar on the table and added a quarter for the speedy service.

She looked down at her plate, then up at him, and sighed. He held out his hand, a peace offering, and she took it.

"I'm full. Just not stuffed. So you owe me some jelly toast."

"Done," he said, tucking her behind him as he walked, and he made a beeline for the door. It wasn't until they'd turned the corner at Bond's clothing store, leaving Short Vincent behind, that he allowed himself to slow and look down at Dani.

She'd kept up, her heels clacking and her hand clasped tightly in his, but the groove between her ginger brows was more pronounced.

"Was it something I said?" she asked, a note of irritation underscoring the soft words.

"What?" He frowned. "We ate. You said you wanted to eat."

"That wasn't a meal. It was a hog and jog. An eat and run. A chow and plow."

He chuckled quietly, in spite of himself. He hadn't heard some of those.

"Yeah. Well. I was hungry."

"Do I embarrass you, Michael?" she asked.

He stopped walking. "What?"

He thought he saw someone dart his head around the corner and pull it back. He shifted Dani to his other side, scanned the sidewalks and the shadows, and started walking again, his pace more measured and his ears peeled for footfalls behind them. It was late, and he just wanted to get Dani back to the car, doors locked, downtown Cleveland in his rearview.

She let him thread her hand through the crook of his arm, and tug her close to his side, but she was quiet for the rest of the way.

When they reached his car, it was the only vehicle still hugging the curb in front of city hall. A couple of coppers stood at the corner having a smoke and talking in comfortable tones, and a man dug through the trash about a block down. His breathing eased. The towering complex was dark against a moonlit sky, and the streetlamps burned faithfully, casting a mellow glow that reflected off his black shoes and the hood of his car. He dug out his keys and opened Dani's door. She hesitated before climbing in and looked up into his face, mere inches away.

"Do I embarrass you?" she asked again, and he realized he'd never answered.

"Why in the world would you think that?" Night had leached the color from her face, making one iris silver, the other black.

"I don't look like the women on Short Vincent."

"Oh, you noticed that too, huh?" His voice was dry, and he meant it only as a compliment, but her shoulders drooped.

"I like being with you, Michael. I could have eaten eggs and toast in that booth all night. Nothing would have made me happier. And you couldn't wait to get out of there."

"Ah, Dani. It has nothing to do with that."

"No?" she challenged.

"No. There isn't anything about that world—or those places—that I like. Except maybe the jelly toast. I've seen too much. I know the underbelly. They make my neck itch and my palms sweat. I got spooked. And I wanted to get you out of there."

She searched his eyes, like she wasn't sure she believed him.

"All right," she whispered.

"Okay?" he asked.

"Okay." But she didn't move.

He leaned down, not allowing himself to think about it too long, and touched his lips to hers. "Now get in the car, kid."

Her lips parted in surprise and her lids were at half-staff, but she immediately obeyed, and he closed the door securely behind her.

"Don't do it, Malone," he whispered to himself. "Don't do it." But it was already done.

21

Malone asked if he could attend Mass with them on Sunday, which pleased Lenka and irritated Zuzana, though Dani noted Zuzana didn't refuse the ride or the ice cream he bought them afterward. The only other time he'd attended, Lenka and Zuzana had sat between them, and he'd gone alone after that. When they entered the sanctuary at Our Lady of Lourdes, and Lenka began positioning herself to force them together and Zuzana attempted to keep them apart, Malone put his hand on Dani's elbow and guided her into the end of a full row with enough room for only the two of them. The aunts had to move two rows down.

Malone sat through Mass with the same expressionless concentration with which he seemed to approach everything, his eyes heavy lidded and his hands clasped in his lap, but for the first time in Dani's life, Mass was a heady experience. Things she hadn't particularly enjoyed before became pleasurable. Repeating the prayers and hearing his voice rumble the words. Bowing her head and seeing her skirt against his thigh. Breathing deeply and smelling the soap on his skin and the mint on his tongue.

Sitting quietly with nothing to occupy her hands had always been a challenge, but it occurred to her that it was not lack of focus or a tendency to fidget that had always beset her. It was the constant, nagging worry that she wouldn't get it all done or, even worse, that there would be no work to do. But in the church, with the drone of Father Kovak's homily and Malone at her side, she felt nothing but a mellow hum and a blissfully empty head. He didn't reach for her hand or run his arm along the back of the bench, but his presence was a balm beside her.

He helped her at the morgue Monday morning but was gone for the rest of the day, returning late and leaving as soon as breakfast was over on Tuesday. He spent both days down in the Run, wearing his old boots, a work shirt, and a pair of coveralls she'd given him, along with the checkered hat that had once belonged to poor Ready Eddie.

She had more than enough to keep her occupied but waited anxiously for him to return at the end of each day.

"What are you doing down there?" she asked, sitting across from him at the kitchen table as he inhaled the plate of food she'd set in front of him.

"Listening," he said. "It's what you do, isn't it?" His eyes met hers briefly. "Two detectives walk down there with their notebooks and their shiny shoes, and nobody is going to tell them anything, whether they know it or not. It's just not worth it."

"Why?" she asked. "Surely the men in the shantytowns want the Butcher caught most of all."

"As a general rule, if you want to get along in a place like the Run—or sadly, any of the neighborhoods around here—you don't go to the police. Especially if you don't know something for certain. Nobody likes a rat. Especially of the human variety."

"I wish I could come with you."

"Yeah . . . that's not going to work," he said with a small smile.

"I can't wear a few layers and an old hat? Dani is a boy's name." She was half teasing with the hope that he might shrug and give in.

"There isn't a man in that camp that would fall for that. But if you can spare some time tomorrow, I could use you."

"I could get away at about four. Will that work?"

He nodded. "I also . . . had another idea." He said the words slowly, like he wasn't sure he wanted to say them. "You ever heard of the Spring Gala at St. Alexis?"

"St. Alexis is right across the street, Michael," she said. Of course she'd heard of it.

"I had Eliot get me two tickets."

"Are you teasing me, Michael Malone?" she whispered.

"No, Dani Flanagan." His lips softened in the barest of smiles. "Would you like to go?"

"The Rockefellers still go to the gala. It's . . . swanky."

"Do you think you can find something to wear?"

"I am a clothier, Michael," she said with a haughty lift of her chin and a slight eastern European accent. "Of course I can find something to wear."

"You are not just a clothier, you are a Kos, Daniela," he said, mimicking the flavor of a true Bohemian, and making her laugh.

"You are better at that accent than I am, and I've been hearing it all my life," she marveled.

She sat back in her chair, considering her options, and her excitement grew. "You must wear one of your silk suits. The one with the chalk stripe."

"Shouldn't I wear tails?"

"Tails are a step down from a suit like that. And I have just the dress."

"Good. We might have to work a little . . . but I think we could squeeze in a dance and maybe some free champagne."

"Do you like to dance, Michael?" she squeaked, hardly daring to hope.

"Yes."

"Really?"

"Yes." He shrugged. "Does that surprise you?"

She tipped her head to the side, trying to imagine it.

"It doesn't surprise me, no. You're an actor, after all. But I'd like to see it."

"I didn't say I was good. I said I enjoyed it. At least I did, once."

"With Irene?" She didn't mean to sound jealous, but she did.

It didn't appear to bother Malone. He even smirked at her a little. "Yeah. With Irene. And long before that. Molly taught me. She loves to dance, and I was her practice partner. My mother loved to dance too."

"What was she like, your mother? I can't picture her."

He was quiet for a minute, his eyes distant. "You know . . . I don't really remember. It was a long time ago. I was brokenhearted when she died. I remember that much." He rose and rinsed his plate, like he'd made himself uncomfortable with his admission.

"I'm sorry," she said.

"No need. Like I said . . . it was a long time ago. I learned how to . . . move on." He set the plate in the rack beside the sink and shook off his hands.

He shifted his weight like he wanted to stay, and still he headed for the door.

"Good night, Dani," he said, not looking back.

"Good night, Michael."

~

"Flo Polillo was in a rooming house on Carnegie, and Rose Wallace rented a single on Scovill," Malone explained to Dani the following afternoon. "They aren't far from each other. The rooms have been rented out. I checked a while back, but the landlords might still have some of their possessions. We'll go see what we can find."

He'd considered taking the streetcar—he didn't like the attention his car garnered in the poorest neighborhoods—but they had a few stops, and he didn't want Dani walking in the parts of town where they were headed. They would just have to be quick.

"We'll go to Scovill first," he said. "Rose Wallace was missing for almost a year before her remains were found under Lorain-Carnegie Bridge, but her landlord wouldn't have known she was dead, so maybe they're still boxed up somewhere.

"She was last seen doing her laundry. A friend stopped by and told her someone was asking for her at the bar around the corner. She dropped everything and went. Maybe we'll get lucky, and you can get your magic hands on that laundry."

"What's our story? Are we just going to ask for her things?" Dani asked as they pulled up in front of a grimy building that butted right up next to the street. If someone tried to take his car, he could reach out and smack them without taking a step.

"Nah. You're a friend. You're wondering if any of her things are still around. You're looking for something you lent her."

Rose Wallace's landlord was not impressed with Dani's story. Malone wouldn't have believed her either if he were the woman. Dani was too sweet and prim. The residents of this rooming house were neither.

"You didn't know Rose. You're just trying to claim her things. That's low down, if ya ask me," the woman growled. She was missing three of her front teeth and two of her fingers, but she stared at Dani's eyes like Dani was the odd one.

"We'd be glad to pay for them," Malone chimed in. "It's not an issue of money."

"Oh yeah? How much?"

Malone handed her five dollars.

"Well, when you put it like that, I'm a little more willing to take a look. I think Mr. Morgan put her things in a box in the basement." She put Malone's fiver in the pocket of her skirt. "It's down three flights of stairs, though. You'll have to go with me. I'm not lugging it back up. If there's something there, you can have it all. Nobody else wants it. Rose's clothes are too small for me."

Malone tossed a fleeting look at his car and considered making Dani wait for him there. He decided she was safer with him and took her hand before following the woman into the bowels of the building. He didn't think they would get jumped. Swindled? Yes. But not jumped. And as Dani had so aptly put it, his holster was not empty.

The basement was littered with the detritus of years. No one dared get rid of anything anymore. Scarcity did that. A pile of junk felt like a pile of possessions, and possessions felt like safety.

The woman knew exactly what she had.

"Here ya go. That's everything." She pushed two boxes toward them, one large and one small, and both labeled *Rose Wallace*.

He opened them, unwilling to lug them up the stairs if there was nothing they could use. The woman snorted like he was challenging her integrity.

In one box was a frying pan, a teapot, and assorted dishes. That one wouldn't do them any good. He shoved it aside and opened the next one. The second box was half-empty. It contained a lipstick and hair pins, a straw hat, and an empty perfume bottle. The only items of clothing, besides the hat, were a hair scarf, a single silk nylon, and a threadbare nightgown that was probably pink at one time but had been washed into beige. It was something, but not much. Malone closed the small box and hoisted it onto his shoulder.

"We'll take this one," he said. "Someone else might be able to use the dishes, seeing as Rose isn't coming back."

The woman pulled out the frying pan and tested its weight.

"Is there a chance we might see the room she occupied?" Dani chirped up. Malone knew she was angling to feel up the drapes.

The woman looked at Dani like she'd just asked if she could have a nap in her bed.

"No, you may not. I have a boarder in that room now. And why in the world would you need to go in her room? Are you one of those ghost hunters? Because I'll have none of that."

"Thank you very much for the box," Malone interrupted. He handed the woman another dollar for her trouble. She made the sign of the cross and shot another dirty look at Dani and ushered them up the stairs with her new pan.

"We don't need to do this right here," Malone said when they were back in the car. "But we might as well see if these things were really hers at all."

Malone handed Dani the nightgown, and she balled it up in her hands and stilled, the way he'd almost become accustomed to. A moment later, her cheeks grew flushed.

"What?" Malone grunted. "You're blushing."

"It's hers."

"How do you know?"

"She must have worn it near her last day. It hasn't been laundered." She paused. "She likes how Willie calls her *Roses*. Not Rose, but Roses, like she is a whole bouquet."

"All right. That's good." But that didn't explain Dani's warm cheeks and glassy eyes.

Her voice dropped, almost like she was hearing Rose Wallace in her head. Even the cadence of her words sounded like someone else.

"He makes better love than any man she's ever been with, and he only has one arm. He makes her feel good. If she could make love all the time, she would. It's after the loving that Willie gets mean. Never during and never before."

Malone took the nightgown from her hands and put it back in the box. Her eyes cleared slightly, and she frowned.

"What?" she asked him. "Isn't this helpful?"

"Let's go," he said, terse, and closed the box. She would have to tell him more about the nightgown, but he didn't think he could listen to her talk about "making love all the time" in that breathy voice without losing his mind. Dani would have to see what else remained in the fibers of the cloth later. Without him.

The building at 3205 Carnegie, where Flo Polillo had resided, was the same color, the same shape, and the same condition as the one Rose had lived in, but two girls sat on the stoop playing with their dolls, making the place seem a little less ominous, even though the building sat right on the edge of the Roaring Third, a part of town known for its depravity and despair. The girls were clean and cared for, though their clothes were plain and a little too small.

When they rang the bell and knocked on the door, nobody responded.

"Excuse me," Dani asked the girls, "do you live here?"

"Mother went upstairs," the older girl said. "Mrs. Brewster's having a baby. We're listening for the cry." She pointed up at the open window just right of the entrance.

Malone turned around and headed back down the stairs, not wanting any part of that, but Dani hung back.

"What's your doll's name?" he heard her say.

"Louisa." The little girl said it with a lisp, making it *Lew-ee-tha.*

"That's a very nice name. And what a beautiful dress that is," Dani said.

"My dolly's name is Genevieve," the older girl inserted. "I don't like it much. But I didn't name her."

"No?"

"No."

"Can I hold them?" Dani asked. Malone checked his pocket watch. If they hurried, he might still be able to swing by Hart Manufacturing. It was late in the day, but if Steve Jeziorski was working a swing, he might catch him. He turned back to the front steps where Dani had taken a seat by the girls. She was holding the dolls and straightening their clothes, her head bowed. He groaned.

"Genevieve is a special name," she said, and her voice sounded pained.

"Why?" the older girl asked.

"Because it was Miss Polillo's middle name."

"You knew Mith Polillo?" the little girl with the lisp asked, dumbfounded.

Dani nodded, but Malone wasn't sure she'd heard. Her hands had stilled.

"Dani?" he called, unnerved.

"It is one of a collection," she said slowly.

"Mith Polillo had loth of dollth," the little girl said.

"Mother let us have them," the older girl said, a note of fear in her voice, like she thought Dani might be there to claim them.

"That's good," Dani said. "She would have wanted you to have them." She handed the dolls back to the two girls, who stared at her, wide-eyed. Dani dug in her pockets and pulled out a few pennies and set them on the stairs.

"Thank you for letting me hold them for a minute," she said. She descended the stairs briskly and moved past him, her heels clicking and her hands fisted. She climbed into the car without a word. Malone followed, slid behind the wheel, and pulled away from Carnegie before darting a look at her face. He sighed. Tears were streaming down her cheeks, though she was trying desperately to control them.

"Ah, Dani."

"Louisa was an old d-doll. She was like a friend that never complained and was up for anything. That's what Flo thought."

"How did you know they were hers?"

"When I touched her coat, I saw her dolls. Remember? She hoped they would be taken care of. She knew she was going to die, and she thought of her dolls."

He'd been under the impression she'd been talking about sex when Flo Polillo "hoped he'd be quick." She'd been talking about death.

"Well, damn."

He took out his hanky and blotted at her cheeks, trying to drive at the same time. He didn't want to hand the handkerchief to Dani. It would give him away the moment she pressed it to her palms, so he wiped her tears for her.

"She loved them. I can see them all, the way she saw them. She brushed their hair and made them clothes. She gave them names, Michael."

"Ah, Dani," he said again. "You sat through three hours of bloody evidence last Friday, the toughest bird I've ever seen. But you're crying over dolls?" he asked, shoving his hanky back into his chest pocket. He thought maybe Hart Manufacturing would have to wait for another day.

She swiped at her cheeks and kept her gaze straight ahead.

"You need to hold on to something?"

"Yes, please."

With his left hand on the wheel, he reached across her with his right, hooked her around the hips, and bodily slid her over until she was pressed up against him on the seat. Then she wrapped her arms around his bicep, turned her face into his shoulder, and cried her heart out.

~

Later that night, when Malone had girded himself up and Dani had long since dried her eyes, they went through the rest of the box.

"You catching a whiff of anything?" Malone asked after she'd held Rose Wallace's scarf every which way and gotten nothing.

"You say that like I'm a bloodhound." She looked up from the scarf and gave him a small smile. He relaxed a little, grateful there would be no tears. His chest had hurt all evening.

"You were the one who described it that way," he reminded her, voice mild. "Not me. I told you to stop touching things. You wouldn't listen."

"The whole box smells like mildew and mothballs, but there's something beneath it."

Malone couldn't smell anything.

"It's hair tonic. Something Rose used on her curls. And a particular brand of cigarettes."

Malone sighed. None of this was going to tell them anything.

"Do you think it was Willie who killed her?" she asked.

"No."

"Rose felt his meanness as keenly as his . . . care," she said. "Care" wasn't a great substitute for "lovemaking skills," but Malone didn't need it spelled out.

"Willie's mean is different from the Butcher's mean. Not to mention most of the murders would have taken two arms, unlike lovemaking."

"Maybe Willie just killed Rose," she said softly. "She was small."

"I've thought about that. What better way to get away with murder? Just cut 'em up, toss 'em in a feed bag, and throw them in the water. Everyone will blame it on the Butcher."

Dani nodded like she'd thought of that too.

"It's just . . . not that easy to cut someone up, Dani."

"I never assumed it was."

"Whoever is doing this knows what he's doing. The marks on the neck and around the joints display knowledge. And he always sections the torsos the same way. On Victim Number Nine the blade appears to have been getting dull. I think that frustrated the killer. He started hacking. Eliot thinks he's losing control. But I don't know. Bottom line, it's the same guy doing all that cutting. All ten—all eleven—victims have telltale marks that somebody trying to pull a copycat wouldn't know or be able to replicate."

"I see."

That reminded him of something. Malone strode to his desk and dug through the ever-growing stack of files. He found the one for Victim #9, the man whose pieces had been found in the Cuyahoga a month after Rose Wallace's bones were found under the bridge. He scanned the details until he found what he was looking for. A woman's silk stocking and the top half of a man's torso wrapped in newspapers dated three weeks earlier were fished out of the water. A single stocking.

He stared, not knowing what to make of it, not knowing if he *should* make anything of it. At this point, everything felt like a clue . . . and a cruel joke.

22

Her dress was a sleeveless purple silk that was so deep it was almost black. It didn't grip, but skimmed, from the drape of the neckline to the fishtail skirt that swished around her calves, and it would allow for dancing if Malone was sincere. The dress had belonged to a client who had abandoned it when she couldn't pay for the desired alterations. It'd been hanging in a closet of similar discards since the stock market crashed almost a decade before. It had just needed a shortening of the straps, a tuck at the waist, and a press, which she'd easily accomplished.

She wore a long pair of black gloves and black pearls at her ears and throat that Zuzana claimed were gifts from the emperor himself. She'd copied Greta Garbo, complete with vivid lips and sweeping lashes, and she'd been confident about her appearance until she'd heard Michael climbing the stairs to fetch her. Zuzana poked between her shoulder blades with her cane, scolding her about her posture, and Lenka fretted about the fact that she didn't have a stole.

"Shall we go?" Malone held out his arm.

"I just need to get my glasses and my coat," she said, suddenly nervous.

"You don't need your glasses," Zuzana snapped.

"Or your coat," Lenka moaned. "That dress demands furs, and we don't have furs."

"All right. No coat. But I need my glasses," Dani insisted.

"It will ruin the look, girl," Lenka protested. "You don't want to ruin the look."

"You represent Kos Clothiers," Zuzana agreed. "These people might be future clients."

"No one will notice the dress if I don't wear my glasses. They'll be too busy staring at my eyes," she worried.

"Let them stare," Lenka said. "You look so glamorous. And no one will notice your eyes except for those who get close enough to say hello . . . and then they won't be able to forget you."

Malone's brow furrowed as if he'd made a miscalculation.

"The people there will be the political, the wealthy, and the connected," Zuzana said. "And if they ask where you got your dress, you will tell them Kos Clothiers. It is publicity we can't buy."

They would not go unnoticed, that was for certain. And she'd been right. Her dress complemented Malone's suit perfectly. They were about a decade behind current fashion, more roaring twenties than late thirties, but the statement looked intentional instead of tired.

She'd even added a ribbon in the same shade as her dress to his white fedora, which pulled out the white chalk stripe in the silk, and added a pocket square to match. He looked as though he were having second thoughts, but she wasn't sure if it was the attention they would garner or the fact that the aunts were hovering. He was so handsome, dark-eyed and distinguished, she caught herself staring, and Zuzana prodded her between the shoulders again. He acted as though he wasn't sure where to look, though his hooded eyes had widened when he'd reached the top of the stairs and seen her standing there, waiting for him.

"It will be easier to walk than drive," he said. "The line of cars for the valet is already a block deep, and if we don't bring a car, we won't be waiting for it to be brought around when we're ready to go."

"Have a good time, dears," Lenka said as they turned to leave.

"If she's not back by midnight, Mr. Malone, I will ring the authorities," Zuzana threatened.

"Oh, Zuzana, do you really think the authorities would come?" Lenka sighed.

Malone simply grunted, and they escaped into the dark night, her hand linked through his arm and the lights of St. Alexis beckoning them.

"I imagine that's what the *Titanic* looked like before it sank," he said, tone dry, as they made their way up the long, circular drive.

"Isn't it magnificent?" Dani said. She'd always thought it so.

"You are magnificent," he said quietly, almost begrudgingly.

"I am?"

"You are. So we'll be steering clear of Ness . . . and everyone else . . . as much as possible. Unfortunately for your aunts and your shop, drawing attention is not my goal."

"Why?"

He sighed. "It's complicated."

"You don't want any obvious association between you and Ness."

"Yeah."

"So what is your goal?"

"We're going to take a stroll through the cloakroom after I get a good look at everyone in attendance. And after we dance."

Their tickets put them at a table of eight near the dais with a congressman named Sweeney and his wife, Marie, who had the burr of an Irish birth to her voice and kept darting nervous looks at Michael like she thought him delicious and dangerous. The congressman ignored them altogether, his attention consumed by the Catholic bishop on his left and a man named Higbee, whose family established the department store of the same name on Public Square, seated on Dani's right. Higbee's wife, Constance, was seated between her husband and her unmarried daughter, who took the final chair at the table, a balance to the unaccompanied bishop.

It was Constance who made sure names were exchanged and pleasantries offered, but Michael introduced them as Mike and Daniela Kos, inferring that they were married and he was the Kos, but gave no explanations as to why they were there or who had invited them. He was quick to pull Dani out onto the dance floor after only a few sips of champagne and that single, stilted exchange.

"Are you good at everything, Michael?" she asked, as he swung into the steps with perfect ease, leading like he knew exactly where he was going. She had only to follow.

"I'm not a particularly good seamstress, and I'd rather not do the Lindy Hop," he murmured, his lips near her ear.

She laughed, and her heart was as light as his feet.

"I also don't have magic hands," he added, but his hand resting lightly on her back felt almost miraculous.

"Magic?"

"You are like an ancient oracle."

She smiled, but she wasn't sure it was a compliment. "Didn't the oracles sleep most of the time and only grant people one question and always at a price?"

He grinned. "That's definitely not you."

"No."

"But you have always been ancient."

"Is that good?" she whispered. It was lovely to talk this way, heads close together, everything else a backdrop.

"Didn't you tell me all the best things are old?" he murmured. "You are ancient. And wise. And you know who you are. I find that even more remarkable than your voodoo."

"Don't you know who you are, Michael?"

"I do. Yes."

"Then why do you marvel that I do as well?"

"You have always known, and I had to figure it out," he said, and he spun her into a new dance.

The room around them was a blur, the music unremarkable, the celebrity attendees almost invisible. When her aunts pressed her for details afterward, it was only Michael she would remember, his hand at her back, his cheek to her hair, his scent all around her. It was Michael and his ease on the dance floor and her ease in his arms. In the end, he was all she would remember.

~

He was allowing himself to forget. To forget his past and forget his present. To forget that he would move on to the next mess and the next mark, and that he was not free. He was not young and hopeful or even *available*. But the music was fine and his skin was warm with champagne, and he had a beautiful woman in his arms.

His thoughts didn't race and his eyes weren't scanning. He was simply enjoying the sway of the steps and the swish of satin as Dani moved with him. Maybe he was not forgetting after all but remembering. Maybe he was allowing himself to remember what it felt like to live a little.

He kept trying to find the old Malone, but she made him laugh. He tried to rein himself in, but she made him run headlong. He would tighten up and shift away only to step toward her again. And he could not be cold. He could not be firm. He could not say no or even say maybe. *Okay, Dani. All right, Dani. Yes, Dani. Please, Dani.* And worst of all, he couldn't find the fear he'd lost, that healthy fear that warned of pain and loss, that kept a child from touching a stove or climbing too high. It was just gone, and he teetered above the earth, looking down, knowing he was going to fall, or worse, perish, and he just didn't . . . care.

He danced, blissfully uncaring, until Dani lifted her chin and told him Eliot had arrived. Alone. And the room was buzzing. Reluctantly, he turned his attention to the crowd, identifying the players he knew. Eliot was shaking hands with Mayor Burton, who was seated three tables over from Congressman Sweeney. Malone wasn't sure how he and Dani had managed to be seated beside him, but better Sweeney's table than Ness's, which he'd been a little worried would happen, considering Eliot had procured the tickets.

Mayor Burton was an affable enough sort, the kind of staid politician that nobody hates and nobody remembers. There was a place for his type. Folks preferred boring to bold most of the time. But Burton was as ambitious as the next; that had become apparent. Malone reminded himself not to mistake his sedate affability for lack of ambition.

Congressman Sweeney was a former judge who had been in Congress for a while. He reminded him of the Irish rabble-rousers of his father's generation, the men who sat around American tables and talked of Irish freedom, seven hundred years of British oppression, and Irish patriots, but who wouldn't go back to Ireland if you paid them. It was an identity. People needed that. But it wasn't grounded in anything but nostalgia and a desire to connect.

Sweeney was no Michael Collins or Eamon de Valera, but he played the same strings and used some of the same tactics. Malone didn't mind it, but he didn't buy it either. He recognized that most politics required manipulation and overwhelming self-interest.

He supposed that was why he liked Eliot, who looked a bit like a kid at a church dance, though he was dutifully making the rounds and shaking hands. He would likely make the social page the next day for coming to the event by himself.

"Poor Eliot," Dani murmured, and he pulled her closer in a pretense of not being able to hear her over the band.

"Yeah. Poor Eliot," he agreed. "But nobody knows how it all works better than he does. In Chicago, Eliot knew he had to court the press. It's a propaganda war. He had the picture with the axe, breaking down the door of the distilleries. He knew he had to frame his job a certain way, tell the story he wanted printed. He who controls the narrative wins the game. It backfired a few times, and he was embarrassed a few times. But he won more rounds in the press than he lost. I don't know if that will happen here."

"What about you? Anybody ever take your picture and talk about your heroic adventures?"

"No. And it's a good thing. I wouldn't be able to do my job otherwise. Eliot can hardly do his."

"We're hardest on our heroes, aren't we?" she said.

"Eliot never took a bribe, and that made him a legend. He set an impossible standard for himself and made every other politician look bad in the process. They haven't forgiven him for that."

"It's the reason people secretly adore villains. Villains make them feel better about themselves. It's why the Butcher never gets caught," she mused.

"Give the lady a big, gold star."

"Well, really. The Butcher is no threat to the people in this room," she said, warming to her subject. "If he were . . . he'd have been snagged long ago. The politicians use him to rouse the base and excite the crowd. But they aren't concerned. Not really. He's useful to them."

"Ah, Dani. You're starting to sound like me. I'm afraid I've been a very bad influence," he murmured, spinning her out and drawing her back to him. They let the subject rest for the remainder of the song, swaying to a Bing Crosby number called "Sweet Leilani" that he didn't even like. But damn did he like dancing with Dani.

He found himself changing the words. *Sweet Daniela. Sweet Daniela.* And though he felt like a fool, it stuck in his head.

The song ended and the nuns of St. Alexis began to file up onto the dais as the audience clapped for the orchestra. No more dancing tonight. At least not for him and Dani. The speeches and arm twisting were about to begin, and it was time to do a little snooping.

~

"Every year we gather in this hall, in this hospital, in this city, to support an institution built on the faith and fortitude of two good sisters who lived the commandment that we love our neighbors. At St. Alexis, no one was turned away. Everyone was a neighbor. Everyone had value. Everyone, regardless of their status in life, was cared for," Congressman Sweeney intoned.

Michael had swiped two flutes of champagne from the table, and Dani had drunk it a little too fast. She liked the bubbles more than the taste, but all the dancing had made her thirsty.

"Members from my own family have served at this hospital . . . ," Congressman Sweeney continued as they left the ballroom and headed for the coat check. Just as Michael had predicted, there was no one in sight.

A prim bell was centered on the counter in case someone wanted to duck out early, but Malone shoved it aside and hoisted himself up and over the counter in one smooth motion.

She gasped.

He reached over the counter, put his hands on her waist, and said, "Give a little jump on three."

She jumped on three, and he plucked her off her feet and swung her over the counter like she was Ginger Rogers.

"What if they see us back here?" she said when he set her on her feet.

"Then we'll pretend like we're here for a tryst. I promise you, it won't be the first time someone retired to the cloakroom at a Catholic fundraiser."

A tryst?

"You have too much confidence in me, Michael," she worried, following him to the first row. "There are too many. There have to be hundreds in here." The champagne and dancing had left her delightfully soft around the edges. She didn't think she could focus. Especially after he mentioned trysting. From the easy way Malone smiled, she didn't know how steady he was either. She liked him this way, looser and more relaxed, his sad eyes a little less sad, his grim mouth a little less grim.

"It's a long shot. No pressure," he reassured her. "Don't bother with the hats or the women's coats. Just the men's. Touch and go, Dani. Touch and go."

"What am I looking for?"

"Dr. Frank." Ah. There he was again. Grim Michael. She didn't blame him. The thought sobered her up immediately.

She skimmed her hand across the shoulders instead of the lapels. Lapels might cover the heart, but the contact at the back was constant, and if she had to be quick, that was where to focus.

It felt like flipping through face cards and trying to spot the joker. Colors and names, fears and frustrations. Treatment plans, antiseptic, stitches, and sleep deprivation.

"You're right. Most of these men are doctors," she murmured.

"What'd I tell you?"

She kept going, in and out of the rows, Malone beside her, keeping watch on the counter as he kept track of her progress.

It wasn't until she'd groped her way through four sections that she felt a frisson on her fingertips. She'd begun to let her touch bounce from one hanger to the next, trying to cover as much area as she could. It was nothing more than an icy pinprick, but she halted and stepped back, reaching for the overcoat again.

The bell began to ring, *pling, pling, pling, pling.*

"Time to go." Malone tugged her behind a numbered partition, his arm around her waist. It was enough to hide them from the view of whomever stood waiting for service, but not enough to give them cover the moment a porter returned.

The ringing became strident. Whoever had arrived at the coat check was not pleased.

"Do you have my claim ticket, Marie?"

"No, Martin. I don't. I told you to give it to me," Marie reminded him, voice patient.

"And I did. See? That's it right there," he said, triumphant.

"That's not yours. That's Francis's. You didn't give me yours. Check your breast pocket."

Pling, pling, pling, pling.

"If we don't leave now, we'll have to wait in the queue. Where is my infernal ticket? And where is the attendant?"

Malone pulled her into another row as a portly man in coattails, nicotine trailing him like a fog and a bit of toilet tissue clinging to the bottom of his shoe, came bounding through a door somewhere in the back and hurried toward the clanging bell.

Pling, pling, pling.

"He gave his speech, now he's ready to go. Can't say I blame him," Malone muttered.

"Who?" she whispered, but Malone was still listening to the exchange at the counter.

"I'm so sorry, Congressman," the attendant said. "But . . . I really do need your claim ticket. I won't be able to find your coat without it."

"It's the one right next to my wife's. She has her ticket." *Tap, tap, tap.* "That's it, right there. Just grab the gray overcoat and the black bowler hat beside it. Those'll be mine."

"But, sir . . . it doesn't always work that way."

"Fine. Go with him, Marie," the congressman snapped. "So he doesn't grab the wrong ones."

The attendant made a gurgle of protest and then must have thought better of it.

"Very well. If you would accompany me, madam," he said. The whoosh of a door being opened and the swish of a woman's skirts followed. Malone hesitated, his hand on her arm, waiting to see which way they would go.

"Well damn," he muttered as they rounded the corner.

The attendant stopped so abruptly that Marie Sweeney let out a little oomph of surprise as she bumped into his back.

"You should not be back here," the attendant stammered, his gaze pinging from Dani to Malone. He tugged at the bottom of his coat, indignant, like he was gearing up to blow a whistle or sound an alarm. Marie Sweeney peered around him, and her mouth dropped open.

"I needed my hat. You weren't where you should be. I was tired of waiting," Malone said, his voice so sinister the attendant took a step back and trod on Mrs. Sweeney's pea-green dress.

"Oh. Oh dear," she said, giving the poor man a little shove and staring dejectedly at her torn hem.

Malone took a step and plucked his hat from a cubbyhole just above the attendant's head. The man flinched.

"Lucky for you, I got it." Malone dropped the fedora on his head and drew his claim ticket from his pocket. He held it out to the attendant like he was serving a warrant, though there was nothing but the ticket in his hand and the flattest gaze Dani had ever seen on his face. The man's hand shook as he accepted it.

"Now, if you'll excuse us, we'll let you apologize to Mrs. Sweeney," he sneered, taking Dani's hand, and moving around the attendant.

"Ma'am," he said sweetly, touching the brim of his hat as he passed the congressman's wife.

"What in the blazes is going on back there?" Congressman Sweeney bellowed, punching the bell with the flat of his hand as they approached the counter.

Malone didn't vault it this time. He simply opened the door to the left of the counter and escorted her out, the way Marie Sweeney had been let in.

"I enjoyed your speech, sir," he said to the congressman, slowing slightly. "Very powerful. My people are from Mayo too." He added something in Gaelic and winked, like they had a secret.

Sweeney cleared his throat. "Yes, yes. Well. Thank you."

"Your people aren't from County Mayo, Michael," Dani whispered as they walked away. "You said your father was from Belfast and your mother was from Dublin. That's not Mayo."

"I was tweaking him, Dani. Mayo is a bit of a rallying cry here among Cleveland's Irish. He uses his heritage when he needs the votes."

"What did you say to him?"

"Imigh leat, amadán."

"Yes. That."

"I called him an idiot and told him to, uh . . ." He cleared his throat. "Sod off."

"But he said thank you," she said.

"Proof that he is, indeed, an idiot. He's made Eliot's life hell."

"Ih-mig lath oh-mah-don," she murmured, trying it out. "I like that."

He groaned like he'd taught a child how to curse, like she'd just given him another example of his "bad influence," and she frowned at him.

"That reminds me. I thought if we got caught, we were going to fake a tryst," she scolded him. "I feel swindled."

Malone laughed out loud.

23

It was laundry day, Margaret had reminded him at breakfast, and he'd dutifully put his hamper in the hall. The house was muggy and too warm, and he'd thrown open his bedroom windows to combat it.

The same thing had been done in the rest of the house, for the sounds reached him differently, both from within and without—chatter from the shop, whirring from the sewing room, and the clank and sizzle of Margaret's iron. The hum of a busy house mixed with birdsong from the trees and noise from the street was a strange symphony, and the sounds of life soothed him as he reexamined the dead.

He heard Dani walk down the hall from the shop, and his attention instantly strayed. He knew it was Dani from the light tread and the click of her low heels. It was lunchtime, but she didn't go upstairs. He considered taking a break himself, but he didn't think he could eat. He pushed back from his desk and stood, popping a peppermint into his mouth from the candy dish Dani had given him. Since he'd confessed to having a sweet tooth, she'd kept him well stocked.

The peppermint soothed him too.

He'd spent the morning poring over a copy of the coroner's report released late last night, making a new list for the Butcher's latest victim. Official cause of death was still "undetermined," but probable laceration of the neck with severe blood loss—hemorrhage—was likely. In other words, decapitation.

On Monday, a burlap sack had been found in the river, snagged under the West Third Street Bridge. The sack claimed itself to be Wheel Brand potatoes from Bangor, Maine. One hundred pounds of them, but the sack lied. It wasn't one hundred pounds, and the contents weren't potatoes. Both halves of a woman's bisected torso, a thigh, and a left foot, which matched the calf found in April, were turned over to police.

A thought had occurred to him. One he'd not considered before. Many of the victims—or pieces of them—were found in burlap sacks. Dani had never examined the sacks. If she could pull pictures from leather, surely she could draw impressions from burlap, though the time in the water might destroy that possibility for some of the bags. The sacks wouldn't tell them anything about the victims, but they might tell them something about the killer.

He heard Dani's tread again, this time hurried and brief, cutting across the hall from the laundry to his room. She knocked at his door, three quick raps, like he'd summoned her with his musings.

He tamped down his eagerness to see her. It surged hot and sweet in his veins, and he schooled his features and scolded his heart. He'd been careful since the gala. At least . . . more careful. Mass, the morgue, and constant movement had kept him in line.

"Michael?" She sounded breathless, even through the door, and he could almost feel her impatience from the other side.

"Come in. It isn't locked." He sounded surly, even to his own ears. Better that than randy. She poked her head around the door and hesitated.

"Is it a bad time?" she asked. Definitely breathless.

He shoved his hands into his pockets and shook his head. "No. Come in, Dani."

She did, turned the lock behind her, and leaned back against the door. She had a neatly folded stack of his undershirts in her arms and brought with her the dueling scents of bleach and soap flakes. Her curls were tamed in perfect waves that hugged her cheeks and skimmed her shoulders, and she wore a simple brown sheath with narrow lapels that ended in a drooping bow between her breasts. She'd added a slim belt at her waist to avoid the flapper look, but it was a tad faded from too many washes or too many wash days, though the color still warmed her skin. Or maybe that wasn't the dress. Her cheeks were pink, and she was panting, her chest rising and falling like she'd run around the block and not just across the hall.

He frowned. "Did you find something?"

She extended her arms, handing him his shirts without a word, and he took a few steps, and accepted them, puzzled by her behavior. They were alone, the door was locked, and yet she seemed to be struggling to speak.

"I let Margaret fold your things so that I wouldn't . . . intrude . . . on your privacy. But she missed one."

"Oh no," he muttered. "What now?"

She blinked at him and swallowed, and the pulse at her throat thrummed beneath her silky skin. Damn, she was a sight.

"That one on the top?" She fluttered a hand at the small pile.

"Yeah?" He drew out the word.

"You must have worn that one on Saturday night. But Margaret missed it. It was still in the hamper. It hasn't been laundered."

"Huh," he grunted. But he was beginning to understand. She'd been snooping.

"I was just going to bring them to you. Along with your hamper. Though . . . I seem to have forgotten it. I had something to tell you."

"Okay."

"Though I can't remember what it was now."

"You can't remember?"

"No." She shook her head and wetted her lips.

"Why did you lock the door?" he asked, beginning to understand. His heart understood. And his body understood. Beneath the scent of bleach and soap was something else. He set the undershirts on his dresser.

She took a few steps toward him and stopped, but she didn't answer his question.

"What did you see, Dani?" He cut the distance between them in half.

"I saw myself. The way you . . . saw me on Saturday night. You liked the way I looked."

"You needed my undershirt to tell you that?"

She took another step, and the space between them was mere inches. But she didn't touch him and he didn't touch her.

"I'm no good at reading men. Or people. Only cloth. But you thought . . . you think . . . I'm beautiful. And you . . . you *like* me very much," she said softly, resolutely, like she had no doubts about what she'd seen. He suspected she'd seen more than just affection.

The heat in his veins bellowed and blasted like the boiler in the basement.

"Is that all?" He kept his voice level.

She nodded, and she raised her hands slowly and settled them on his chest.

"And what do you think I'm feeling right now?" he asked.

"I don't know. I'm still drunk on your undershirt. I held it to my face for five minutes before I folded it and brought it in here," she confessed. "Are you mad?"

"How could I be mad?" he whispered.

"Please don't make me beg you to kiss me, Michael."

When she called him Michael, he wasn't just the man who'd been wrung out by life, the man who did his duty and little else, the man who had paid the price and would continue paying it. But there was *always* a price, that man warned.

"What will this happiness cost me?" he asked, though he wasn't really talking to Dani.

"Maybe it will only cost a little sleep." She swallowed, nervous, as if she'd said something suggestive. "Or . . . maybe you've already paid."

"Maybe I have."

He kissed her then, shoving his trepidation away with such force that it obeyed and his mind was quiet as his mouth touched hers. Her lips were soft but perfectly still, and her breath fluttered like she didn't know what to do. He was reminded that she was young and he was old, she was sweet and he was salt, she was innocent and he was . . . not.

Her hands rose to his neck and she pulled him in, lifting her chin as she did, and his inner dialogue became nothing more than the rush of surf against the sand. He forgot to judge or justify and simply enjoyed the moment. Her inexperience was not hesitancy, and her eagerness swept him up in weightless wonder. He swept her up too as he floated by, locking his arms around her waist, and taking her weight into his chest. He'd never been one to close his eyes, even when kissing, but his lids were so heavy and his heart so light, he couldn't have lifted them if he tried.

He kissed her until they were both breathless and red-cheeked, gasping and returning for more, and he felt like a boy again, throwing rocks at Irene's window and waiting for her to steal out into the night for a kiss beneath the moon. But that was so long ago, and the woman in his arms and in his heart was new. Her flavor filled his mouth and the press of her limbs made him long to begin that slow and steady climb to the point of no return.

"Why me, Dani?" he asked, almost desperate. He knew what was in his head, but he couldn't imagine what was in hers.

Her lips were watermelon pink and her cheeks were mottled from the roughness of his, but she shook her head, bewildered.

"Oh goodness, we are a pair, aren't we? I see everything and you refuse to see what is right in front of your face," she said.

"Tell me," he pled.

"Why you, Michael? Because you make my heart do this." She took his hand in both of hers and placed it in the valley between her breasts.

It was a hummingbird in his palm, and he curled the pads of his fingers against the skin above the row of buttons, before seeking the flesh beneath them.

"It's not that hard to understand, is it?" she asked, her breath hitching with the caress. Her lids fluttered closed, and her head fell back on a sigh.

No, not that hard to understand at all. No harder to understand than her hips in his hands and his mouth at her throat. No harder to understand than the bed beneath them and the desperate ache in his belly. He needed another kiss. Just one more, and he would stop.

But one became another, and another.

The clanging of a passing fire truck, the flutter of the drapes, the slam of a car door, and the tinkling of the bell as someone entered the shop. None of it registered. None of it intruded. He was in a lust-soaked haze, basking in the details of the woman beneath him.

Dani's skin was especially soft above her elbows. And behind her ears. She wore a lace slip beneath her dress and had a long run in her left stocking. He tugged them off, wanting to touch the silk of her legs. She purred when he kissed her neck, trembled when he stroked her breasts, and cried out in protest when the pounding in his chest became a knocking at his door.

"Mr. Malone? Are you in there?" Lenka called.

He rolled away from Dani at once, the haze parting, and his attention veered to the things he'd ignored.

He didn't know if he should answer. The door was locked. Lenka would go away. Dani straightened her clothing, her movement drawing his eyes. She'd lost her stockings, her lips were swollen, her buttons undone, and her hair tumbled. But no great damage had been done.

"Mr. Malone?" Lenka insisted again. *Knock, knock, knock.*

"I know he's in there. He hasn't left all day. Maybe he's having a little nap," she said, the sound shifting like she'd turned her head away.

"I'll wait for him in front. He probably got past you."

It was Eliot. Eliot was looking for him.

Malone grabbed his suitcoat and stuffed his billfold into the breast pocket before snatching his hat and his keys from atop the dresser. They had been sitting next to the stack of undershirts.

He strode to the window, pushed it up a little higher, and climbed through it. Thoughts of the boy he'd been resurfaced. Rocks on the window, kisses in the moonlight, a girl in his arms, hope in his chest. Those days were gone. And he couldn't go back.

"Something's happened, Dani," he said.

She nodded, silent, and he slipped away, in search of Eliot.

~

Eliot's car was at the curb, and seconds later, he exited from the shop and saw Malone, and his relief was evident. He clapped his hat on his head and pointed at his automobile.

"I gotta talk to you, Malone. Get in."

Malone didn't argue, but he furtively checked his buttons and his collar in the passenger window before he opened the door. He was rumpled and flushed, but no more than Eliot. Eliot looked like he was subsisting on alcohol and hadn't slept since the gala.

The safety director slid behind the wheel and slammed his door. But he didn't turn the ignition. He put his hands on the wheel as if he needed something to hold on to and stared through the windshield.

"Eliot?"

"You look good together, Malone."

"Huh?"

"When I saw you at the gala, dancing with Dani, you looked happy. I've never seen Michael Malone look happy. It gave me hope for myself."

"Eliot, why are you here?"

He sighed and pressed his palms to his eyes. "I need you to tell me what to do."

"About what?"

"You've got a clearer head than I do right now, Malone. I'm not doing so good. I need someone to tell it to me straight."

"Are you drunk, Ness?"

"I wish."

"Are you going to drive us somewhere, or do you need me to?"

"I never took his money. You know that, right?"

"Whose money, Eliot?"

"Capone's. Sometimes he'd have one of his guys leave a thousand dollars on my desk. And I didn't have any trouble turning it down. Because that . . . that shit was obvious. Right and wrong. Black and white. They mighta got me if they'd been a little more subtle about it."

"More shades of gray?"

"Yeah. The thing is . . . I don't know any man who has chosen the right who didn't think it was worth it in the end. And I don't know any man who has sold his soul who thought he got the better deal."

"Eliot . . . what do you need to tell me?" Ness was scaring him a little. He was weary and wilted and taking an awful long time to get to the point.

"The problem is, we don't sell ourselves in one swoop. We sell ourselves sliver by sliver, little by little, until one day it's all gone. This feels like that. Like taking a bribe that's so small I can pretend it isn't a bribe at all."

"Eliot! What the hell is going on?"

Eliot took a deep breath. "You know Martin L. Sweeney has been a thorn in my side."

"Yeah."

"Since I got here, he's done everything he can to get me fired, to make me look like a flunky, a stooge, an incompetent."

"Yeah."

"He's got a lot of sway in this city, and he doesn't like me."

Malone grunted. Ness was picking up steam now.

"I told you that there was a group of businessmen who were funding this operation. Kind of like the Untouchables."

"The Unknowns," Malone said, mocking.

"Yeah. Well. Most of them are big donors too."

"Big donors to who?"

"To everyone, Mike. The money is spread nice and thick."

"Like jelly toast. All you can eat."

"Huh?" Ness said. Malone just shook his head.

"The thing is. I'm out on a limb here, all by myself. They aren't going to like what I've done."

"What have you done, Eliot?"

He took another deep breath. "We got that list from Dr. Peterka after your tip about the apartment. Thing is, there was a name on it. A doctor who was a partner and lived upstairs for a while. It was a name I was already familiar with."

Malone just waited. Eliot seemed intent on circling around the issue, for whatever reason.

"This guy grew up over on Jessie Avenue, not too far from here. A guy who knows the Run. A doctor. Smart too. Brilliant, even, according to his school records. His wife has petitioned the court—twice—about his mental state. She divorced him in 1934, right before all this garbage started going down. He did his internship at St. Alexis, though his work history has been spotty. He's got an alcohol problem. Barbiturates too."

"And you knew all this before you came to me in Chicago and asked me to take this job?"

"Yeah."

"And you didn't think to put an asterisk by his name . . . maybe give me a heads-up about him going in?" Malone asked softly. "I don't remember seeing that guy in the files."

"I thought about it. But I told myself that woulda been wrong."

"Why?"

"Because his name is Francis Sweeney."

"Sweeney?" Malone asked, voice flat.

"Yep. Francis E. Sweeney. First cousin to Martin L. Sweeney."

"Ah, shit," Malone hissed.

"He goes by Frank. He even introduced himself as Dr. Frank when I met him at the gala last Saturday. He said he's a 'big fan' and told me to 'keep my chin up.' Shook my hand with both of his. Looks a lot like his cousin. Same big nose and receding jaw. Same wide forehead and blue eyes."

"He was at the gala?" Malone asked, stunned.

"Yeah. He was at the table right next to Sweeney and his wife. A table full of distinguished alumni." Ness's voice was wry. "He blended right in."

"When did he live in that apartment?" Malone shot his thumb toward Peterka's clinic.

"In 1934, when his wife booted him."

"That lines up with Emil Fronek's story."

"Yep. A few weeks ago, an inquest over Francis Sweeney's lunacy was brought forward by another doctor. A concerned family friend. It was immediately quashed."

"And you've ignored all this because he's a Sweeney, and you know you're going to get torn up by the press."

"I'm damned if I do, damned if I don't."

"You also know the money men funding your special investigation aren't going to like it. That's why the description of the car that took down Peter Kostura bothered you so much. A politician's car. You don't know who to trust. This isn't Al Capone, public enemy number one.

This isn't the T-men versus the gangsters. This guy's inconvenient for them."

"I've got nothing on Sweeney, Malone, except my gut and what I just told you. And I can't decide if the thing that's holding me back is my own neck. 'Cause that would be like taking a bribe."

"Are you asking whether I think you should pull him in?" Malone asked, grim.

"Yeah. That's what I'm asking."

"You have to, Ness. You don't need me to tell you that."

Eliot's shoulders sagged, and he rested his head on the steering wheel for as long as it took him to breathe deeply and let it out. Then he turned and looked at Malone, his burden visibly lightened.

"Well, I'm glad you think so. Because right now, I've got Dr. Francis Sweeney in a suite at the Hotel Cleveland. He drank himself into a stupor at a bar in the Third on Tuesday night. I've had a man on him since the gala. We scooped him up, carried the son of a bitch right out of that bar early yesterday morning, and he's still sleeping it off."

Malone felt his jaw drop.

Ness reached over and closed it.

"I have his suitcoat in my trunk. I need Dani to have a look-see. If Sweeney's the Butcher, I need to know. If he isn't . . . I need to get him out of the Cleveland before all hell breaks loose."

~

Malone ended up going back inside alone and waiting for Dani to finish with a customer. She'd changed her stockings and buttoned her dress, but the flush in her cheeks deepened the moment she saw him.

The aunts were squabbling in the sewing room, Margaret would be upstairs, and he didn't want to bring the coat into his room or even into the house. The moment the customer left, he turned the lock on the door and flipped the sign in the window to *Closed*. Dani's eyes widened and she bit her lip.

He scowled even as his stomach dipped. "I'm not going to ravage you in the shop, Dani."

"Oh." She sounded disappointed.

"Eliot's here. He's got something he needs you to look at," he said, but he couldn't resist dipping his head and stealing a quick kiss. Eliot could wait for a few more seconds.

She rose up on her toes and kissed him back, and his arms snaked around her waist. It was instant combustion, and he set her back from him ten seconds later dazed and done for. He swiped at his mouth with his palm, checking for lipstick, and strode out of the shop before he lost his wits altogether.

"I need you to do that every time you see me," she said, slipping her hand into his. "From now on."

"All right," he said. *Yes, Dani. All right, Dani. Anything you want, Dani.*

"And will we do other things too?" she whispered as he tugged her down the hall and out the back door.

"I really can't imagine myself telling you no," he muttered.

He led Dani into the stable, where Eliot was waiting, his hands in his pockets, his eyes hopeful. He'd turned the suitcoat inside out and tossed it over an old dress form so Dani didn't have to hold it.

"Eliot," Dani greeted.

"Dani."

"What have we here?" she asked, pointing at the rickety dress form.

"I need you to tell me what you see on that suitcoat, Dani. And it might not be pleasant" was all he said, and she accepted his request with a nod.

She didn't ask him whose it was or where he'd gotten it. She didn't even comment on the stench, though her nose wrinkled in distaste and she pursed her pretty lips when she moved in closer. Malone followed.

"I'm going to stand right behind you. But go slow, okay? Go easy," Malone instructed, terse.

She flattened her palms, her fingers flared, and ran them up the front of the coat from the hem to the shoulders.

"It belongs to a man named Francis Sweeney," she said immediately.

Considering he hadn't said a word to her about Francis Sweeney or Eliot's suspicions, that the name had never once come up between them, her declaration was its own witness. Eliot's exhale was audible, and Malone's gut twisted.

"Yes. It does," Malone said. "But who is Francis Sweeney?"

Dani allowed her palms to rest on the cloth, but her fingers flexed and curled, like she was strumming a harp. "He doesn't know," she said. "Sometimes he can't remember. He prefers Frank. Most people call him Frank. Dr. Frank."

She dropped her hands and stepped back, coming flush against him.

"No more?" he asked.

"I just need . . . a minute," she whispered.

"Is it the same Dr. Frank, Dani?" Eliot asked. He didn't have to explain to her what he meant.

She curled her fingers into the garment again. A second later she nodded. "It's him. He was there in Flo's coat and Andrassy's socks. In the curtains too. The same cold. The same . . . void."

"Do you know the name Francis Sweeney, Dani?" Malone asked. "Have you ever met him before?"

"I'm not sure. The name sounds familiar. Mrs. Sweeney mentioned a Francis at the coat check. Is he related to her?"

"Yeah. He is," Eliot answered, grim. "And I don't think I have to tell you how sensitive that makes all of this."

She nodded, but Malone wasn't sure she really understood. Her focus was on the garment.

"What else?" Malone asked, wanting to be done. Wanting Dani away from the whole mess.

"He's cold. That's why he drinks. It makes him warm. And when he's not drinking, the voices drive him mad."

She gripped the coat like she'd clutched the drapes.

"He is Frank and Francis and Sweeney and Doc. He is Robert and Raymond and Eddie and Ed. Carlos and Chuck and Douglas and David." The names started tripping from her tongue.

Malone put his hands over hers.

"It's okay, Michael," she soothed, glancing up at him. Her eyes were unfocused, the colors dominated by her huge pupils. "I'm okay."

He removed his hands but remained at her back, wishing he could shield her and realizing in the same instant that she was the one shielding him.

"He is Rose and Flo and Catherine and Dorothy too, though he doesn't like that they are there. He cuts them into smaller pieces so they won't come back."

Goose bumps had begun to rise on her bare arms, the little golden hairs standing at attention. She radiated cold.

"He doesn't know who he is," she said. It was the same thing she'd said before. Multiple times.

"What does that mean?" Eliot asked.

"I'm nobody. Are you nobody too?" she quoted.

"Emily Dickinson?" Malone frowned.

"Yes." She nodded, her hair tickling his chin. "He likes that one. It makes him chuckle."

"Is he killing them, Dani? Is he the Butcher, or is Francis Sweeney just a sad, sick drunk?" Eliot asked, needing it as plain and unambiguous as she could make it.

"Francis Sweeney is a sad, sick drunk," she said. "And he is most assuredly killing them."

24

Francis Sweeney was sprawled across the bed, legs and arms wide, mouth open, wearing a pair of trousers and a white dress shirt and natty striped socks. The dress shirt was ringed with sweat and partially untucked, and sometime in the last two days, he'd soiled himself, leaving his trousers stained and the room reeking.

"We tried to wake him up this morning, but he wasn't having it. Dr. Grossman thinks it better to let him come around on his own," Eliot had explained when he'd led Malone into the suite, "but if he doesn't start coming around soon, we're going to have to get creative."

Dr. Royal Grossman was a psychiatrist Eliot seemed to trust, a man who had worked with the Cuyahoga County Probation Department and had attended the Torso Clinic the first coroner, A. J. Pearce, had organized. Malone recognized his name and had read through his assessments in the files.

Eliot had secured the whole floor. Malone didn't ask what it was costing him—or who was footing the bill—but he was glad of it. The fewer people aware of what was going on, the better. A guard sat at the door and another at the elevator making sure no one got off on the wrong floor. Neither man was anyone Malone recognized, but Eliot claimed they were two of the "Unknowns," which meant *Don't ask*.

The bedroom of the suite opened up into a separate sitting room where Dr. Grossman and David Cowles sat, an ashtray between them, comparing notes. They looked up when Eliot and Malone arrived. Eliot tossed the soiled suitcoat into the corner of the room and made quick introductions.

"Mike, you know David."

David Cowles nodded once. Whatever he thought of Eliot's maneuver, he was present and accounted for. His shirtsleeves were rolled and his pate was shiny with perspiration, and from the look he'd tossed at Sweeney's coat, he knew where they'd been and whose advice they'd sought.

"Royal Grossman, Mike Malone," Eliot continued. "Dr. Grossman, I know Mike from Chicago. Best undercover man in the business." That was it. *Best undercover man in the business*. And Grossman didn't ask for elaboration.

"I've called in another favor from Chicago too, Malone."

Malone dropped into an empty chair, but Ness remained standing as though his nerves wouldn't allow the rest. "Leonarde Keeler is on his way with his machine."

Malone knew Leonarde Keeler. He'd developed what was known as the Keeler polygraph, a lie detector machine that indicated whether a subject, who was connected to the device via a chest belt, an arm band, and a tube that measured respirations, was being truthful. Keeler was respected, and his machine had been widely tested—Malone had been subjected to it in training a time or two—but the polygraph was no more accepted in a court of law than Dani's magic hands.

"He's the best. And he's agreed to help us," Eliot said.

"Well, we're going to need all the help we can get," Cowles muttered.

The big man on the bed tossed and the four men stilled, waiting. Hopeful.

But it would be another full day before questioning could even begin.

~

"Do you know who I am?" Francis Sweeney shouted on the morning of the third day. He'd come awake in stages, none of them pleasant. He begged for a drink and they gave him water. He threw that against the wall and begged for a bath. A male nurse from the psychiatric hospital had arrived—someone Grossman knew and trusted—to help the man bathe and administer aid should he need it, only to be tackled by a furious Francis Sweeney, who accused him of having romantic inclinations.

Around and around they went. Sometimes Malone was convinced the man was a genius. Other times a drooling idiot. But he was coherent enough, wily enough, that he teetered between denial and demand and answered nothing directly. He threatened them with exposure and then thanked them for the sumptuous accommodations. They brought him clean clothes when he complained of his filth, but he refused to put them on because the quality was inferior.

"I have very sensitive skin. I will break out into a rash."

He wrapped himself in the curtains after that, huddling in a corner though the mattress he'd soiled had been stripped, turned, and remade. Malone wondered if wrapping himself in the curtains was a common practice. It would explain Dani's reaction to the ones in the apartment.

"I'm freezing. I'm so cold I can't feel my toes or my fingers," he whined. The room was so hot that every other man had lost his tie, and his sleeves were rolled up to his elbows. They didn't dare open the windows for fear of someone hearing his shouts, and there remained the very real possibility that Francis Sweeney might try to hurl himself out one of them.

Keeler had arrived with his polygraph, but he sat waiting, unable to perform any kind of assessment on Francis Sweeney until he was more stable.

"How can a man be so drunk that even when he wakes, after days of being unconscious, he acts like this?" Cowles marveled.

"This is why he's probably never sober," Grossman responded. "The alcohol makes him functional. But he doesn't know when to stop."

Malone did his best to ignore the dark smear that clung to Sweeney's shoulders and moved with his bulk every time the man was awake. He'd never seen a shadow quite like it, and it unsettled him deeply.

They slept in shifts in a suite across the hall, and Malone had only been back to the house once. He'd washed and changed his clothes, kissed Dani like they were both drowning, and left again to sit in a stinking hotel room and watch Francis Sweeney sweat and shake and shout.

To Dr. Grossman: "You are a doctor? What kind? Couldn't cut it in surgery, eh? Afraid of a little blood?"

To Leonarde Keeler: "I've heard about your little machine. This isn't science. It's a parlor trick. I don't have to answer your questions. Do you know who I am?"

To Malone: "What's your real name? Why are you here? Have you been following me?"

"My wife is here. Isn't she?" he would babble. "Mary? Mary? I know you're here, Mary. She put you up to this, didn't she, Ness? She told you lies about me. She spends all my money, yet I cannot see my sons. You don't have any sons, do you, Ness? And your wife left you too. I saw you at the gala. All alone. We should have gone together. Two bachelors about town."

He demanded to be let out of the room, yelled about his civil rights, threatened Eliot with public crucifixion, and yet seemed almost flattered by his circumstance, as though he was living out a fantasy. His fixation with Eliot was obvious.

∼

"What are you gonna do when this wraps, Mike?" Eliot asked. It was 3:00 a.m. and the two of them were the only ones awake. Grossman and Keeler had retired to beds on the empty floor, and Cowles was asleep in his chair, the lamplight reflecting off his bowed, bald head. Sweeney's snores buzzed and burbled from the other room.

"I'm going to do what I always do, Ness."

"What do you always do?"

"I go on to the next job. The next assignment. There's always another job."

"And leave her here?"

Malone didn't have to ask who Eliot was talking about. He'd thought of little else for days. Months.

"You should tell Elmer about her," Eliot suggested. "They'll make a whole division for her. Maybe call it the Extra-Sensory Division. The ESD. Daniela Kos, ESD agent. Or maybe Dani Malone, ESD agent." He waggled his eyebrows. "You could be partners."

"Eliot." He sighed at the outlandish suggestion. "She's a seamstress. She's a . . . goddamn child. And she has a business, two old biddies, and a terrorist named Charlie to take care of."

"That hasn't stopped you from kissing her, though, has it? You had lipstick on your collar the other day when you brought her out to take a look at Sweeney's suitcoat. You're attached. Both of you."

"Yeah. Well." *What could he say?*

"But . . . if you're determined to move on, like you are inclined to do, then I will be making my own bid for Miss Daniela's skills, maybe as a consultant," Ness mused.

Malone scowled at him.

"What? You don't want her, but nobody else can have her?" Ness grinned.

"I didn't say I don't want her," he whispered.

Ness was silent, letting Malone's declaration hang in the air. And though Malone knew the tactic the man was employing, he wanted to tell him. He needed to tell someone.

"You've heard it said, 'Be careful about what you ask for'?"

"Yes."

"Well, I don't ever ask for anything. Ever. That way God can't exact a price."

"You don't pray?"

"Not really. I'm Catholic. I just confess."

Eliot snorted like Malone was kidding. He wasn't.

"I would never have asked for her, Eliot. I would have kept my feelings to myself. But she *knows* everything. I couldn't hide it from her." Even saying the words embarrassed him, and he didn't look at Ness.

"And she likes you too?" Eliot asked.

"She seems to. Yes."

"Well, hallelujah." Eliot raised his cup toward the ceiling.

Malone groaned, but the words came a little faster. A little easier. "She could do so much better, Ness. She's young. And she's beautiful. And smart. And kind. Her goodness makes me . . . itch. *She* makes me itch."

"Itch?"

"Yes. When I'm not with her, it's like this . . . itch. And when I'm with her, I itch. When I *think* about her, I itch. It's just this incessant . . . *itching*."

"And she's the only one who can scratch it?"

Malone dug his palms into his eyes and ground his teeth so he wouldn't slap the man. "Are you laughing at me, Ness?"

"Yes. But I'm happy for you too."

"She knows too much," he said from behind his hands.

"About you?"

"Yes. About me. About every goddamn thing she touches. And she's still good. I don't know how she stays that way. I sure as hell couldn't do it."

"But you did. That's exactly what you did. What you still do. That's why you're locked down so tight. You're protecting the good," Ness said softly. Kindly.

He needed to walk. To move. He set down his empty cup and stood. Eliot looked up at him, compassion in his gaze, and Malone sat back down. "I have never been *known*, Eliot."

Ness frowned at him. "I don't understand, Malone."

"Is it just a human trait, do you think, to think no one knows us? Really knows us, deep down. And almost being afraid that if they did, they would back away?"

"She knows you. And she hasn't backed away," Eliot summarized.

"No. She hasn't. And God is laughing at me."

"Don't be so dramatic, old boy."

"I'm not bitter. At least . . . I don't think I am. I never thought I deserved better, so how could I resent what I was given? But I *am* suspicious. Things always go bad. It's nature. Fruit rots. People age. Things decay. Nothing lasts."

"So when this is over, you'll just . . . let her go?"

"It would be for her own good."

"Maybe." Ness nodded. "Maybe it would."

Several seconds passed.

"You're not supposed to say that," Malone said. "You're supposed to tell me it could work."

"Could it?"

"I'd have to get a new job."

Malone raised his gaze to Eliot's, and for a moment the men studied each other silently.

"Yeah. Well there's the rub, huh?" Eliot said. "What do men like us do without our work? I mean . . . somebody's got to do it."

"If we don't do it, who will?" Malone agreed.

"I'm not the guy to get advice from. Not on love," Ness said. "Maybe it's just like you said. Edna knows me, and she doesn't want me anymore. And she says I don't want her."

"Do you?"

"Yes. But not enough to be the man she says she needs. I would have to be someone else entirely."

The silence from the other room was suddenly jarring. Malone wasn't sure when the snoring had ceased, and he and Ness both stilled, listening.

"Do you know who I am?" Francis Sweeney boomed. "Because I know who you are."

"Sounds like someone's awake," Malone said, rising.

~

Since the night on Short Vincent, she'd seen Darby O'Shea twice. Once it was just the reflection in the front window at the market on East Fifty-Fifth. She had paused to buy a paper poppy from the woman selling them by the door. She couldn't resist the poppies since "meeting" Ivan at the morgue. Ivan had bought one for his Johanna every chance he got.

Dani tucked the flower in her pocket, thanking the woman, who thanked her back, and she saw her uncle, across the street, watching her. The same hat. The same stance. But when she turned, he began striding away at a good clip, and she wasn't sure anymore.

The second time was in the line of cars waiting for attendees at the gala. He was propped against a car like many of the other drivers waiting for their passengers, having a smoke. She didn't tell Michael. When she'd mentioned Darby at the Coney Island Café, he'd gotten tense and marched her out of there so fast she didn't even get to finish her toast. She didn't want to ruin their night, and unlike her aunts, and maybe Michael too, she wasn't worried about Darby O'Shea.

She would be going to the morgue alone again today. Michael was holed up somewhere with Eliot Ness doing who knew what. He'd only been home once in three days to bathe and have dinner with her and the aunts, but he'd kissed her the moment they were alone. She didn't even have to ask. He'd simply gathered her up and kissed her until she was climbing him the way Charlie climbed the curtains.

When she left the shop at noon, hoping the workload at the morgue would be light and she wouldn't have to leave her aunts minding the shop for too long, Darby was standing at the curb. He acted as if he were waiting for the streetcar to pass before crossing, but she knew he was waiting for her. She kept walking, pulling her wagon, and waited for him to follow. Follow he did.

"Did you think I wouldn't remember you, Uncle Darby?" she called when they'd moved beyond view of the house and she'd turned the corner on Mead.

"I hoped you would." His voice made her breath catch and her eyes instantly tear. He sounded just like her dad. Or maybe . . . he sounded like Darby, and she just couldn't separate the two.

She stopped walking and turned toward him, still clinging to the handle of her wagon. Everything about him was faded. Eyes, hair, skin, clothes. He was in his midfifties, she guessed, but he looked older. He wore a suit that didn't fit and a pair of shoes that were laced so tight, she suspected they didn't fit either. He was still tall, though she had grown since she'd peered up at him last, so even his size felt diminished. He stopped walking too, allowing the wagon to remain between them.

"I've missed you," she said.

His chin wobbled and he ducked his head. "I've missed you too, Dani."

"This isn't the best place to talk," she said. "And I have work that can't wait."

"Yeah. I know. I've been keeping an eye on you, wanting to say hello since I got into town. But I didn't know how. I didn't want to scare you . . . or that man you've taken up with."

"How long have you been in town?"

He scratched at his face like he wasn't entirely sure.

"Awhile I guess. I have a little place down in the Run. It's not much. But it's mine. George and I used to come to Cleveland all the time, back in the day. That was before he met Aneta. George was always good at rustling up the work. Meeting people. Making a go of it. He had big plans."

"Yes. He did."

"He got all the talent in the family. The looks too." He smiled, revealing that his teeth had not fared much better than he had. "But he took care of me. And I tried to take care of him." His face cracked. "I didn't do a very good job. I'm always too late. But I woulda taken care of you, if they'da let me."

"I know, Darby."

"You look like her, Dani. So much . . . I almost thought you were her when I saw you again."

"And when was that, Darby?"

He smiled at her again, almost sadly, like he knew she had to be cautious around him and hated that it was so.

"You were shoveling snow. Out front. With the fella. I was freezing my arse off. But there you were, looking like your mother the day George and I walked into that shop. And it made me warm."

"Do you need some money, Darby? Or some clothes?"

"No. No." He seemed appalled that she would even ask. "That's not why I'm here, Dani. That isn't it at all."

"I know. But if you do need something, you let me know. You don't need to hide or creep around. Come into the shop. I'm all grown up now, and I don't need permission to see you. You are my family."

He seemed flabbergasted by that, and his lips trembled again. "That's the kinda thing George woulda said. He was all the family I had. And I haven't had anyone since."

Dani swallowed back the lump in her throat. "I'm sorry, Darby."

He nodded. "I'm sorry too. But . . . that fella . . . I've seen you with him a few times now. I don't think he'd like me coming around."

"You let me worry about that."

He took off his cap like there was something he wanted to say. "He was a copper, wasn't he? He looks familiar to me."

Dani wasn't sure how much to say or what Michael would want her to say. It was hardly a surprise that Darby would recognize him.

"A long time ago. Yes."

"That's good then. That's good. He'll keep you safe."

"I need to go now, Darby."

"Okay, Dani. I'll be around," he said, turning away. As he strode off, hands in his trousers, his tattered coattails flapping, she wanted to call him back. Darby wasn't so different from the unclaimed dead she cared for. He was also the kind of man the Butcher preyed upon. Isn't that what Malone had said? *His victims are loners with no intact families. They're nobodies. It takes days for people to realize they are missing if they realize it at all. And even then they don't go to the police.*

Should something happen to Darby, no one would know who he was.

"Darby. Wait," she called. "Just wait for a minute, please. I have something for you." She'd slipped on the St. Christopher medallion Darby had given her that morning. It'd been hanging over the corner of the photograph; she'd been afraid of losing it and rarely wore it. It'd been a whim, but now she wondered if she'd been expecting him with Malone gone so much.

Darby turned around and walked back toward her, almost shy. She pulled the chain over her neck and extended it to him.

"Wear this. Please. It would make me happy if you did."

"You tryin' to protect me, Dani girl?"

"You are dear to me."

"You wear it," he insisted. "That's why I gave it to you."

"I have a copper to keep me safe. Remember?" She smiled. He smiled too, and took the chain, slipping it over his head and dropping the medallion beneath his collar.

He whistled as he walked away, a new bounce in his step.

25

Cowles started an official interrogation on the fourth day, but Francis Sweeney sulked and stormed and refused to answer. He'd taken a dislike to Cowles and wanted Eliot's attention.

"I don't want to be questioned by an underling."

"Do you know your name?" Cowles inquired.

Sweeney's mouth opened and closed, like a fish in a tank, and he didn't answer.

"Please state your name for our records," Cowles repeated.

"Ask Eliot Ness!" the man bellowed. "The man who got Al Capone but can't catch the Mad Butcher of Kingsbury Run. What a disgrace. Cleveland deserves better."

"What is your name?" Cowles repeated, weary.

"You know my name. My question is, What is your name? You can be assured I will be shouting it from the rooftops when we are through here."

"Do you understand why you are here, Dr. Sweeney?" Cowles asked him for the umpteenth time.

"Because Eliot Ness has an axe to grind. Do you know who I am?"

~

By the sixth day, Sweeney was considerably less manic, but they were running out of time. They were already on very shaky legal ground, and the longer they occupied that room, the more likely word would get out to the press.

Leonarde Keeler began a round of testing, trying to coax cooperation from a very unmotivated subject. Sweeney was connected to the device, his arms folded, his expression petulant.

"I want Mr. Ness to ask me questions," Sweeney said. "I want to match wits with the director himself."

Eliot ignored him.

"Or Mike. I want Mike to ask me questions. He's hardly said two words. My feelings are hurt." Sweeney used Malone's name with glee.

The interrogators had been careful not to address each other, but over five days, it was bound to happen.

Malone rose to leave; he was obviously a distraction, and he could hear just fine from the adjoining room. Eliot followed him.

"Don't leave, Mike. Where are you going?" Sweeney protested. "Do you have a lady you need to get home to? I heard you and Eliot talking about her. You love her, don't you, Mike?"

Malone's heart lurched. Sweeney was indeed wily. But Malone continued through the door, Eliot on his heels.

"Are you a T-man too, Mike? A famed Prohibition agent from the glory days? Is that how you know Eliot Ness? We met once, Mike. At the Lexington Hotel. Don't you remember? You wore the same suit you wore the other night at the gala."

"What the hell?" Eliot whispered.

"You aren't in the papers like Eliot. Eliot enjoys being in the papers, don't you, Eliot?" Sweeney's voice grew more boisterous, projecting so they would not ignore him.

"I followed the Capone case. And the trial. Fascinating. That's when I became a fan of our boy, Eliot. When the government sets its sights on you . . . it's over, isn't it?" He chuckled.

"I wanted to come up and shake your hand at the gala. But I thought maybe you were undercover. I did tell Martin and Marie I thought you might be a spy. I'm not sure they believed me. Were you there watching me? This is so exciting."

Eliot was frowning. Malone was rigid. And they stood, facing each other, listening to the man in the other room. Sweeney kept talking.

"Martin got me into the trial. Did you know he was a judge? He has lots of pull, Martin does. Our fathers were brothers. Martin and I are like brothers. You know his father wanted him to be a doctor and my father wanted me to study law? We both disappointed our fathers. We laugh about that."

"Did you kill Edward Andrassy?" Keeler asked Sweeney, redirecting his attention with a voice that was perfectly mild.

"I don't know who that is."

"Did you kill Flo Polillo?"

"I don't speak Spanish."

"Are you Francis Edward Sweeney?"

"Only when my mother was cross with me."

"Did you reside at 5026 Broadway in 1934?"

"What year is it now?" He laughed uproariously. "I don't even know what day it is."

Leonarde Keeler persisted, but Sweeney wanted to talk to Malone, and continued flinging questions toward the adjoining room.

"Does anyone know who you really are, Mike? It's sad, honestly. Eliot takes all the credit when men like us run circles around him."

"Did you work at St. Alexis Hospital?" Keeler asked.

"Are you there, Ness?" Sweeney called. "Are you angry?"

"Did you kill Rose Wallace?" Keeler continued.

"Mike? Do you know Rose Wallace?"

"Are you the man they call the Butcher of Kingsbury Run?" Keeler intoned, undeterred.

"Am I the Butcher? I'm nobody, who are you?" he chortled. "Are you nobody too? Then there's a pair of us—don't tell! They'd banish us, you know."

~

"We've got nothing, Eliot," Cowles said. David's hair stood out in little tufts above his ears, and discouragement rimmed his eyes and bowed his shoulders.

"We'll get a warrant to search his residence," Eliot said, jaw set.

"His current residence is listed as Congressman Sweeney's house," Cowles reminded him. "And if we do that . . . what's the point of all this? We've gone to great lengths to keep this quiet. You want to storm the congressman's house now?"

"My professional assessment is that he's suffering from psychosis. But . . . I can't tell you whether he's a killer," Grossman said.

Eliot frowned. "Keeler? What's the ruling?"

Leonarde sat back in his chair. "He's not being truthful."

Cowles moaned. "That's not especially helpful, Leonarde."

"I couldn't get a good baseline, David. If I don't know what the truth looks like with a subject, I can't very well assess when they are lying."

"And he lied on almost every single question we asked him. He even lied about his own name," Ness added.

"Did he kill those people, Leonarde?" Malone pressed Keeler. "Yes or no?"

"According to the polygraph . . . yes. He did. If he didn't, I might as well throw my machine out the window. But I agree with Dr. Grossman. He's psychotic. And that makes the test a whole lot more unreliable. It makes his responses more unreliable. He is severely unwell."

"We've got to shut this down, guys," Cowles worried. "We've got to shut this whole thing down."

~

Malone went for a walk. He just needed a little air. Some time away from Sweeney and the sweat-soaked suite. What a mess. Keeler was packing up his machine. Grossman was talking forced confinement in a mental institution. Malone supposed if a suite in the Cleveland could be finagled for almost a week, forced institutionalization might not be out of the realm of possibility. Sweeney was demanding to be released, and Ness wasn't talking.

What a mess.

He wasn't surprised. He always expected the worst. He planned for it. For that reason, he was always the most capable guy in the room and the most unassuming. He did not look on the bright side, because in his experience, there wasn't one. You could always make the best of things, but most of the time, that wasn't saying much. He was actually comforted by bad news, because he could go about making things better. When he got good news, all he could do was wait for the tides to turn.

The tides were turning.

The point was driven home when a kid, running at full speed and looking over his shoulder like he was being chased, barreled into him, driving them both back around the corner Malone had just turned.

Malone recognized his hat before he recognized the bundle of sticks in his arms. Steve Jeziorski still wore Malone's fedora. It made him look even younger than he was. He tried to dart left, but Malone saw the feint and moved right, and backed the kid up into the wall in three steps.

"Who you running from?" He scanned the large square and the streets that fed into it. The Cleveland was a high-rise hotel that sat on the south corner of the diamond-shaped thoroughfare. It anchored the upscale shops and restaurants on every side, and it was rife with pickpockets. It was also a long way from Broadway and East Fifty-Fifth and a considerable distance from Hart Manufacturing, where Steve supposedly still lived and worked.

"Not running from anybody. Need to catch the streetcar," the kid panted.

"You're running the wrong way."

"Huh. Yeah. Well. I know a shortcut."

"Where you been, Steve?"

"I go by Jez now. Jazzy Jez."

"That's a stupid name, kid."

"What would you know, Lepito?" Jeziorski spat, trying to wriggle away.

Malone frowned down at him, and the kid wilted.

"What did you just call me?" he hissed.

"That's your name, right? Lepito? That's what the guy told me."

"What guy?"

"Your tail. He came around again. He asked me some questions, gave me some money, and told me you were a gangster named Lepito."

"A gangster named Lepito," Malone repeated. "Are you lying to me, Jazzy?"

"About what part?"

Malone was too tired to play word games with a punk kid.

"When was this? And why didn't you tell me?"

"You told me you didn't want my information. Remember? But if you want it now, I might know something . . . for a price."

"How much money we talking?" Malone opened the billfold he'd lifted from the kid's pocket.

"Hey!" Steve yelled, patting at his baggy trousers.

Malone raised his arms out of reach. "How about I don't drag you out into the square and flag down a patrolman, and we'll call it even?"

"I told you what I know, Mike," the kid whined, but Malone was no longer listening. His eyes were drawn across the square to the entrance of the hotel. Elmer Irey was climbing out of a long black car. As he watched, two more cars pulled up. Both long, both black, both filled with people he didn't know but immediately recognized.

All hell had just broken loose.

He handed Jeziorski the pilfered wallet and headed for the war zone.

"Hey, thanks, Mike," Steve Jeziorski shouted. "You're a good guy. That's what I told the other fella. You're a good guy. Not as scary as you look. If I hear anything else, I'll come find you, okay? No charge."

~

Cowles had made a call.

By the time Malone reached the suite, Sweeney was being spirited down the back stairs, Grossman and Keeler were gone, and Irey was waiting for him. Cowles and Ness sat in dejected silence, the detritus of the last week pooled around them.

"I'm sorry, Malone," Cowles said. "We were in over our heads. We needed reinforcements."

"Where are they taking Sweeney?" he asked.

"Go home, Ness. Cowles," Irey said, his tone firm, even consoling. "It's all been handled. It's over. I'll take care of everything."

Ness raised bruised eyes to Malone's, shrugged into his rumpled blue suitcoat, and walked from the room, leaving the door of the suite gaping.

Cowles followed him out, and Malone could hear him apologizing down the long hall.

"We didn't have anything to hold him on, Eliot. I just couldn't see any other way forward. I did this for you."

"I know you did, Cowles. I know you did," he could hear Ness say. Then Irey walked to the door of the suite and shut it firmly.

Malone didn't sit. The windows had been opened to air the place out, and evening was falling gently through the drapes that had survived Sweeney's confinement.

Irey didn't sit either. He surveyed the room like he couldn't believe what he was seeing and flipped on a lamp as if he needed a second witness.

"Cowles filled me in, Malone. I think I have the basic gist of it all. I'm just wondering why it was David who called me. And not you."

Malone was silent. To defend himself would have meant throwing Eliot under the bus. And, try as he might, he didn't know what else Eliot could have done. When every choice was rotten, you had to make a rotten choice.

"You had a respected doctor—" Irey began.

"He isn't respected, Elmer. His wife has petitioned the court for him to be committed to an institution twice."

"That is not the point!"

"You said he was respected, sir. As if that protects him from the law."

"You aren't the law!"

"I'm not?" Malone frowned, baffled.

"Not in this matter, you aren't. You're a Treasury agent, in case you weren't aware."

"I'm aware that I had no communication from you indicating there were any protected persons in the case you *knew* I was assisting on." Malone was more surprised by Elmer's agitation than he was angry, and he easily kept his voice level and his own temper under control.

"You never take a vacation. Your wife had just died. You needed some downtime," Irey said.

"In Cleveland?" Malone snorted. "I was in the Bahamas, Elmer, but you readily agreed for me to go to Cleveland. If it was for my emotional well-being, you and I have far different definitions of 'rest.'"

"You were not lead, you were not point, you aren't even here officially. You have had no oversight—"

"But a month ago, you told me to do whatever I needed to do to end it. You said the big guy wanted it wrapped up."

"I regret that now."

"Why?" Malone asked. He'd never seen his boss so agitated, and he'd never given such mixed signals. "We've never been an agency that went about investigations in the regular ways. I daresay it's one of the reasons we've been successful. The reason *you've* been successful, Elmer."

Elmer took off his spectacles and rubbed a large hand over his square face, as though he could reform his features into something less reproving. Then he dropped into a chair. His next words made Malone's heart sink.

"Lie detector machines and palm readers?" he asked. "Is that the best you could do?"

"Palm readers?" Malone hissed.

"What is it that Daniela Kos does, Malone?"

Malone did not answer. He stared at his boss, not understanding, and for the first time in his career with the department, not . . . *trusting*.

"You and Eliot Ness pulled a respected doctor into a clandestine interrogation for six days." Irey raised his hand to quell Malone's argument. "A doctor whose only documented crimes are that he drinks too much and his wife doesn't want him anymore. That describes most men, doesn't it, Malone? Including you and Eliot Ness. You aren't one to drink too much, but your wife wasn't too keen on you either, now was she?"

Malone stilled, biting back his affront. Irey getting nasty and personal was the most baffling thing of all. Malone hadn't believed any part of his life was truly private. The agency didn't work that way. When you signed up, you turned your life over for inspection, every embarrassing moment. But for Irey to pull out Irene's rejection and use it as leverage was new.

"What the hell is going on here, Irey?" he whispered.

"You don't have a real suspect," Irey said. "And you resorted to methods I can't condone or defend."

"Francis Sweeney has killed a dozen—and probably a whole lot more—men and women. He's hacked off their heads, chopped up their bodies, and deposited them all over Cleveland."

"You have no evidence."

"Yes, we do." They had plenty. Just nothing they could use.

"You kept the man prisoner in a hotel room for almost a week. Against his will."

"He was detained for good reason. We were unable to question him for days because he was so drunk. He was not tortured or mistreated."

"His cousin is a US congressman," Irey ground out. "A US congressman who has been very vocal about the president's preparations for war and American isolationism. The president needs him on board."

"So I hear. It's the reason Francis Sweeney wasn't hauled in like every other suspect. Special treatment for a special suspect. A whole week in a luxury hotel."

"You were in the room with Francis Sweeney?"

"Yes."

"So he can identify all of you—you, Ness, Cowles, Leonarde Keeler, and Royal Grossman? And what about Daniela Kos? Does she know who you are and who you work for?"

Malone knew better than to react to references to Dani, but Cowles had filled Irey in. All the way in. Cowles didn't work for the Treasury's intelligence division anymore, but he worked for the Scientific Investigation Bureau, and he knew both worlds and all the players.

"Frank Sweeney was unconscious, sleeping off a drunk, for much of the time that he was in that room. I observed. His interactions were mainly with the psychiatrist, Mr. Keeler, Cowles, and Eliot."

"What a story that will be. Eliot Ness targeting his political enemies."

"That isn't what this is, Elmer."

"No. It isn't. I am sure of that. But the truth doesn't matter in an instance like this, because your actions—all of them completely outrageous and sensational—speak louder than the truth."

"The truth is that we know who the Butcher is," Malone shot back. "And we're trying to stop him."

Irey sighed and sat back in his chair. "Come on now, Malone. You are not a foolish man. You know how this works."

Malone didn't respond. The axe was coming, and he simply waited for it to fall.

"You're done in Cleveland. Case closed."

"The case is not closed, as you've so plainly outlined," he said.

"We're done in Cleveland," Irey reiterated, changing the pronoun. *We're done.* Meaning the agency was done. "And I need you in Chicago."

"Why?"

"Big money is going into US Steel, money not making it to production levels. With the war coming, the president wants to know why." Irey's voice was brisk, matter-of-fact.

What in the hell was he going to tell Dani? What in the hell was he going to tell himself?

"I'll expect you in Chicago tomorrow. You've got somewhere you can stay?" Irey knew he did.

Malone nodded once.

"We're done here, Malone," Irey said again. "It's over."

26

She was waiting up for him. His lamp was burning, and she was sitting cross-legged on his bed, a dress in her lap, and a tin of beads beside her. She was attaching them, one by one, her needle flying, her hands sure.

He walked into the bathroom without greeting her, needing a minute alone. He washed and shaved, brushed his teeth, and gathered his things. He didn't have much.

He didn't look at her when he walked back in the room, but Charlie twined himself around his legs and then shot under the bed when he stumbled.

"Damn cat," he muttered. He crouched down and lifted the spread. His suitcases were where he'd shoved them back in January. Both were speckled with Charlie's hair. He unzipped the empty one and laid it open. The other was still packed with things he hadn't used, costumes for characters he hadn't needed.

"He's going to sulk for hours now," Dani said, still beading. "I'll never get him out."

He grunted and straightened. She thought he was worried about Charlie. He shrugged out of his shirt, exchanging it for a new one. His fingers flew over the buttons, and he tucked it into his trousers, snapping his suspenders back in place and turning down his collar.

"He likes you, you know. He just doesn't know how to tell you. So he makes a nuisance of himself." So far his actions had not alerted her that something was amiss.

"I have to leave, Dani," he said, tugging open his drawers. He didn't look at her, but from the corner of his eye, he saw her pause, her needle upraised so her beads wouldn't slide off the string.

"Where to?" she asked. "And when will you be back?" Her voice was easy, trusting.

He kept moving. His drawers were emptied—one, two, three—in all of twenty seconds.

"Michael?" She secured the needle in her fabric and put the lid on the tin of beads.

He folded his suits on top of the contents of his drawers and added his dress shirts before zipping it closed. His files were already in the trunk. He didn't know what he'd do with those. He didn't need them anymore. His boots were in the trunk too. He'd started keeping them there, away from Dani's curious touch.

"Chicago. I have to go to Chicago," he said, his answer distracted. Belated.

He tossed his shaving kit, his spectators, and his white fedora into the valise he'd had since he was eighteen years old. It'd been everywhere with him. The white handkerchief Irene had initialed and Dani had returned was already tucked in the inside pocket.

"Michael?" Her voice was sharper now.

"I'll just run these out to the car. Give me a minute," he said. "Then I'll tell you everything." Dani's feet were bare, and she wouldn't follow him. He strode out of the room, the two suitcases in his hands, and was through the back door before she was even off the bed.

She was ready for him when he returned, though, holding his valise like she was taking it hostage, her eyes bright, shoulders stiff, mouth unsmiling.

He took it from her and set it by the door. His hat was on his desk, his overcoat slung over his chair. His suitcoat was still in the car. He hadn't even worn it inside. He was ready.

"What happened, Michael?" she asked.

"I have a new assignment in Chicago and reason to believe that I've been made, or Michael Lepito's been made. And that's not safe for you or your aunts."

Her brow furrowed. "What about Francis Sweeney?"

"He's not my problem anymore. He really never was. This was all . . . temporary. You knew that."

"Whose problem is he?" she whispered.

"His family has been notified and advised."

"Of what?"

"His mental condition. He's being taken to an institution as we speak. He'll continue to be monitored. Watched. He won't be getting out anytime soon." He shrugged and reached for his hat.

"I see," Dani whispered. He could see that she did.

"You're not coming back?" she asked, but it wasn't really a question.

"No." His heart had begun to race.

"You will leave. And I will stay. And we will be through," she said.

"Yes." He couldn't breathe. Short, blunt answers were best when one couldn't breathe.

"Is there nothing about me . . . about us . . . that you would like to keep?"

Leave it to Dani to pose the question that way, to cut to the heart of it all. The parts of himself, all the neat compartments that he kept so cleanly divided, were beginning to touch. They were beginning to hover at the edges of one another, sparking and grinding, and he could not simply walk from room to room, closing doors on one matter to attend to the next.

"I would take you with me if I could. If you could," he confessed in a rush. It was a suggestion, a cruel one, because she would not leave. But he couldn't help himself from making it. He would take her with him, everything else be damned. If she said, *I'm coming with you,* he would let her.

"I can't leave them," she said.

"I know. I can't stay, and you can't leave," he said.

"I have responsibilities here. I am not free to go wherever I wish."

He didn't lecture her and say, *I told you so.* It would have been insincere. He *had* told her. And he'd told himself, and they had still done what people do. They'd become attached to one another.

"Do you think someday we might be . . . together again?" she asked.

"You will find someone else."

"No. I won't." She shook her head once, vehement. "And I wish you wouldn't say such things. It makes me feel as though you don't know me at all."

"I know you, Dani. And you know me. No pretense, remember? You have become . . . dear . . . to me. You will always be dear to me." It was true. But it was weak. Limp. And only a fraction of the truth.

"So we will part as friends, then?" she asked. "Is that what you want?"

"You are not just my friend," he confessed.

"No?" Her voice was faint.

"No. I'm in love with you. So you aren't just . . . my friend." And he was a bastard for admitting it. Love confessed and then denied was not a gift.

"You are in love with me. And I am in love with you. But you're still going to go?"

"Yes." A *bastard.*

Her gaze was steady, but her blue eye was brighter, her dark eye deeper, and he could see her fighting for her composure.

"I've made my choices, Dani. I don't live a life that I can share. I knew, going into this job fifteen years ago, that there would be no room for anything or anyone else. I chose that. It is what I wanted."

"But . . . is it what you *want*?" she challenged, her voice bleak.

He reached for her then, needing one last embrace, one last kiss. He would pay attention to every detail. He would catalog it. Make a list so he wouldn't forget. But she stepped away. She bristled, like she couldn't bear his touch. His hand fell, and her eyes followed, clinging to the floor.

"You say you know me, and I'm not sure you do. But I *do* know you," Dani insisted, her voice shaking. "I know every line of your face and wish in your heart. I *know* you. And you will go, and you will never come back. You will convince yourself that I am foolish and that you are undeserving. You will continue in the way you have done, and you will die alone. We will *both* die alone."

"Don't say that, Dani," he said, aghast.

She pressed her palms to her eyes and breathed deeply, fighting, struggling, winning. She dropped her hands, straightened her back, and met his gaze again.

"Forgive me," she murmured.

His heart ached and his spirit howled, but he picked up his hat and put it on his head. It was time to go.

"I will call if that's . . . all right," he said. "To see how you are. Maybe I could . . . send a letter, now and again. But only if you want me to."

"Do you have to go tonight?" she asked.

He hesitated.

"I would very much like for you to stay. With me. Just . . . tonight."

"It will not change anything."

She was silent as though she thought it might.

"It will hurt more," he warned.

"I can't imagine that it would."

~

She'd asked him once not to make her beg. She would not beg him now. And she would not chase him. But she had flinched when he'd reached for her, and it was not how she wanted to part. She had not flinched because she didn't want his touch. She wanted it too much, and she didn't want to weep in front of him. Not for herself.

He set his hat back down and approached her, his eyes wary.

Once, he had yearned for pretense. So pretense was what she would give him. She would pretend his leaving was what they both wanted. That it was for the best. She would pretend she was steady. And she would take whatever he would give her.

He lifted his hands to her face, the pads of his thumbs bracketing her mouth. Then he leaned in and laid his lips on hers. So kindly. So gently. And when he withdrew, she was angry.

"I am not a child," she said, keeping her voice low so it wouldn't quake. "And I am not glass. I am not sending you away or begging you to stay, so don't kiss me like I am. Don't kiss me like I will break."

"How should I kiss you, Dani?" he whispered, still holding her face in his hands.

"You *know* how to kiss me, Michael. You know! Why do you act as if you don't?"

"Why don't you show me?" he said.

She did, flattening her lips against his and gripping his coat in her hands. It was too hard and too angry, too much passion and not enough pleasure, and not at all what she wanted.

"Are we fighting or kissing?" he ground out against her mouth.

She pulled away, but he tightened his grip on her jaw, his fingers curling in her hair, and brought her back to him. He coaxed her lips to yield with a soft mouth and sweet pressure, and when they did, he sank into her, deep and deliberate, and there he stayed. He was not frantic. He did not kiss her with pent-up desire or a pending goodbye. He simply kissed her, thorough and slow, like he had nowhere else to go and nowhere else he wanted to be.

The pull in her belly and the heat in her breasts betrayed her, weakening to him when she needed strength, and desperation rose in her chest. She grew bold, chasing his tongue and letting her hands rove, daring him to deny her. He didn't, though he shuddered, his lips still seeking and his eyes closed, like the pleasure was dragging him under.

She let herself memorize him, the smoky clean scent of his skin, the contrast of his silken mouth and his freshly shaved cheeks. Wide shoulders, long biceps, strong forearms, big hands. His fingers flexed against hers, but she didn't cease her explorations. He was lean, and the knobs of his shoulders, elbows, and knees were sharp, the ridges on his back and the ribs beneath a well-developed chest too defined. She'd seen him eat—he ate heartily—but he allowed himself no glut, no vice, and very few comforts. He was harsh with himself. Unyielding and unforgiving. It made it easier to accept what he withheld from her, knowing it was his way.

His hands had fallen to her bottom, urging her against him. Then he swooped her up and laid her on the bed, a magnanimous bridegroom, but he did not cover her body with his own or lay down beside her. He stood, bent over her, his mouth on hers for a minute more before burying his face in her neck, one hand stroking her hair, one hand resting low on her belly, as if he knew the heat he'd kindled there and wished to protect it.

She pressed her hand over his, urging him downward, silently begging, but he turned his palm and stayed her motion. Then he lifted his head and looked down at her. His throat worked, and his lips were wet from her kisses. And she knew what he was going to say.

"I love you, Dani Flanagan. I . . . adore you," he whispered, emphatic. "But I won't make love to you and then leave. You would not thank me when it was all said and done, and I would hate myself. This way is better for both of us."

He kissed her again, a fleeting touch with closed lips, as if he didn't trust himself to linger, and then he straightened and stepped away, his hands falling to his sides.

She could not speak. She could not even look at him. She rolled to her side, away from the door, away from him, and waited for him to go.

~

When he'd said it would hurt more if he stayed, he'd known with certainty that it would. In the space of mere minutes the situation had gone from terrible to intolerable, and he'd learned long ago that the only way to deal with intolerable was to move. And keep moving.

Dani had turned away from him, giving him her back. But he understood. There was nothing to say, and no good way to say it. In the soft glow of the lamp, her hair was copper, and the line of her back, the curve of her waist, and the flare of her hips were desert dunes draped in soft pink. She glowed.

She was a painting in sunset shades, her colors melding into the shadows of the room, and he let himself look for a moment more. The dress she wore was the same hue as the apples of her cheeks and the plum of her mouth. He'd noted both when he tore himself from her lips. It was the same dress she'd worn the night she'd roused him with kisses on the sitting room floor, Debussy having put him to sleep.

Oh, to go back to that moment, when he'd been hazy with sleep and easy with dreams, awakened by a lover's touch. He'd run from her then like he was running from her now. But it was not because he didn't want to stay.

When he dropped his hat on his head and his coat over his arm, he made himself turn away for good. He would call when he reached Chicago. Just like he'd said he would. He would even write to her. He would enjoy that. He would allow himself that. And if or when she failed to reply, he would know to let go.

He picked up his bag, still waiting by the door, and reached for the knob.

"Good night, Dani," he whispered, one last time.

He was in the hallway when he thought he heard her reply. "Good night, Michael."

∼

When he'd left Chicago in '23, he'd left behind a woman who had wanted him gone. She'd begged him to go. She'd screamed and wept and threatened and cajoled. And she'd never once asked him to come back. He would have. He'd remained faithful to her, as faithful as a man could be when the object of his loyalty has given up all claim to him.

Molly said he should comfort himself with the fact that Irene did not reject him for the love of another. Irene had never strayed either, as far as he knew. She gave him up because she preferred to stay broken, and a marriage, a true marriage, required constant mending. But Irene's isolation had never been a comfort to him. Isolation was not fidelity.

He'd left Chicago with nothing but heartbreak behind him.

It was different leaving Cleveland.

He found himself inexplicably checking his rearview mirror, like the city would follow him. Like he would still be able to see it, the signs and the skyline, the hollowed-out Run, and the odd-eyed woman he'd kissed goodbye. No, it was not like leaving Chicago at all.

He drove in silence, not whistling or humming, not muttering to himself or listening to the push-button radio that was a luxury in most cars. He drove that way for hours, stopping for fuel and then continuing on, silence sitting beside him, just like it had done for the last fifteen years.

But something had changed.

The silence was no longer empty. It was no longer a relief. It gnawed at him now, biting and tugging and twisting in his gut. And it got worse the farther he traveled.

At one point he pulled over, convinced he was going to be sick. He rolled down the window and let the air whoosh through the windows. It was going to be a beautiful day and nothing like his miserable trip to Cleveland in January had been. The foliage was lush, the skies clear, and dawn was coming. Yet his discomfort grew with every mile.

He retched, trying to force the feeling to abate, and suddenly there were tears on his cheeks and a moan in his throat. His chest began to heave, the writhing in his belly rising to his lungs. He wasn't sick. He was *crying*.

And it shocked him.

He pulled out his handkerchief and mopped at his face. More tears replaced the ones he dried. "Good God, Malone," he said, but the tremor in his voice embarrassed him, making it a thousand times worse. The tears were coming so hard he would not be able to drive. He sat behind the wheel instead, shaking and shuddering, his fists to his eyes, fearing he'd lost his goddamn mind.

A few cars slowed on the highway as they passed, curious about the car pulled to the shoulder of the road. Most gaped, a few gestured. One man even stopped, probably thinking he was having car trouble. Malone waved him on through his open window, and the man mercifully veered back onto the road.

His eyes were raw and red, his nose too, but eventually the streaming ebbed, and the pain in his throat became a dull ache. He had not cried since Mary died. And even then, he'd bit his sorrow back and shoved it away so often that eventually it had only lurked at the edge of his thoughts and plagued his sleep.

He'd thought all his grief had gone. He'd thought it had moved on. And suddenly . . . it was back. Maybe grief was always like that. Maybe it kept coming back until you released it. He suspected it had always been there, under the ice, just like Dani said. Maybe now, it would finally go for good.

He pulled back onto the highway an hour after he'd stopped, but his eyes continued to well and his chest continued to ache. By the time he reached Molly's house in Chicago, his head was pounding, and his legs shook as he took his valise from the car. His other things could wait.

Molly made him breakfast—he'd just missed Sean—and bustled around him, cleaning and chatting and needling him for news about the Butcher. If she noticed his battered countenance and exhausted reticence, she didn't say, and Molly would have said. Having the face of a hound dog had its advantages.

He was weary enough that rising from the table was too much work, and he sat with his hands clasped and his head bowed, knowing he needed to call Dani. He'd said he would. But he didn't think he could. Not today.

"You know I never pry in your work, but do you think you've caught him?" Molly asked, sitting down across from him with a pot of tea. "Is that why you've left Cleveland?"

"Caught who, Molly?"

"The Butcher!"

"Now why would you think I had anything to do with that?"

"Eliot Ness was here, brother. He was here for an hour, and he gave you a box of files. Eliot Ness is in Cleveland now. He has some job as a bigwig police commissioner or some such thing. And why else, in God's name, would you have gone to Cleveland?"

"Why indeed?" he muttered.

"So . . . have you caught him?"

"In a way," he sighed, deciding it did no good to deny his involvement when Molly had it all figured out.

She frowned. "What way is that?"

"The case is . . . closed. For me, it is closed. I have another assignment."

"Another assignment *here*? That surprises me," she said, concern furrowing her brow. "I thought Chicago wasn't safe for you."

"The anniversary of the massacre is in a couple of weeks." That wasn't anything Molly wouldn't know. Ten people had been killed and a number seriously injured on Memorial Day in Chicago last year when hundreds of sympathizers at a steelworkers' strike clashed with police. "Roosevelt is worried about the steel industry with war coming. He's been giving the union what it wants, but I'm guessing the Treasury Department wants to make sure the money is going where it's supposed to be going."

"Do you really think war is coming?" Molly said.

"Whether the US gets involved with the fighting or not, we'll still be supplying weapons, ships, and planes. War is big business, and America wants its cut."

"You're quite the cynic, Michael Francis Malone."

"Yes. I am. But I'm also right." He heaved himself up from the table. "Can I stay here for a few days? Until I know what's what?"

"Of course you can. Sean and I are bored out of our minds. At least your gloom is new."

"Ha." He paused by the telephone in the hallway and looked down at it, thinking of Dani. Molly was still watching him.

"Are you all right, little brother?" Molly asked softly. So she *had* noticed.

"I'm the same as I ever was, Molly girl," he responded and turned away from the telephone. He would call tomorrow.

"Hmm. That's what I was afraid of," Molly muttered. He didn't acknowledge her teasing but proceeded toward the bottom of the stairs where his bag sat waiting.

27

Neither of them were equipped to handle a prolonged goodbye. But whether from kindness or cowardice, in the days that followed, Dani bounced between anger and disappointment like a yo-yo on a string. There was work to do, always work to do, and she was grateful for the demands that kept her from curling up like Charlie and refusing to move.

The grief was not unlike the grief she'd felt when her parents died, and that surprised her. She'd been left behind then too, though not by choice.

Malone had left her by choice.

She wasn't sure what that said about her or him. Maybe it said nothing at all, and maybe it said everything. He loved her. Surprisingly, she did not doubt that. He loved her as greedily and obsessively as she loved him. His mouth, his hands, his eyes, his attention had all matched hers, and she'd felt the truth of it in his clothes. What Michael did not have was courage.

Her anger would always flare with that thought, but then her compassion would drag it down again. "Courage" was not the right word.

Michael was not a man of weak character or selfish intentions, and a man who worked undercover in Al Capone's circle for eighteen months was not short on mettle. It was not courage he lacked. She suspected it was confidence. He'd never recovered the faith to love again, with all that love demanded. That he'd fallen for her at all was miraculous. That he'd admitted it was yet another wonder.

If they'd had more time, he might have allowed himself to wade deeper, to swim farther, and not panic when he could no longer touch the bottom. If they'd had more time, he might have found the faith in himself—and her—to stay.

But the taskmaster had called, tugging the leash he'd been on for fifteen years, and he'd been dragged back to dry land. She was still treading water, hoping he would return.

Some days were easier than others, and she floated. Other days she felt like she was riding an anchor to the ocean floor. She knew she would have to wade back to shore sooner or later to face the prospect that the love he'd given her was all the love she was going to get.

But she had so much more to give him. *She had so much more to give.* And that kept her standing in the surf, looking out to sea.

For the first few days after he left, Lenka kept asking if she'd heard from him and when he was going to call. When he finally did, she'd demanded to know every word of the conversation. But Zuzana must have scolded her, for she stopped bringing him up.

The warmer weather meant less death from exposure but quicker decomposition, and without Michael's help, her work at the morgue was suddenly intolerable. Smells were stronger as the days grew longer. Every day, at least one body was too ripe to touch or wash. She would write a few meaningless words—a line by Dickinson that she loved or a bit of scripture—and tuck the papers in soiled pockets and fill out her forms. She hated when she could do nothing for the dead but make a notation on a ledger no one would likely ever read.

May rolled into June, and June became July. She received three letters from him, all of them short, vague, and rather meandering, as though he composed them over days as new lines occurred to him. She loved them because they signaled he was thinking about her. She hated them because they were empty of detail and devoid of hope. He didn't speak of seeing her again or tell her he missed her, but he signed them Michael, and that made her weep.

They were all postmarked in Chicago, and that was everything she knew about his current situation. She wrote back, using the post office box he'd provided her, and he seemed to have gotten her letters, though he never referenced anything she talked about specifically. He'd left her a telephone number too, but she didn't call him. She had asked him to stay. He had refused. She would not ask again.

The Cleveland papers crowed about "Eliot Ness's Secret Suspect" on May 31, but when no arrests were made and no official comments were forthcoming, the summer heat seemed to deflate that story. The summer heat had deflated *every* story. There was little talk of the investigation at all.

Darby didn't come by the shop like she'd told him to do, but once she found a bunch of yellow flowers in her wagon and another time a big brass button with St. Christopher stamped on the surface. A thin book of poems by Emily Dickinson was there another day. She ran her hands over the leather cover, but the volume was new, and she felt nothing but the brush of a bookseller's hands. Still, she had no doubt the items were from him.

Unemployment rose. Minimum wage rose too, though no one was working, so it was mostly a useless gesture. Dani was weary of useless gestures. Problems didn't get solved, they just got covered up, repackaged, or shoved to the side.

Hitler demanded that the Sudetenland, a part of Czechoslovakia with a large population of "ethnic Germans," be annexed, and the local Czech newspaper shared arguments for and against it, though Dani wasn't sure anyone really cared all that much. It was too far away, and they were Americans now, with American concerns.

"They will give it to him," Zuzana said. "No one wants war. So they will give it to him. And he will just keep taking and taking. You mark my words. You can't appease tyrants. You have to defeat them."

"We appease you every day, Zu," Lenka had scoffed.

But Zuzana's words struck a chord with Dani. With Michael's sudden departure, she'd been distracted by her own misery and hardly thought about the consequences of what had occurred. She had no doubt about what she'd seen and felt on Francis Sweeney's coat.

Michael had believed her. Eliot Ness too. But nothing had been done to hold the man accountable. Maybe nothing could be done. But why would he stop? If no one defeated him . . . why would he stop?

~

Malone was assigned to undercover detail at US Steel. He worked in a mill in coveralls and a cap, getting a firsthand look at the capacity and the conditions of the place. It had recently received an influx of money that didn't seem to be making it into production or the workers' pockets. It was going into someone's pockets, and Irey had a fair idea whose, but the strategy was not to prosecute—that took too long—but to plug the hole and get rid of the problem.

Malone was grateful for the physical nature of the work. It kept the silence at bay. He fell into his bed late and woke early, with little chance to stew or compose lists of all the reasons he was a fool.

He'd achieved a new level of grim.

Molly had worried about him taking an assignment so close to home, but he'd told her what Irey told him. The people who had known him as Michael Lepito didn't know him well, and those people weren't going to be in the mill.

He'd only called Dani once. It was better that way. But he found himself adding a line here and there to a letter, bits and pieces of nothing. He couldn't talk about his work.

One Sunday in August after Mass, he found himself standing beneath a theater marquee, hands in his pockets, staring at the ticket window. A new Errol Flynn movie in Technicolor was being touted. *Robin Hood.* Just what America needed in the midst of a depression that hadn't let up for almost a decade. Robin Hood, a man who takes from the haves to give to the have-nots. The concept had always appealed, especially among the poor, and since everyone nowadays was poor, it would appeal to most. He liked the pictures for the reason he guessed most people did. They were a beautiful escape from yourself for a couple of hours.

He bought a ticket, but he didn't manage to escape. He sat for most of the picture in a haze of longing, his hands clasped in his lap, remembering eggs and jelly toast and Dani's joy at the outing, replaying their discussion about systems and programs, about dignity and division. Dani would love Robin Hood.

He left before it was over and walked aimlessly, not wanting to be still, and ended up back at Molly's, the telephone in his hand, desperate to hear her voice. He didn't breathe as the operator connected him, and then felt faint when Dani's hello echoed over the line.

"Dani. It's Malone. Are you well?" he barked.

"Yes."

"And Lenka and Zuzana?"

"They are fine too. Lenka tries to read your letters, and Zuzana pretends to have forgotten your name, but they are well."

He smiled at that, though when he caught his reflection in the mirror, he realized he wasn't smiling at all. His mouth held the same straight line, and his eyes were not creased in mirth.

"How are *you*, Michael?" Her voice was gentle, and he marveled that she could be so kind. He'd expected her to be stilted and a little cold after months without a call. She wasn't, and it made him ache all the more.

"Are you sleeping? And eating? Are you smiling sometimes?" she asked.

"Not as often as I did in Cleveland." He'd slept so well in her old room. "But I'm busy. I have to sleep quickly or I won't sleep at all."

They talked for a minute more, saying nothing, and then he made himself say goodbye. When he hung up the handset and walked into the kitchen, not certain when he'd last eaten, his sister was sitting at the table.

"Was that Daniela?" she asked.

He scowled at her. "Why is it that every woman in my life is a snoop?"

"Is *Daniela* a woman in your life?"

He sat down at the table and laid his head on his arms. He was too tired to match wits with Molly. She had always been able to read him like a book. She hadn't even needed to touch his goddamn clothes.

"How did you know about Dani?" he muttered.

"I called Eliot."

"You called Eliot," he said flatly. "Why does everyone call Eliot?"

"Because he's the only friend you have," she snapped. "And he's the reason you were in Cleveland in the first place. He shows up here, you run there, and now you're back, looking like the Mad Butcher himself hacked you up, and you tried to sew yourself together. You run yourself ragged, Michael Francis. Ragged. And for what? For who?"

"I will be done soon, Molly. Then I will be out of your hair."

"I don't want you out of my hair! I want to know why you aren't in Cleveland when that's clearly where you want to be."

"Nobody wants to be in Cleveland."

"Eliot says you are in love with a woman named Daniela. You were a boarder in her house for all those months, apparently?"

He stared at her glumly, wondering why in tarnation Eliot, who was a master negotiator, couldn't hold his tongue with Molly.

"Oh, my dear brother. Have you not learned anything from your suffering?" She tsked.

"What suffering?"

"You have carried your share of burdens, to be sure," she said, and he could see she was warming up for a good lecture.

"Molly—" he groaned.

"But responsibilities should not be avoided." She stabbed her finger at him.

"So I work too hard, but I'm avoiding my responsibilities?" he snapped.

"You are afraid of commitment," she said. "And it's understandable, really, after Irene. But I must speak plainly to you, brother. You avoided Irene too."

"I didn't avoid Irene."

"You did."

When he began to protest in his own defense, she raised her hand, halting him.

"I am not accusing you. I am not judging or condemning. Don't misunderstand. I know Irene told you to go. I know she pushed you away."

"Yes. She did," he said, surprised that it still wounded him and more surprised that Molly was picking at the wound.

"So, in response, you have taken on burdens that require no emotional commitment. For the last fifteen years you have solved one problem after another, and I am proud of you. But the kind of burdens you build a life around aren't the ones you can set down. You carry them *always*. And in turn . . . they carry you."

"I don't know what you mean, Molly."

"Yes you do!" she cried. "Irene insisted you put her down. And you did. She made you afraid to try again. But you are built to carry heavy loads, Michael Francis Malone."

Suddenly his nose was stinging, and his chest ached, and he cursed the grief that would not . . . let . . . him . . . be. He couldn't even look at Molly. He made to rise, but she clamped her hands over his wrists, demanding he stay put.

"Loving is the greatest burden of all. The heaviest burden of all. And who do you love, Michael?"

"You. I love you, Molly," he said.

"Yes. And I love you. But who else? You are a big, strong man with a powerful heart, and you aren't using it."

He was silent. Everyone he'd once loved was gone. He loved Dani, but it did him no good to dwell on it.

"It is the things we most want to put down, the things that are hardest to carry, to endure, that give our lives the most meaning. Sometimes our burdens are taken from us. And sometimes we walk away from them. Sometimes, not having that burden might even feel good. We might feel relief. But it doesn't take long to realize that the things we call burdens are most often ballast. Our burdens give weight to everything we do. They shed light on all that we are. And the moment we lose them . . . we lose everything."

He had lost everything, once. And he'd made damn sure he couldn't lose it again.

"What if . . . ," he began.

"What if she asks you to put her down?" Molly finished for him.

"Yes. What if she tells me to go?"

"It sounds to me like she's a strong one."

"I think she is. Yes. But she's young too. And naive. And a little blind when it comes to me."

"Is she really?" Molly scoffed. "From the way Eliot tells it, I don't think she's blind at all. I think she sees too much."

"Yeah . . . well. You see too much. And Eliot has a big mouth."

She laughed. "Go to her, brother. Go to her, pick her up in your arms. Take on the burden of love. And don't ever let her go."

"It would not be a burden to love her," he argued, needing the last word since Molly had let him have so few.

"Of course it would. It is a burden to love anyone. And it is a burden to be loved. Stop running from it, my boy. Go back to Cleveland. Go back to your Dani. Be a burden to her. I beg you. And ask her to be yours." She winked. "And now, if you don't mind, I think one of my burdens just pulled in the driveway, and I am going to dish up his dinner. You're welcome to join us."

28

The refrigeration at the morgue was on the fritz. Mr. Raus had all the bodies moved to other facilities or prepared for burial and transported to cemeteries while repairmen sweated in the storage locker, trying to bring the system into working order. On Friday it was working at full capacity, pouring cold air into the storage locker, and Dani documented and dressed ten bodies for burial on Saturday, but by Monday it was back to running in fits and starts, and Mr. Raus was at his wit's end. He and Mrs. Raus left for a convention in Detroit with a warning to Dani that the Mead facility would not be receiving any more of the city's indigent dead until they returned and any necessary repairs had been made.

Mr. Raus asked if she would check the facility Tuesday evening to make certain that no new cases had been delivered.

"I don't want bodies sitting in a faulty fridge for the next week."

Dani was grateful for a brief respite from the work, but worried about the stipend they'd come to rely on. She walked to the morgue, tugging her wagon behind her, more out of habit than necessity. Even with no bodies to tend to, there was still work to be done, and possibly laundry to bring home. But after finding the cold locker empty—and not very cold—with no new dead to be cared for, she made a thorough reassessment of the clothing she kept on hand and added a series of updates in her ledger. By 7:00 p.m., she was ready to leave.

A light rapping at the main door had her frowning up at the clock. Seven o'clock on a Tuesday evening was too late for a delivery, but maybe Mr. Raus had scheduled a repairman to come while she was there and had forgotten to warn her in all the hubbub.

She approached the door wearily. She wanted to go home. But the rapping became scraping in the lock, and she realized whoever was entering had a key.

"Mr. Raus?" she called.

"No. No. Not Mr. Raus, Miss Kos," a voice answered, jovial. "It's just me."

A man stepped inside the facility and hung his straw hat and a white suitcoat on a peg beside the door. It was too hot for anything but shirtsleeves, and he began to roll his as if he was well-accustomed to the work of the morgue.

"I don't think we've ever met before, Miss Kos," he continued, not even looking up at her as he washed and dried his hands.

"There are no dead to attend to, sir," she said, uncertain. "Mr. Raus made other arrangements this week while he's out of town. Did he not tell you?"

"No. No. He didn't tell me. Mr. Raus and I have not talked in years, though I used to help him here and in his mortuary in '33. I'm sure he is not even aware that I have access to this building. Undertaker's privilege." He winked and began pulling on a pair of gloves. "The security is really quite sloppy. He's clearly not worried about his clients." He chuckled.

She could not remember his name, but she recognized him. He'd been one of the doctors at Dr. Peterka's practice for a while. He'd sat with the others some mornings in the lounge, but she couldn't remember ever speaking to him.

He was heavier than he'd been years before, but the puffiness in his face and the ruddiness in his cheeks indicated a fondness for alcohol that had probably contributed to his weight. His faded red hair waved back from a large forehead, and the round spectacles that sat on his prominent nose illuminated the blue of his eyes.

"Forgive me, Doctor. I don't remember your name," she said, retreating several steps. He didn't seem inclined to leave even though there were no undertakings to perform.

"You don't?" He tipped his head at her in amazement. "But I have known your name for so long. And I was sure your friend would have reminded you."

"My friend?"

"Your boarder. Such a fascinating man. I heard him talking about you. With Eliot Ness. I thought he might stay in Cleveland. But men like that don't stay, do they?"

"My boarder?" she asked, her voice faint, and dread pooled at her feet.

"Mike. Michael Malone. He called you Dani. But I prefer Daniela. A beautiful name for a beautiful girl. You look like your mother. Aneta Kos and I were friends, you know, when we were young. Edward Peterka introduced us. But she left Cleveland, didn't she? Got swept off her feet. And she never came back. I was sorry to hear of her passing. But that was years ago."

"Can I help you with something, Doctor?" He was too close to the door. She would not be able to get past him. Her mind scrambled for options, should she need them.

"I don't know, Daniela." He paused, studying her, one gloved hand cupping his chin, one wrapped around his middle. "I have something for you. And a confession of sorts."

"You do?" A bead of sweat scuttled from the base of her neck to the waistband of her skirt.

"Yes. I am a fan of your work, though I've never quite understood it."

"Have you worn one of our suits, Doctor?" she asked, voice faint.

"No, I confess I haven't. I've never worn anything with the Kos label, though I suspect I've been missing out. You have such a delicate and distinct hand."

Dani looked down at her fingers and back up at the man, who was smiling at her in such an odd, benevolent manner. Her hands didn't tremble and her gaze stayed steady, but her knees were knocking beneath her skirt.

The doctor turned back to his suitcoat and took a small stack of papers from the breast pocket. He walked toward her, clutching them, but stopped several feet from her, his arm extended. Her eyes darted to his offering, and she froze. The papers in his hands were obituaries. Her obituaries. The ones she made for all the unknowns.

"I've startled you, haven't I?" he asked. "I'm sorry." He pulled the papers back and fixed the spectacles on his nose, as if he were preparing to remind her of the words she'd written.

"These are just my favorites, but I've read them all. For years now, I've read them all. And I've wondered about you." He read a few out loud, and she remembered each one. He'd taken them from her dead.

"It seems we both have a fondness for Dickinson. So witty. So droll. I think she must be like us. 'I'm nobody, who are you? Are you a nobody too?'" he quoted. "This place is a home for the nobodies, isn't it? But you and I, we take our work very seriously. We make the nobodies into somebodies." He smiled and shook his head. "You name them all and give them lives. It's delightful."

"I don't know what you want," she whispered. "Or why you would take those from the dead. They have nothing, and you took even the little I could give them."

"And you still don't know who I am?"

She hesitated.

"Ah . . . I thought so." He waggled a finger at her. "You shouldn't lie about such things. Names are important."

"Are you Francis Sweeney?" she said. "Is that your name?"

"Yes. Francis Sweeney. But my friends call me Frank. Dr. Frank. You may call me Frank too. That's what your mother called me." He added in a conspiratorial whisper, "And I called her Nettie."

He waved one of the white obituaries in the air, and his voice resumed a jovial tone. "Just like the other Nettie. The one wrapped in a quilt. I took her, you know. I couldn't resist when I saw her name, though she was already dead."

"You . . . took Nettie?"

"Yes. Months ago. I left her for Eliot, but it seems I hid her too well. So . . . I had to put her somewhere he could find her." He shook his head indulgently. "I leave him so many clues . . . but he never understands them. But you understood them, didn't you, Daniela? You understand me."

She didn't answer. She didn't understand him at all.

He smiled and put the stack of obituaries back in the pocket of his trousers.

"You helped them find me. You told them who I was. I would have left you alone to do your work. Why couldn't you leave me alone to do mine?"

∼

Malone had just pulled into the driveway at five on Wednesday afternoon when Molly came rushing from the front door, waving her arms and calling his name.

"Thank God you're home early. She's been calling all day. All day. And I haven't known what to tell her. She's on the line now."

He stepped out of the car and slammed the door. "Who, Molly?"

"It's an old woman. She's asking for Michael Malone. I didn't know whether to admit I even know who that is, but she's insistent."

He followed Molly into the house, an odd weightlessness in his chest, a cold heaviness in his gut. He picked up the receiver and placed it to his ear.

"Hello?"

"Mr. Malone?"

"Lenka?"

"No, Michael. It is Zuzana."

Zuzana was calling him. And she'd called him Michael. He hardly knew what to make of that, but in a millisecond his mind tripped over the possibilities. She would beg him to come back. She would tell him to never come back. She would call him a cad. An Irish dog. A miserable fool.

But she did none of those things.

"Mr. Malone . . . Daniela is gone. And we don't know where."

~

He couldn't douse his terror, and speed didn't help. He drove straight through, from Chicago to Cleveland, stopping once for fuel and crowding the poor attendant who couldn't pump the gasoline any faster than he was. He threw a wad of cash at him and pulled away a mere five minutes after he'd stopped, frothing at the mouth and unable to feel anything but the fear that soaked his shirt and dried his mouth.

He couldn't even think about her without his hands slipping from the wheel and sweat dripping in his eyes. By the time he pulled into the driveway at 5054 Broadway, it was nearing midnight, and he had half convinced himself that she would be there waiting, simply because he could bear no other thought.

If she was there, he would fall down at her feet and beg her to have him, if only to douse the burning in his veins. He was smoldering, yet he still had hope. The hope just made the burning worse.

But when he walked into the house, reeking of six hours of agony and horror, Lenka, Zuzana, and Margaret greeted him with hollow eyes and shaking hands. Dani had not come home, and the police had been slow to respond.

"She went to the morgue, just like she always does, but she never came back. And Mr. and Mrs. Raus are out of town."

"Her wagon is here, by the back door," Zuzana said. "She must have come back."

"It was there when I arrived this morning," Margaret interjected. "There was a bit of paper in it. A few lines from a poem, something in her hand. But I never saw Daniela."

"She was not at breakfast," Lenka moaned.

"She must have come home last night . . . but her bed has not been slept in," Zuzana said.

"We didn't know she wasn't home." Lenka shook her head, aghast. "We ate supper without her last night and retired early."

"I heard that damnable squeaking, though. It woke me up. I know she came home," Zuzana insisted.

The women were piling the details one on top of the other, and he threw up his hands, silencing them.

He started at the beginning, making sure he understood the timeline.

"Dani went to the morgue on Mead Avenue yesterday?" *Yesterday.*

Lenka nodded. "She left at five, when we closed the shop." *Thirty-one hours ago.*

"You're sure?"

"I watched her leave when I locked the front door. She was pulling her wagon," Lenka said.

"Mr. Raus is out of town, and the building is locked," Zuzana insisted again.

"She must have come home. Her wagon's here," Margaret reminded.

"Let me see the paper that you found in the wagon," Malone directed. Margaret pulled it from her apron pocket and handed it to him.

"Unable are the loved to die, for love is immortality," he read. It was in Dani's handwriting, a slip of paper like the ones she tucked into the pockets of her dead. He stared at it, helpless. The paper was creased and soiled, and when he lifted it to his nose, it carried the sticky, sweet smell of rotting flesh. He recoiled violently.

"It's Emily Dickinson," Margaret said. "I know that. Just yesterday she was reading a book of her poems. She must have liked that one and copied it down."

"She didn't write this yesterday," he whispered.

"We rang the safety director . . . but he hasn't responded," Lenka added, shaking her head.

"They've found another body," Margaret blurted out, and Lenka broke down.

"Two. They found two," Zuzana said. "At the dump near the Exposition site. That's why no one has come to help us. Nobody has time for two old women when the Butcher's been busy."

"Oh no," he groaned. "Oh no. Oh, Dani."

"But you'll help us, won't you, Michael?" Lenka asked, tears winding their way through her wrinkles and dripping from her trembling chin.

"I should have let her go," Zuzana said, her voice dull. "I should have let her go with you. It's all my fault. I was afraid to be alone. Now she's dead. The Butcher got her. I know it. The Butcher got her."

~

The man was standing by his car when Malone rushed from the house, after telling the distraught women he would get help. He had to find Eliot, and he had to see the bodies. He had to know whether there was anything left to search for.

Malone skidded to a halt.

"What happened to Dani?" the man said, his Cork accent as marked as it must have been three decades before. He held his hat in his hands, and even in the darkness, his fear was evident.

Malone didn't answer but approached the man with careful tread. The man asked the question again, his voice adamant.

"Tell me what happened to Dani. I heard the women crying. They've been up and down the block today, talking to the neighbors. They can't find her. And now you're back. Where did you go?"

"We don't know where she is," Malone said, hardly able to admit the words out loud. "She's missing. Do you know anything that might help us find her?"

"I'm always too late," the man moaned. "I'm never where I need to be. I didn't know she was in trouble."

"What's your name?" Malone asked, but he already knew.

"Darby," the man said. "Darby O'Shea. Dani's father was my cousin."

"Why are you here, Darby O'Shea?"

"I check on her sometimes. I've been back every year. Every year. Just to see how she fares. I stuck around a little longer this time."

"When did you see her last?"

"I don't know." The man shook his head. "I thought you were going to look after her," he accused. "Where've you been?" He was angry, and his words punched the air and knocked the breath from Malone's chest.

Malone opened his car door. He didn't have time for O'Shea. He didn't have time for any of it. Darby O'Shea wrenched open the passenger-side door and slid in beside him, undeterred and still talking.

"I know who you are, Michael Malone. Michael Lepito. You took care of Dani when her folks died. You brought her to Cleveland. I saw you again when you were working for Capone. I knew you were a copper. But I didn't say nothin'. Because I owed you."

"Get out of my car, O'Shea," Malone warned, but O'Shea just talked faster.

"When you came back here . . . I worried. I didn't understand it. Couldn't figure out why you were here. So I followed you a bit. Asked that kid about you. He said you were asking questions about the Butcher. Then I saw Ness pick you up one day. Made me feel better. But I kept an eye out."

Malone started the car. He didn't have time for this. *He didn't have time.* Malone knew where Eliot would be. Where they all would be, and bile rose and burned his throat. Darby O'Shea would just have to come along for the ride.

"I saw the two of you on Short Vincent," O'Shea babbled. "She saw me too. Scared me a little. I thought you might think I was up to no good. Maybe send someone after me. So I took off for a few days. But I came back."

"When did you see her last?" Malone asked.

"I don't know . . . she gave me her medallion. Told me to take care of myself. I thought she was fine. A little sad about the eyes and mouth. But I'm guessing that was your fault. I should have warned her offa ya, like I warned that kid. You got enemies. You got enemies . . . and now she's gone."

Malone stared straight ahead, his hands gripping the wheel.

"Where did you go?" O'Shea shouted. "Where the hell you been?" He had a hand braced against the dash and the other hanging on to the door. Malone was not driving cautiously. "I'll kill you, Malone. If something's happened to that girl, I'll kill you."

If something had happened to Dani, Malone would kill himself.

Darby O'Shea fell back against the seat, releasing his death hold on the dash and covering his face. "Oh God," he moaned. "George. George, forgive me. I'm always too late. I'm always too late."

~

Malone drove to the city morgue. The Butcher's latest victims would have been brought there, and that's where Ness would be. Where they all would be if there were new remains to examine. Darby O'Shea rode beside him in introspective silence, and when Malone pulled into the parking lot, the man followed close on his heels. Malone did not protest.

In April, Malone had waited outside the city morgue for news on Victim #10. He didn't wait now. He walked through the front doors and past the sign-in desk without slowing his stride. It was something he'd learned long ago: look like you know where you're going, and no one will stop you.

No one did.

No one yelled, *You can't go in there*, or asked for his credentials. No one even turned their head. He walked down a long corridor, past doorways and gurneys and evidence tables, past technicians and policemen. He even walked past Coroner Gerber, who was huddled with a group that hung on his every word. Malone did not slow to hear the discussion, and no one looked up as he passed. He must have looked like he belonged. Confident. In control. Unconcerned. But when Malone saw Eliot, he felt none of those things. His legs went numb, and his head swam. He didn't know how he remained upright for the final few steps.

Ness looked like he hadn't slept since Capone. Maybe he hadn't. His hair stuck up on the sides like he'd been sitting with his hands gripping his head. His tie was loose and his trousers creased in a thousand places.

"Mike?" Eliot asked, baffled. "Why are you here?" Then his eyes skipped to Darby O'Shea, still at Malone's heels, but Malone was too distraught to make introductions or give explanations. Instead he asked, "Is it her, Eliot. Did you find her?"

"Who?" Eliot asked, bewildered.

"Did you find Dani?" Malone insisted, gripping Eliot by his rumpled lapels. He needed *something* to hold on to.

"What are you talking about?" Eliot gasped.

"Dani's gone."

Eliot blanched, but he shook his head.

"Yes!" Malone hissed. "Yes! She hasn't been seen since five o'clock yesterday. And you have two new victims. So I need to know if you found her, goddamn it."

"We found a body, Mike. Two of them. But not Dani. The woman's remains are old. Four months old, at least, David says."

Malone released Eliot's lapels and staggered back into Darby O'Shea, who was praising Jesus, Mary, and Joseph beneath his breath. But Malone's relief was a wave that slapped the shore and instantly receded. Dani was still missing.

"We found them yesterday," Eliot continued, rushing to reassure him. "Two people. Dumped at the same site. Corner of East Ninth and Lakeshore. Not too far from city hall. The remains of a woman and a man. Not together. Not even dead the same amount of time. But they were placed there sometime yesterday, we think. We got a head in a tin can, thighs in butcher paper, and a torso wrapped up in a yellow quilt like a baby." He rubbed at his face, and for a minute, Malone thought he might break down.

"Eliot," Malone whispered. "Where is Francis Sweeney?"

29

She ran from him.

The building was spacious, and the corners were dark and empty, and there were a number of places to hide, but she raced to the only place with a lock on the door.

"Come back, Daniela. Whatever are you going to do in there?" he called.

She pulled the heavy door of the cold locker closed behind her and turned the bolt. Sweeney had a key. He'd unlocked the front door. Did he know his key would unlock the cold storage too? She held the bolt down with shaking fingers. A moment later, she felt tension in the lock. He knew.

The tension immediately released, and he knocked politely.

"Daniela? What are you doing? You can't stay in there. You'll get cold. And I want to visit."

She didn't answer him. The locker was empty, the drawers for the dead held nothing but lingering scents and fetid air. And it wasn't cold.

"I'll wait out here," he said. She heard him moving around and the scrape of a stool. "Maybe we can just visit through the door."

She heard the slosh of a bottle and the sound of an uncorking. "I don't like being cold," he said, smacking his lips.

"How long can one remain in the cold locker? You're wearing that pretty dress. It won't keep you warm." He sighed, and she heard him take another long pull from whatever he was drinking. For several minutes he didn't speak at all, but he was there.

She leaned against the door, still clutching the lock.

"Did you help him find me?" he asked. She jerked, knocking her head against the frame.

"Miss Kos?" He snickered. "Are you there?"

"Yes."

"Ahh. You answered. Good. Good. I thought maybe you had already succumbed to the cold. You must keep moving. That will help stave it off."

Francis Sweeney clearly did not know the refrigeration wasn't working. If anything, it was uncomfortably warm in the locker. How long could she stay in here? It was not airtight. She supposed she could stay inside a good while, as long as she kept Francis Sweeney out.

"Did you help Mike find me, Miss Kos? I think maybe you did," he said. "That wasn't very nice of you. I did not interfere with your work. Why did you interfere with mine?"

"Mike?" she asked. She couldn't help herself. She wanted to moan his name. To cry his name. He would suffer when he found her gone. He would mourn, and there would be no one to comfort him.

"Michael Malone. Michael Lepito. He has many names. He's a spy, you know. Of course you know. He works with Eliot Ness. But now he's gone, isn't he?"

"Yes." He was gone.

"I don't think Eliot will be around much longer either. Cleveland deserves better. But I've so enjoyed our interactions. I will miss him when he goes. I have given him a few names too. Helpless Ness. Silly Ness. Hopeless Ness. Clueless Ness."

Another long pause.

"Are you like me, Miss Kos? Or can I call you Daniela? Or Dani. Mike calls you Dani. I heard him talking about you. At the Hotel Cleveland. Did you know they kept me imprisoned at the Cleveland for a week?" He sounded delighted. "He and Eliot talked about you at great length when they thought I was sleeping. So foolish of them. Mike seemed quite taken with you. But so pessimistic. He also said you see everything. Do you see everything, Daniela? Is that how they knew about me?"

"No. I don't see everything."

"You don't?"

"No."

He was silent for a moment, considering. "I confess . . . I was quite upset at you when I realized. I saw you at the gala, dancing with him. Daniela Kos and Michael Malone. Together. The undertaker and the spy."

He'd seen them at the gala. He'd been watching them before they were watching him.

"I left you alone all these years. Let you write your little notes and play with the dead. There was room here for both of us. I did not interfere with your work. Why did you interfere with mine?" he repeated.

He'd used the morgue.

It was the perfect spot. And she'd never felt him. Why would she? His dead and hers were not the same. His dead did not arrive via the city morgue. They came drugged and trussed and . . . alive. Then he scattered his dead all over town. He didn't leave his victims for her to clean and dress. And name.

"I know all about you, Daniela. I've known you for years. I know your family. I know everyone in Kingsbury Run. But do you . . . know . . . who *I* am?" he asked.

He was not asking her if she knew his name. They'd already established that.

"You're the Butcher," she said. No need to pretend any longer. It wouldn't save her to play dumb.

"Yes. I am," he said. "And I am Francis and Frank and Edward and Eddie."

"You are not Edward and Eddie. You killed Edward and Eddie."

"Yes. But they are still here. They won't leave me alone." He grew quiet again, drinking. She heard his weight shift and settle, and for a moment she thought he might have drifted off. She pressed her ear against the door, straining to hear him.

"Would you like to come out now?" he asked suddenly, his voice loud, and she bit back a cry and bore down on the lock.

He laughed and sighed. "No? That's a pity."

Another hour passed in silence. Francis Sweeney drank, and Dani sat and then stood, the room growing more and more unbearable.

"I'm going to go now, Daniela. You've made it so easy for me. I will miss you. I suspect many will. Do you think Mike will come back when he hears? I hope so."

She heard a clanking and a rattling of the handle, and a small scream escaped her throat.

"I'm not coming in. Don't worry. But you're not coming out either. Farewell, dear girl."

Then he retreated, his tread heavy. She held her breath, trying to track his progress. She thought she heard the entrance door open but couldn't be sure. A high, narrow window covered by a metal grate sat at the southwest corner of the wall, and she pulled out the locker drawers, climbing them like stairs until she could see out through the window. In the moonlight, she could see Francis Sweeney walking down the street, pulling her wagon behind him. She frowned, puzzled, and then she began to weep.

He was actually leaving.

~

Her hope was short lived. Sweeney had wedged something through the door handles, barring her escape, and when Dani unbolted the door and tried to open it, it didn't budge. If she could break the glass on the window she could scream for help. Not that anyone would come. The street was as dead as the regular inhabitants of the morgue. She climbed back up, but the holes in the grate covering the window were barely big enough to peer through, and she couldn't loosen it, though she tried until her fingertips began to bleed and she was sweating profusely.

She remained atop the shelves where at least she could see the street, where at least she could observe whether he returned, but after several hours, she feared she would doze off and fall, and she'd begun to shake with fear and fatigue. She climbed down on wobbly legs and sat with her back against the door so she would hear Francis Sweeney if he came back.

The room was not completely airtight—Mr. Raus had complained about cold air escaping into the cavernous warehouse and costing him money—but it *felt* airtight. The air was close and dry, hot from the August heat, and Dani spent the remainder of the night trying to conserve her energy and control her emotions. Tears were a luxury she couldn't afford, not when she had nothing to drink and her dress was stiff with perspiration.

The faulty refrigeration suddenly kicked on sometime around dawn, and she moaned in horror. It felt so good, but it would kill her. Sweeney was counting on it.

It became too cold very quickly, and she rose and began to pace to keep warm.

From the sunlight poking through the grate-covered window, she tracked the passing of the day. Her aunts would know she was missing by now. They would know she'd never made it home. They would come. Mr. Raus was out of town, and the aunts would not be able to get inside, but they would get help. Someone would surely come. Someone other than Frank Sweeney. Oh, please God. She had no doubt he'd left her for dead but feared he would come back to see for himself.

The faulty refrigeration groaned to a shuddering halt after two hours, and she almost wept in relief again, but her eyes were dry and her throat drier. The floor was concrete, and the metal drawers where the dead were kept weren't any warmer, even if she'd been willing to crawl into one. She managed to fall asleep sitting on her haunches, her arms wrapped around her legs and her head tucked into her knees as the room warmed again, the August heat of the warehouse outside the cold locker slowly raising the heat inside of it.

She dreamed of clothes. Piles of them. Whispering to her. Weighing her down.

She thought she heard Sweeney return and rolled against the door and clung to the lock, knowing that if he came back now, she wouldn't have the strength to stop him.

But the door did not rattle, and the stool was not removed, and she considered climbing the shelves once more, but her head spun and her legs trembled when she tried to rise, so she stayed put, her back against the door.

The temperamental system whirred up again at nightfall, and she hardly noticed when it clanked off again. Or maybe she'd simply gotten too tired to feel it.

～

"Where is Francis Sweeney?" Malone repeated, louder. Eliot flinched but met his gaze.

"I don't know," he confessed, crestfallen. "I have several units walking the Third and scouring the Run and surrounding streets looking for him, but no word yet."

"You don't know?" Malone shouted. The activity around them ceased as the whole room stopped and stared.

"He was released last week, and I've been trying to get a court order to get him locked up again. We've had a tail on him ever since, but he's enjoying himself, jumping on and off the streetcar suddenly to make his detail scramble, buying drinks for his 'shadows' at the bars and then slipping out the back door. He's loving every minute of the chase, and we keep losing him. Then this happened." Eliot tossed his hands toward the evidence tables. Flesh, bones, buckets, and battered clothing were being photographed while clinicians watched with clasped hands and blank faces.

"Find Francis Sweeney," Malone bellowed, including the gawkers in his command. Policemen, medical examiners, lab technicians, officials, insiders. They all stared.

"Malone!" David Cowles was pushing toward him, panic in his stride, but Malone didn't care.

"His name is Dr. Francis Edward Sweeney. He's your guy. He's your Butcher. He did that!" Malone pointed at the remains of the two most recent victims. "He's done all of it. And none of you—none of us—have stopped him."

Eliot tried to pull him back, but he lurched toward the macabre exhibit, ready to upend the tables. A soiled yellow quilt was spread beside a greasy display of bones, like a picnic for the Butcher's dead, and for the first time, Malone's eyes focused on what he was seeing.

He froze, his fury giving way to shock. His thoughts scattered and then merged, and that's when . . . he knew. He knew where Francis Sweeney killed his victims. He understood the clue.

"Eliot?" he asked.

"Yeah?" Eliot's arms were still wrapped around him, but Malone was perfectly still.

"Where did you find that quilt?" It was a bright patchwork, frayed at the edges and dirty with the gristle and grime of death, but he recognized it all the same.

"It was wrapped around the torso of the dead woman. Cheerful, isn't it?" Eliot whispered.

"Nettie," Malone moaned.

"What?"

"That's Nettie's quilt."

"I don't know who Nettie is, Mike. Who's Nettie?" Eliot kept his grip on his shoulders. Malone was grateful; he couldn't feel his legs.

"Check those remains, Cowles," Malone barked. "That woman in the quilt was already dead when Sweeney got to her. He didn't kill her, he just took her body and hacked it up. He's messing with us, Ness. He's toying with us."

"What are you talking about?" Eliot begged, still not following.

"Remains were taken from the indigent morgue on Mead Avenue where Dani works. Back in April. I saw that quilt wrapped around a dead woman's body *months ago*. Dani said her name was Nettie."

Sweeney took Nettie. *Oh God. Oh Dani.* But taking the body was just theater, one of Sweeney's merry stunts. The theft itself wasn't what shook Malone. It was the realization that Francis Sweeney, the Butcher of Kingsbury Run, had been using Dani's morgue all this time.

"That's where he's killing them, Ness," Malone insisted. "Where he's killed . . . all of them."

Eliot dropped his arms and stepped back, understanding lighting his raccoon-rimmed blue eyes, and Malone turned toward the door.

"Get a team to the morgue on Mead, Ness. We're all at the wrong goddamn morgue."

"But, Malone, what about Dani?" O'Shea shouted, trailing behind him.

He had to keep moving. He had to. He pushed out of the building, knowing Ness wouldn't be far behind him, but he couldn't wait.

"Malone?" O'Shea persisted, wrenching the passenger door open and climbing inside as Malone started his car.

"If we don't find Francis Sweeney, we won't find Dani," he said, and the words were like hot coals on his tongue.

∼

Someone was calling her name. Michael. Michael . . . and someone else. Many voices. Many voices and pounding feet. Calling her name. Calling Frank Sweeney's name.

The voices got closer, and the stool was wrenched free and tossed aside, clattering against the concrete floor.

"Dani. Where are you, Dani? Are you here?" That was Michael. That was Michael's voice, right outside the locker.

She tried to answer, but she suspected he wasn't real. It was probably the rattling of the refrigeration starting up. She would be freezing before too long. She didn't know if she could bear it again. She was so thirsty. So tired.

The door rattled.

Sweeney was back. He would unlock the door.

"No," she gasped. "No." She dragged herself up and clung to the bolt. "Go away."

"Dani?"

"Michael?" she cried.

Her mind was playing tricks on her. Sweeney was playing tricks on her.

"Dani," he shouted. "Are you in there?"

"Michael?" she moaned. Not Sweeney. Michael. It was Michael.

"It's me, Dani." His voice cracked over his words. He sounded as though he was weeping. Or exulting. "Dani . . . can you open the door?"

Michael was telling her to let go. And she'd promised him she would. She'd promised him that when she felt the cold, she would let go.

She turned the lock and let him in.

~

Dani's skin was drawn across her pale face, and her eyes were huge and darkly rimmed. She was there among the empty drawers and shelves that should have held the dead but instead housed her, wilted and wan, but alive and looking at him like she didn't trust her sight. She was wearing the same dress she'd worn the day she came to his room with a stack of his undershirts and a glazed expression, having realized exactly how he felt about her. Her dress was streaked with sweat and dust, and her curls were corkscrews around her face, but she was still standing. Standing and . . . swaying . . . and then she was in his arms. He lifted her up against his chest and carried her from the room.

Oh God. Thank you. Thank you, God.

"He took their names," she moaned into his neck. "And he knew me. He knew you too, Michael."

"I know, sweetheart," he said. "I know. But I've got you now." He brought her to the sink and laid her gently on the table where she sorted clothes, resting her head on a pile of laundered shirts. O'Shea, Ness, and a dozen others crowded around them.

"Who was it, Dani? Who did this?" Ness asked, needing her to be clear and unequivocal.

"Francis Sweeney," she answered. "It was Francis Sweeney. He's the Butcher."

"Search everywhere," Ness yelled, directing the milling officers. "High and low. It wouldn't surprise me if he has a hidey-hole somewhere nearby."

"I saw him go. I saw him leave. He took my wagon," Dani rasped. "I don't think he wanted anyone to know I was still here."

Malone found himself unable to think or speak and left that up to Ness. His rage and his relief were too big. He busied himself bathing Dani's face with a wet cloth, and O'Shea produced a tin cup filled with water. Eliot waited for Dani to drink deeply before he proceeded with his questions.

"I need to know what happened," Eliot pressed. He was bristling with impatience, yet his voice was mellow and unhurried.

"He had a key," Dani explained. "He surprised me, but I ran into the locker. He told me . . . that he's known me for years. And he . . . admires my work." She was shaking, panting, and Malone urged her to drink again. She couldn't hold the cup without assistance, and he helped her even as his own throat swelled and his fury billowed.

"He didn't know the refrigeration wasn't working," she continued after a long pull. "I'm sure he thought I would die in there, and no one would know it was him that barred me inside. He didn't come back. No need. I was afraid he would . . . but he didn't."

Darby O'Shea leaned down to Dani, his blue eyes bright and his cheeks ruddy with emotion. "Dr. Frank did this to you?" he pressed again, like he needed to be certain.

"You know him?" she gasped.

"I know of him. Seen him. Heard people talk about him. But I didn't know he was the Butcher."

Dani's eyes bounced to Malone's. "He knows I helped you. He saw us dancing at the gala. He heard you talking about me when you thought he was sleeping. The undertaker and the spy. That's what he called us. He said he left me alone to do my work, so why didn't I leave him alone to do his?"

"Son of a bitch," Ness swore.

"He killed them here, Michael. All that death, and I never . . . had a clue. This is his . . . workshop . . . and I never knew. I never knew him. But he . . . knew me."

Darby O'Shea straightened away from Dani and turned to Ness, his gaze flat and his jaw tight. "He has a place in the Run. I've seen him there before. Everyone down there knows Dr. Frank. He writes prescriptions—anything folks need—no charge. Free doctoring. Man like that comes and goes as he pleases, and folks keep quiet. They want him around. He has a little shanty he uses. He calls it his clinic. Keeps some supplies there. Bandages. Pills. This and that. He has a lock on the door, but nobody touches it. Everyone kinda respects him down there. Thinks he's one of the good guys. I'll show you where."

"This ends now. We don't wait. We don't ask. The Run is coming down," Ness said.

30

The newspapers excoriated Eliot, though he was mostly unbothered by it. He even read one article aloud to Malone, sitting at the kitchen table two days later while Margaret made them eggs and toast with jelly that was even better than the kind they served at the Coney Island Café. Malone had not joined Eliot and his men on the raid of Kingsbury Run. He'd been unwilling to leave Dani, and he'd had to wait to hear how it all went down. O'Shea had never reported back or returned, and other than a brief phone call to check on Dani's condition, Eliot had been putting out nonstop fires—literally and figuratively—until now.

"In the early hours of August 18, less than forty-eight hours after the remains of two more bodies were found at the dump at the intersection of East Ninth and Lakeshore Drive, director of safety, Eliot Ness, and what looked to be the entire Cuyahoga County fire department and police force, blocked the streets leading in and out of Kingsbury Run and descended into the unsuspecting shantytowns," Eliot read, his voice mild, his shoulders hunched over the paper.

"Armed with clubs and flashlights, Ness and his officers moved from hovel to hut, pulling confused residents from their pitiful homes.

Men were herded into trucks and transferred to county holding facilities where they were questioned and detained, many unable to return to the place they have called home for many years.

"'We just wanted to get our possessions,' a longtime resident of the Run, Joseph Gorsuch, told the *Plain Dealer*. 'But he wouldn't hear it. The whole place is gone now. They burned it down.'"

"Good riddance," Malone grunted. Eliot kept reading.

"Eliot Ness did not apologize for the order that left Kingsbury Run in ashes. When questioned, he had this statement for reporters: 'We have made accommodations available around the city. Conditions in the Run have bred sickness and suffering and are a breeding ground for all manner of crime. People in the Run have been preyed upon for years. It is not compassion to ignore it or allow it to continue. As safety director, it is my duty to make Cleveland safer. That is what I've done. As a city and as a department, we will do our best to help those who have been displaced, both in halfway houses and shelters in and around the city, but the Run is no longer inhabitable, and I intend to keep it that way.'"

"Not a bad response," Malone said, judicious.

"The mayor wasn't impressed. Neither were the reporters," Eliot said. He continued reading.

"Director Ness was not as forthcoming when questioned about the Butcher's latest slaughter. When asked if he had any new developments on the identity of the victims found on August sixteenth or their killer, Ness had nothing to say. The Butcher's tally has reached a staggering twelve victims, with no end in sight."

"I get the feeling they hope there's no end in sight. Life will be so dull if it's over," Malone interjected. Eliot just shook his head and kept going.

"The man believed to have succumbed to the smoke and confusion of the late-night raid has not yet been identified either. He was wearing a St. Christopher medallion around his neck and is thought to have been a vagrant simply passing through Cleveland and taking shelter in Kingsbury Run. At this time, authorities have not released any other identifying information."

Ness put down the paper and dug into the eggs Margaret set in front of him. "He wasn't wearing the necklace," he added after she bustled away. "He'd been strangled with it, according to Cowles."

"You think it was Sweeney?" Malone asked softly.

"The body was burned beyond recognition. Nothing to identify him but the medallion and his teeth . . . though as of right now, we don't have Sweeney's dental records yet, if they even exist. Francis Sweeney was big on trading services. But yeah. I think it was him, Malone. Someone got him."

Neither of them offered speculations on who that someone was. They ate in silence for several charged seconds.

"O'Shea brought us to Sweeney's clinic, just like he said he would," Ness continued. "We hit it first. It was just a hut made of tin and tires not far from the Eagle Street ramp. But there wasn't much there. Some booze. Some bandages. A lockbox with some tonics and pills inside. We didn't find the body until the next day, after the fires were all put out. It was discovered on the other side of the Run beside a pile of tires."

"Whoever killed Sweeney started the fires," Malone said.

"Yeah. Most likely. It wasn't us, though we got blamed for it. We'd cleared everyone out before a shout went up. I thought for sure it was Sweeney, covering his tracks." Ness shrugged. "Guess not. But the whole Run is gone . . . and I can't say I'm sorry."

"Sweeney's next of kin notified?" Malone asked, sarcasm dripping.

Ness snorted. "In a way."

Malone raised his brows.

"I don't think the congressman is going to be running to the papers. In fact, I'm guessing his whole family is hoping the dead man *is* Frank Sweeney. But the gag order is in full effect. Every officer has been read the riot act. No talking to the press. No speculating. And those orders aren't coming from me."

"Did you find any evidence on Mead? Anything that connected the Butcher's victims to the indigent morgue?"

"Nah. But Raus verified Sweeney volunteered there years back. He knew the place well. What better way to dispose of death than at a morgue? He drugged them somewhere else but killed them there, then washed his evidence down the gutters with the blood and gore of a thousand others, and left their bodies around the city. I don't know where he kept the remains of the woman in the quilt, the one you called Nettie. We got a report back on her. She died of natural causes. Unlike the others, he chopped her up posthumously."

"Why?" Malone shook his head. It wasn't really a question he expected Ness to answer.

"Hell if I know. But I'm guessing it was one of his clues. He was telling us where he killed them."

"And where he planned to kill Dani. He asked her if she thought I'd come back when she was dead."

"Dani's death was his revenge on you, Mike."

"And on her. She helped us find him." He paused, not wanting to continue, but knowing it needed to be said. "You have Dani's word that he was there, Eliot. He confessed to her. That's evidence."

"You want me to give the papers Dani's name? You want me to take her name to a judge? To put her in the crosshairs of the machine?"

"You'd have to kill me first," Malone said. He wouldn't expose Dani to get Sweeney. He supposed that made him no better than the politicians.

"That's what I thought," Eliot said, his smile wan.

"Though the way Irey feels about me—and you—and this whole thing, you'll have to get in line," Malone continued. "They want this all to go away. And you can bet that it will. Immediately. Poof. Nobody will talk about it. Nobody will ever really know the truth. About anything."

"Yeah." Ness nodded. "Yep."

"So that's it, then? You're not going to say a word?"

"No." Ness shook his head. "Cowles won't either. It's over. Unless . . . the body wasn't Sweeney."

"They'll never let you live this down," Malone said. The thought bothered him greatly.

"Nope. I'll be the man who got Al Capone but couldn't get the Mad Butcher of Kingsbury Run."

"But you did."

"Well, someone did."

Margaret was back again and both men fell silent while she refilled their coffee and fussed over them before retreating once more.

"So what's next for you, Malone?" Ness asked, folding the paper with finality.

"I'm thinking of adopting a pain in the ass named Charlie."

"Oh yeah?"

"Yeah. And a couple of old ladies. Margaret too. And it's probably time for a new name. Michael Malone is a liability."

"Maybe something a little more eastern European. Say . . . Michael Kos?" Ness grinned.

"Yeah. Maybe."

"It has a ring."

"Well, I've always wanted to learn to sew."

Ness laughed and scooped up his last spoonful of eggs. "If that doesn't work out . . . you can always come work for me."

"Nah. This last time didn't go so well," Malone shot back.

"I don't know about that." Ness sipped his coffee and raised his eyes to Malone's. "The way I look at it, you owe me big."

"Yeah," Malone grunted. "Maybe I do."

"Maybe you do. And you know I'll be calling that marker in."

~

He was lurking at her bedroom door again, like he'd done over the last few days. Dr. Peterka said she needed rest and liquids—he'd checked on her several times since they'd brought her home—and she'd gotten plenty of both. The Rauses checked on her as well. The story was that Dani had been accidentally trapped in the faulty freezer. Privately, Malone knew Peterka and Raus were questioned at length, but Ness was handling that. Sweeney's name never came up when Raus or Peterka made their calls on Dani. He knew because he hadn't been far from her side since the night he'd found her at the morgue.

Her aunts had hovered too, and Dani had patiently borne their anxious fluttering and Malone's constant presence. She'd told him and Eliot everything that had occurred—word for word, minute by minute—when Francis Sweeney strolled into the morgue on Mead.

Yet there was so much that hadn't been said. He'd been waiting for the horror to ebb, for the quiet and privacy his feelings required.

"Michael?" Dani called.

He stuck his head around the frame. "Can I come in?"

"Yes."

He shut the door behind him and moved to stand beside her bed. She was sitting up, her back against the headboard, and she looked beautiful. Well and rested. Her face was scrubbed, her hair loose, her nightgown fresh. A pitcher and a glass of water sat beside her on her nightstand.

"How do you feel?" he asked. She'd been asked the same thing countless times in the last few days. She had to be weary of answering, but she answered all the same, reassuring him.

"I'm bored silly."

He gave her the barest of grins, but his heart contracted. "Have you ever been bored a day in your life?"

"No. I haven't had time."

"That's what I thought."

"I'm not spending another day lying in bed, Michael. Tomorrow, life must go on."

"All right," he whispered, nodding. He chewed his lip, eyeing her glass of water, and then he took it and gulped it down. Lenka had refilled it before she went to bed as well as the pitcher beside it. He poured Dani another glass and set it down before shoving his hands in his pockets.

"Michael? Did you want to talk?"

He cleared his throat. They'd talked at length about the Butcher and her ordeal. They'd talked about the burnt remains that Eliot believed were Frank Sweeney. But they hadn't talked about what came next. "I just need . . . I just need to hold on to you for a while. I'll be gone when you wake, I promise." He was trying for easy, for lighthearted, but when he met Dani's gaze, she shook her head.

"No," she said.

"No?"

"No. If I let you hold on to me again, Michael Malone, you need to be here when I wake. And every morning after that."

He nodded, his eyes holding hers. "All right, Dani."

"All right?" she asked. They studied each other, taking each other in, conversing silently.

"All right," he repeated.

"And I think maybe we should move downstairs," she said. "To your room."

"Oh yeah?"

"Yes. There's a little more privacy and a much better tub. But we might have to make things more official if . . . that's . . . going to happen."

"Sign another six-month rental agreement?" he teased, but his heart was in his throat, and the ring in his pocket was burning a hole in his leg.

"I was thinking sixty years," she said. Firmly.

"Sixty years in Cleveland? I'll be one hundred years old."

"Lenka and Zuzana will be almost two hundred years old. Not to mention Charlie. Do you think we might let Darby have a room in the stable? It wouldn't take much to make it a nice little cottage."

"So now you're going to take on two jobless men as part of your load?"

"Yes. Absolutely."

He sat down on the bed beside her and reached for her hand. "I don't think Darby is going to stick around, sweetheart."

"No?" She sounded so disappointed.

His eyes were drawn to the picture of George Flanagan and Darby O'Shea, side by side, trying to be serious and failing. The St. Christopher medallion on the rusting chain was no longer slung over the corner of the frame.

"And what about you, Michael? Are you going to stick around?" Her voice was quiet. Mild. But when he looked back at her, her mismatched eyes were turbulent. Blue sky and dark earth, the whole wide world in one small face. For a moment he just allowed himself to look, to study the landscape he wanted to call home. Then he brought their clasped hands to his mouth and pressed a kiss to the space between her knuckles and her wrist.

"Yes, Dani. I am."

He took the ring from his pocket and without waiting for permission or dropping to his knees, he slid it on her finger.

Her breath hitched, but he kept his gaze fixed on the ring, suddenly so nervous he couldn't look at her.

It was too big. He'd been afraid of that, but they could get it sized or trade it for something she liked better. He'd walked into the jeweler on the corner of East Fifty-Fifth and Broadway that afternoon and walked out again fifteen minutes later, his wallet much lighter. It was a nice ring—a gold filigree setting with a garnet center—but he had no eye for such things. It was the girl he was sure of. The ring was just a formality.

Dani didn't squeal or flare her fingers to study the effect as he'd seen other women do. She closed her hand into a fist, curling her fingers around the loose band as if she was afraid it would slide right off again, or worse, that it didn't mean what she thought it did.

He brought her clenched fist to his chest, pressing it to his heart, and made himself meet her gaze. She was silent as her eyes searched his. She needed him to say the words.

"Will you marry me, Dani Flanagan?" he asked, his throat tight.

"Yes, Michael Malone. I will." No hesitation. "But we're going to have to live here. You know that, don't you?"

"I do."

She exhaled in gusty relief. She must have been holding her breath because she hiccuped and then giggled.

Joy bubbled up in his throat, and his heart swelled beneath her fist. He smiled, unable to help himself, and Dani pulled her hand from his and gripped his face, pressing her mouth to his. But she was smiling too, making the kiss more shared laughter than intimate caress. He wanted to kiss her senseless, but try as he might, his mouth would not form the proper shape to accomplish the task. So he let himself grin like a fool and nuzzled her throat instead, wrapping his arms around her and tugging her down onto the bed.

The scent of her skin, so dear and so distinct, flooded him, and he stilled, his face buried in the crook of her neck. He wanted to pray. He wanted to confess. To moan the Rosary in humble adoration, but he suddenly didn't trust himself to speak. His emotions were too close to the surface. Dani was whole and well and in his arms, and he was home.

"You aren't going to tell me no again, are you, Malone?" she asked, her pulse thrumming against his lips, her hands stroking his head.

"No, Dani," he said.

They laughed again, like children up to no good, awake past their bedtime, struggling to be quiet yet unable to quiet their delight in each other. He just wanted to touch her. To trace every beloved line.

He brushed his fingers over the tip of her nose and the swell of her lips, his mouth following his hand. He continued down her throat and across her breasts, resting his rough face against her soft heart, and their mirth dissipated into the mellow light of the room and the reverence of adoration.

He rose over her and kissed her the way she loved, the way *he* loved. He kept his mouth on hers even as he dispensed with her nightgown and slid her silk underthings from her body. He proceeded slowly, aware of the house breathing around them, the creak of old walls and old women, and when he reared back slightly, just to drink her in and find his self-control, she divined his thoughts.

"They won't disturb us," Dani whispered. Her languid eyes and parted lips beckoned him, and he withdrew from her long enough to check the lock on the door and to shrug out of his clothes. He watched her as she watched him, rosy and rumpled, naked and trusting, and his love swamped him again, making him quake and struggle for breath.

"Ah, Dani," he murmured, completely ensnared, completely undone. "Are you sure, lass? Are you sure you want me? Because I won't survive you changing your mind. I won't be strong enough to leave again. I won't be able to. Even if you tell me to go."

He was babbling. He didn't babble. And yet . . . he babbled on. "I'll drive you crazy. I'll be constantly underfoot, like that damn cat. You won't get any rest. Or space. I can't stand the space even now." She was only a few feet away from him—lips and limbs, smiling eyes and copper curls—and he couldn't bear it. "I'll be a burden," he warned, folding his arms to hold himself back.

"Oh, Michael. Come here, my darling," Dani said, reaching for him, and his name, uttered so tenderly, was all the urging he needed. He obeyed, a man committed, and stretched himself willingly on the rack of his devotion, his body covering hers. Dani welcomed him, undaunted, meting out the torture and the transcendence with her hands and her mouth and her trust. And he returned it in full measure.

~

Beyond the room in the aging house on Broadway, where Dani slept with his kiss on her lips and his scent on her skin, past the morgue where the nameless were brought, and down the steep gully into Kingsbury Run, the embers of shanties and the stink of burnt rubber permeated the soft summer air. A few men moved through the rubble, kicking at the debris, looking for treasure where no treasure remained. Where no treasure had likely ever existed. Malone moved among them, peeking at the sooty cheeks beneath soiled caps, looking for Francis Sweeney. He couldn't help himself. He wanted to be sure, and he didn't know if he ever would be.

He'd been unable to stay asleep, happy as he was. Buoyant as he was. It was something he would have to get used to. He'd lain in the darkness listening to Dani breathe, so weightless he thought he might float away. After a while he rose and tiptoed through the house and down to his room, Charlie padding behind him. He thought Dani might wake and follow him, and he briefly considered rousing her so that if she found him gone from her bed, she wouldn't think he'd been eager to leave it. But she didn't wake, and he was grateful. It was better if he went to the Run alone.

He left a note on his desk.

I know I promised I'd be here when you wake, but if I'm not, don't worry. I needed to walk. I won't be gone long.

The note had seemed cold and impersonal, considering that he felt neither of those things, and he stared down at the words. He added, *I love you*, and felt like a child. But he left it.

He headed back home before dawn, wishing he'd never gone. It'd done him no good. He should have stayed in bed beside Dani and let the Run rest.

He had just passed the sandwich shop and turned onto Broadway when he realized he was being followed. It didn't frighten him. He had a good idea who it was; the man had followed him before. He stopped and turned, waiting for his shadow to show himself.

"Is that you, O'Shea?" he asked.

"Why you kicking through rubble down there in the Run, Malone?" Darby O'Shea asked, approaching him with his head cocked and his steps cautious. "What do you think you're going to find?"

"Where've you been, O'Shea?" The birds were starting to squawk in anticipation of the morning, and the streetlight was sputtering on the corner. Darby O'Shea's stomach growled.

"I haven't seen you since we found Dani," he continued. "And Ness said he lost track of you during the raid. I thought maybe something had happened to you." He hadn't really. Darby O'Shea had a knack for disappearing. And reappearing. Malone hadn't been worried at all.

"I've been around. Waiting. You know." Darby shrugged. "I wanted to come see her. But I knew I wouldn't be welcome."

"So you're coming now?" Malone asked, voice wry. "It's a little early. Or late."

"Look who's talking," Darby shot back. "Some things can only be done in the dark. You know that. I saw you and thought maybe . . . I'd just pass a message along."

"Come on. I'll make you breakfast," Malone said, taking a few steps. "Nobody will say a word. And Dani will be glad to see you, regardless of the hour."

"Nah. Hold on. I have some things for her. But I'll just give 'em to you. It'll be better that way."

Malone paused, and Darby O'Shea closed the distance between them. He looked both ways, as if making sure they didn't have an audience. The streets were dead, but he lowered his voice to a murmur anyway.

"You can quit looking for Dr. Frank, Malone. That's what you're doing, isn't it?"

Malone waited, not answering, but his heart had quickened.

"He's dead," O'Shea said, voice so flat it floated like a paper plane and landed with a whisper.

"How do you know for sure?"

"When he wasn't in his . . . clinic . . . I checked somewhere else."

"Where?"

"I can't really say. You know how it is. One shanty looks like another."

"Huh."

"He wasn't dead when I found him," Darby hedged.

"No?"

"No. He was passed out. Snoring like a bear. And . . . he had these in his pockets." Darby reached into his trousers and pulled out a small stack of papers, covered in Dani's handwriting. "I thought maybe Dani would like them back. They're hers, ain't they?"

"Yeah. They're hers," Malone said, unable to pull his gaze from the pages.

O'Shea handed them over like he was glad to be rid of them. "Why does she do that?"

"You know how Dani is . . . don't you?" Malone asked. Maybe he didn't.

"You mean when she touches cloth . . . she knows things?" Darby said, shifting uncomfortably. "Yeah. I know. She's been doing stuff like that since she was a wee one."

Malone fingered the sad pages. "She has a gift. And she uses it to give names to the unknowns brought into the morgue. It's how she gives the dead obituaries, how she keeps a record so that if someone ever comes looking for them, they can be found."

"She takes care of people," O'Shea said.

"Yeah. She does." Malone tucked the papers away. He didn't know what Dani would do with them, but she would be glad to have them back.

"George was like that. Never forgot a name. Never made people feel small. Never made me feel like garbage. I always have been . . . but he still took care o' me."

Darby reached into his pocket again and this time he took out a dangling chain with a medallion hanging from the center. "This is for Dani too. You'll give it to her for me, won't you? She gave me her St. Christopher medal, the one I gave her after her parents died. She was worried about the Butcher coming after me." He snorted as if he found that ironic. "But I lost it . . . somewhere."

"You lost it?" Malone asked.

"Yeah. I did." O'Shea's eyes were level, unflinching, unapologetic. "So I bought her another one. A new one. You can give it to her for me."

"I wouldn't have pegged you as a St. Christopher man," Malone said, taking it. His hands didn't shake.

"I'm Catholic. Just like you. I don't go to Mass. Don't confess. But we need the saints—like Dani. Like St. Christopher. The world needs 'em. And maybe the world needs men like us too, Michael Malone. To save the saints and the angels from the demons. I don't know. But someone put Frank Sweeney out of his misery. Put the Run out of its misery too. And it needed to be done."

"Someone?" Malone pressed.

"Yeah. Someone. A nobody." Darby O'Shea enunciated each word.

"Why are you telling me this, O'Shea?" Malone whispered. "Any of it? You know who I am. Who I work for. Who I . . . worked for," he amended.

"You get fired?"

"I quit."

"Well . . . you ain't a copper anymore then. And you won't say nothin'."

"How do you figure?"

"'Cause it needed to be done."

They were silent then, the truth hanging between them, and Malone could not deny it.

"I wouldn't have said anything either," Darby muttered. "But I figured you needed to know. So you'd stop lookin'. A man like you's got plenty else to lie awake over. To watch his back over."

Darby O'Shea lit a cigarette and offered one to Malone, who shook his head. Maybe he'd enjoy a cigar when he got home. A celebration.

"What now?" Malone asked softly after O'Shea had enjoyed several long draws. Darby ground out the cig on the pavement, blew the ashes away, and dropped the butt into the little front pocket of his vest, ostensibly for later. Times were hard. Nothing went to waste.

"All I ask is that you take good care of Dani so I don't have to keep comin' back to Cleveland," Darby said. "I hate Cleveland."

Malone almost grinned. "Yeah. I felt the same way. But it's growing on me."

"That's what George said too when he fell in love with Aneta. But if you want those old ladies to like you, you better stick around. They made poor George miserable."

"I'll stick around. And where will you be, Darby O'Shea?" he asked.

"I got business in Chicago. Don't worry. I won't tell anyone there that I saw you . . . Your secrets are safe with me. Unless, of course, you don't treat Dani right." Darby touched his cap and turned, but he whistled as he walked away, and Malone recognized the tune.

Beware the lads from Kilgubbin. They'll take what isn't movin'. With a glint in their eyes and a glint of the knife, you can bet your life you'll be losin'.

Epilogue

Dani watched the picture and Malone watched her. She had left her glasses at home—he couldn't even remember the last time she'd worn them—and she'd pinned her curls behind her ears, giving him a better look at the lines of her face in the dark.

She caught him staring once and smiled and looked away. When she realized he hadn't stopped, she raised her hand to his chin and turned his head, and he'd laughed out loud at an inopportune juncture. A few people shushed him, and Dani snickered. But then he reached for her hand, and the mirth became something sweeter as her fingers twined with his.

She had calluses on her fingertips, and her nails were smooth and short. Her palms were narrow, and her wrists were dainty like the rest of her. When she caught him examining her fingers, ignoring the picture once again, she pulled their clasped hands into her lap and rested her head on his shoulder.

"You can look at me any old time. Watch the picture, Michael."

He could look at her any old time. What a novel thought.

He spent the rest of the film staring at the screen obediently, her head on his shoulder and her arm tucked through his, but when it was over, he still remembered nothing specific about it. He had no opinion on whether Errol Flynn was a convincing Sir Robin or whether he liked Technicolor, or even if the theater was full. He'd been focused on her.

They walked up Broadway with unhurried steps, Dani's arm through his. Autumn was here, and Cleveland was beautiful in the fall. God, he loved Cleveland.

Just as he'd predicted, Dani had loved the movie and was caught up in recounting Errol Flynn's impassioned speech to his Merry Men.

"When he said, 'Are you with me?' I wanted to kneel and take the oath with all the others."

"Oh yes. Politicians are very good at pretty speeches," Malone said, needling her. He liked her outrage.

"Robin Hood was not a politician," she huffed.

"No. You're right. He was a rabble-rouser. It's much harder to actually lead."

"But . . . he did lead! He was wonderful."

"He didn't solve the problem. He didn't implement a better system. He didn't create wealth or opportunity. He just took. Taking is easy."

She gaped at him. "But he gave what he took to others."

"And what about when all the bad guys are broke and the money runs out? Who will he take from then?"

"Oh, you! Now you've ruined it for me," she grumbled, giggling. "Why do you do that?"

"I just like to rile you up."

"Well, you're awfully good at it." Her blue eye gleamed and her brown eye deepened, and in the streetlight her hair was gold.

He leaned down and kissed her, not caring that the streetcar was passing and people would see. Not caring that Lenka and Zuzana might be peering out their window, which looked over the front of the house.

A man had the right to kiss his wife whenever and wherever he wished, if his wife was willing.

He dearly loved how willing Dani was.

"Can we go again tomorrow?" she asked when he let her catch her breath.

He laughed and said the only thing he ever said anymore.

"Yes, Dani."

AUTHOR'S NOTE

Eliot Ness died of a heart attack when he was only fifty-four. He was an interesting figure for me, a man I liked. As so often happens in these historical journeys I take, the sadness of the history often overwhelms me, and I wonder how I'm going to give my readers a happy ending—or even a sense of an ending—when history is messy and hard and often sad. The thing that stands out for me with people like Eliot Ness is that he was good. Not perfect. Not by any stretch. But good. He tried. He wanted to make things better. He wanted to do the right thing, and even though he had his flaws and his selfish ambitions, he was not ruled by them. Maybe that is what makes heroes of regular men and what makes regular men (and women) heroes.

Which brings me to Michael Malone. He was a special agent for the Treasury Department, one of the famed T-men. But he is not at all well-known. The rough sketch of his life that I use in my novel does follow the real man. His older sister, Molly, a side character in this story, was a constant in his life after he lost his mother at a young age. He and his wife, Irene, were estranged for most of their marriage after losing two children, and Michael spent the rest of his life embedded in big cases, doing work that very few people ever knew about. His friendship with Eliot Ness was not documented, nor did Malone help Ness with the Cleveland Torso Murders, but I have no doubt that the two knew one another and worked together on the Capone case, where Michael was undercover for eighteen months and served a pivotal role in bringing the organization down. I made him younger than he would have been in 1938—he was born in 1893—and used creative license with many aspects of his life, but the man and his career highlights are factual.

By all accounts, Michael Malone was a quiet, dedicated crime fighter who never received or wanted the credit. I learned about him in a documentary on Al Capone and the mob and started digging into his story. As always happens, once you start pulling on threads, one leads to another and another. He became my leading man, mostly because I wanted to give his story an ending I felt he deserved. His love and life with Dani was all fiction, but the real Michael Malone earned it, and part of me wonders if Dani and Malone might need to go on a few more adventures together, solve a few more mysteries, and pull a few more secrets from the cloth. I think they make a very good team.

And now for the villains of our story. Even though Francis E. Sweeney is widely believed to have been the Butcher, that case was never brought nor proven. All evidence in the eighty years since those murders occurred only strengthens the case against him. His bio, his connections, his employment, his temporary residence above the medical clinic, and his access to the morgue on Mead Avenue are all factual. I left the details of each of the Butcher's victims true to the case—the condition they were found in, the details outlined by the detectives, etc. The circumstances around Victim #12—known in this book as Nettie—were just as I described. Unlike all of his other victims, the Butcher did not kill her. She was dead before he got ahold of her. He simply cut her up and left her remains to be found in that tattered yellow quilt, months after her death.

The timeline was as close to the real timeline as I could make it. Eliot Ness had managed to coerce or corral Sweeney into an institution until that August in 1938, when he was once again on the loose, back in the game, leaving the remains of two bodies to be found not far from Eliot Ness's downtown office. I don't know if Sweeney took the remains from the morgue on Mead Avenue, but seeing as he had access and it was the perfect spot to carry out his murders, it's very probable that he did. He seemed to greatly enjoy leaving clues that no one ever understood.

His cousin, the congressman Martin L. Sweeney, was indeed a vocal critic of Eliot Ness and, as is always true in politics, had pull and power. But he is not here to defend himself, and whatever heinous murders Francis Sweeney might have been guilty of, Martin L. Sweeney was not. So we will leave his role in the events of the time as the book leaves it: highly suspicious, highly likely, and completely unproven.

The interrogation at the Hotel Cleveland, the use of the Keeler polygraph, and the details of the Torso Murders themselves, including dates and known data, were documented by people who were there. The account of Emil Fronek and his drugged dinner is also factual, as is the unsolved hit-and-run on Peter Kostura, one of the youngsters who found Victims #1 and #2 at the bottom of Jackass Hill. What is fictionalized are conversations, coercion by federal officials, and an official intervention by powerful forces of the government.

Francis Sweeney lived on after 1938, though the Torso Murders, at least in Cleveland, ceased. Like Michael Malone, I gave Francis Sweeney an ending that he did not receive in real life, but for whatever reason, his activities in Cleveland *did* cease. He died in a veterans' hospital in 1964.

The mystery surrounding the Cleveland Torso Murders dogged Eliot Ness for the rest of his career. As he said in the story, finding the Butcher wasn't like taking out Al Capone. Ness never talked to the papers or pointed the finger of blame at Sweeney or anyone else, but I think Eliot Ness knew who the Butcher of Kingsbury Run was, and he did his best to bring the carnage to an end. Many believe those years in Cleveland cost him his health, his first marriage, and his career. I wish him peace.

The saddest thing for Dani in *The Unknown Beloved* was the fact that so many of the Butcher's victims were never named. They died alone and unknown. The plight of the unknown was the theme of this book. Unknown people, unknown pain, unknown acts of heroism, and unknown acts of horror. Some of the Butcher's victims were named, most were not, but I tried to make them as real as I could, if only to shine light on the sadness of their stories.

With every book I write, I delve into the people and circumstances that create a setting. Every place has its story, but America, maybe more than any other country, has a patchwork quilt of the world layered over every city and town. It is one of the most fascinating things about writing. You uncover the identity of not only your characters but of every place you write about. Cleveland's founding was dominated by eastern European immigrants, mainly Hungarians, Czechs, and Poles, who brought their own flavor and color to the area. The Kos family are fictional, but their Czech heritage is not. The North Broadway neighborhood has tried to preserve that history and some of the original Bohemian buildings, but sadly, much of it is gone.

So many of the things in this book are true that detailing them would demand a dozen lists. A great resource on the Cleveland serial murders is a book called *In the Wake of the Butcher* by James Jessen Badal, a Cleveland researcher, whose knowledge on the Torso Murders is vast. I have not found a better or more complete compendium of the Kingsbury Run murders.

If you are interested in learning more about the real Michael Malone, research Al Capone documentaries. You'll find him there in the shadows. Other real and fascinating characters of note: Elmer Irey, the first chief of the Internal Revenue Service's intelligence division, and David Cowles of the Scientific Investigation Bureau. I gave David some fictional friction with Michael Malone, but by all accounts, he was a loyal friend of Eliot Ness, a brilliant man, and a dedicated servant of science who revolutionized crime techniques in Cleveland.

A final nod to Miss Emily Dickinson, whose words found place in this book. I have loved her work all my life. She is definitely a somebody to me.

ACKNOWLEDGMENTS

My sincere thanks to Lake Union Publishing, specifically my editor, Jodi Warshaw, and my developmental editor, Jenna Free, who make the writing process a pleasure and a challenge—the best combination.

Continued thanks to my agent, Jane Dystel, who always has my back and reads every book the minute I send it.

To my assistant, Tamara Debbaut, for standing by me though the shine has long since worn off. To my early readers, Sunshine Kamaloni and Korrie Kelley, for making me feel like I have something special to offer, and to Karey White, who has read, edited, and believed in me for so long.

To my husband and children, who surround me with love and life and purpose. Each book feels like a mountain, but you are all there every step of the way. Thank you for that. Now get out of my office and let me work. *wink* *wink*

ABOUT THE AUTHOR

Amy Harmon is a *Wall Street Journal*, *USA Today*, and *New York Times* bestselling author. Her books have been published in more than two dozen languages around the globe. Amy has written eighteen novels, including the *USA Today* bestseller *Making Faces*. Her historical novel *From Sand and Ash* was the Whitney Award–winning Novel of the Year in 2016. Her novel *What the Wind Knows* topped the Amazon charts for thirteen weeks and was on the top 100 bestsellers chart for six months. Her novel *A Different Blue* is a *New York Times* bestseller, and her *USA Today* bestselling fantasy *The Bird and the Sword* was a Goodreads Best Book of 2016 finalist. For updates on upcoming book releases, author posts, and more, join Amy at www.authoramyharmon.com.